Kodi

Jared Cullum

Top Shelf Productions

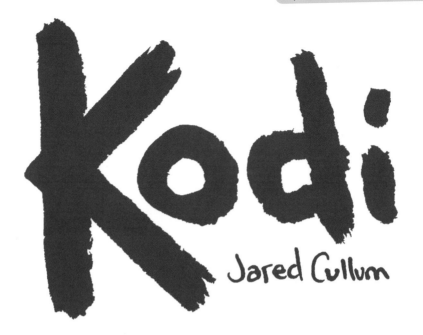

ISBN 978-1-60309-467-2   24 23 22 21 20   1 2 3 4 5

Published by Top Shelf Productions, an imprint of IDW Publishing,
a division of Idea and Design Works, LLC. Offices: Top Shelf
Productions, c/o Idea & Design Works, LLC, 2765 Truxtun Road, San
Diego, CA 92106. Top Shelf Productions®, the Top Shelf logo, Idea
and Design Works®, and the IDW logo are registered trademarks of
Idea and Design Works, LLC. All Rights Reserved. With the exception
of small excerpts of artwork used for review purposes, none of the
contents of this publication may be reprinted without the permission
of IDW Publishing. IDW Publishing does not read or accept
unsolicited submissions of ideas, stories, or artwork.

Printed in Korea.

Editor-in-chief: Chris Staros.
Edited by Chris Staros and Leigh Walton.
Designed by Gilberto Lazcano.

Visit our online catalog at topshelfcomix.com

Kodi

Jared Cullum

Top Shelf PRODUCTIONS

This book is dedicated to my wife Johanna,
who fills my life with inspiration and joy,
my son Oliver, who fills my heart with hope,
and my daughter Genevieve, who raises
the sun each day with her smile.

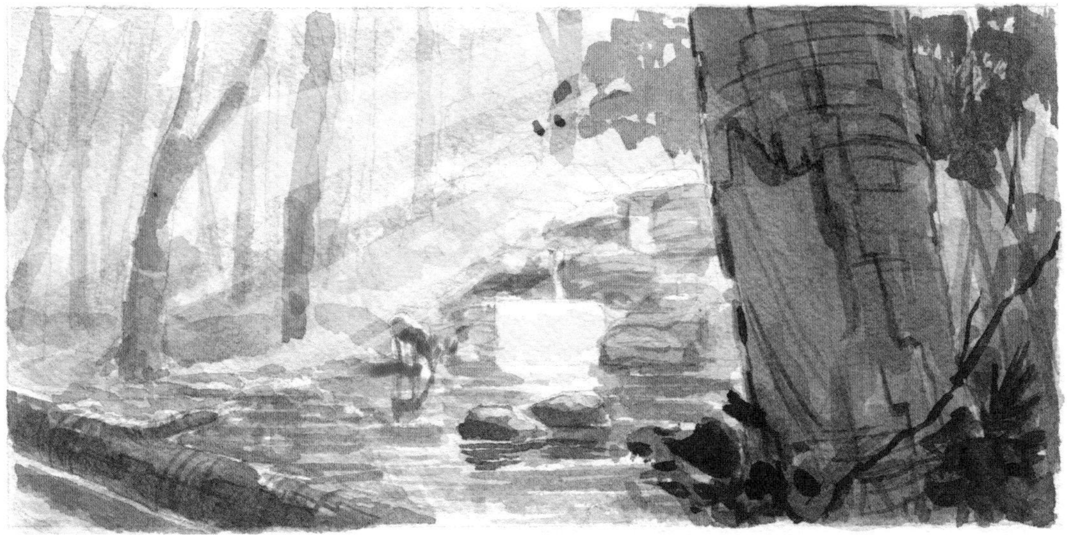

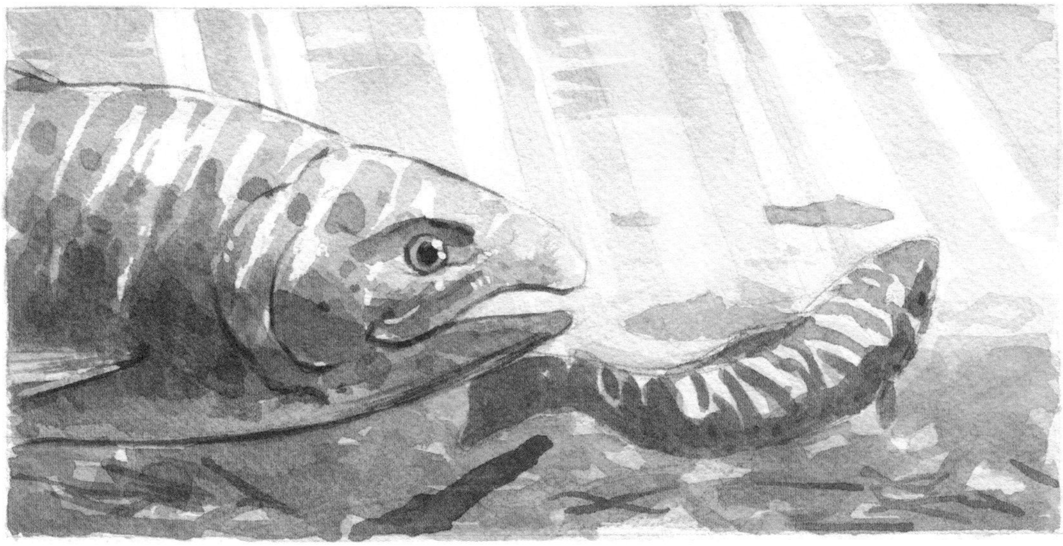

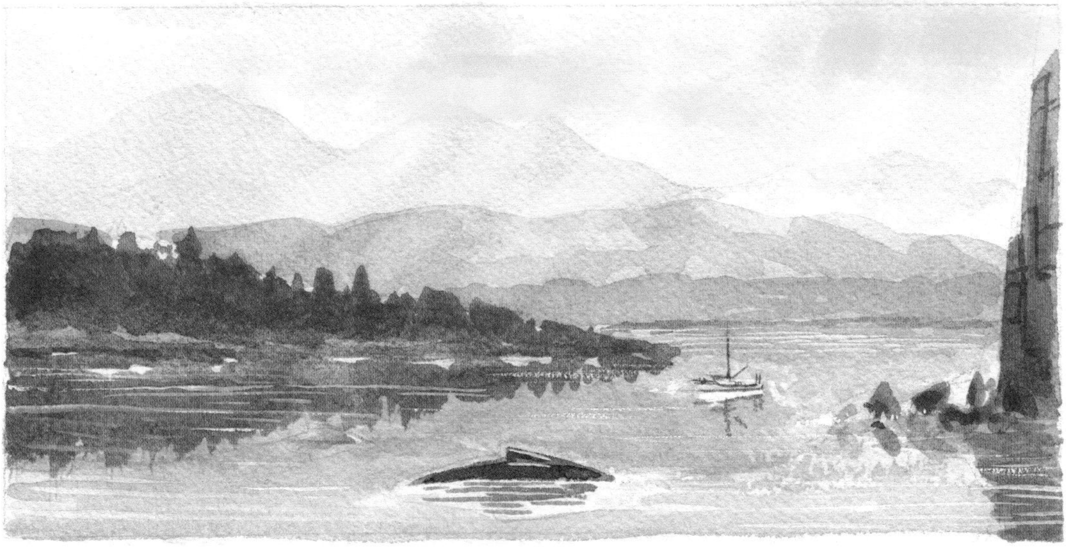

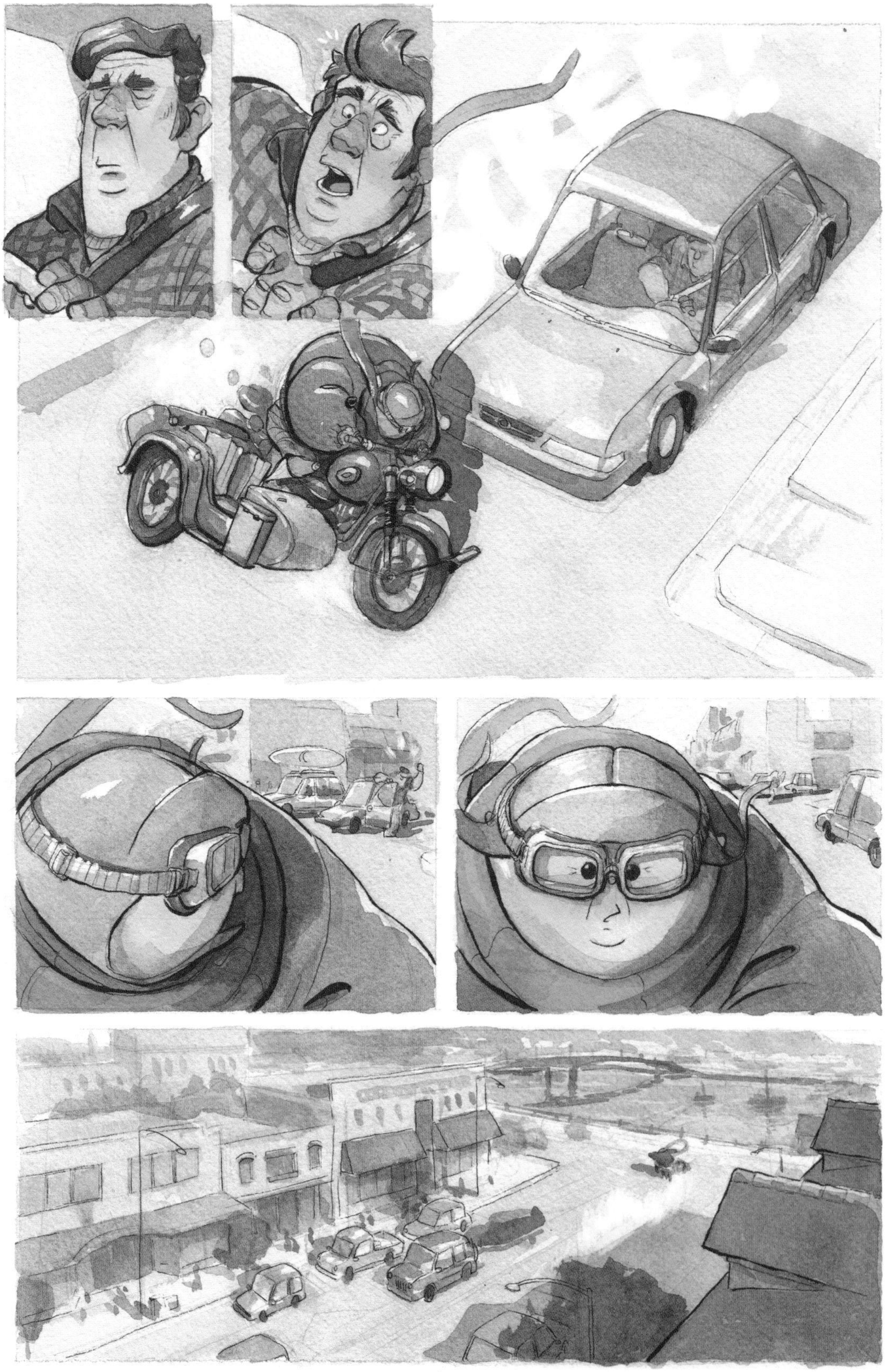

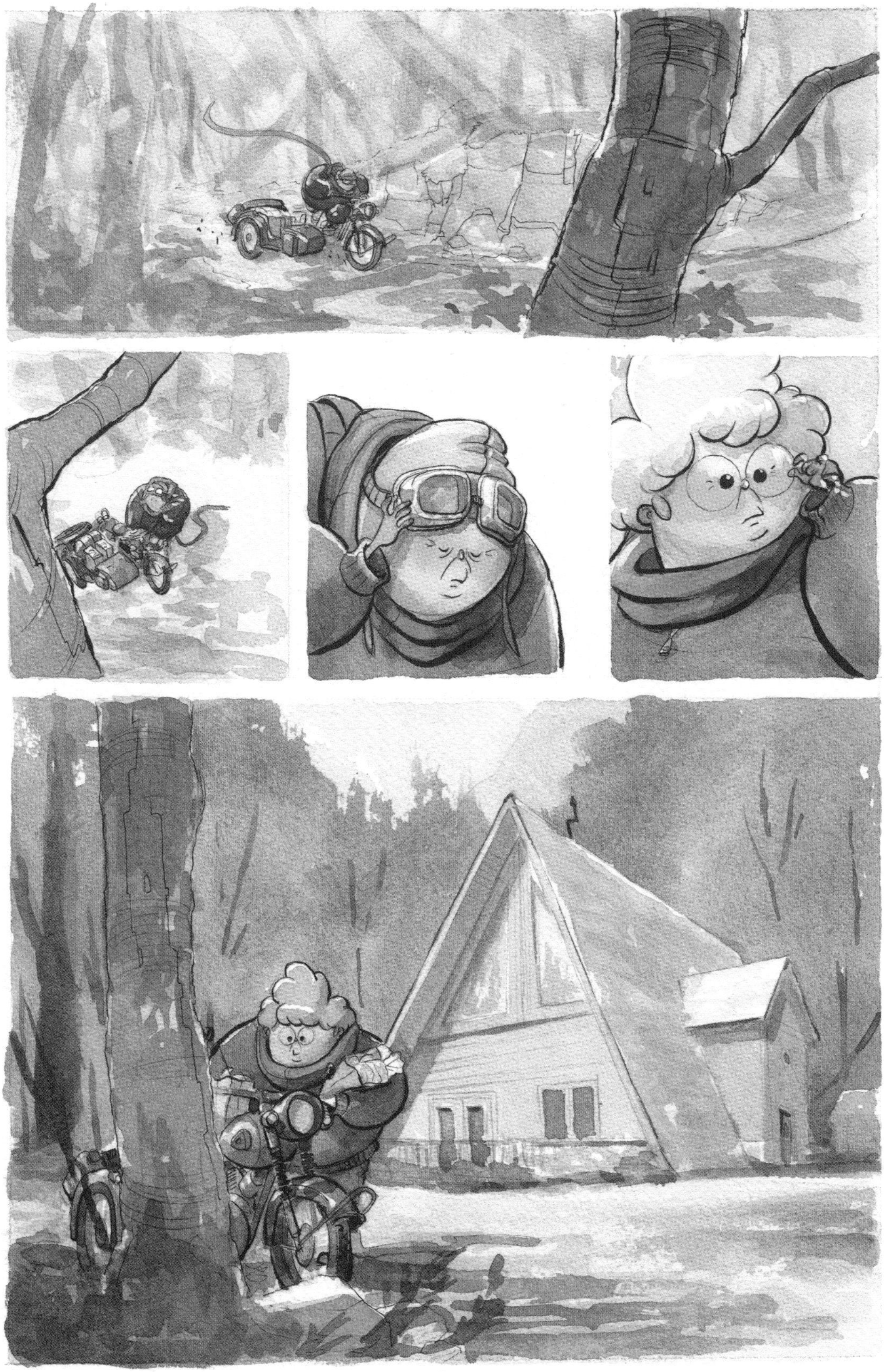

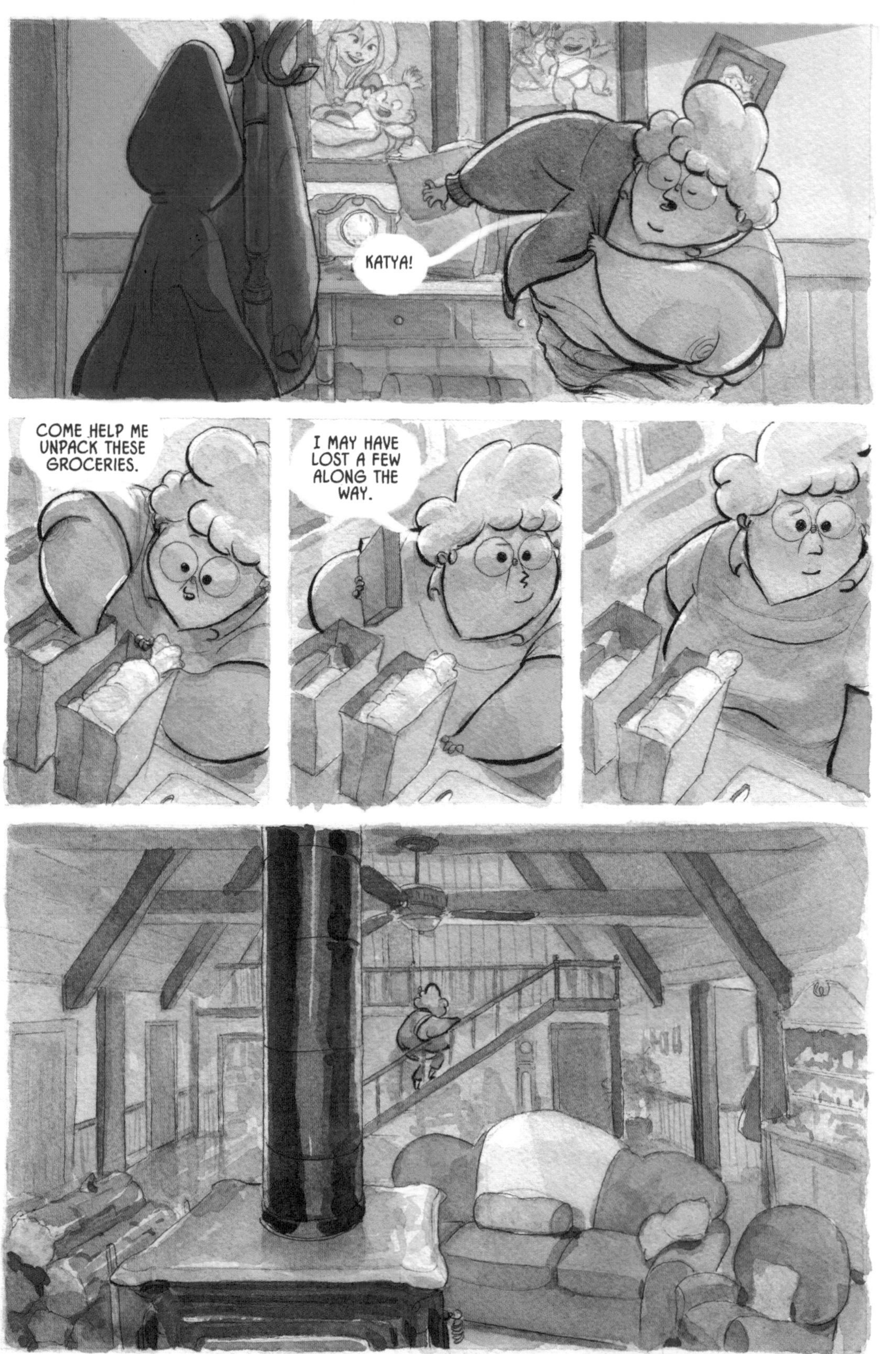

KATYA!
COME HELP ME UNPACK THESE GROCERIES.
I MAY HAVE LOST A FEW ALONG THE WAY.

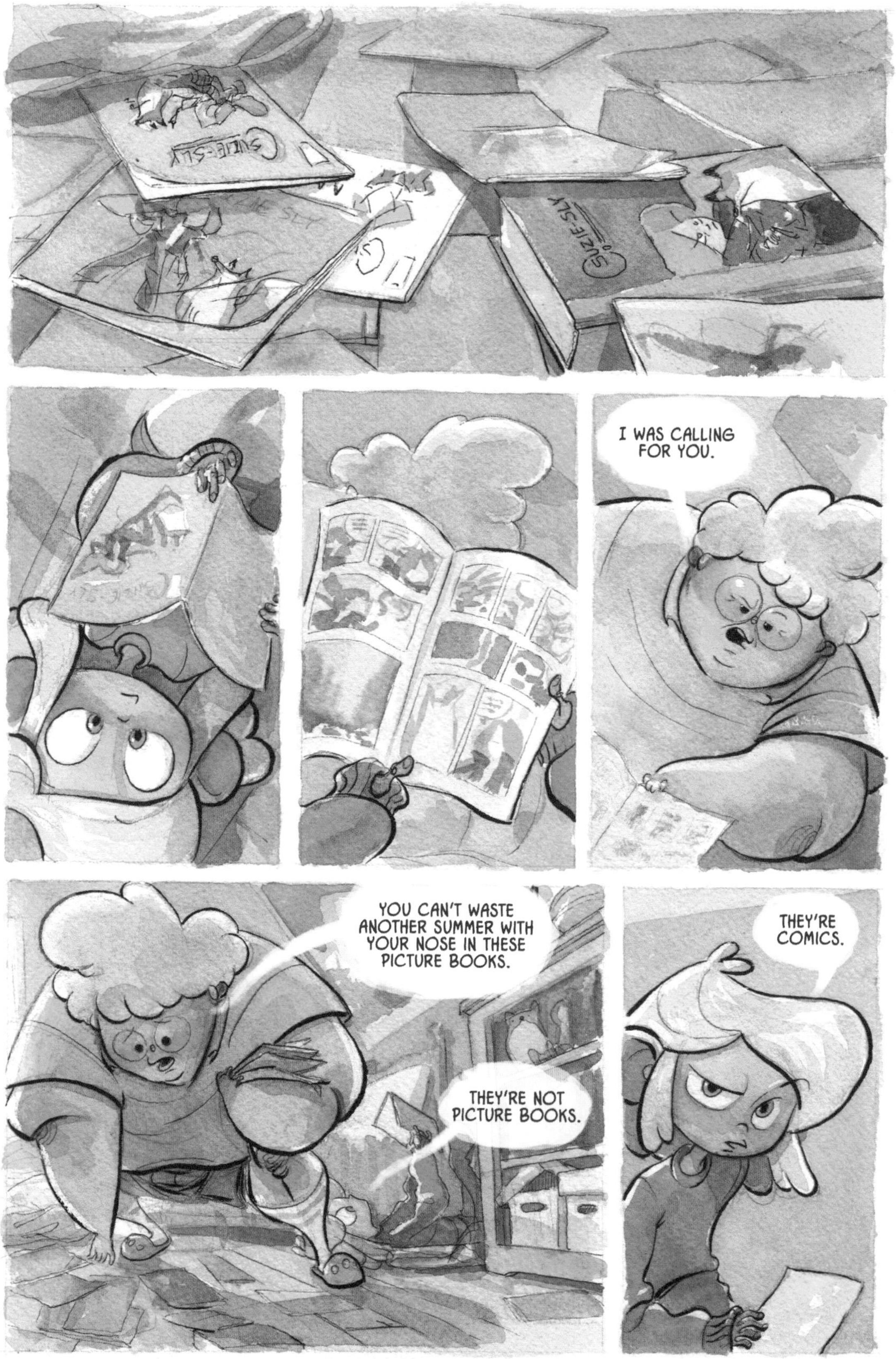

SUZIE-SLY
SUZIE-SLY
I WAS CALLING FOR YOU.
YOU CAN'T WASTE ANOTHER SUMMER WITH YOUR NOSE IN THESE PICTURE BOOKS.
THEY'RE NOT PICTURE BOOKS.
THEY'RE COMICS.

YOU CAN'T HIDE AWAY FOREVER, KATYA.

I WANT YOU TO BE HAPPY AND MAKE FRIENDS.

I DON'T NEED FRIENDS.

DON'T YOU WANT TO BE AROUND KIDS YOUR AGE?

I DON'T LIKE KIDS MY AGE. THEY'RE MEAN.

THEY CALL ME A MONSTER AND FLICK MY EARS.

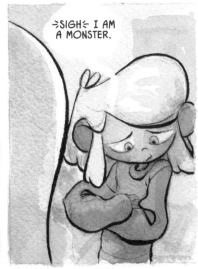

⇒SIGH⇐ I AM A MONSTER.

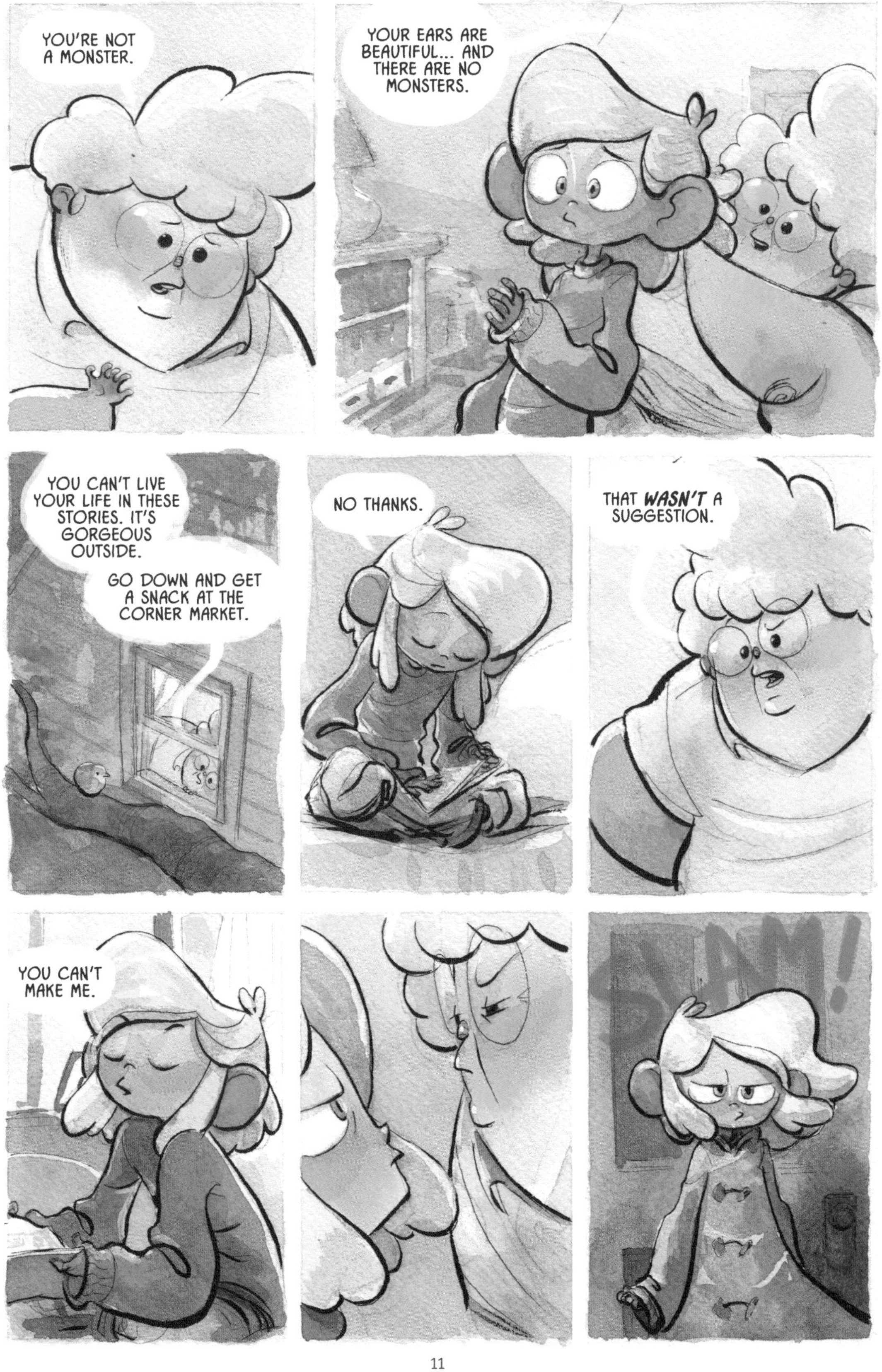
YOU'RE NOT A MONSTER.
YOUR EARS ARE BEAUTIFUL... AND THERE ARE NO MONSTERS.
YOU CAN'T LIVE YOUR LIFE IN THESE STORIES. IT'S GORGEOUS OUTSIDE.
GO DOWN AND GET A SNACK AT THE CORNER MARKET.
NO THANKS.
THAT ***WASN'T*** A SUGGESTION.
YOU CAN'T MAKE ME.
SLAM!

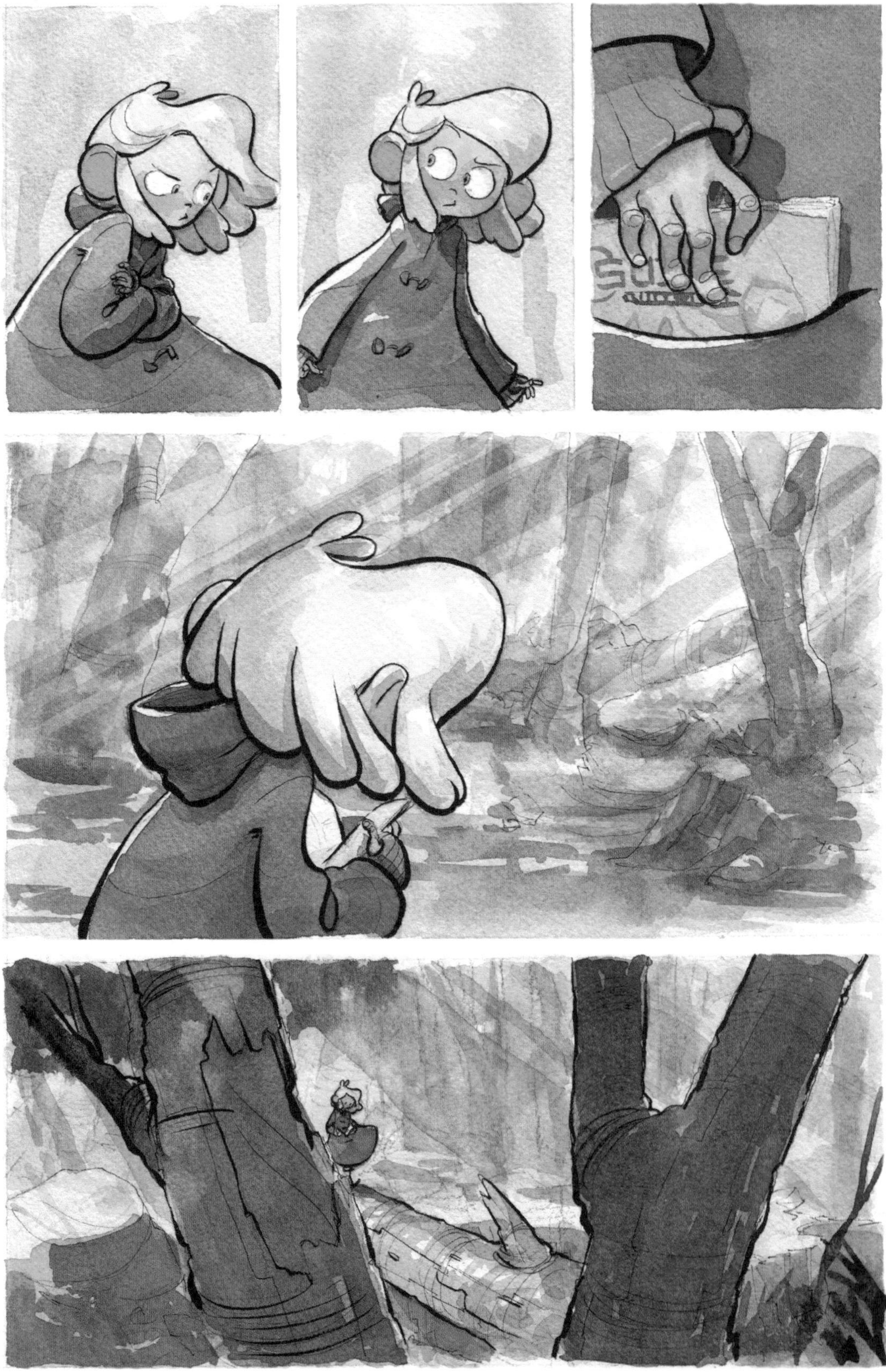

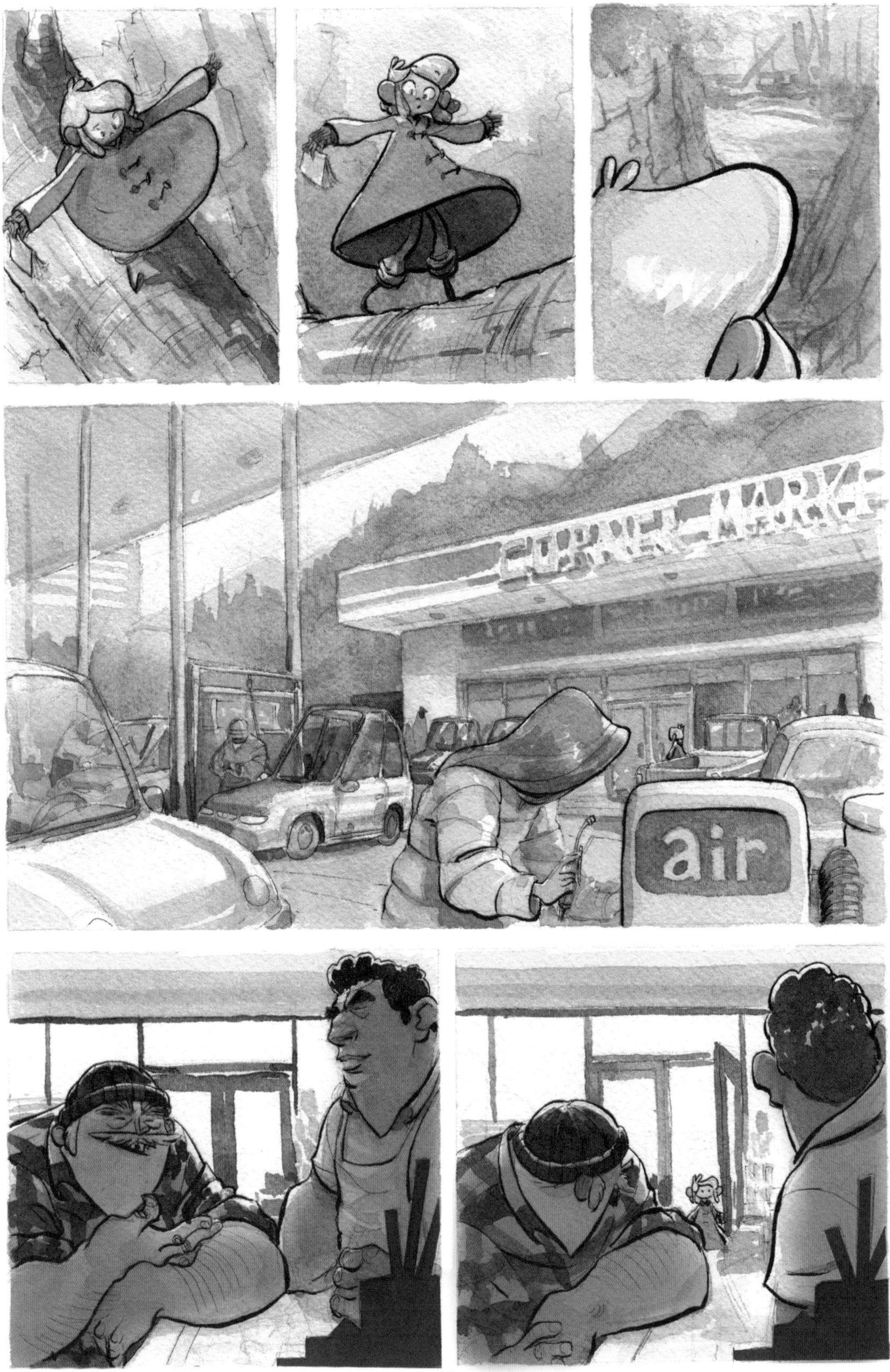
air

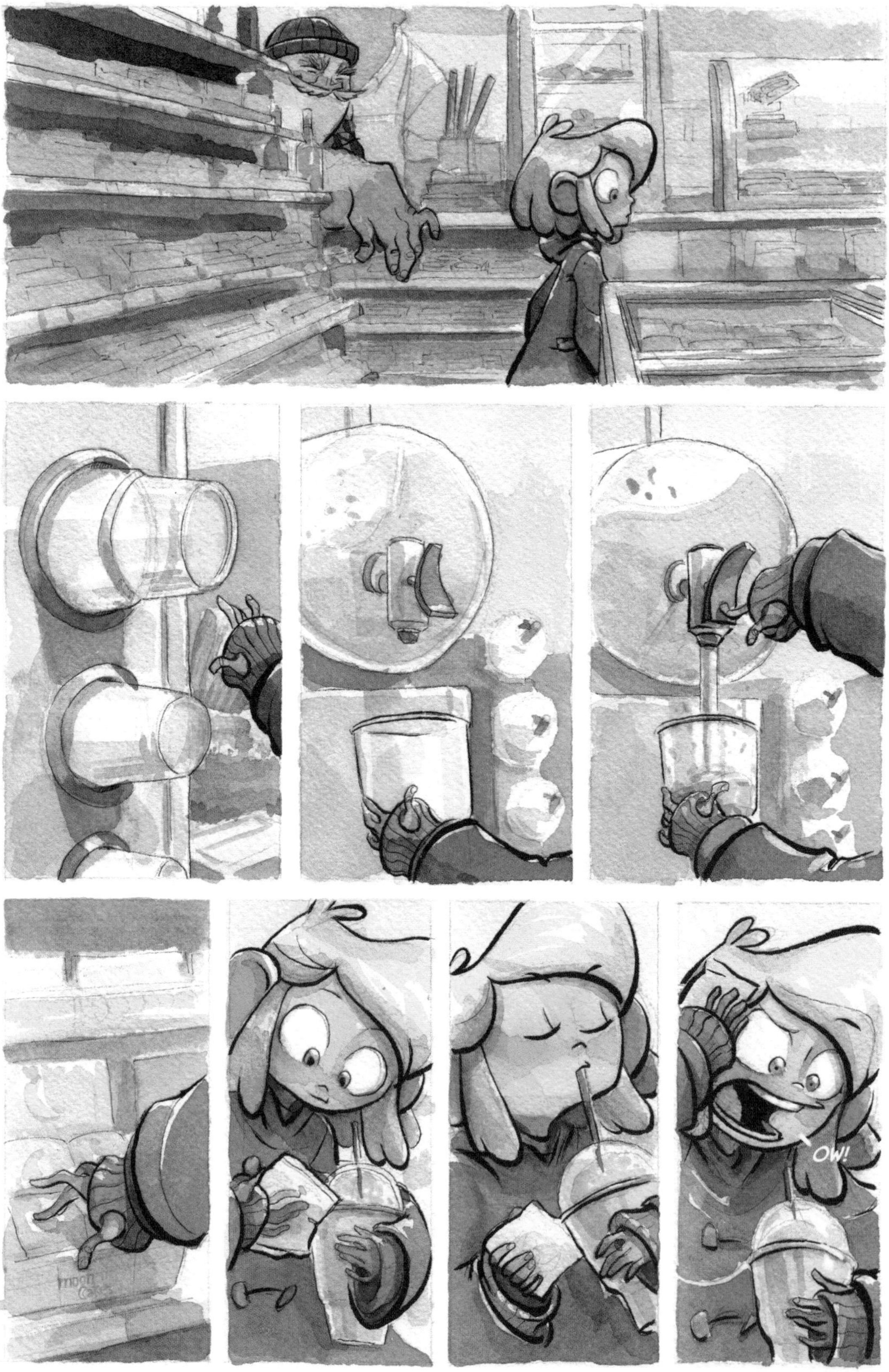
OW!

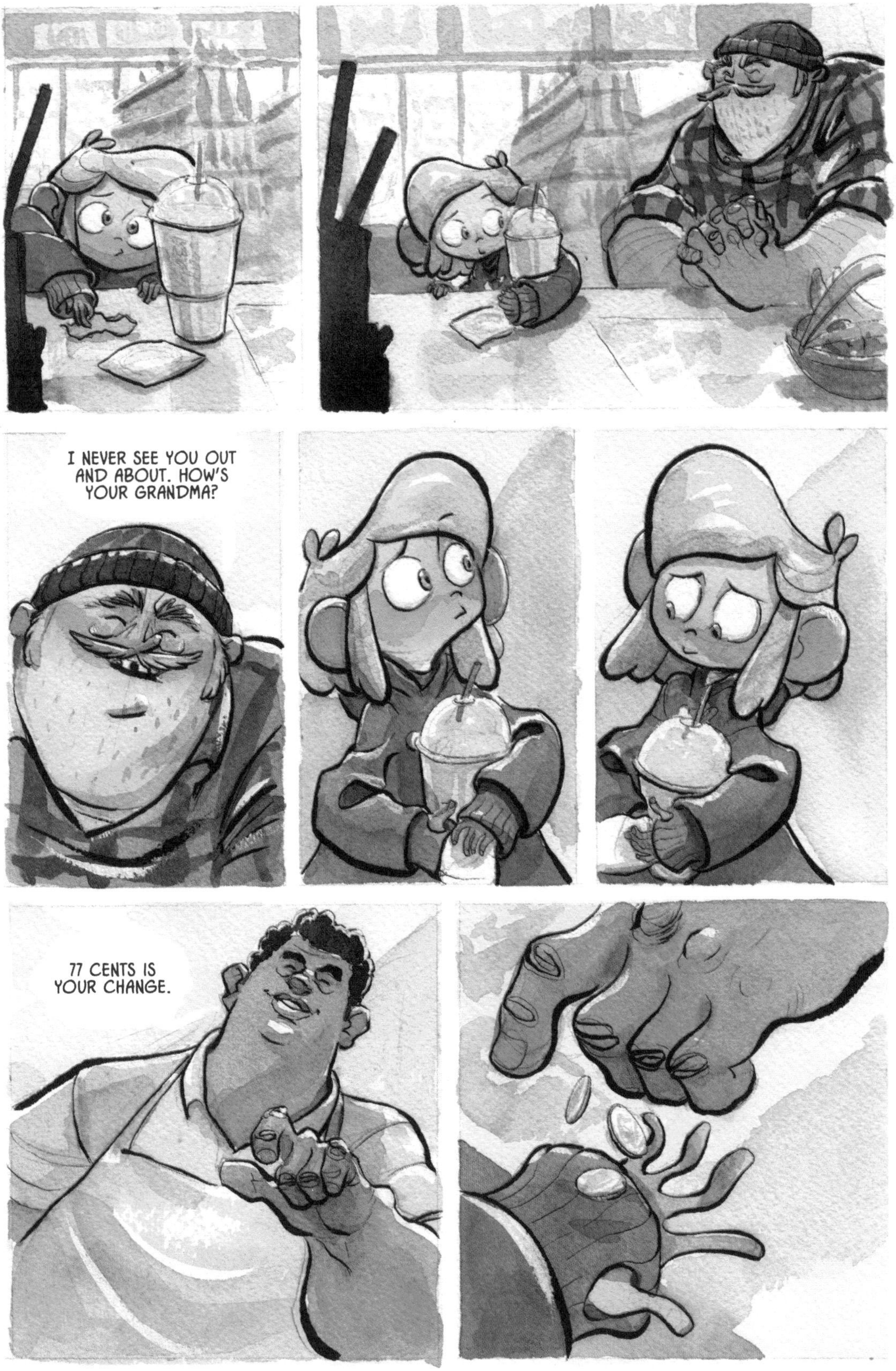

I NEVER SEE YOU OUT AND ABOUT. HOW'S YOUR GRANDMA?
77 CENTS IS YOUR CHANGE.

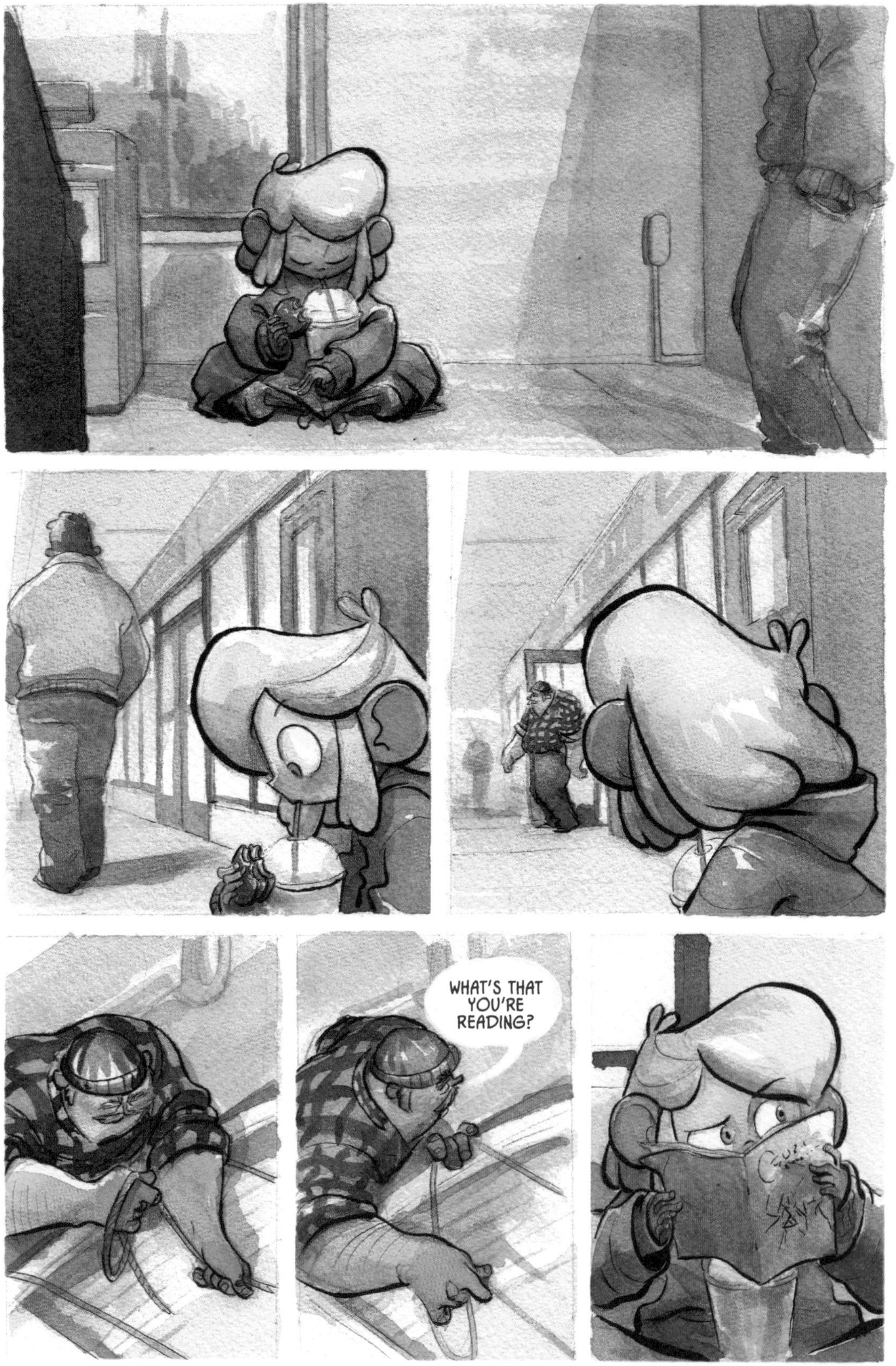
WHAT'S THAT YOU'RE READING?

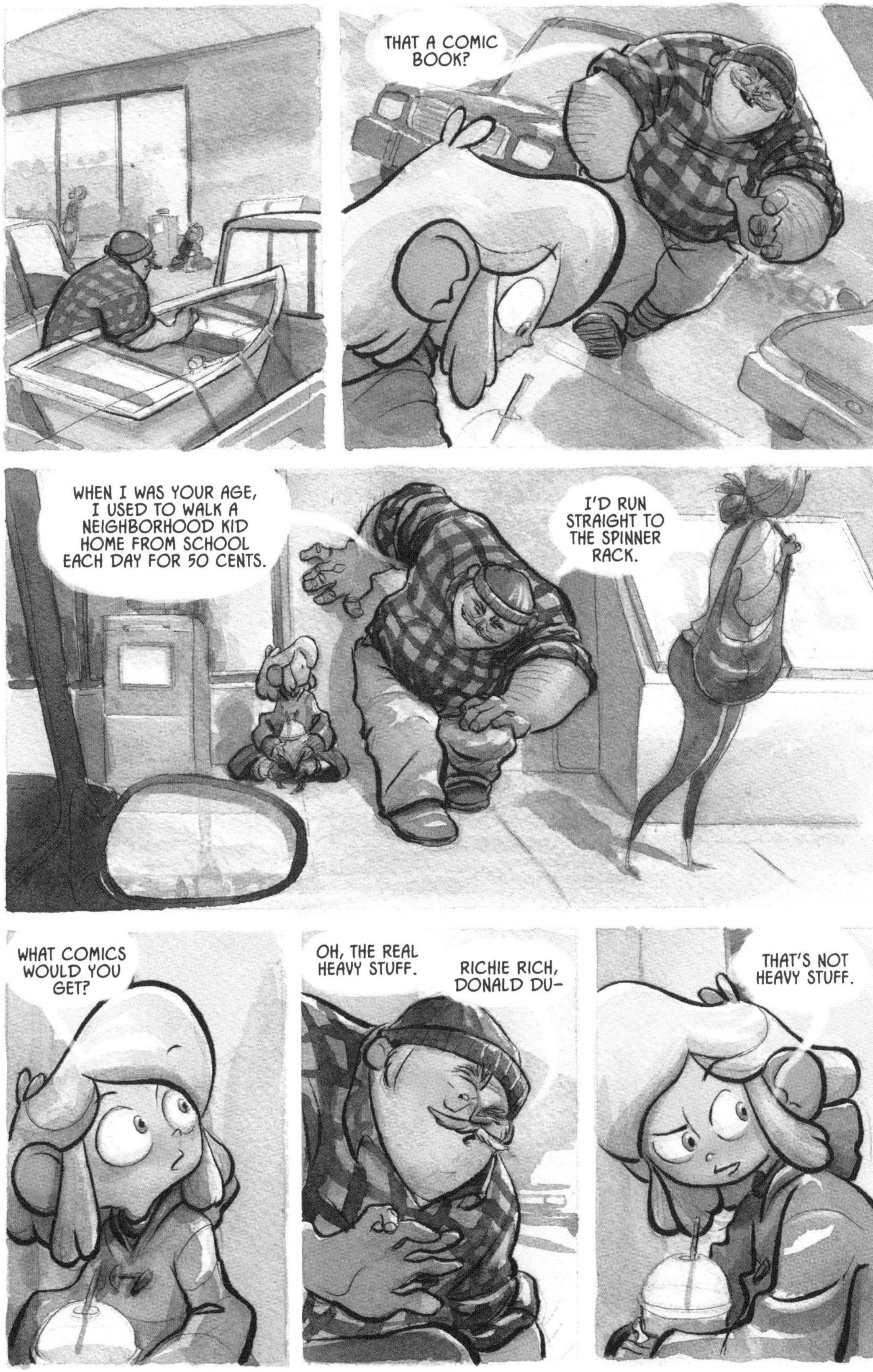
THAT A COMIC BOOK?
WHEN I WAS YOUR AGE, I USED TO WALK A NEIGHBORHOOD KID HOME FROM SCHOOL EACH DAY FOR 50 CENTS.
I'D RUN STRAIGHT TO THE SPINNER RACK.
WHAT COMICS WOULD YOU GET?
OH, THE REAL HEAVY STUFF.
RICHIE RICH, DONALD DU–
THAT'S NOT HEAVY STUFF.

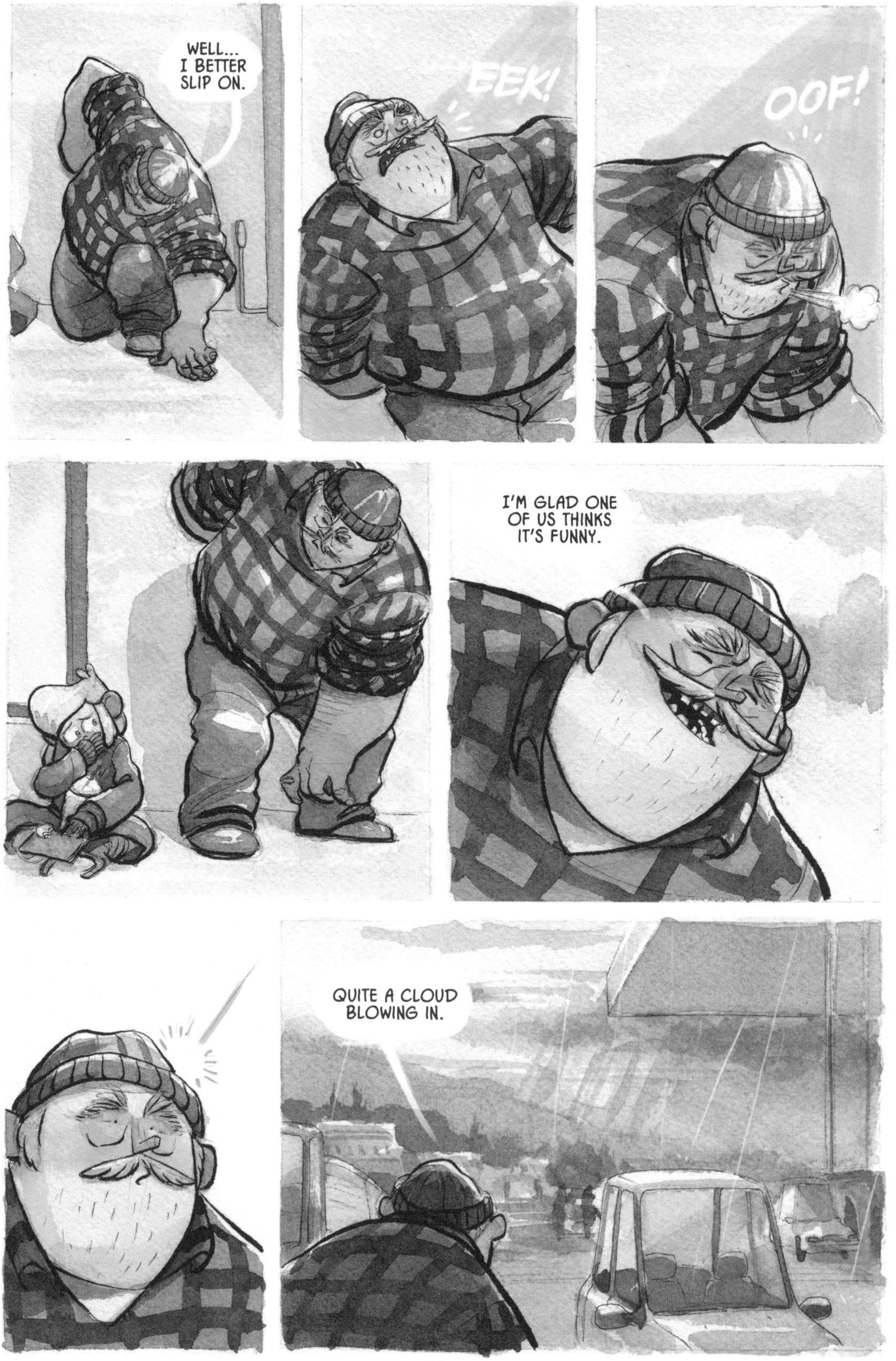
WELL... I BETTER SLIP ON.
EEK!
OOF!
I'M GLAD ONE OF US THINKS IT'S FUNNY.
QUITE A CLOUD BLOWING IN.

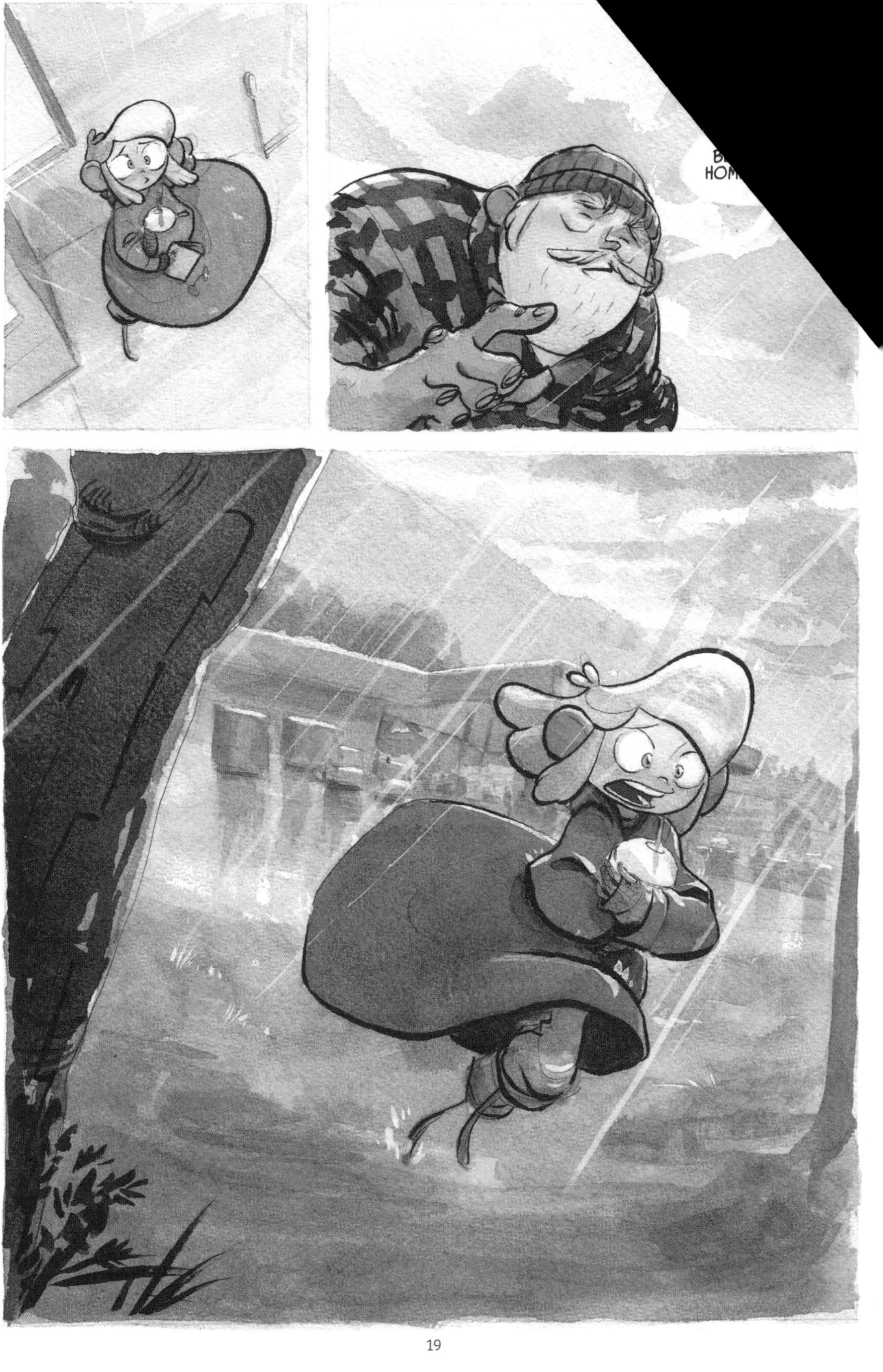

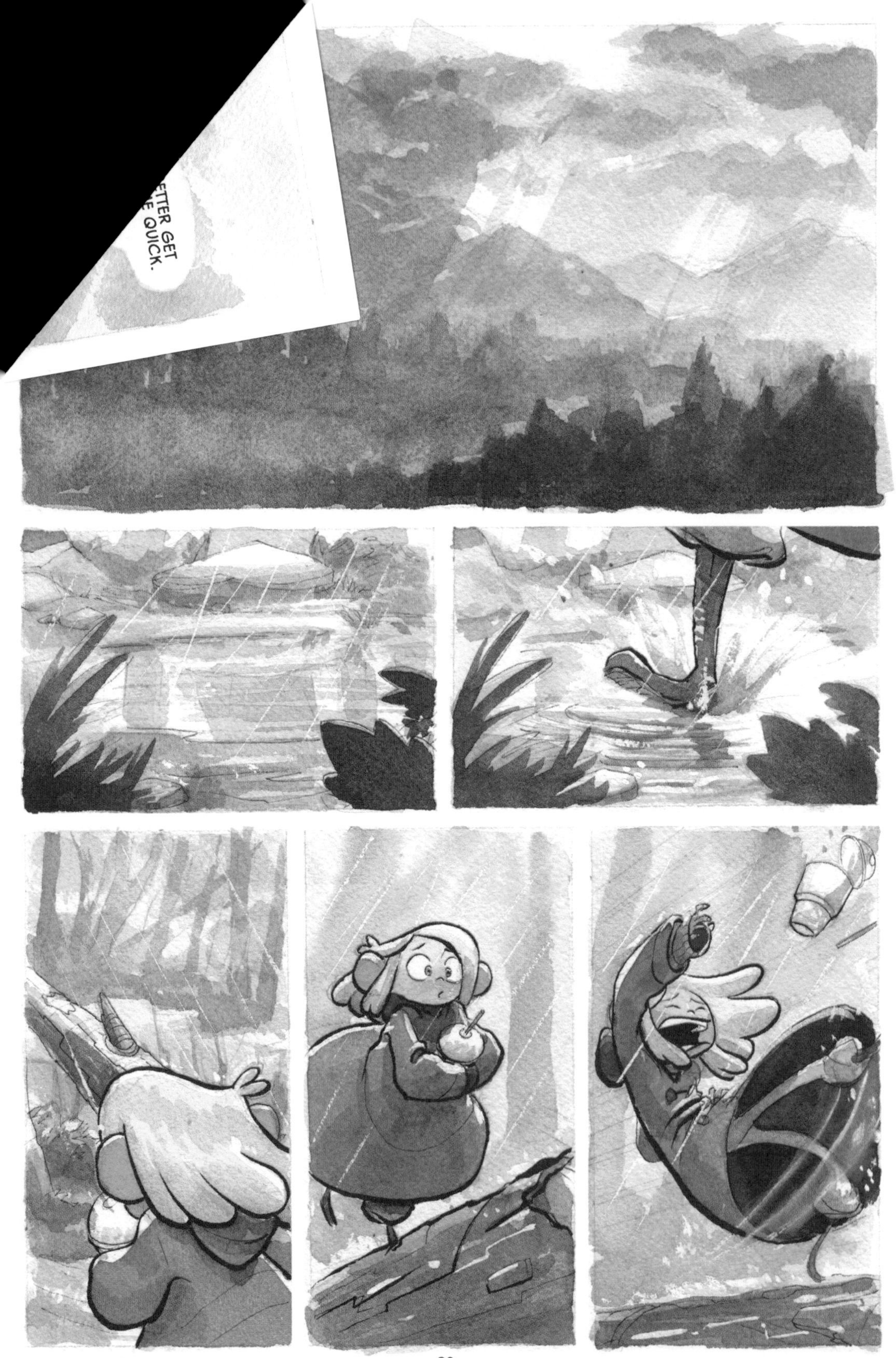

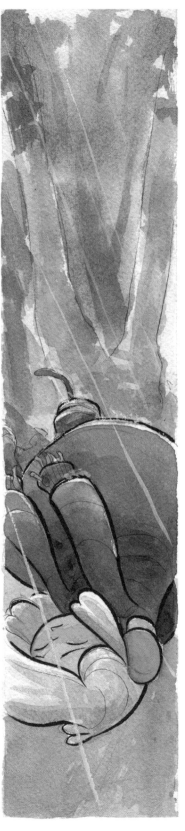

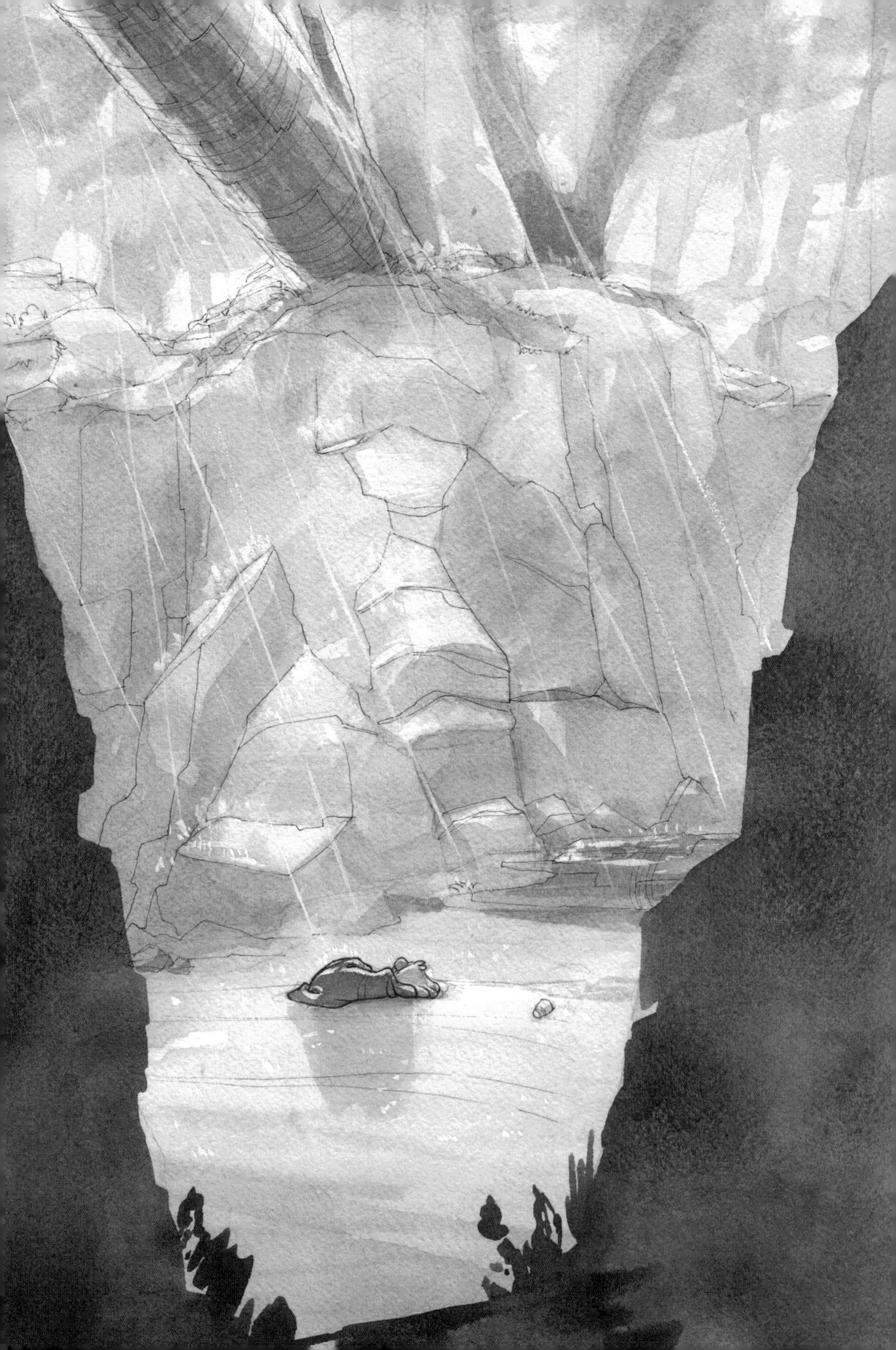

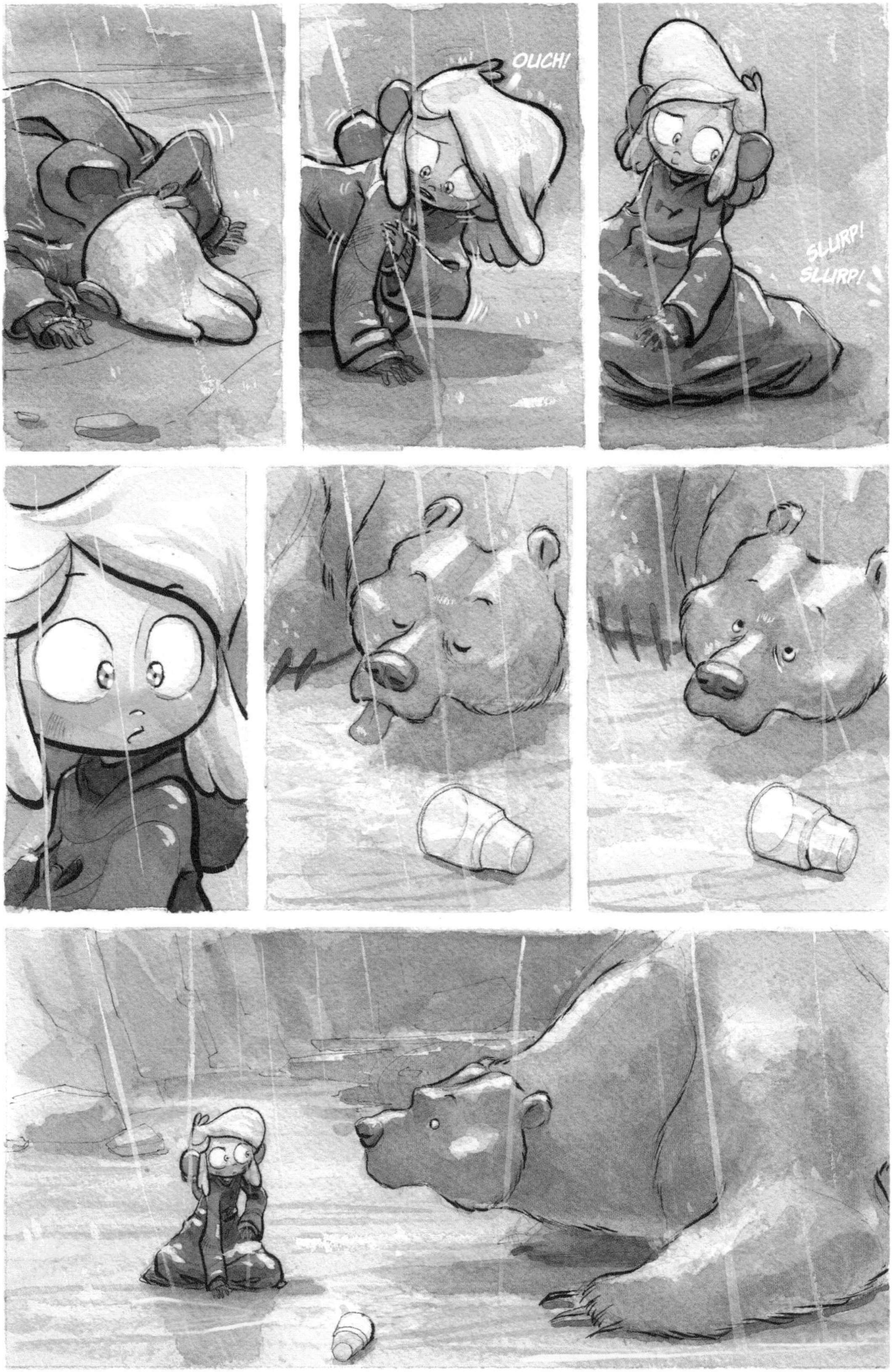
OUCH!
SLURP!
SLURP!

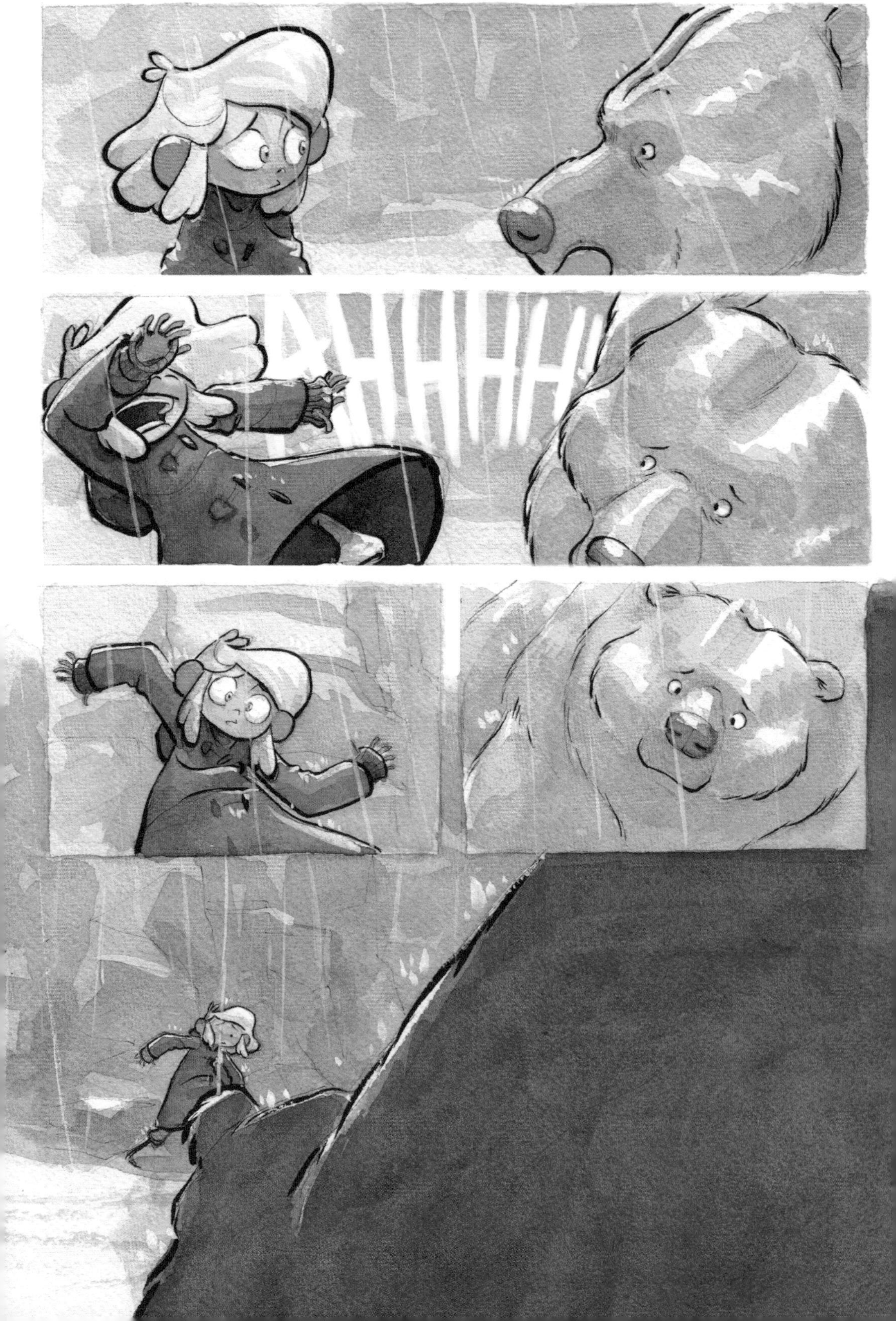
AHHHH!

CRACK!

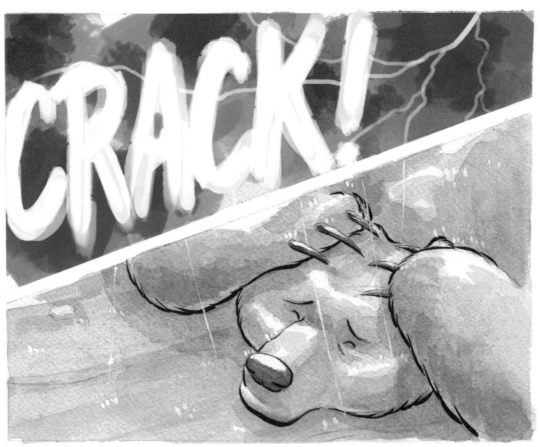

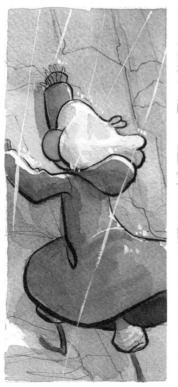

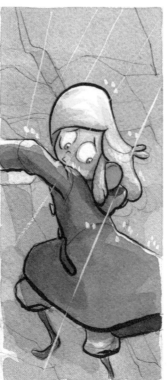

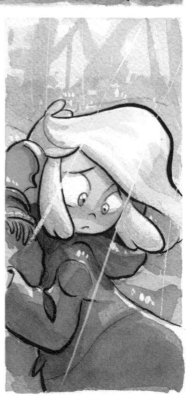

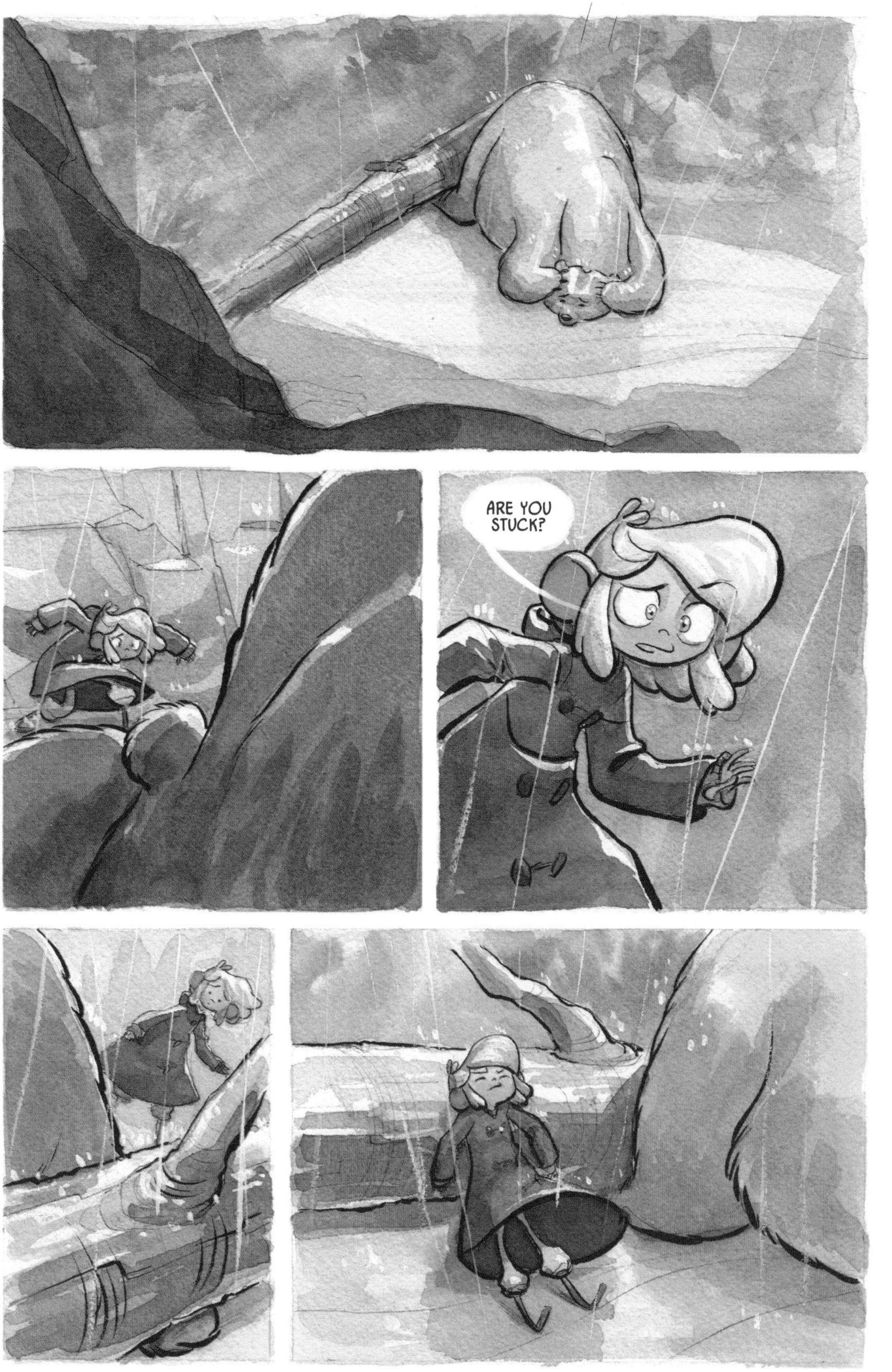
ARE YOU
STUCK?

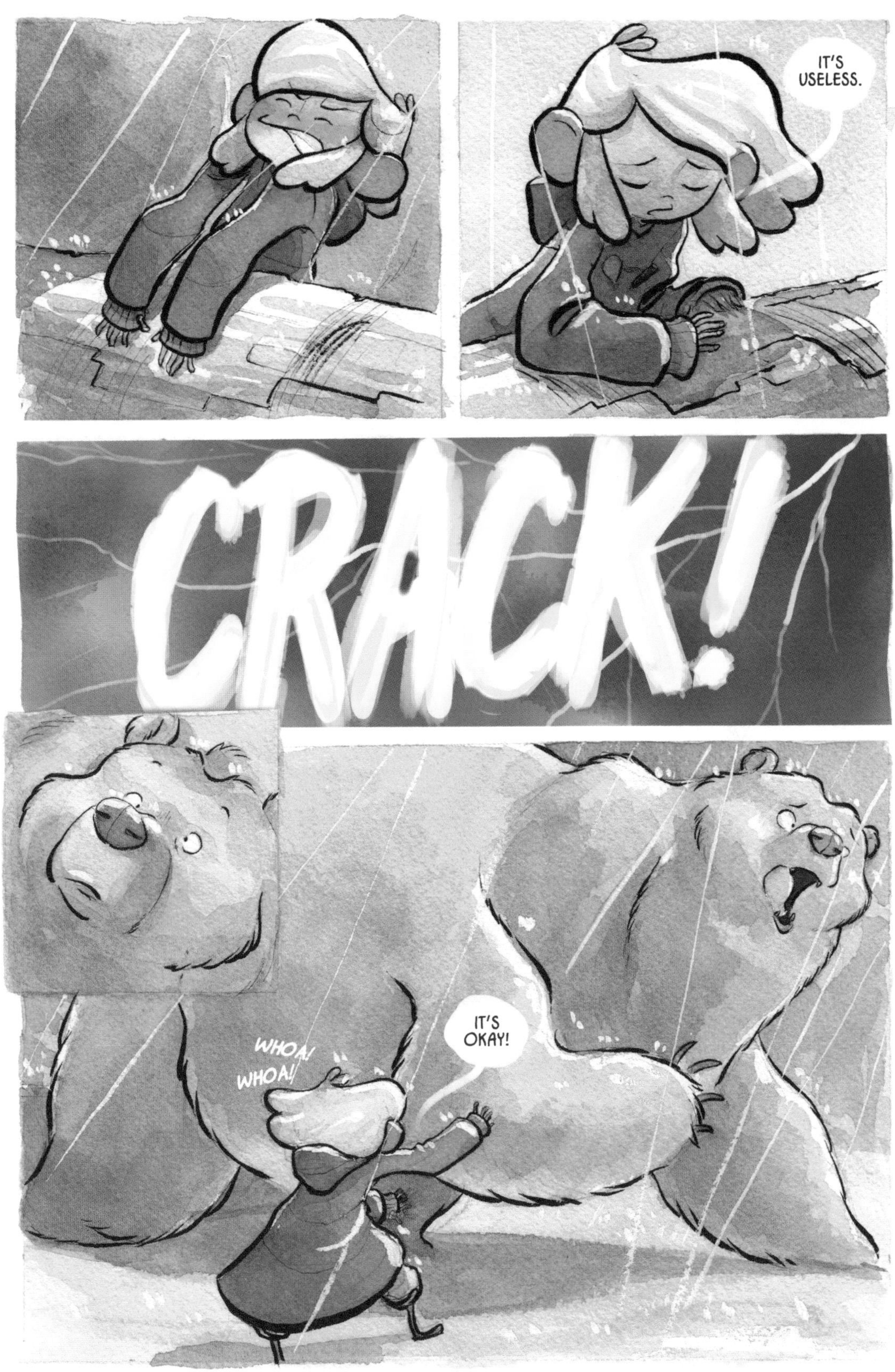
IT'S USELESS.
CRACK!
WHOA! WHOA!
IT'S OKAY!

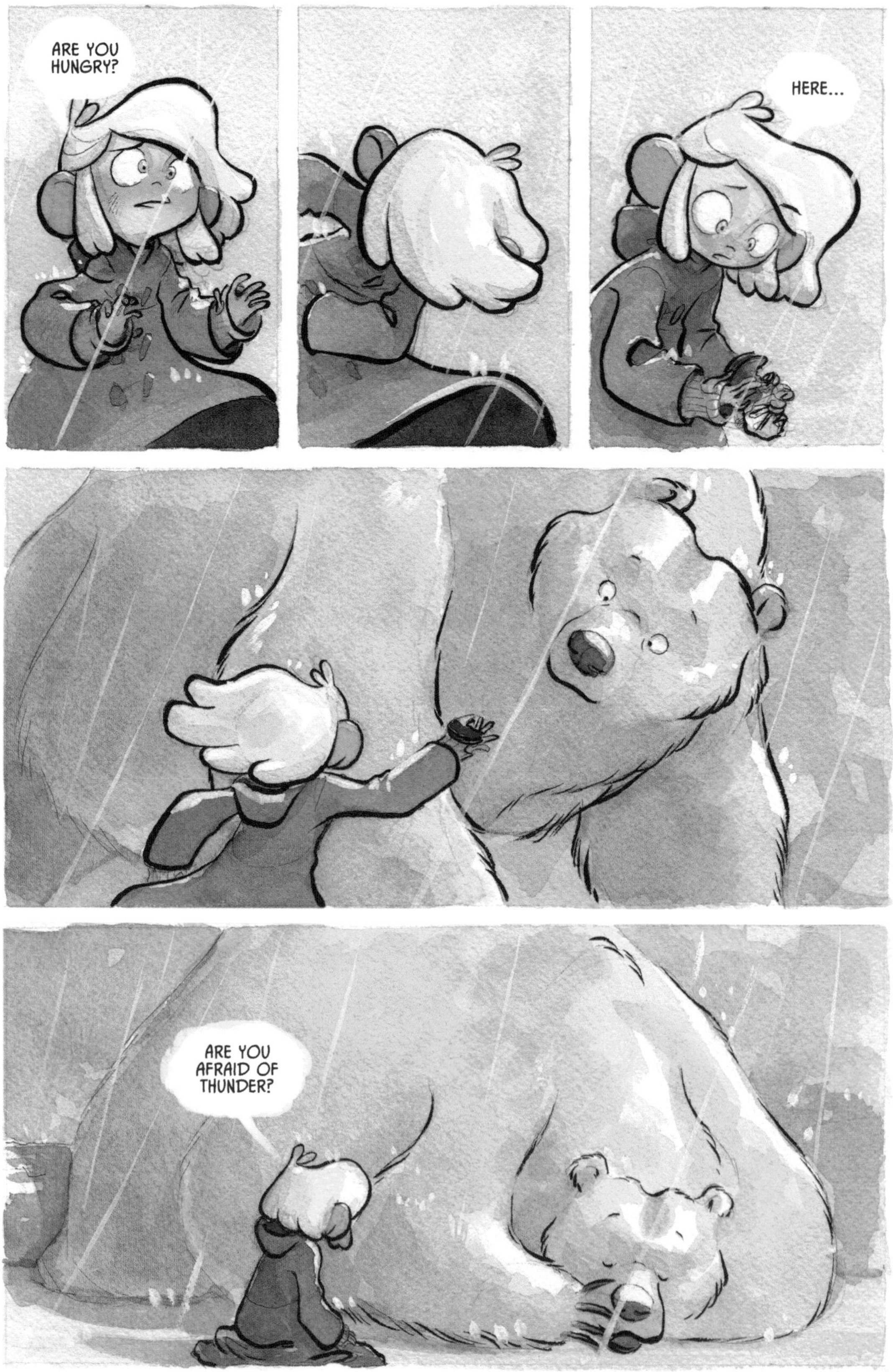
ARE YOU HUNGRY?
HERE...
ARE YOU AFRAID OF THUNDER?

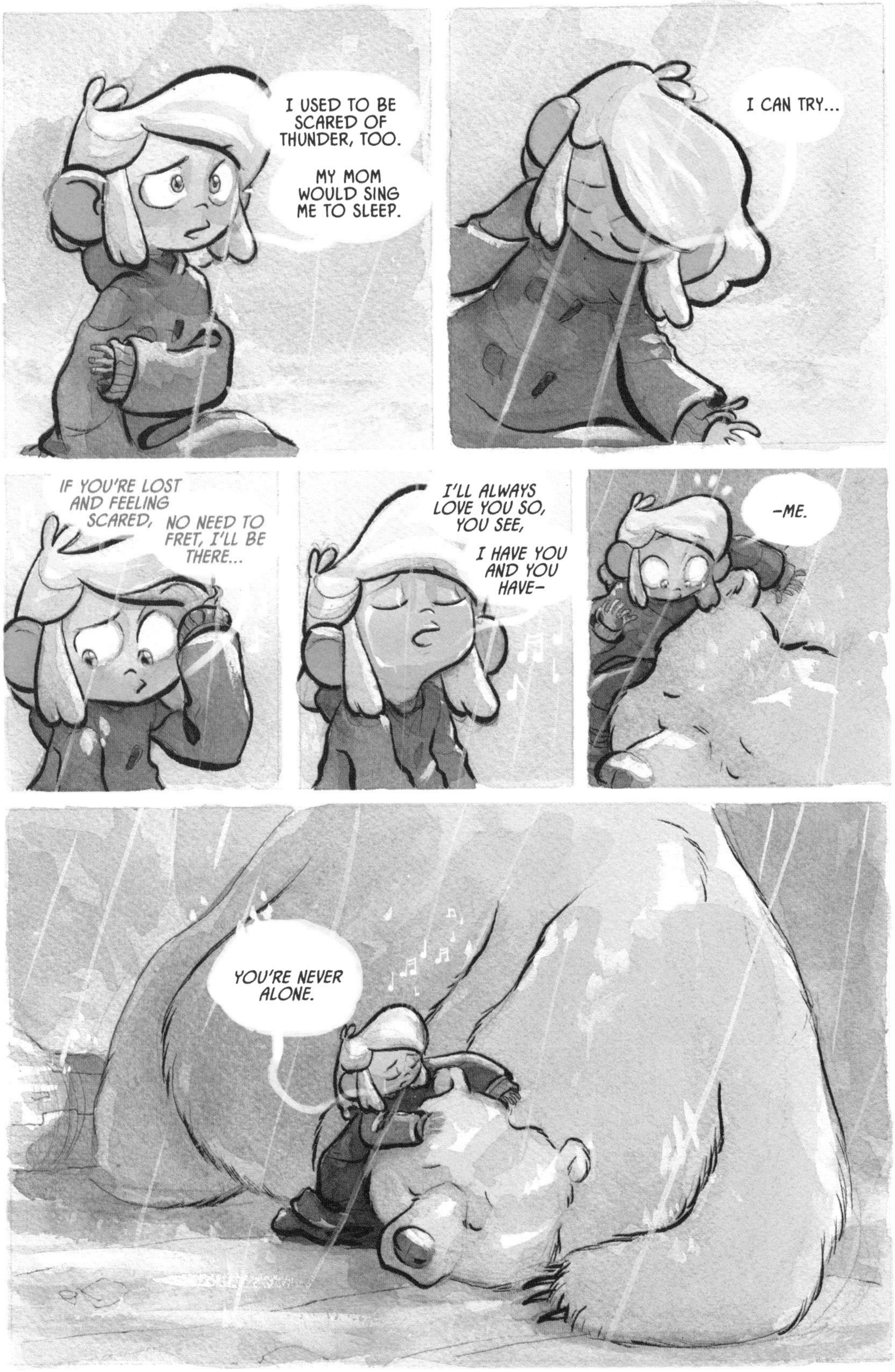
I USED TO BE SCARED OF THUNDER, TOO.
MY MOM WOULD SING ME TO SLEEP.
I CAN TRY...
IF YOU'RE LOST AND FEELING SCARED,
NO NEED TO FRET, I'LL BE THERE...
I'LL ALWAYS LOVE YOU SO, YOU SEE,
I HAVE YOU AND YOU HAVE-
-ME.
YOU'RE NEVER ALONE.

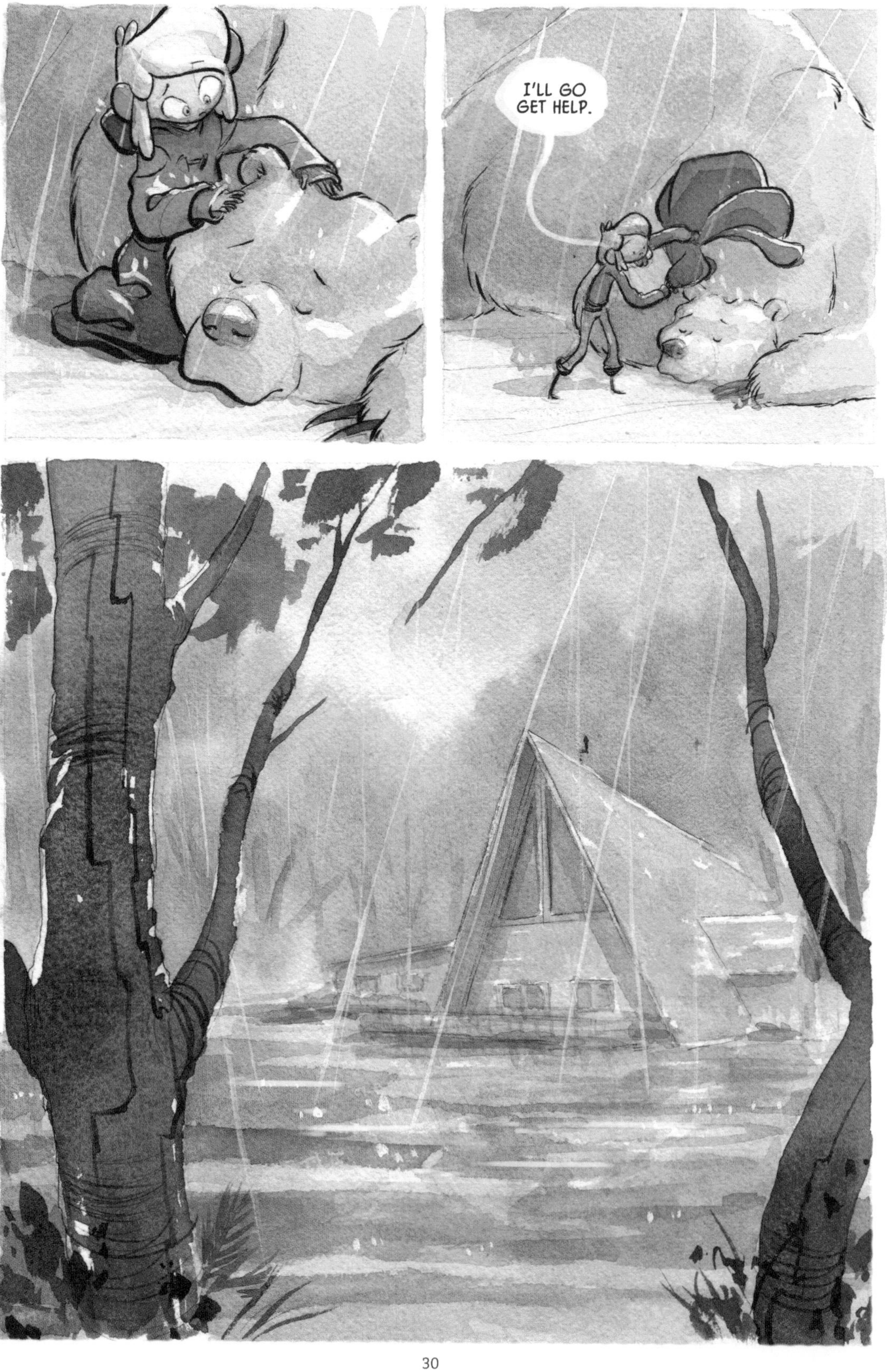
I'LL GO GET HELP.

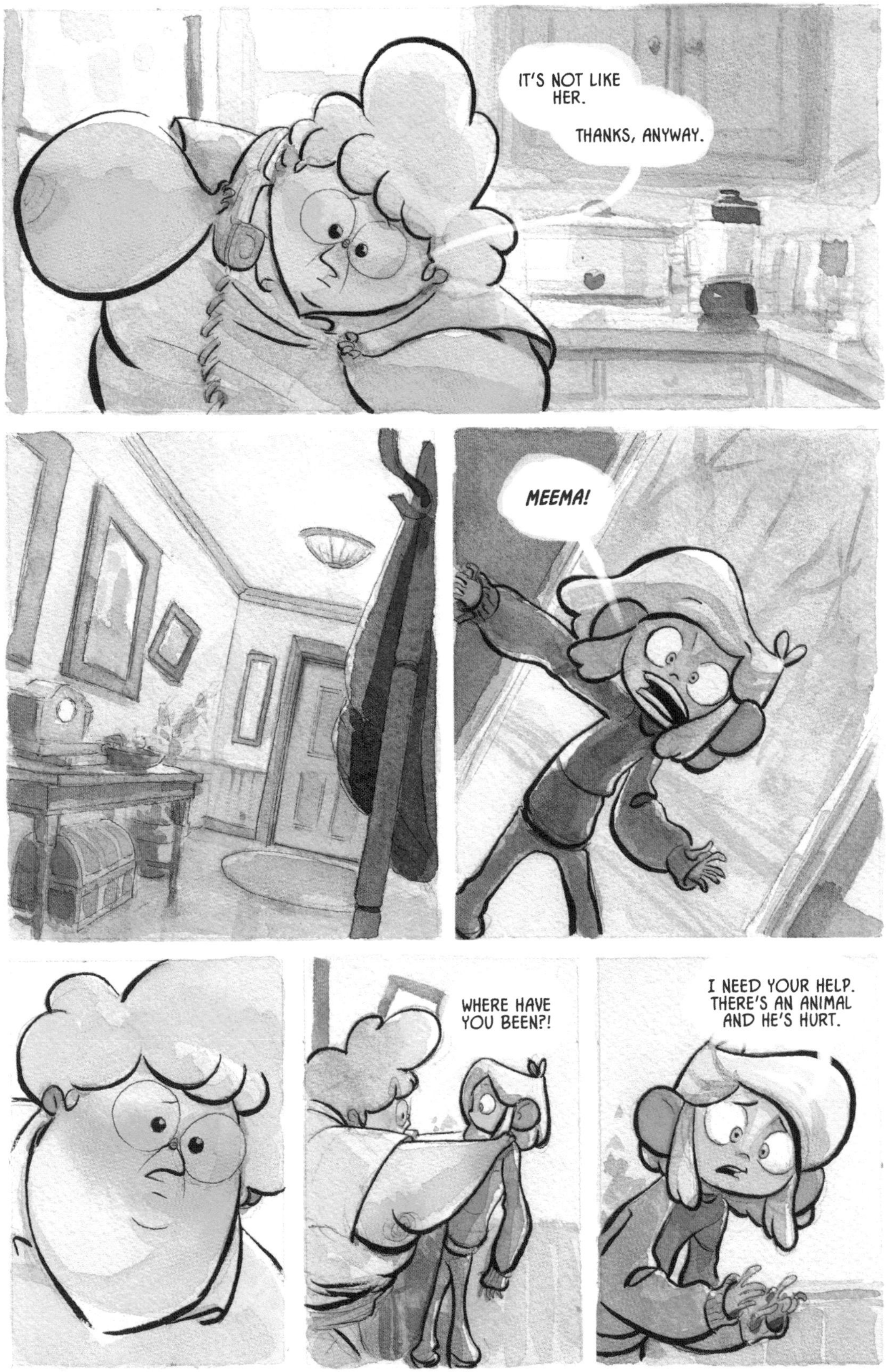
IT'S NOT LIKE HER.
THANKS, ANYWAY.
MEEMA!
WHERE HAVE YOU BEEN?!
I NEED YOUR HELP. THERE'S AN ANIMAL AND HE'S HURT.

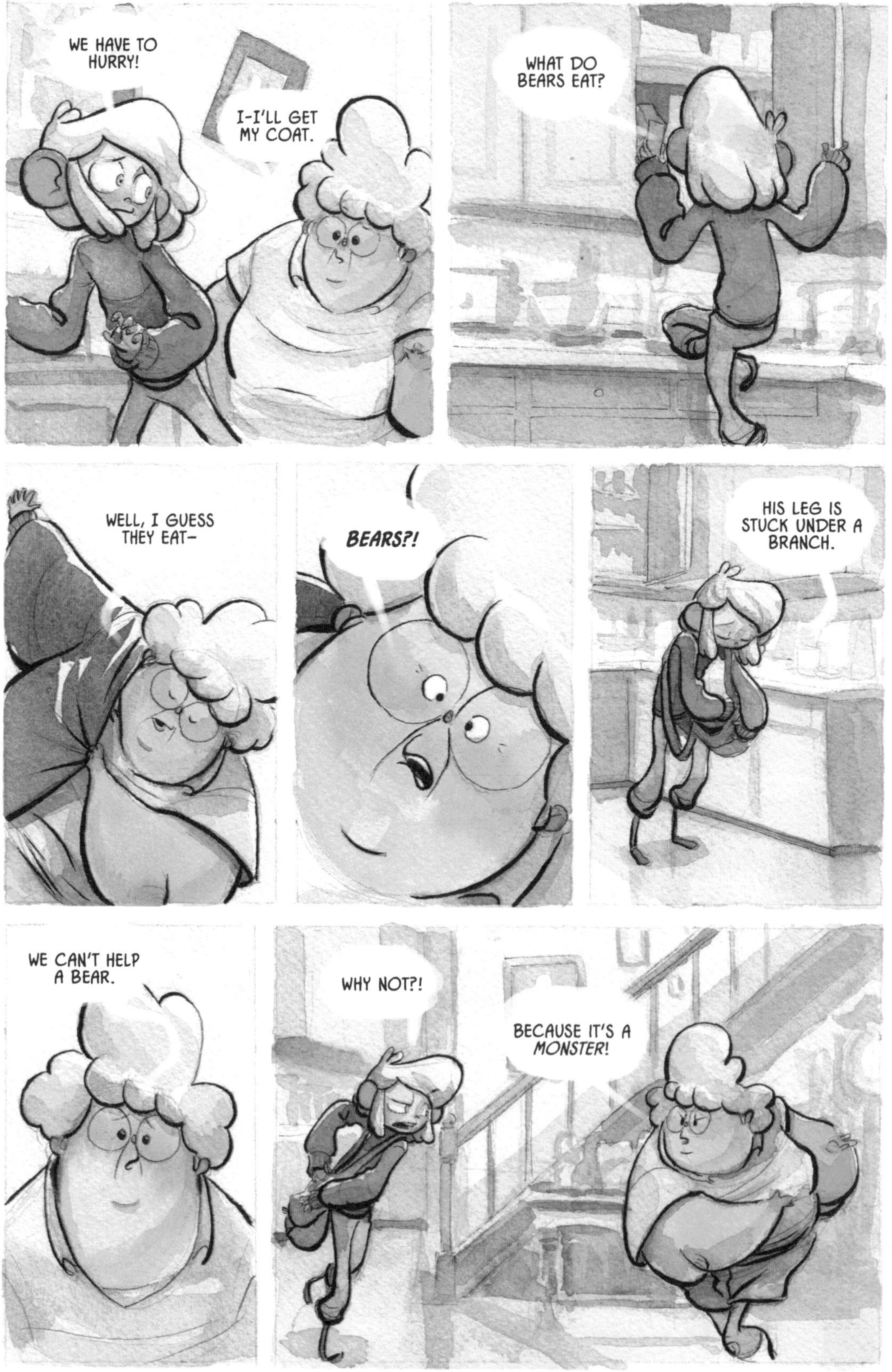

WE HAVE TO HURRY!
I-I'LL GET MY COAT.
WHAT DO BEARS EAT?
WELL, I GUESS THEY EAT-
BEARS?!
HIS LEG IS STUCK UNDER A BRANCH.
WE CAN'T HELP A BEAR.
WHY NOT?!
BECAUSE IT'S A MONSTER!

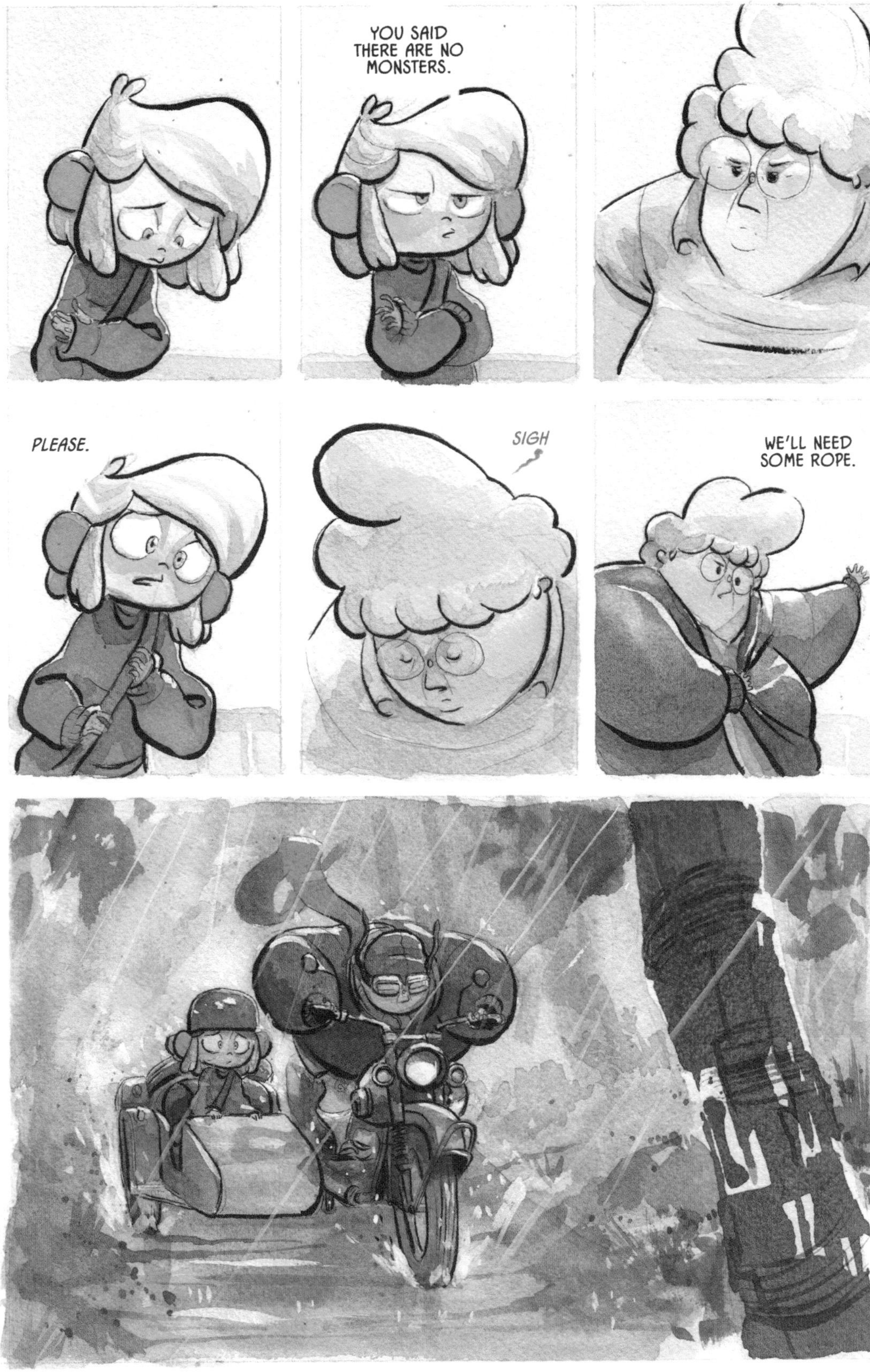
YOU SAID THERE ARE NO MONSTERS.
PLEASE.
SIGH
WE'LL NEED SOME ROPE.

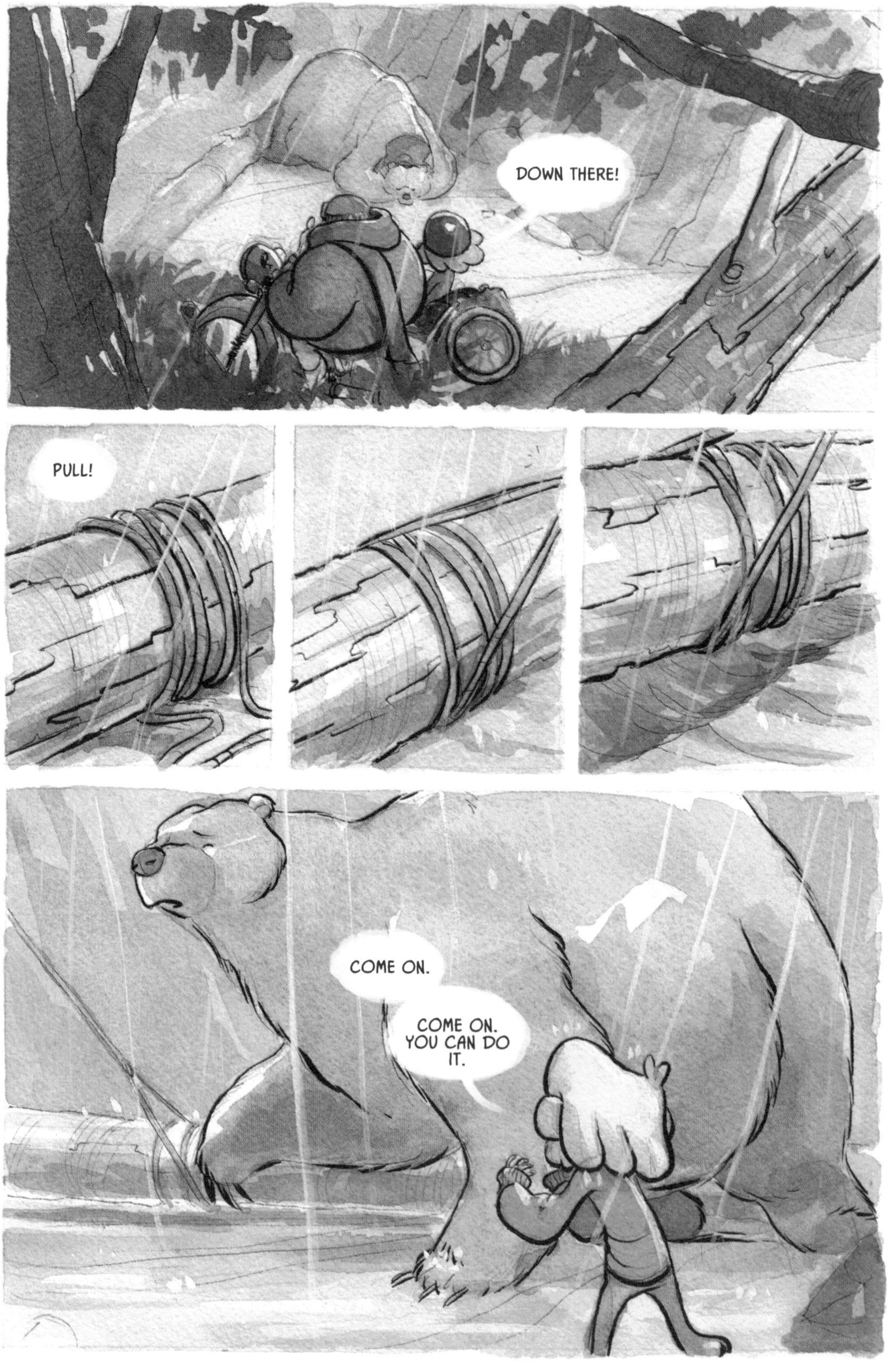
DOWN THERE!
PULL!
COME ON.
COME ON. YOU CAN DO IT.

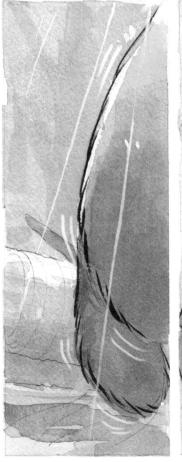

YES!

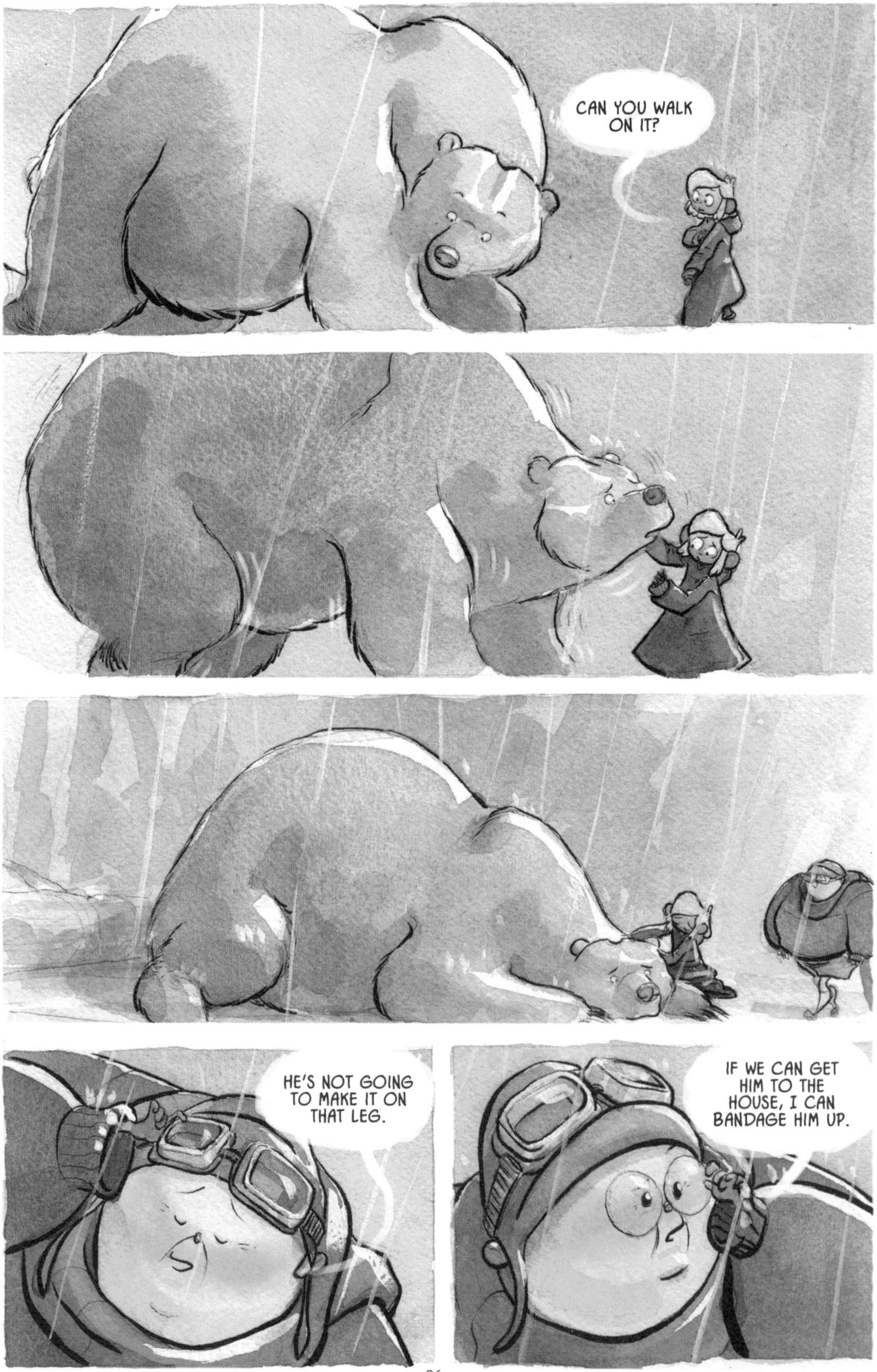
CAN YOU WALK ON IT?
HE'S NOT GOING TO MAKE IT ON THAT LEG.
IF WE CAN GET HIM TO THE HOUSE, I CAN BANDAGE HIM UP.

JUST A LITTLE FURTHER...

STEP BACK, KATYA. THIS MIGHT STING A BIT.

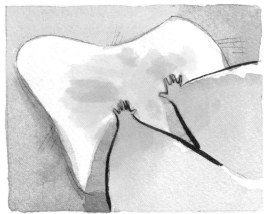

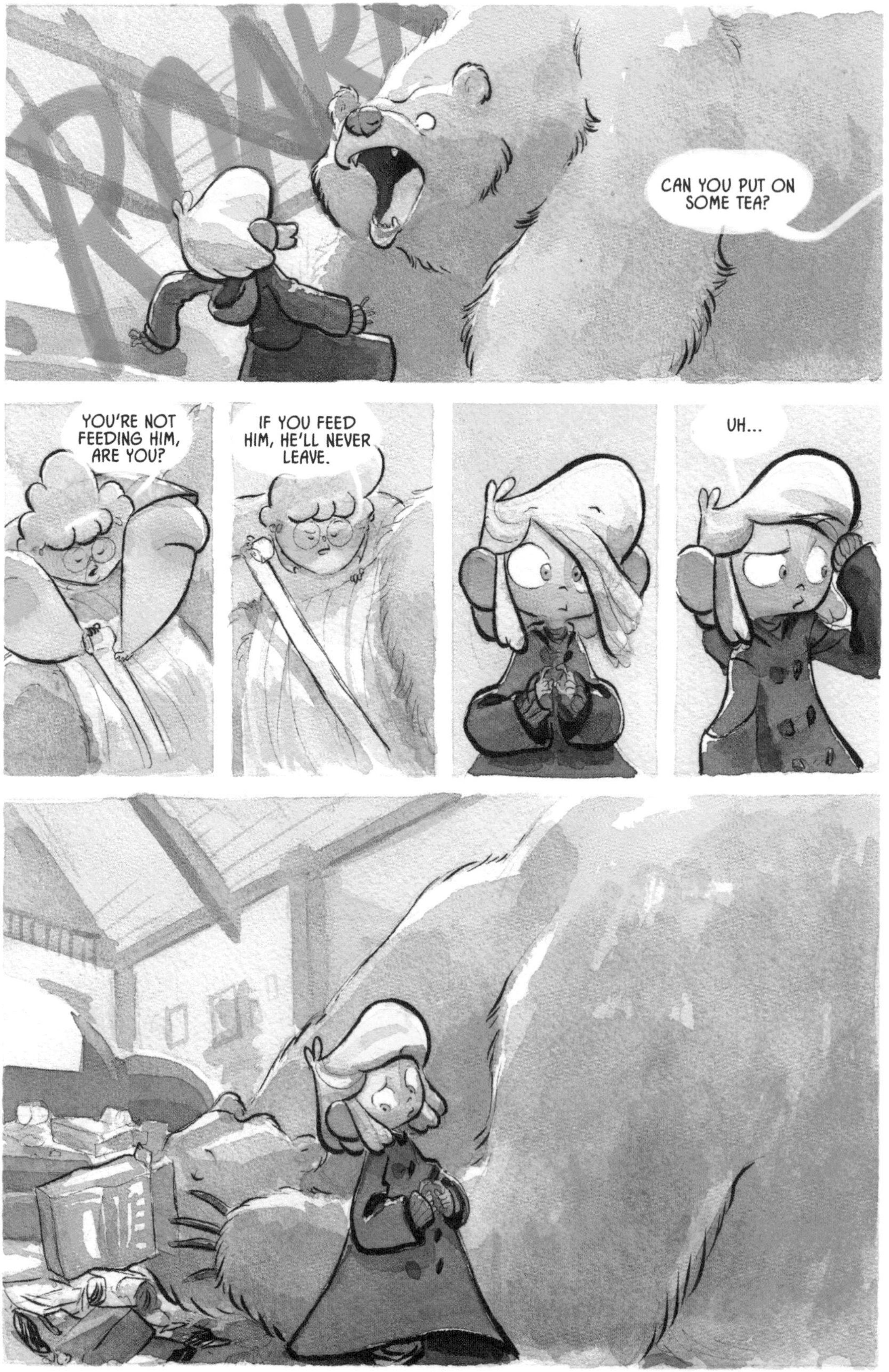
ROAR
CAN YOU PUT ON SOME TEA?
YOU'RE NOT FEEDING HIM, ARE YOU?
IF YOU FEED HIM, HE'LL NEVER LEAVE.
UH...

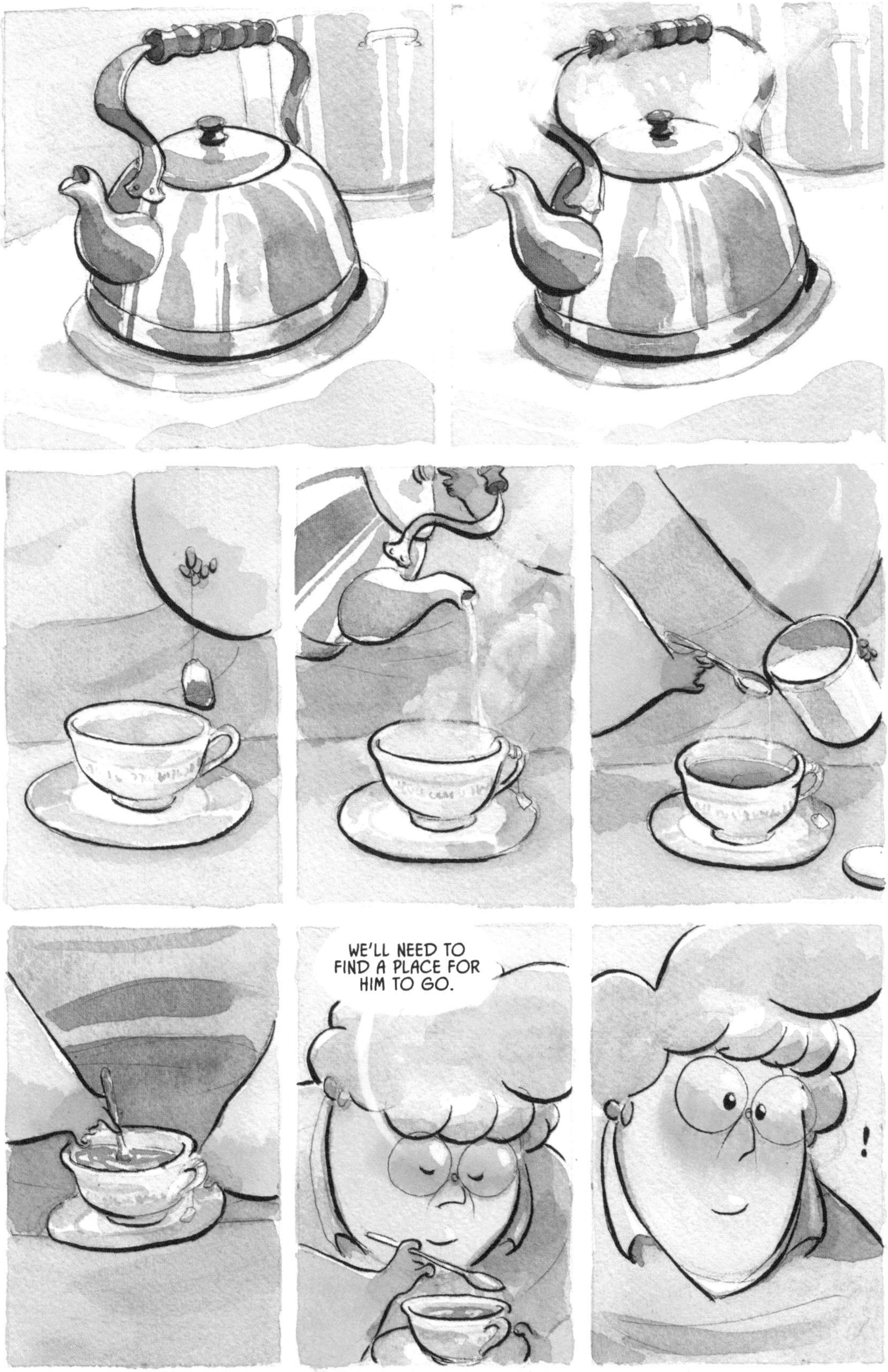
WE'LL NEED TO FIND A PLACE FOR HIM TO GO.
!

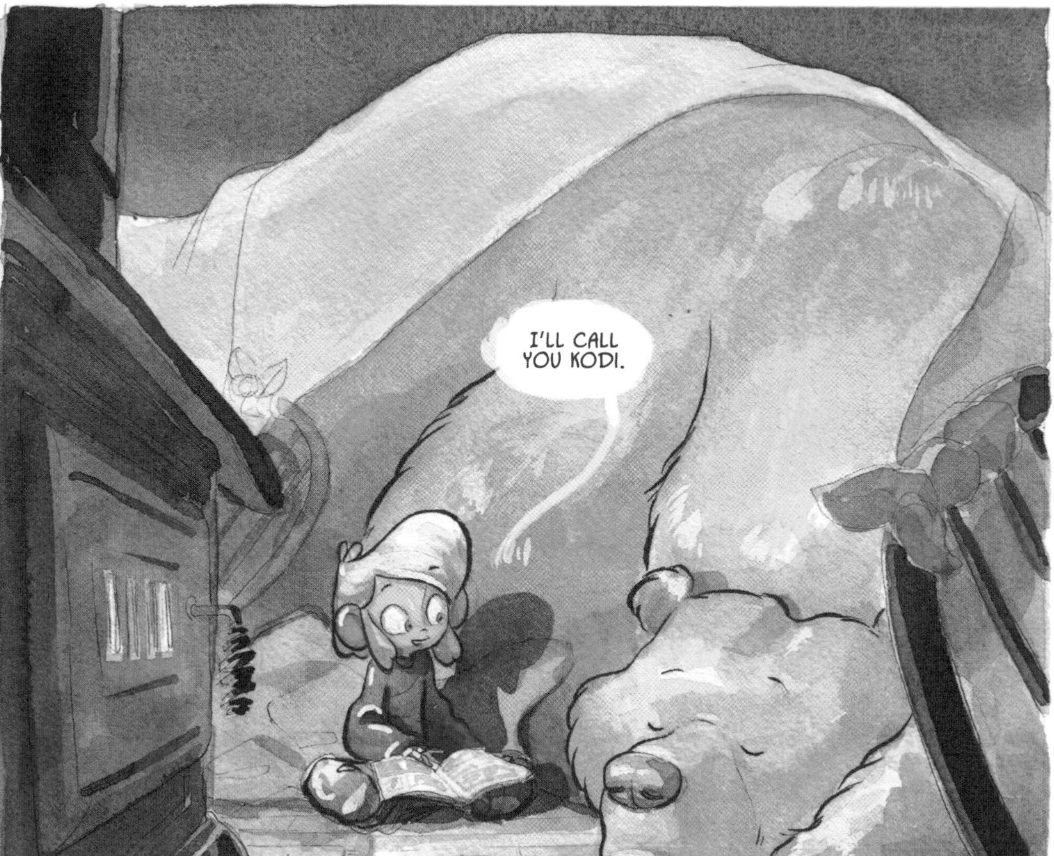
I'LL CALL YOU KODI.

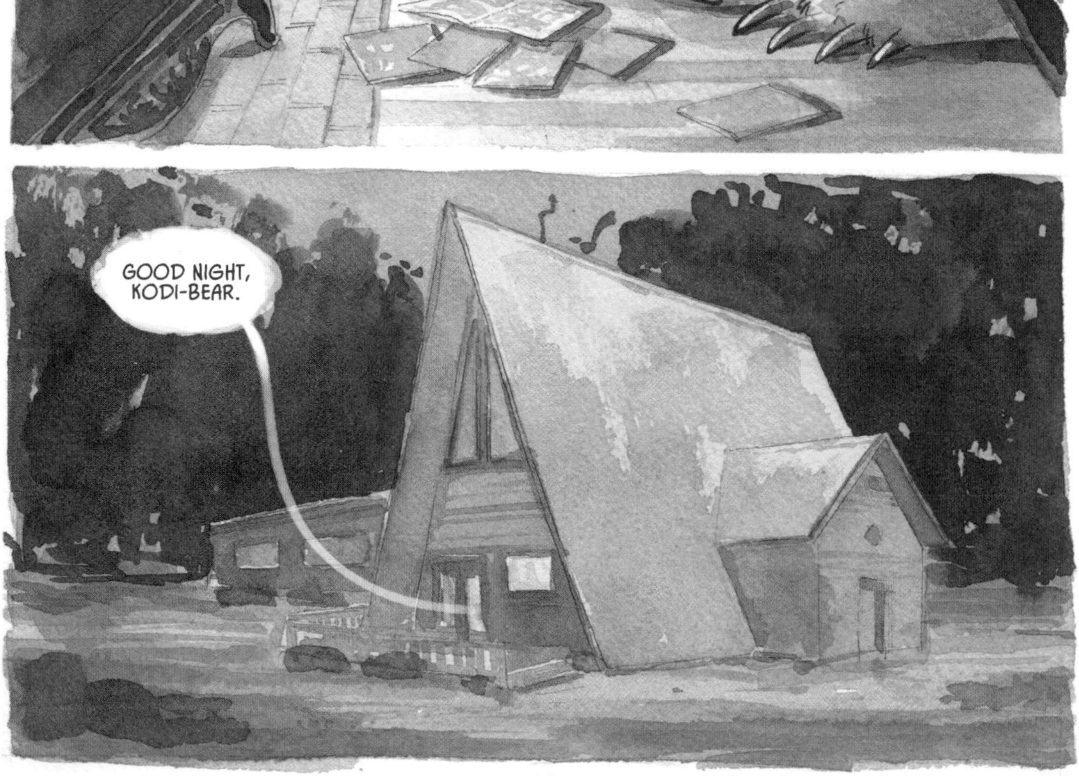
GOOD NIGHT, KODI-BEAR.

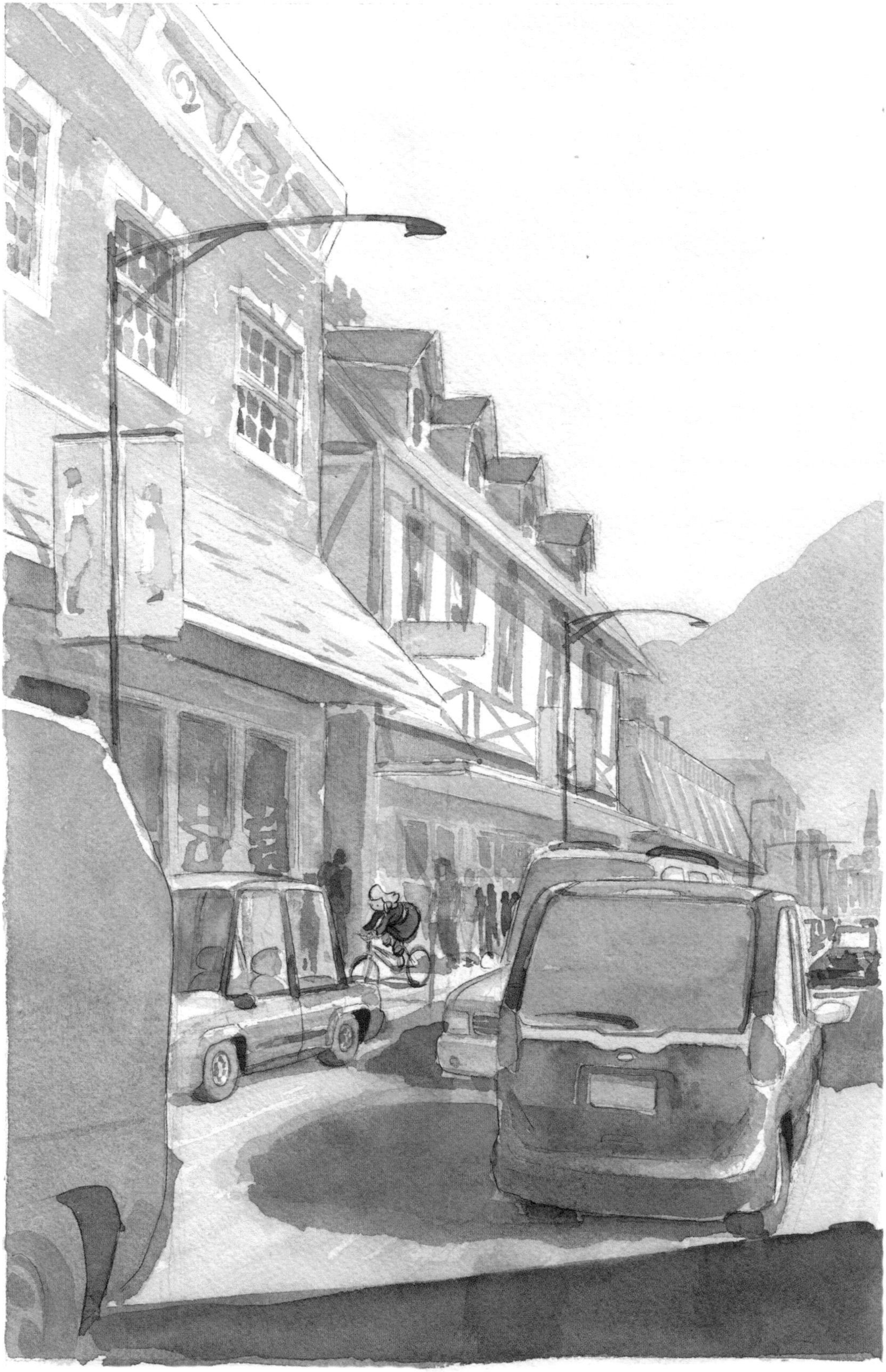

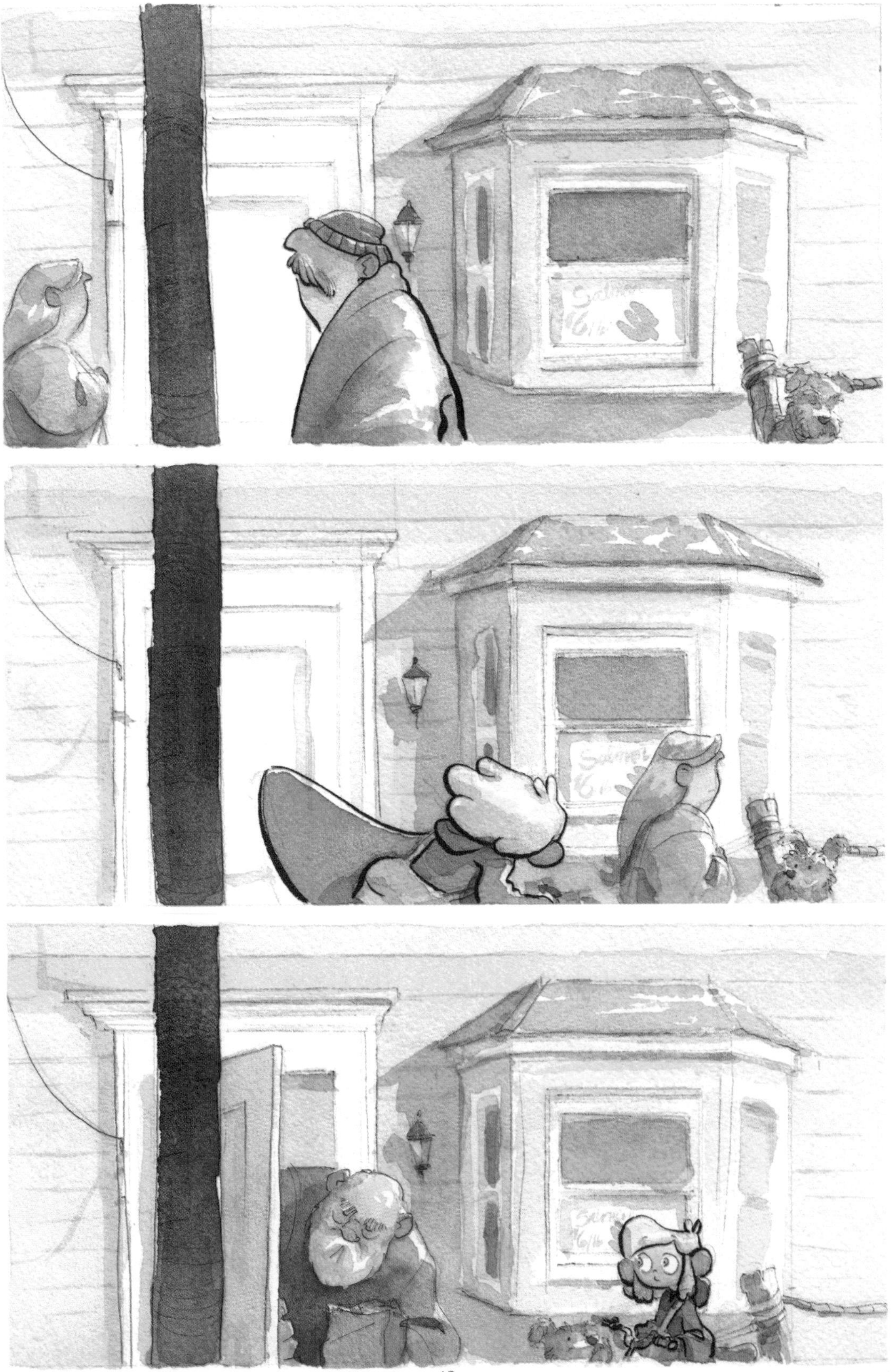

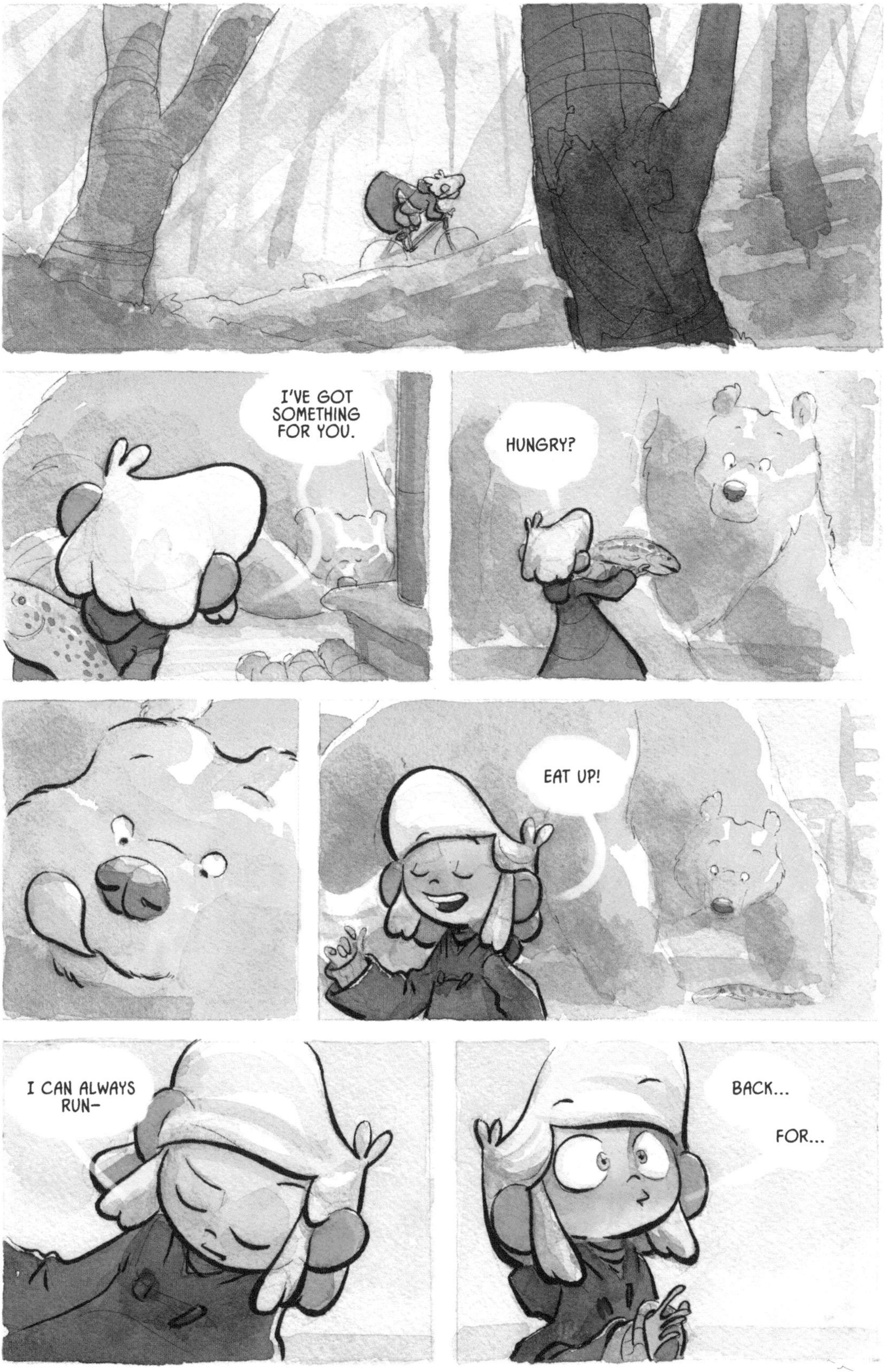
I'VE GOT SOMETHING FOR YOU.
HUNGRY?
EAT UP!
I CAN ALWAYS RUN–
BACK...
FOR...

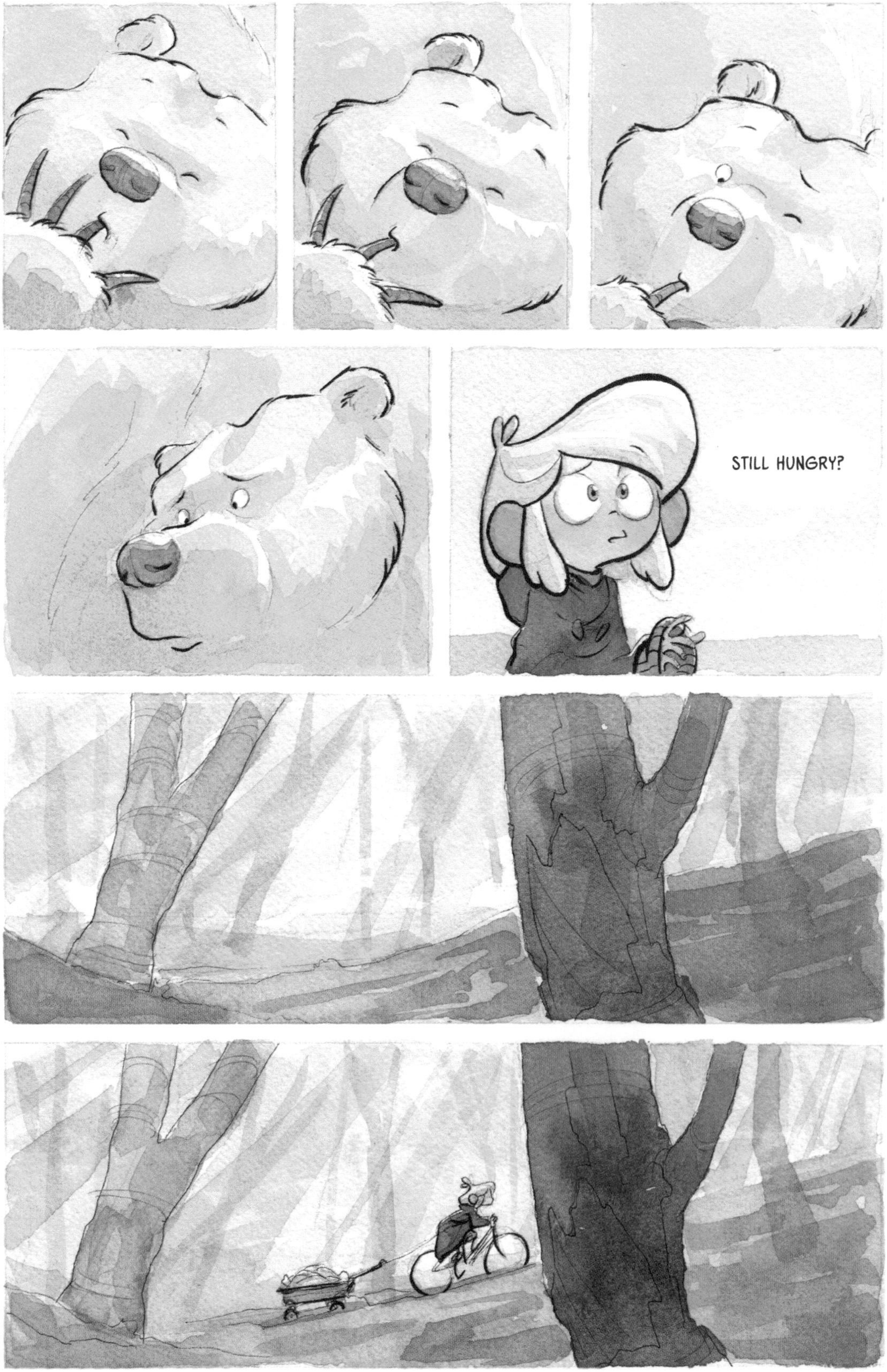
STILL HUNGRY?

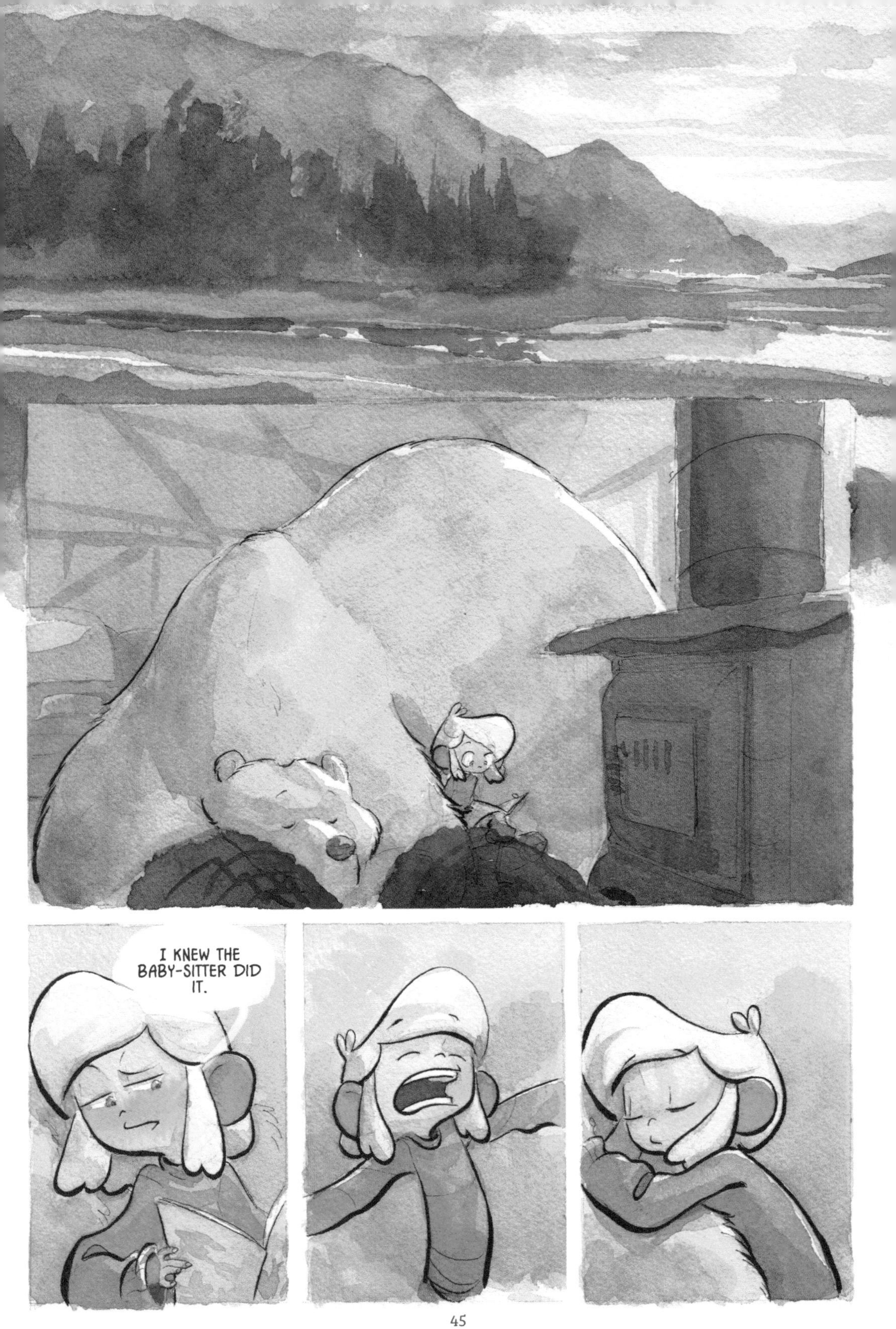
I KNEW THE BABY-SITTER DID IT.

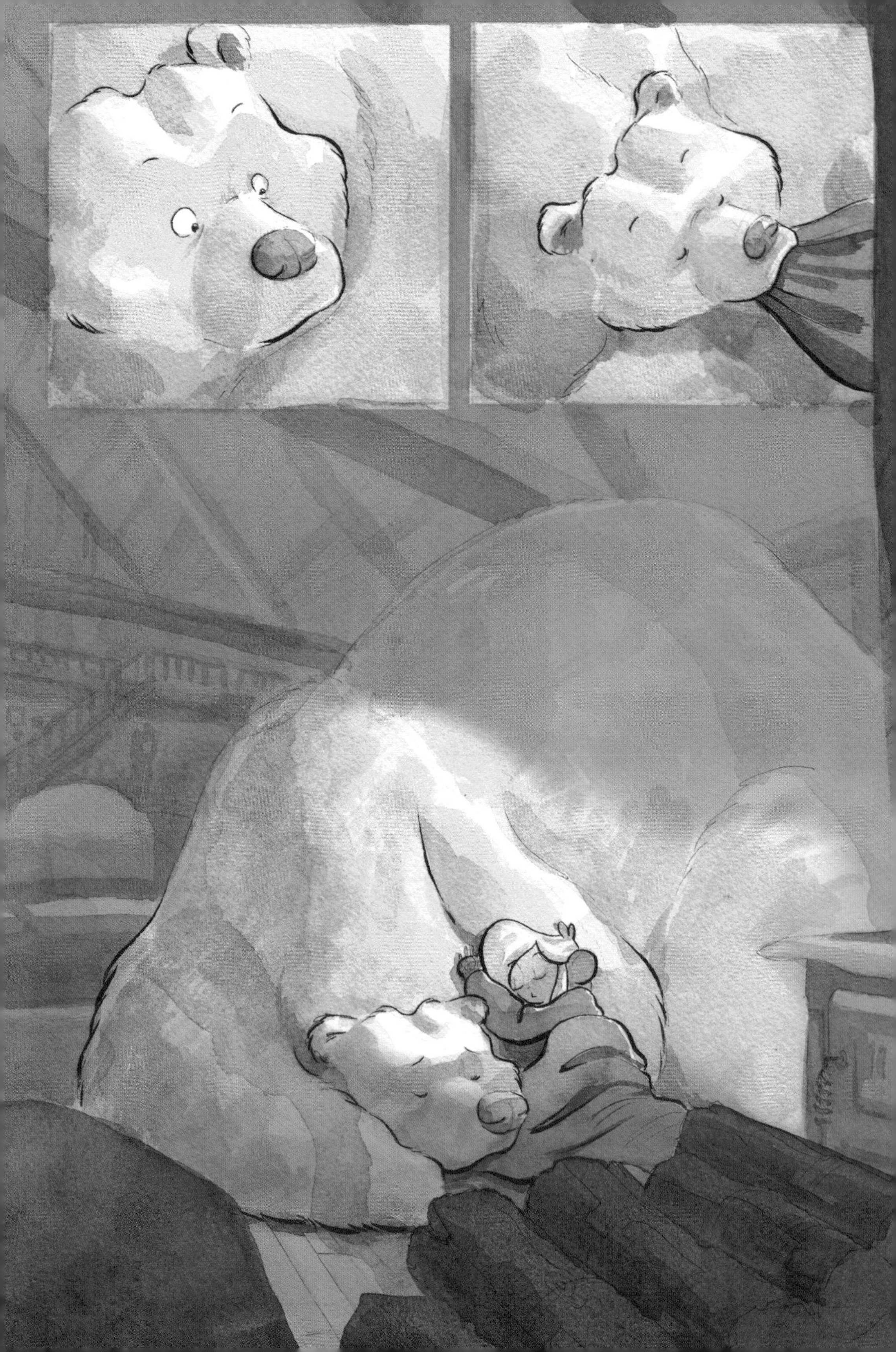

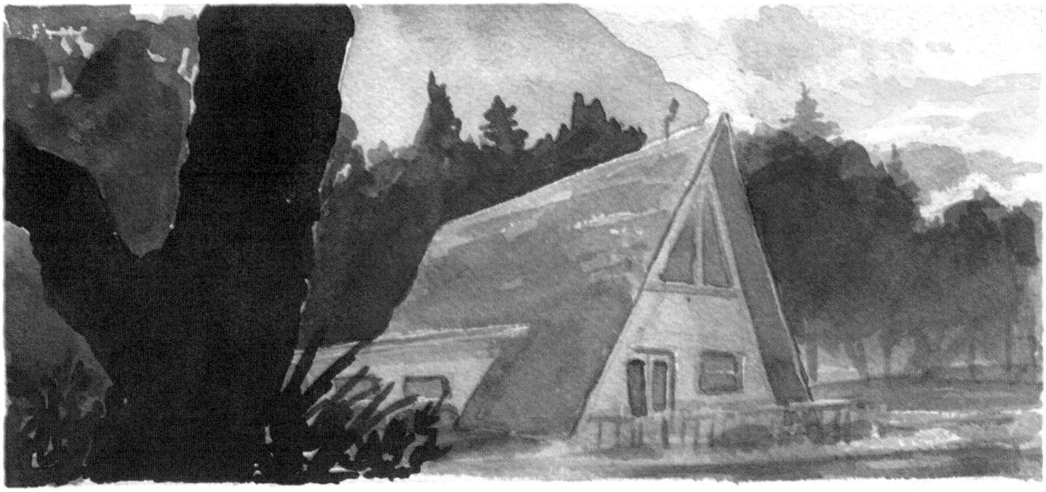
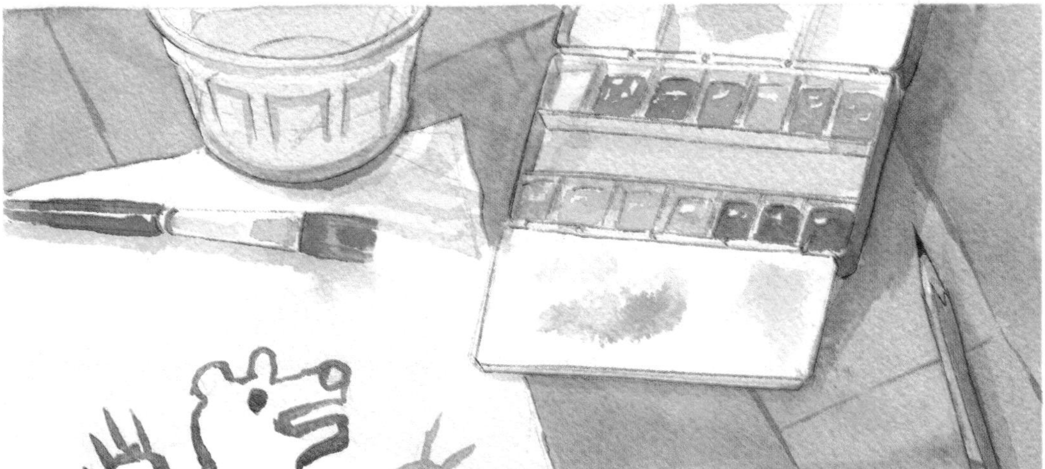
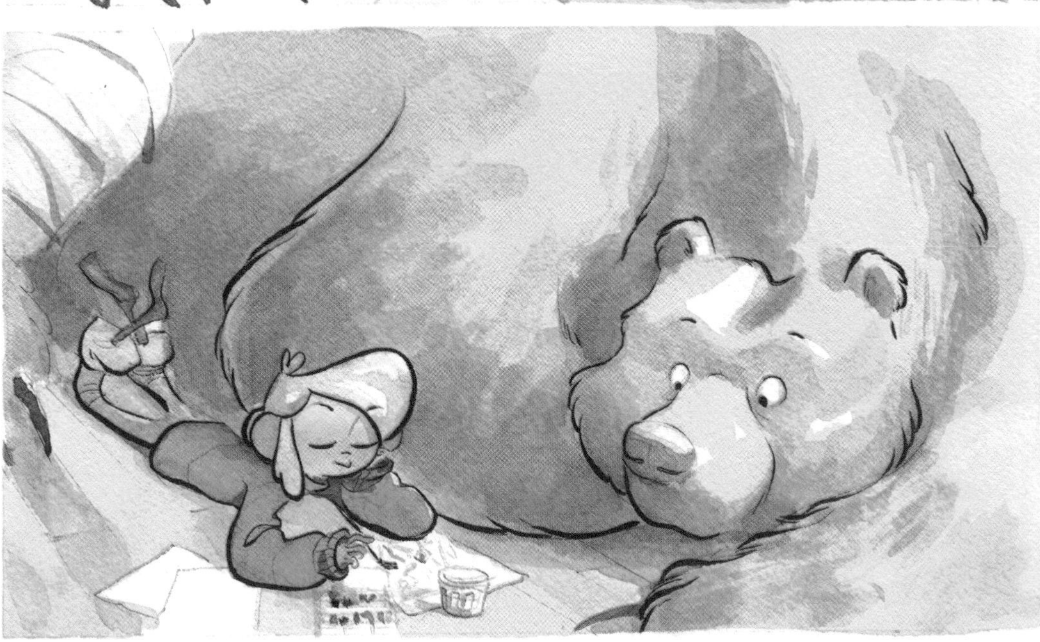

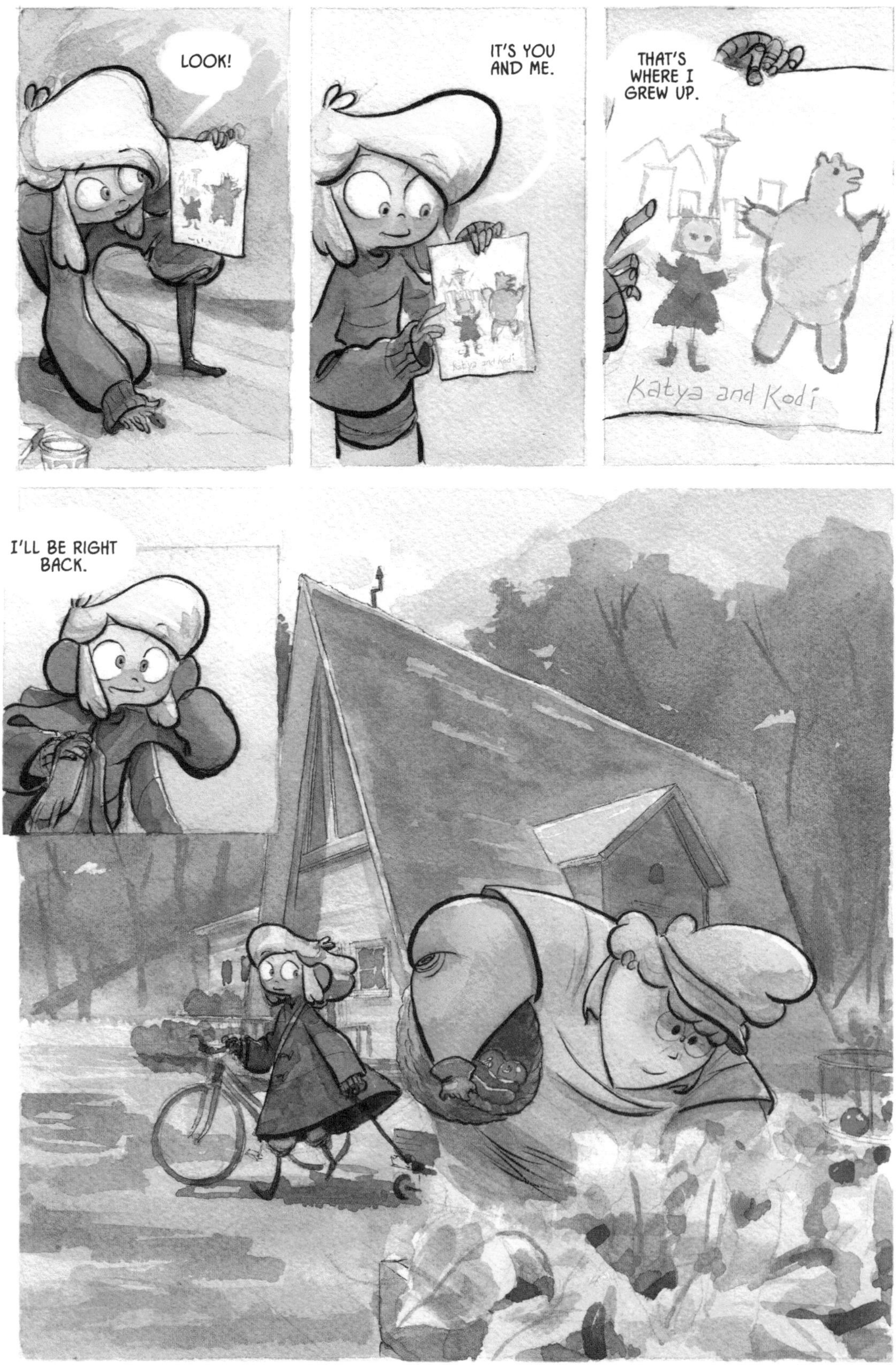
LOOK!
IT'S YOU AND ME.
THAT'S WHERE I GREW UP.
Katya and Kodi
I'LL BE RIGHT BACK.

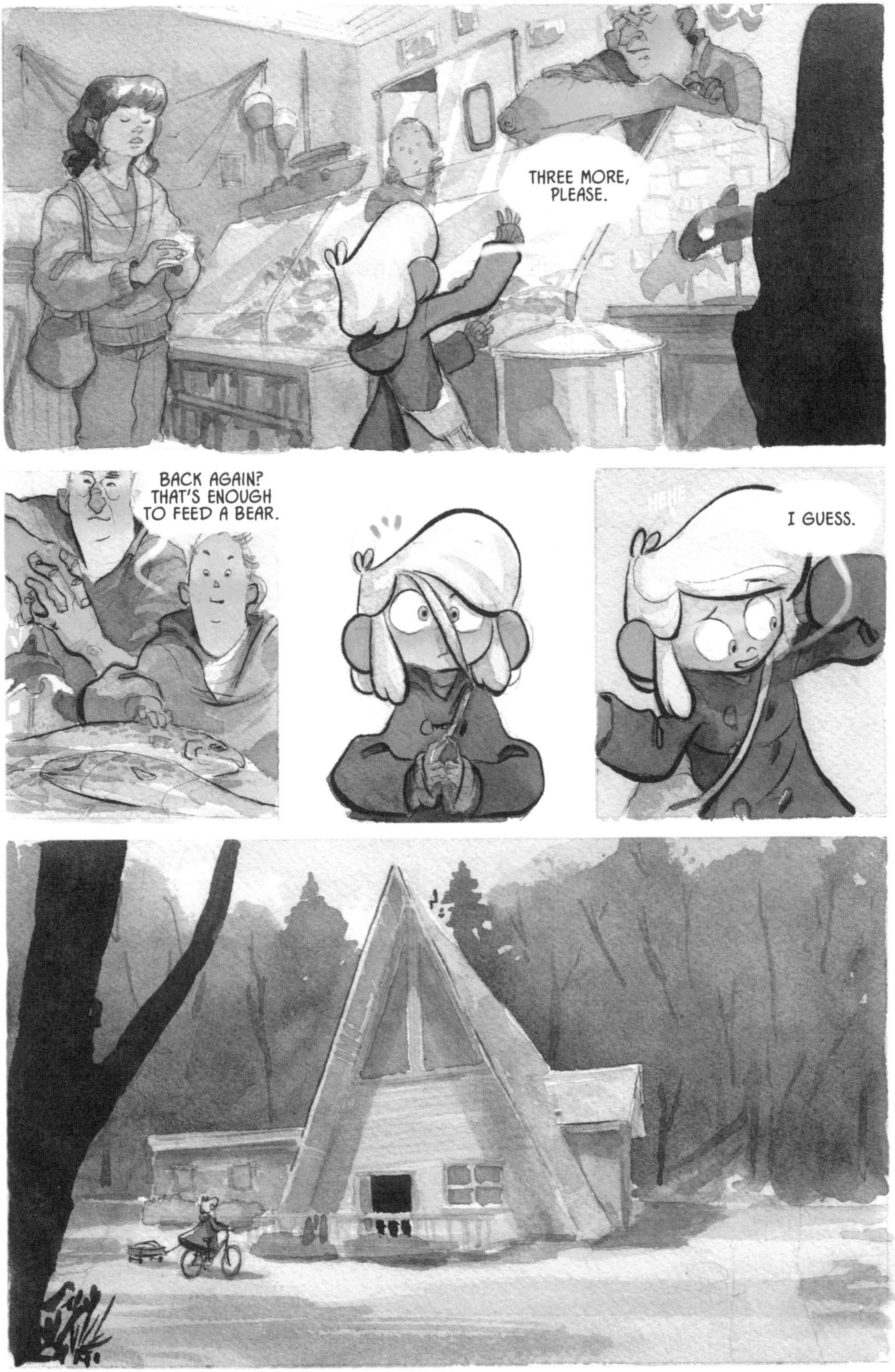
THREE MORE, PLEASE.
BACK AGAIN? THAT'S ENOUGH TO FEED A BEAR.
HEHE
I GUESS.

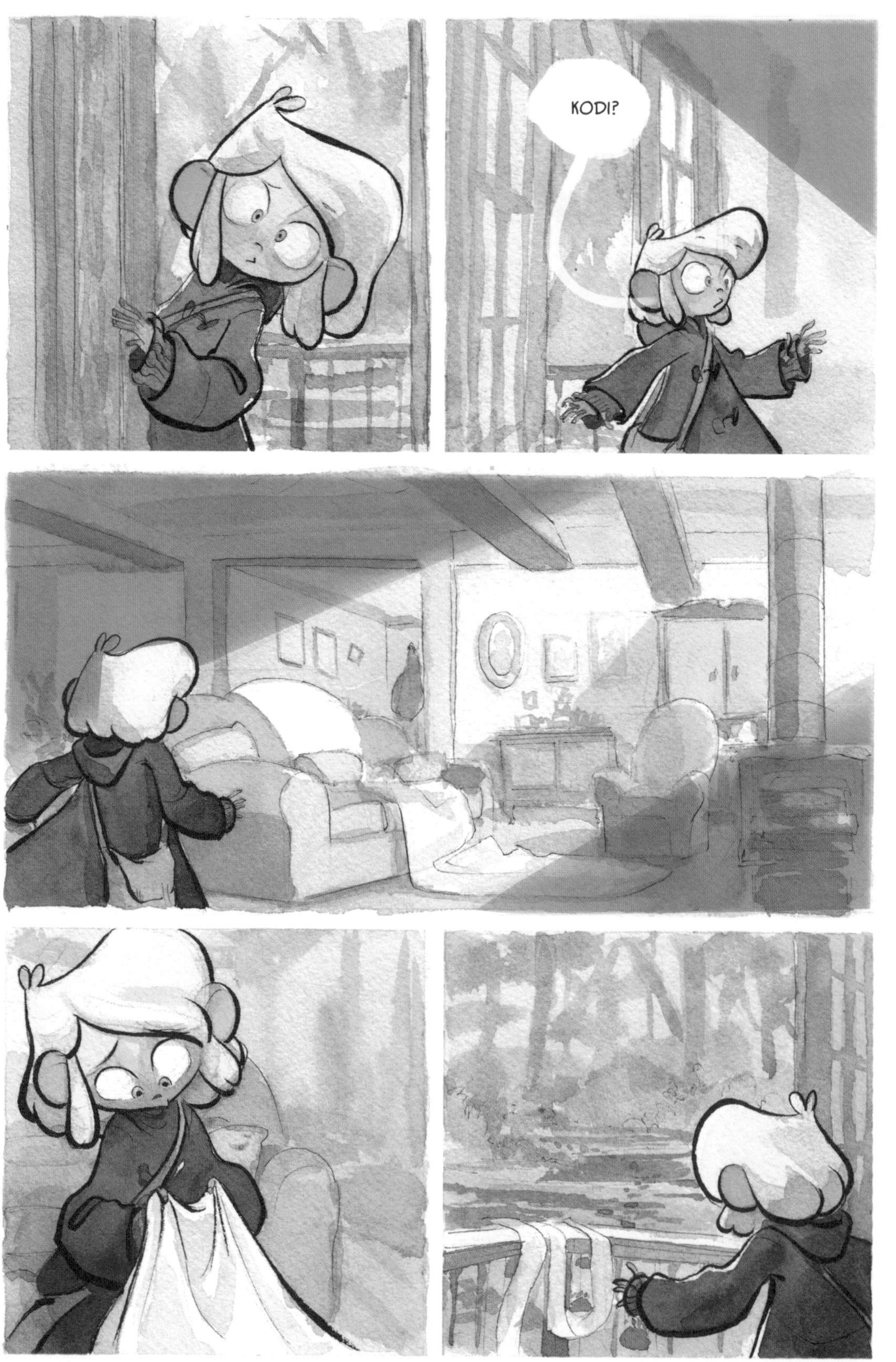
KODI?

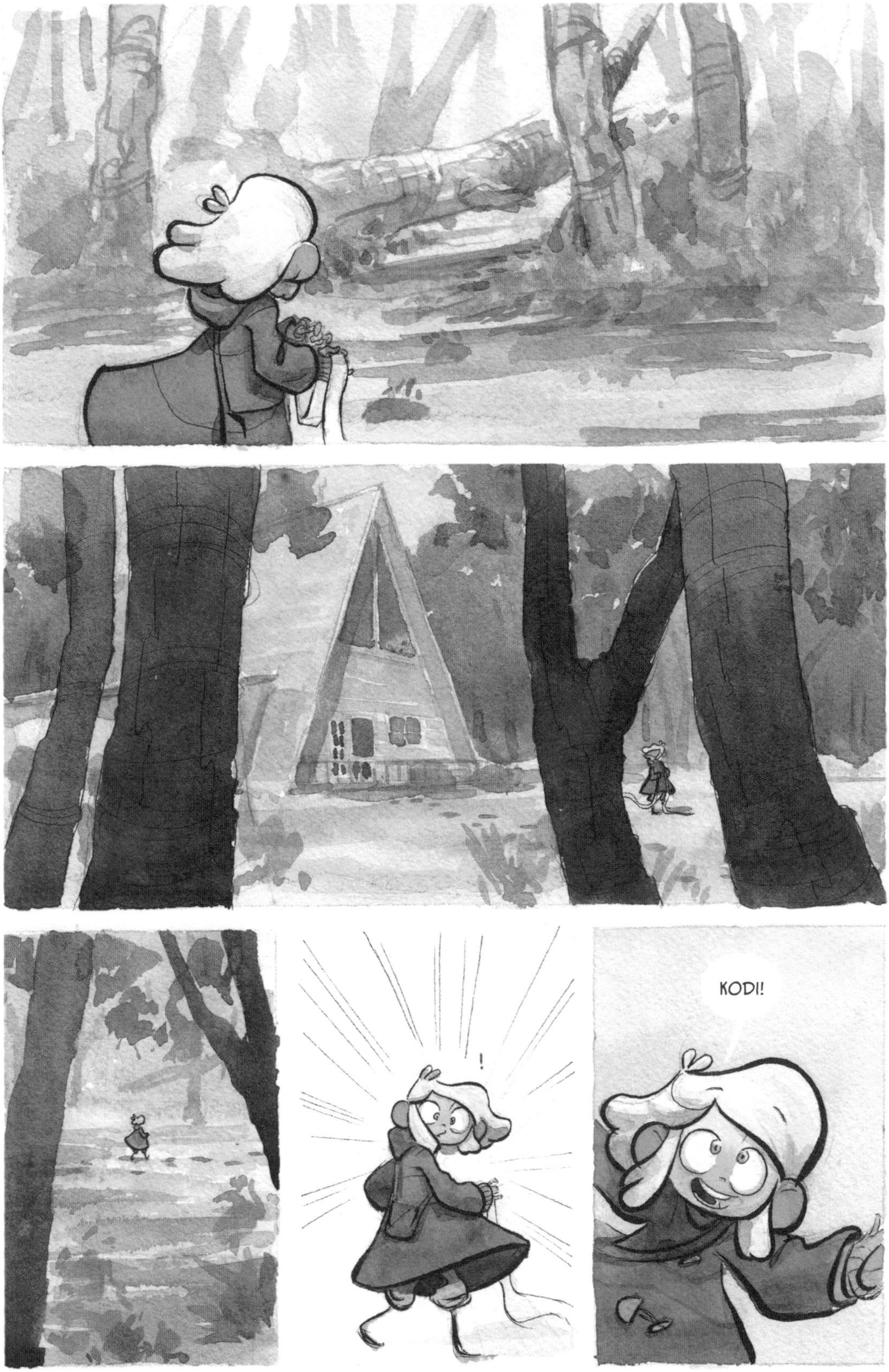
!
KODI!

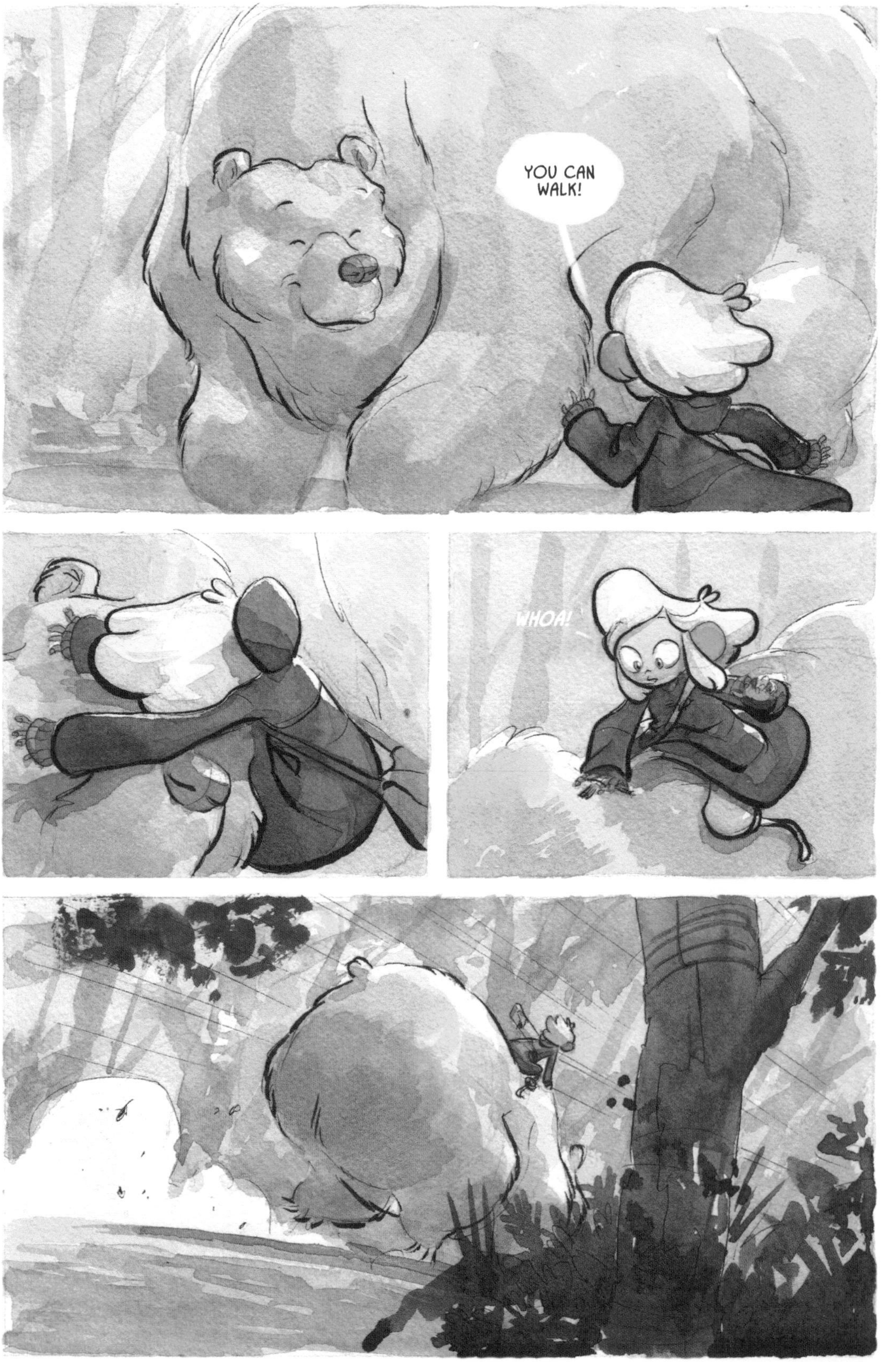
YOU CAN WALK!
WHOA!

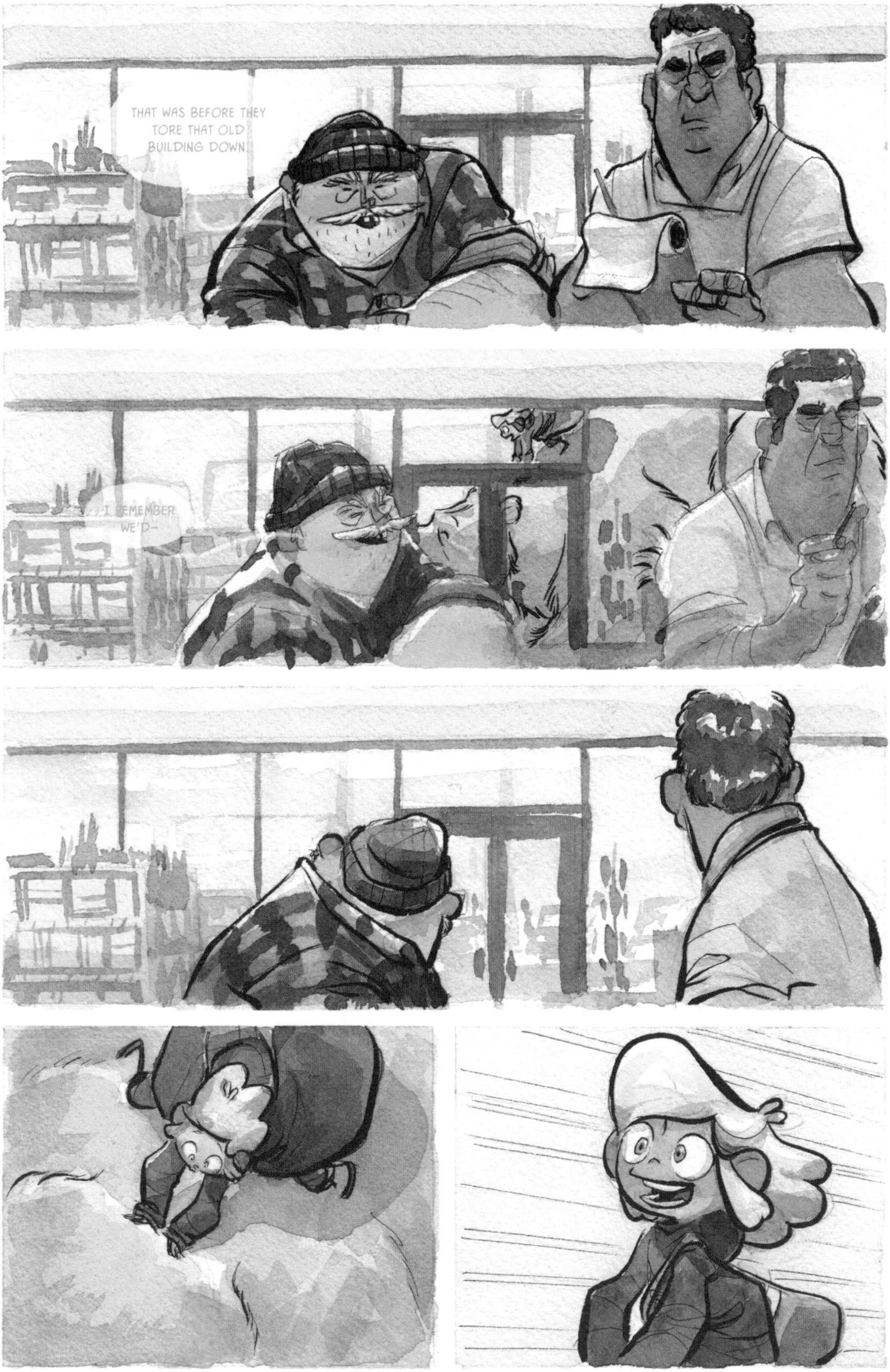
THAT WAS BEFORE THEY TORE THAT OLD BUILDING DOWN.
I REMEMBER WE'D-

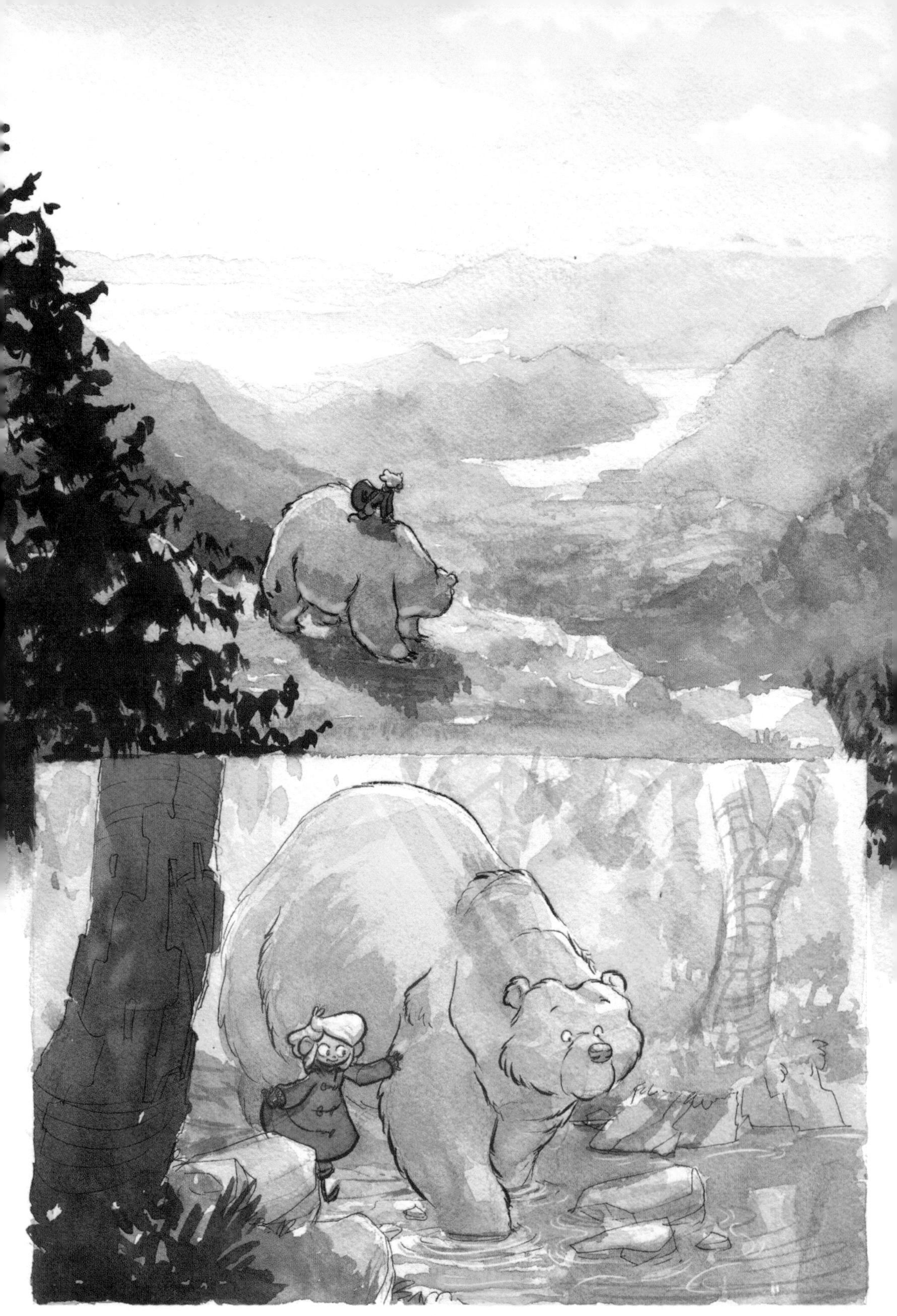

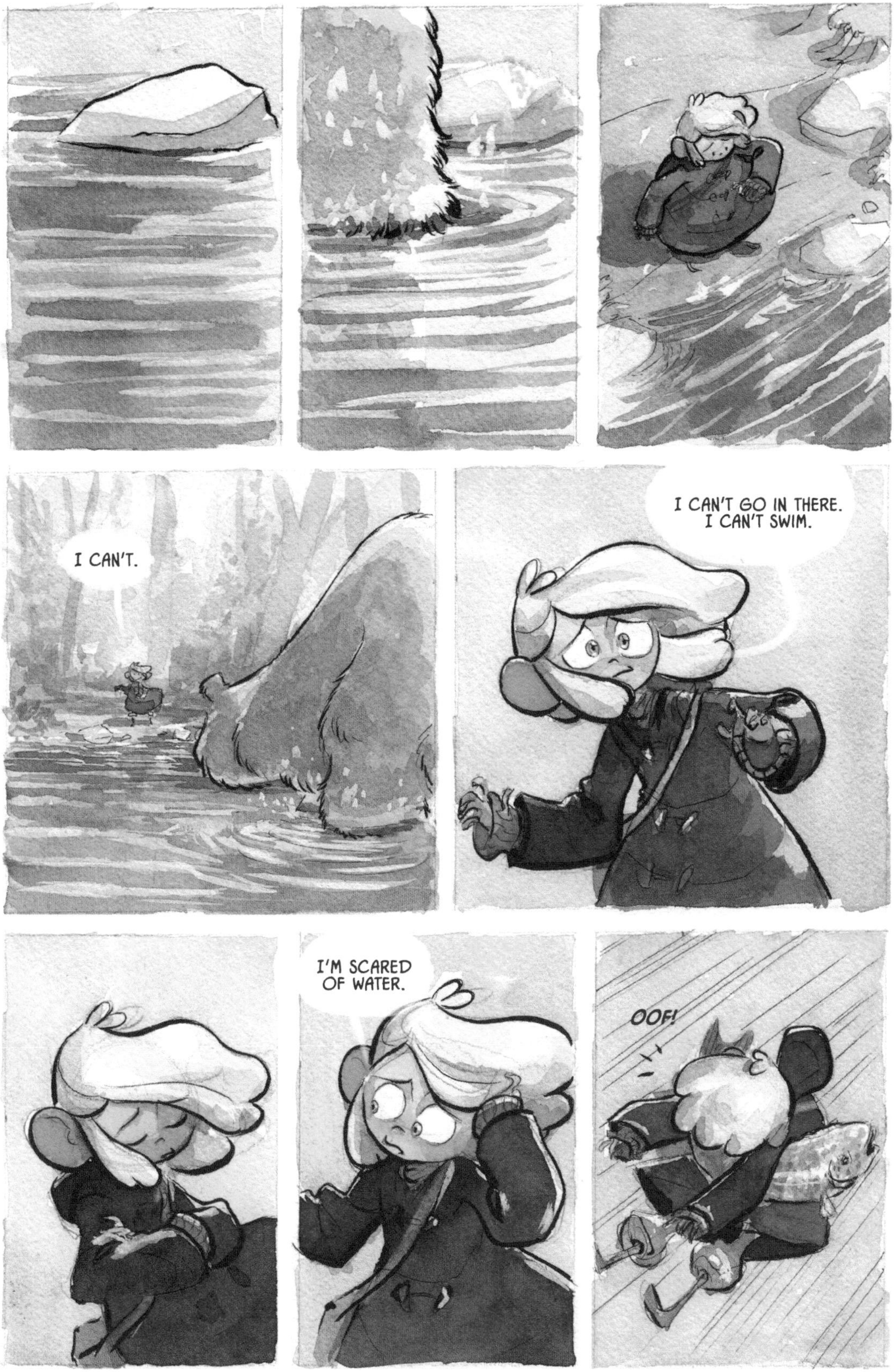
I CAN'T.
I CAN'T GO IN THERE.
I CAN'T SWIM.
I'M SCARED
OF WATER.
OOF!

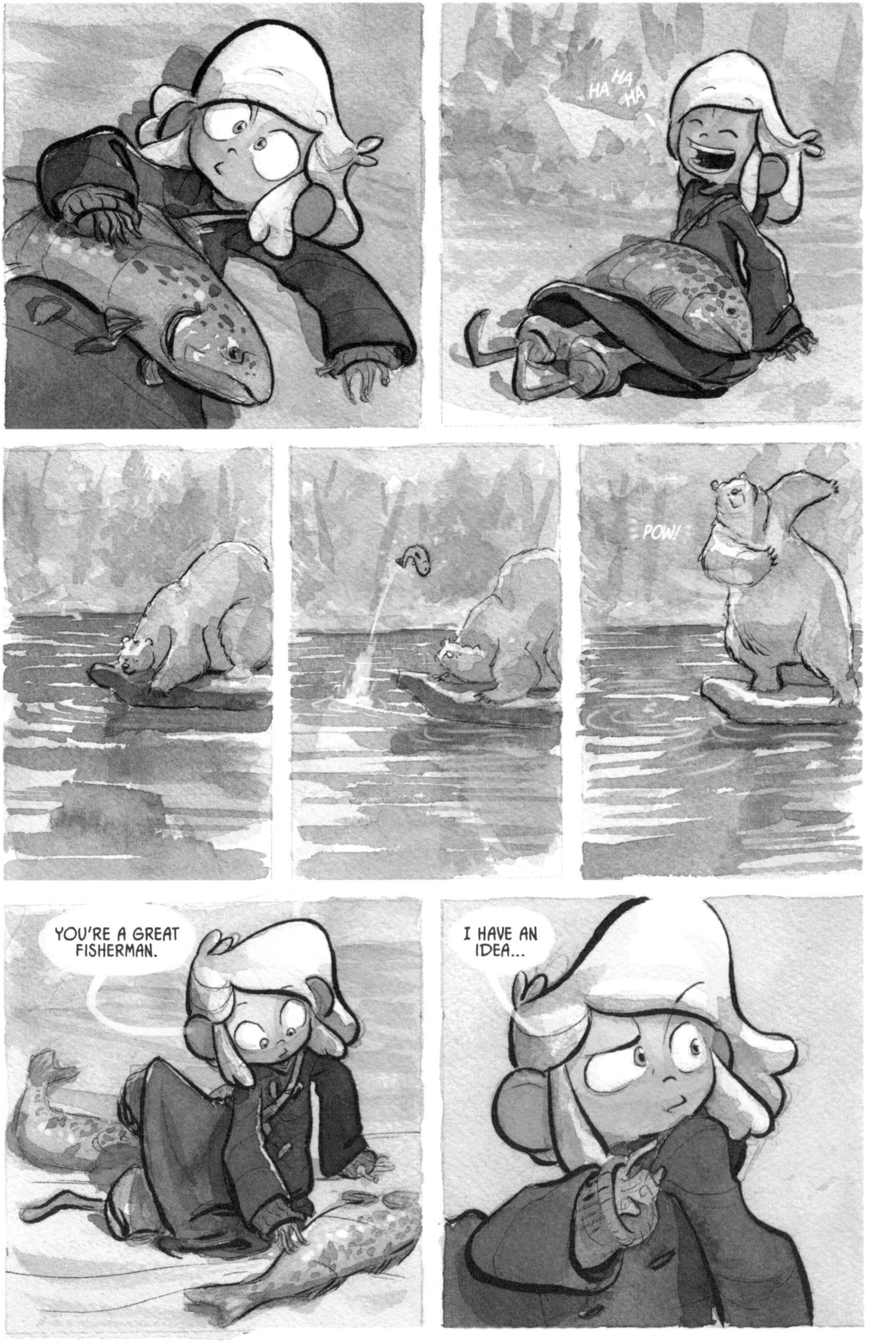

HA HA HA
POW!
YOU'RE A GREAT FISHERMAN.
I HAVE AN IDEA...

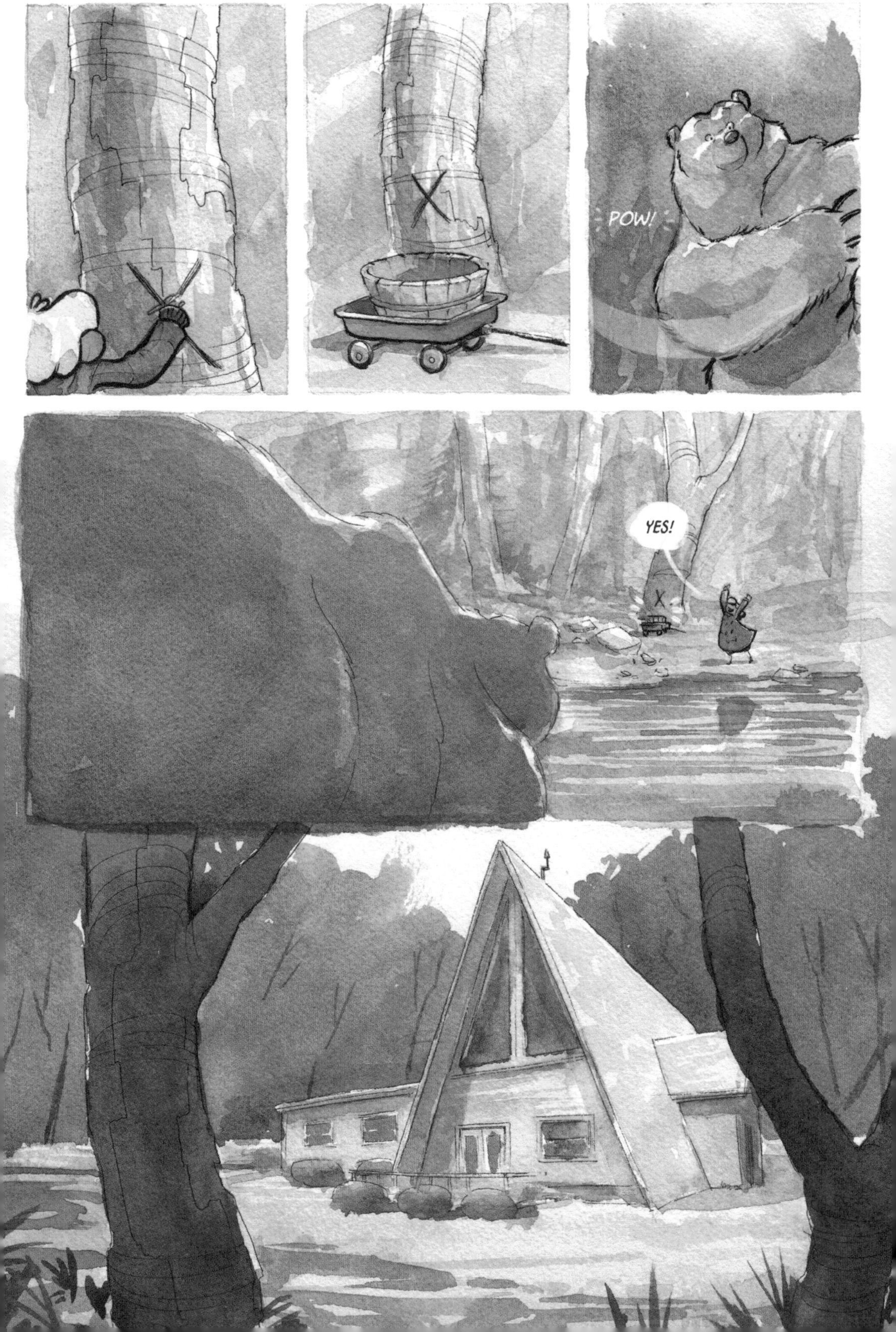
POW!
YES!

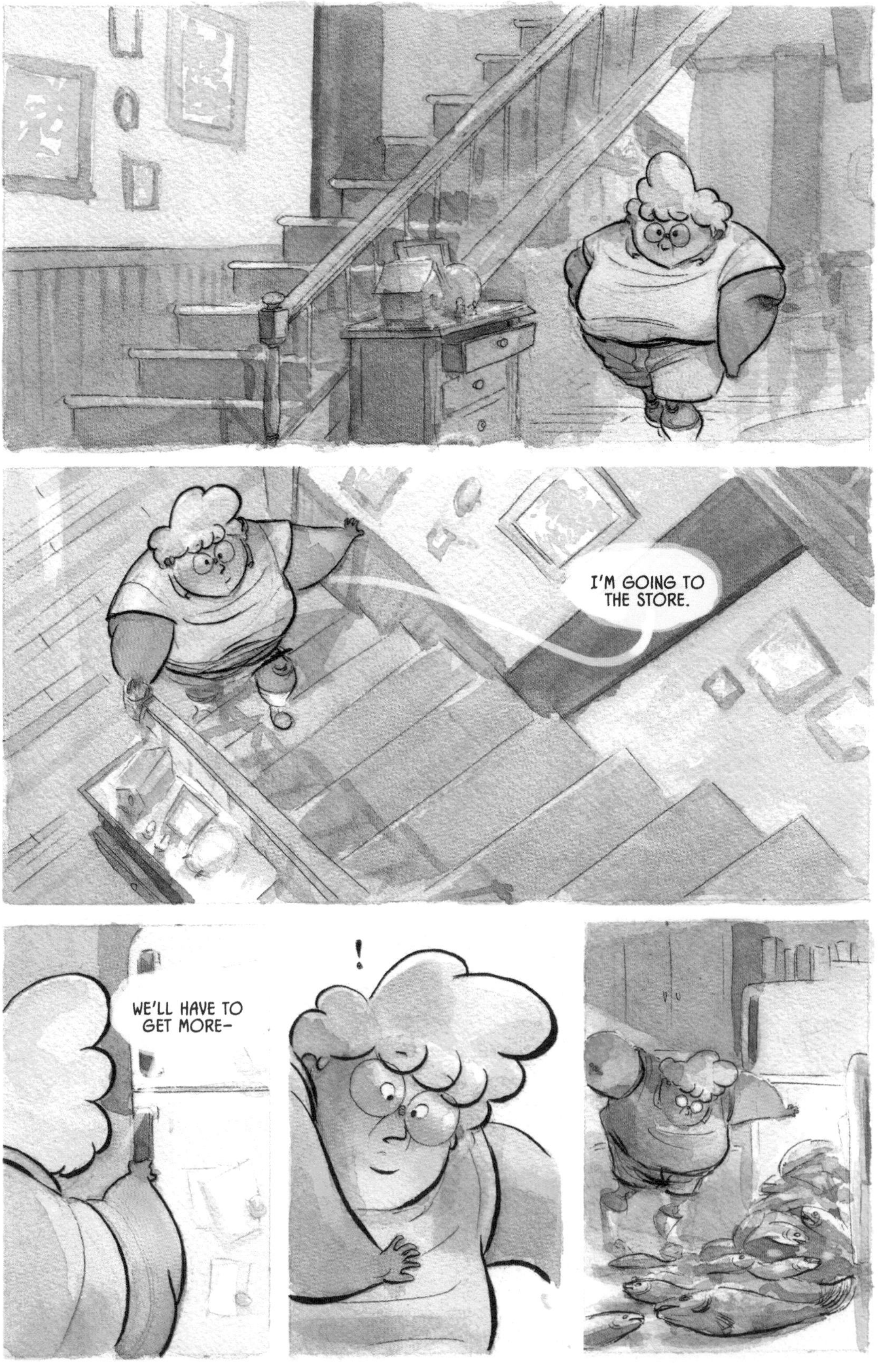
I'M GOING TO THE STORE.
WE'LL HAVE TO GET MORE-
!

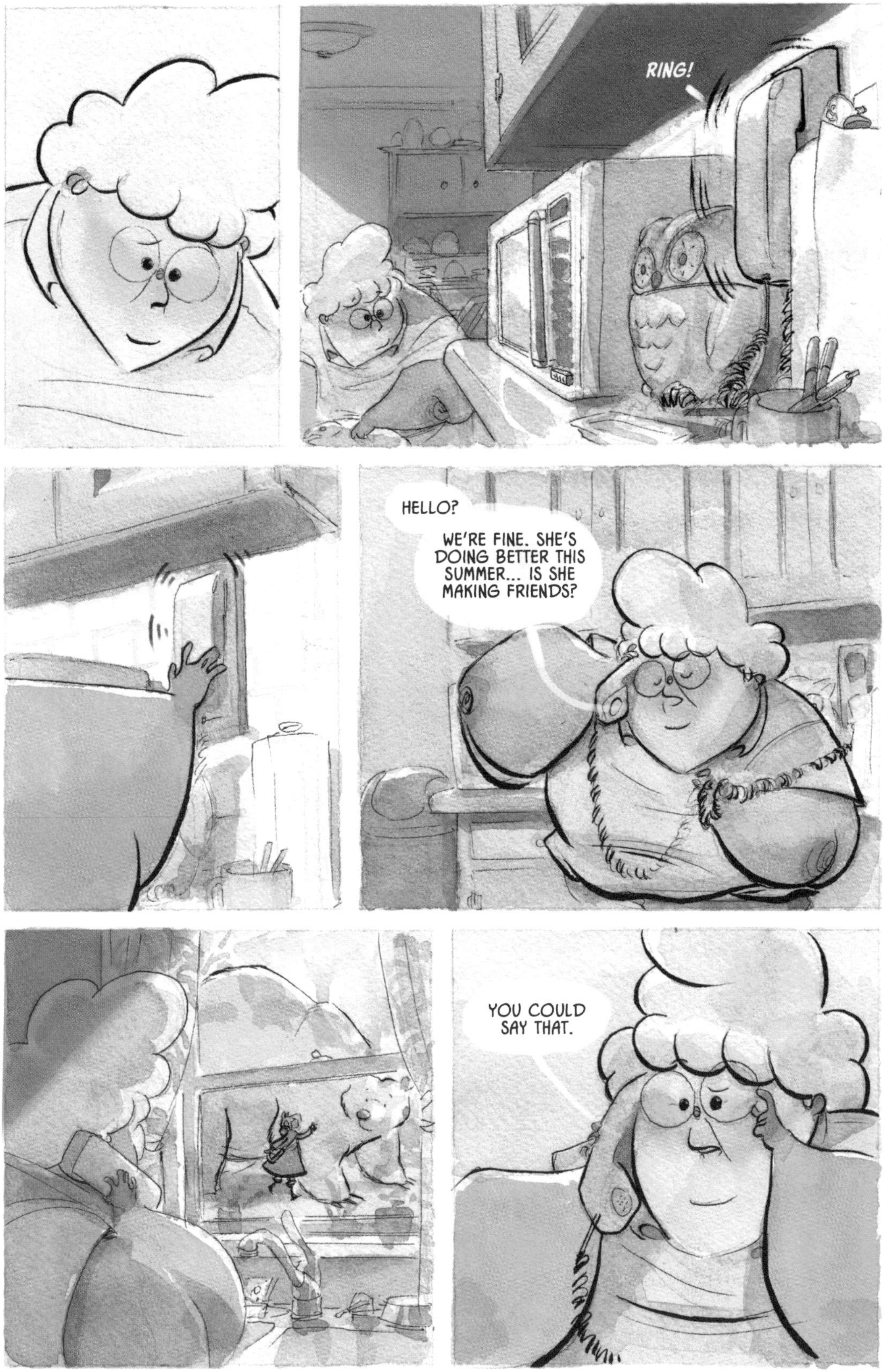
RING!
HELLO?
WE'RE FINE. SHE'S DOING BETTER THIS SUMMER... IS SHE MAKING FRIENDS?
YOU COULD SAY THAT.

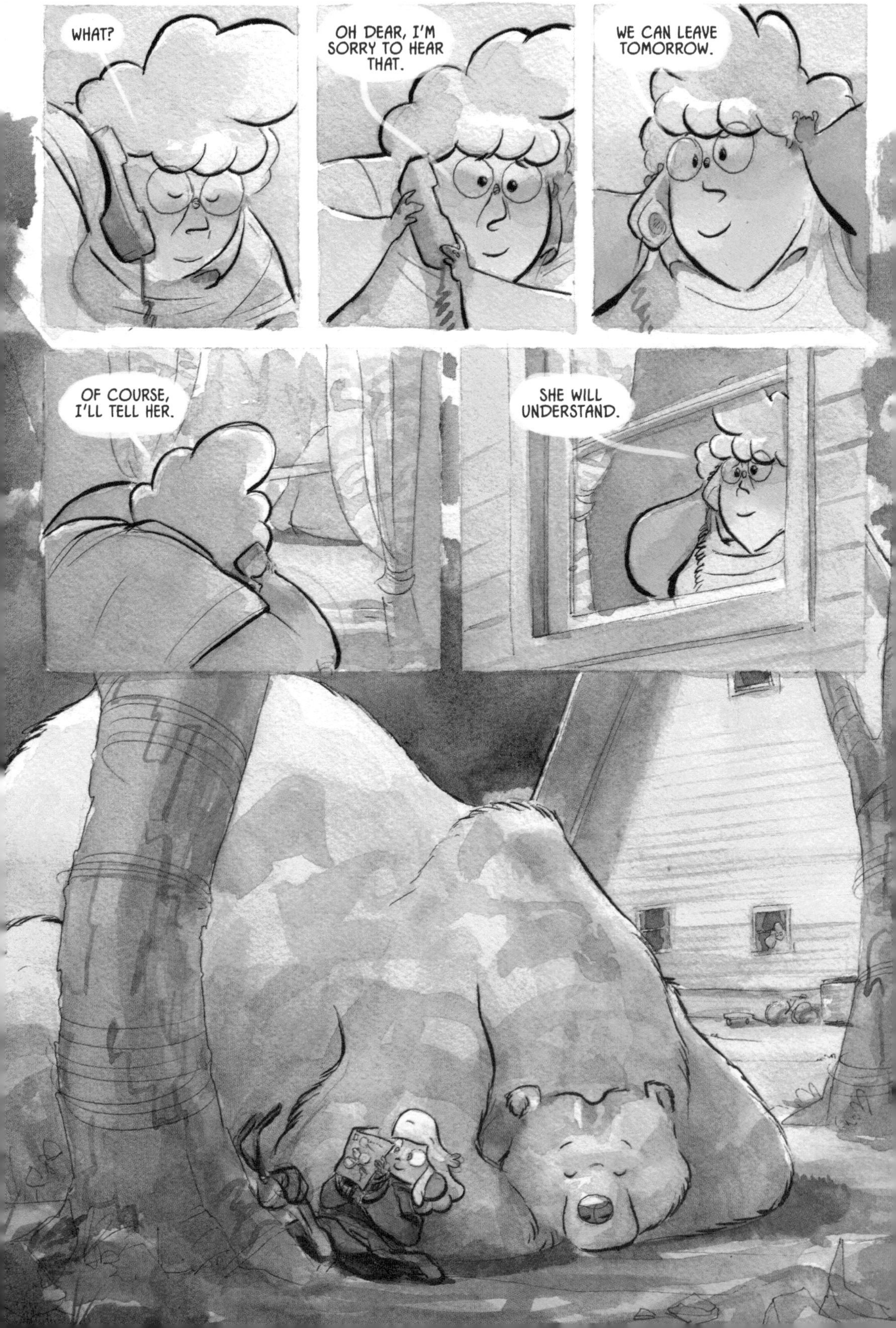
WHAT?
OH DEAR, I'M SORRY TO HEAR THAT.
WE CAN LEAVE TOMORROW.
OF COURSE, I'LL TELL HER.
SHE WILL UNDERSTAND.

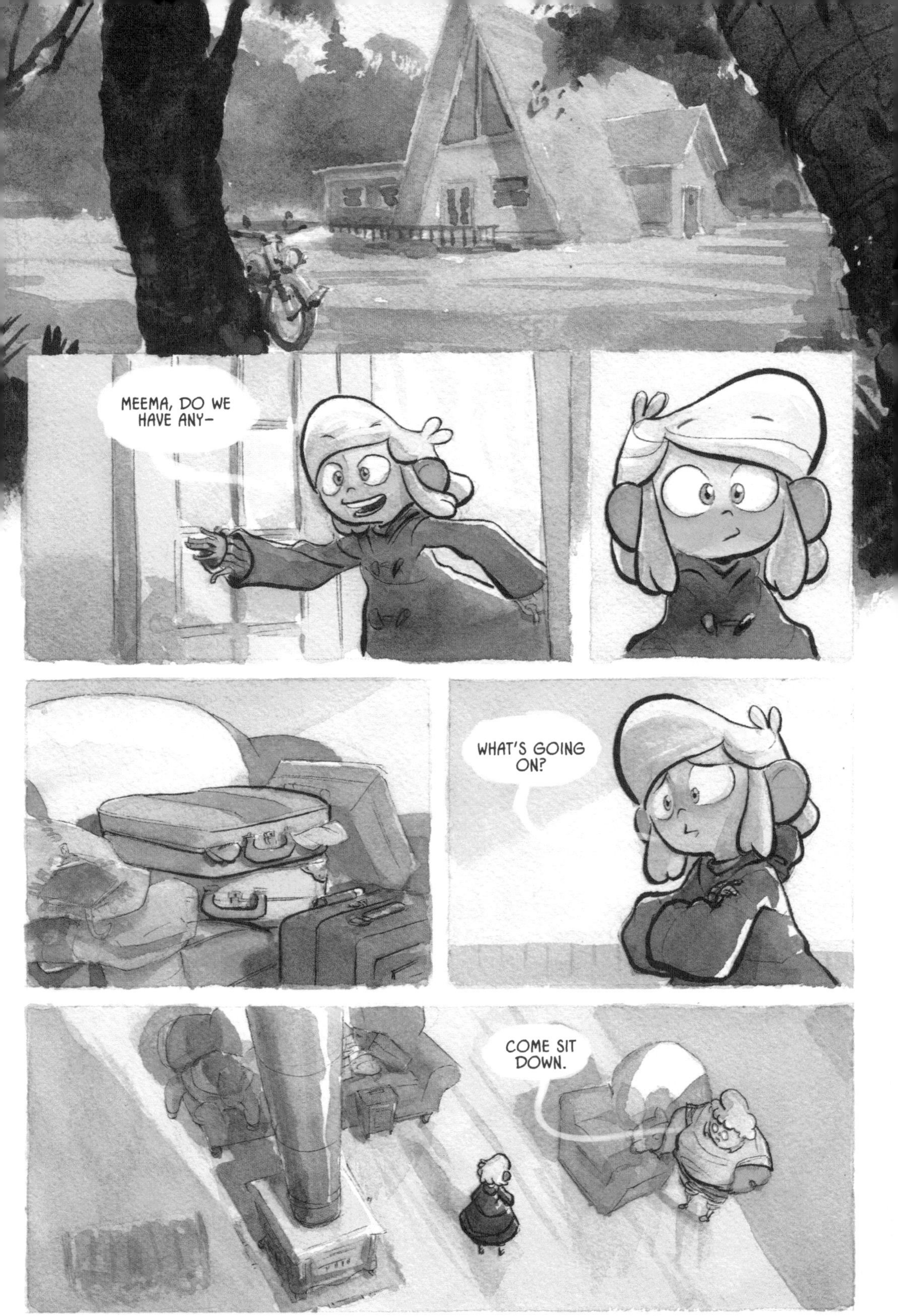
MEEMA, DO WE HAVE ANY-
WHAT'S GOING ON?
COME SIT DOWN.

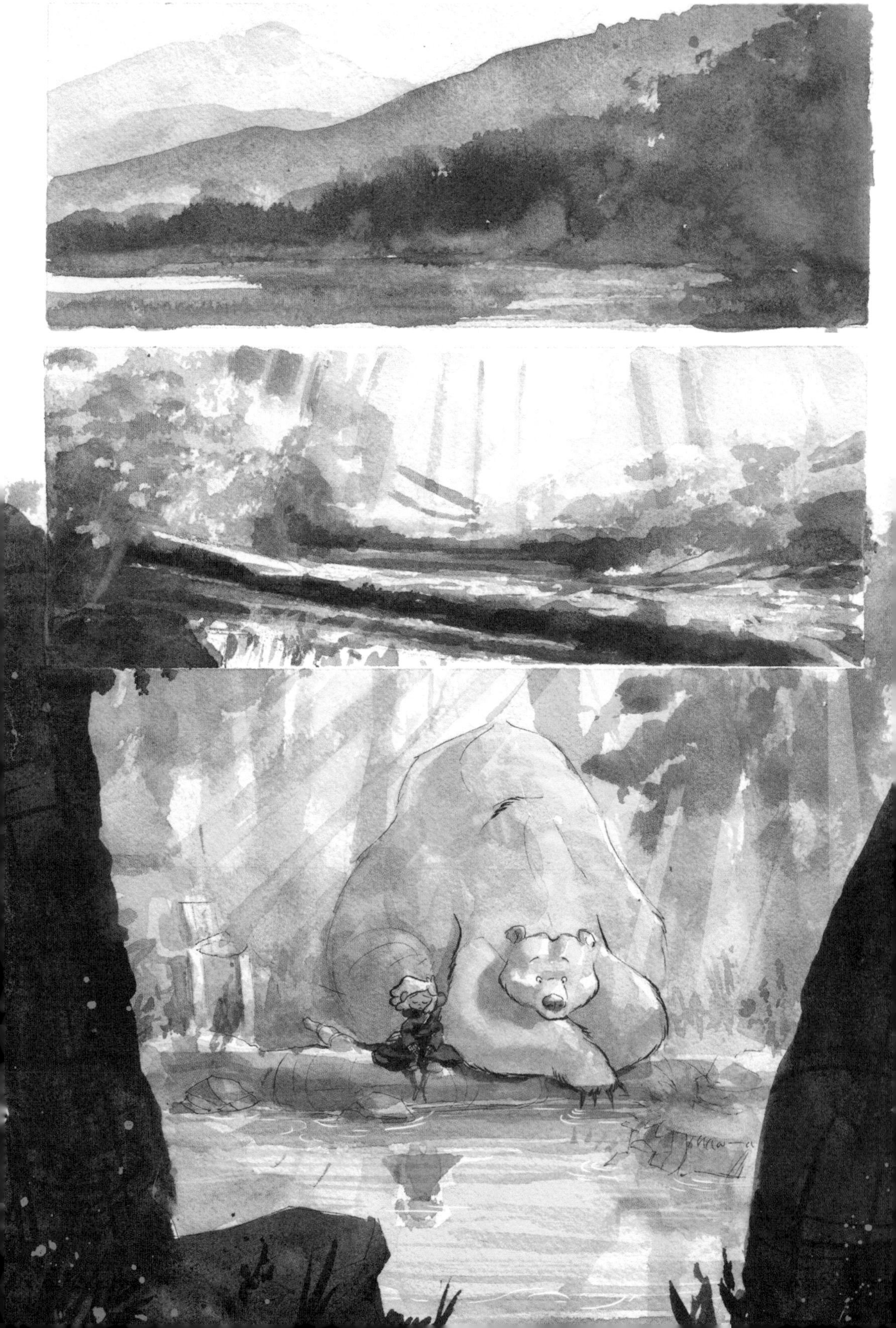

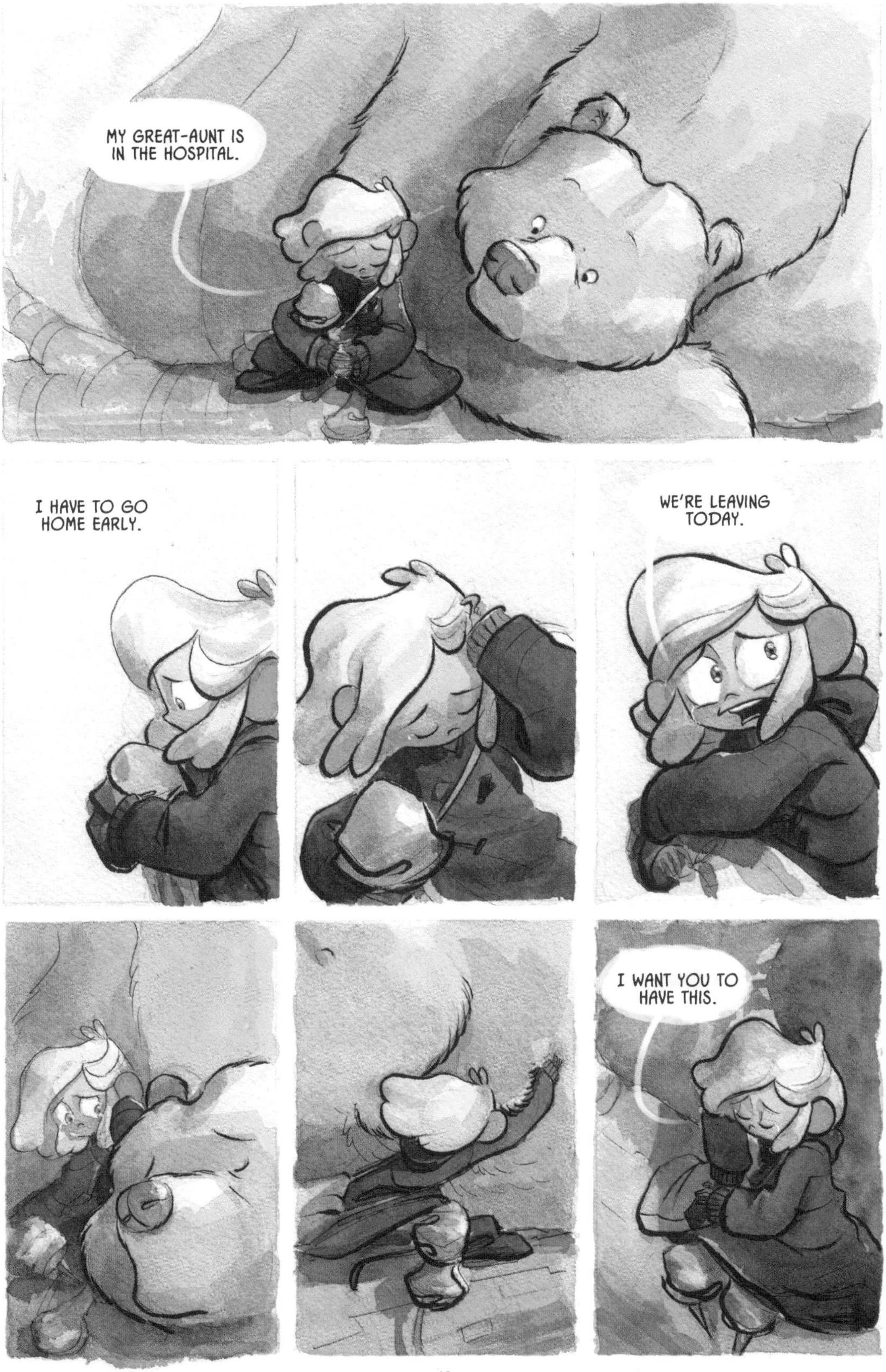
MY GREAT-AUNT IS IN THE HOSPITAL.
I HAVE TO GO HOME EARLY.
WE'RE LEAVING TODAY.
I WANT YOU TO HAVE THIS.

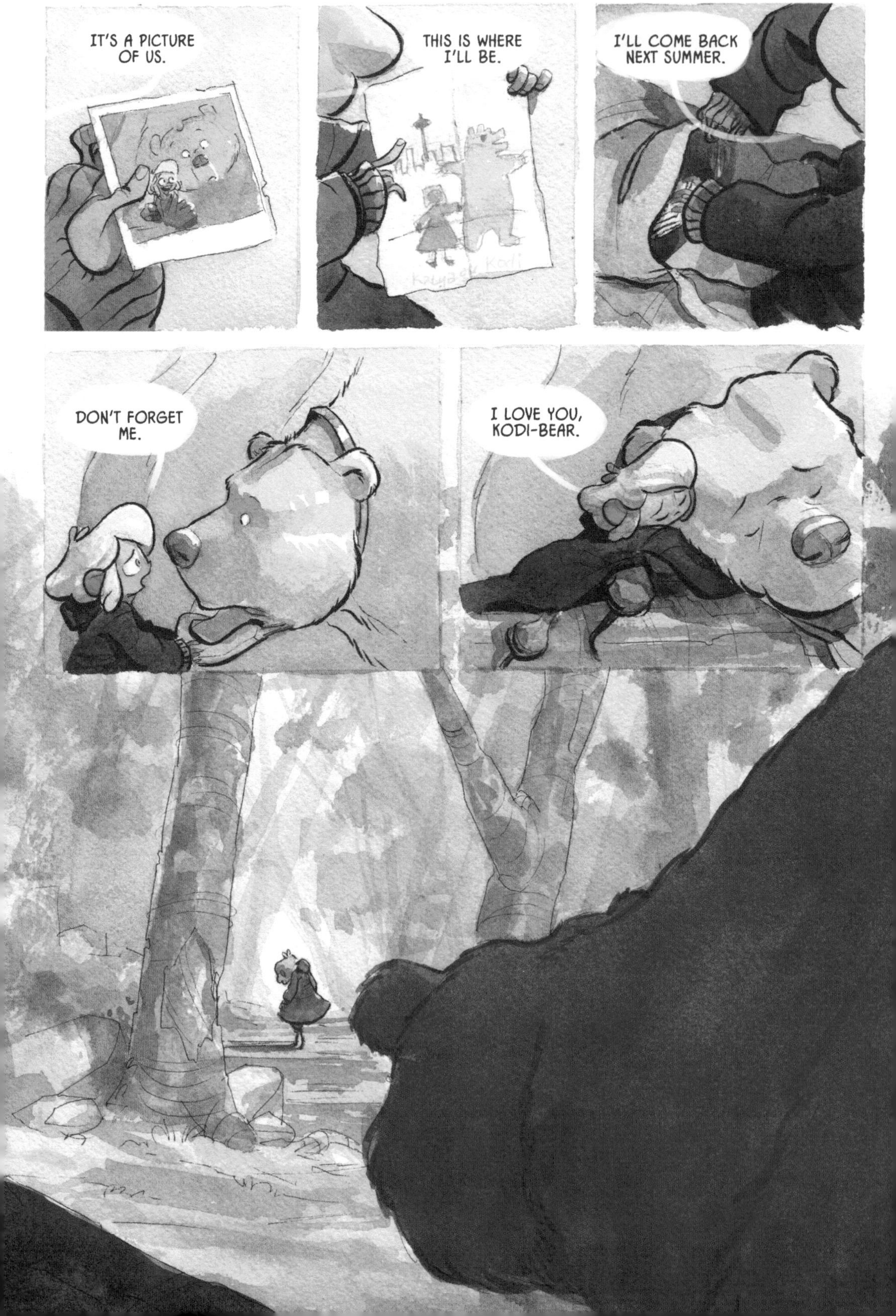
IT'S A PICTURE OF US.
THIS IS WHERE I'LL BE.
I'LL COME BACK NEXT SUMMER.
DON'T FORGET ME.
I LOVE YOU, KODI-BEAR.

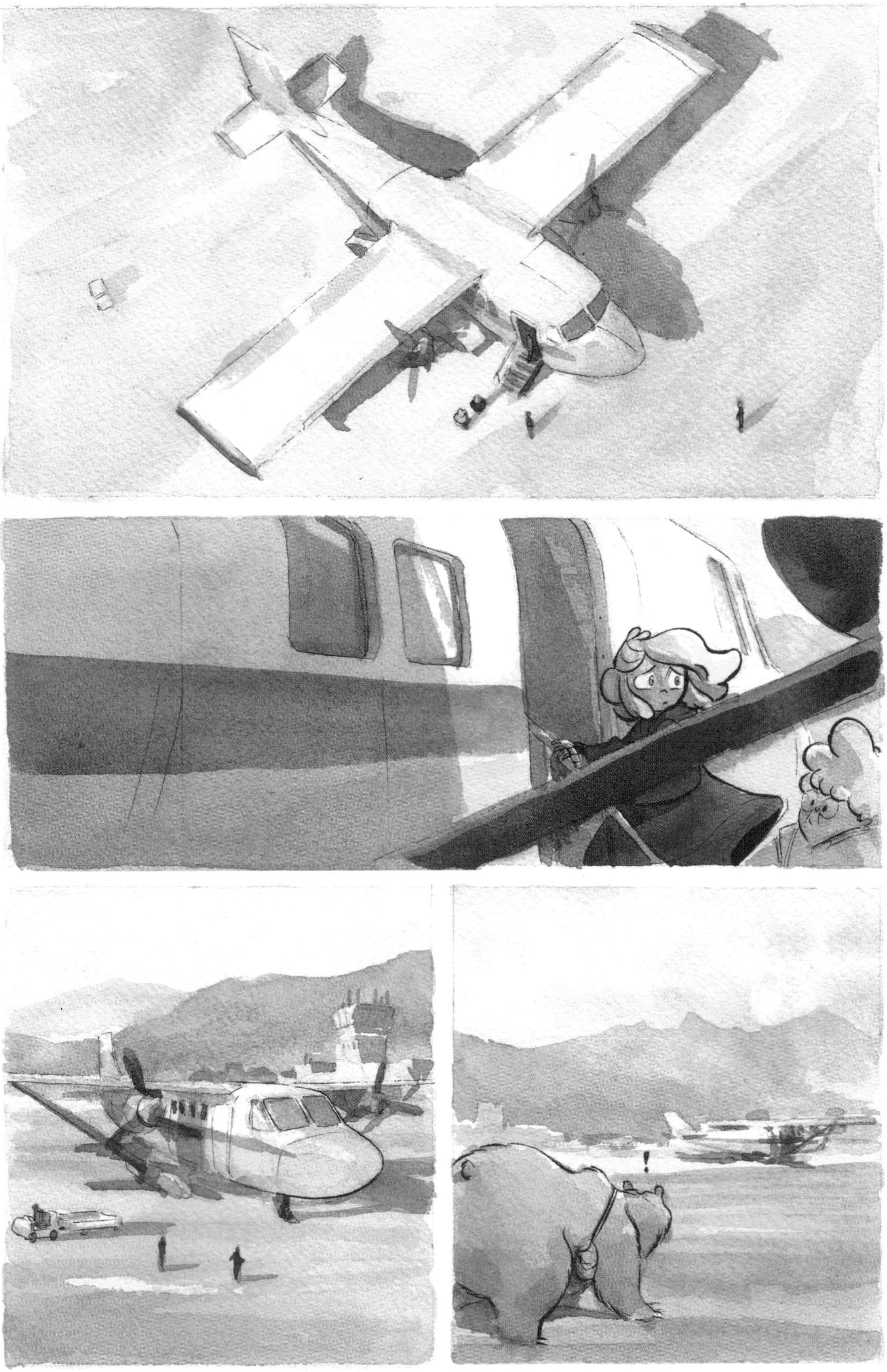
!

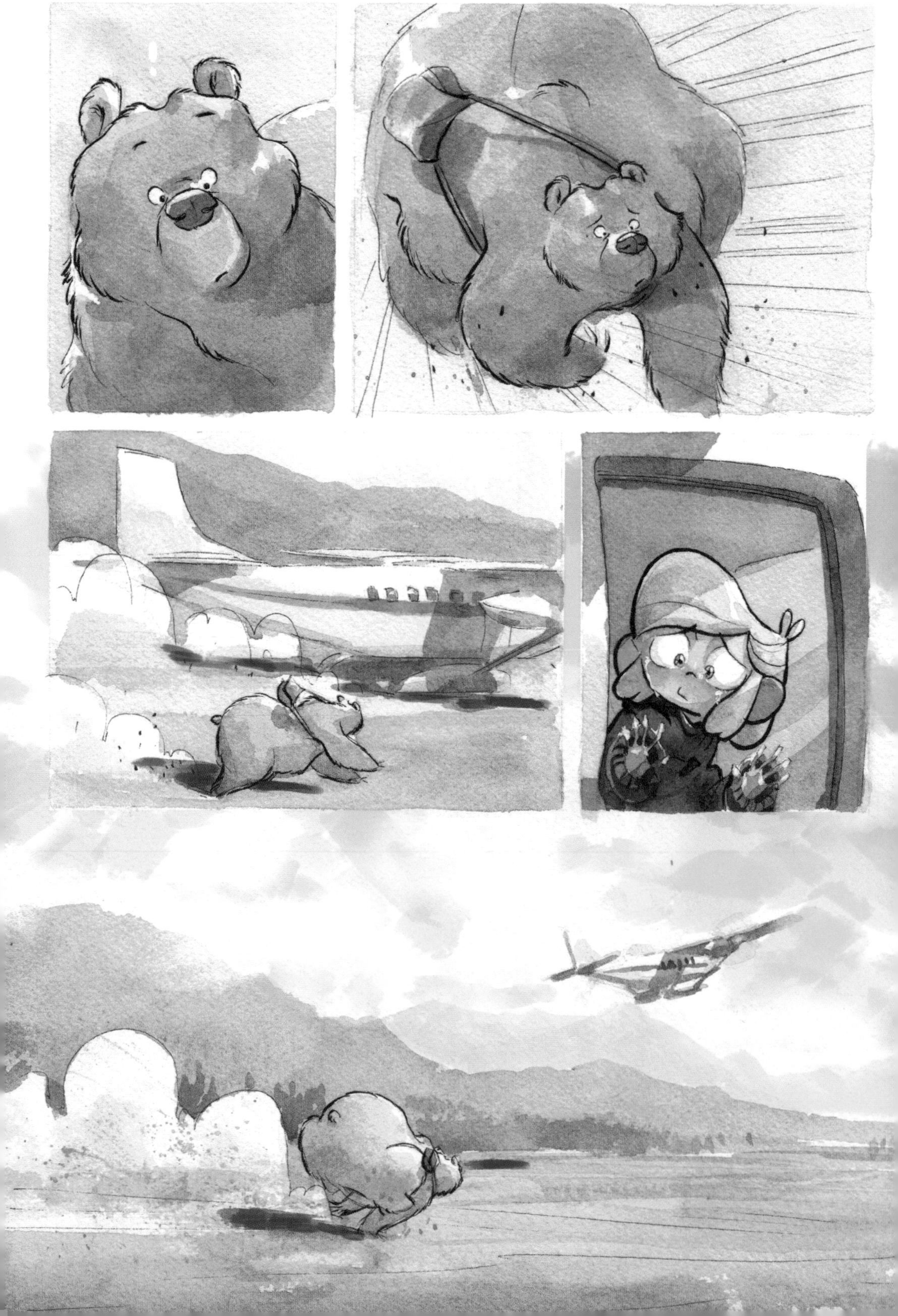
!

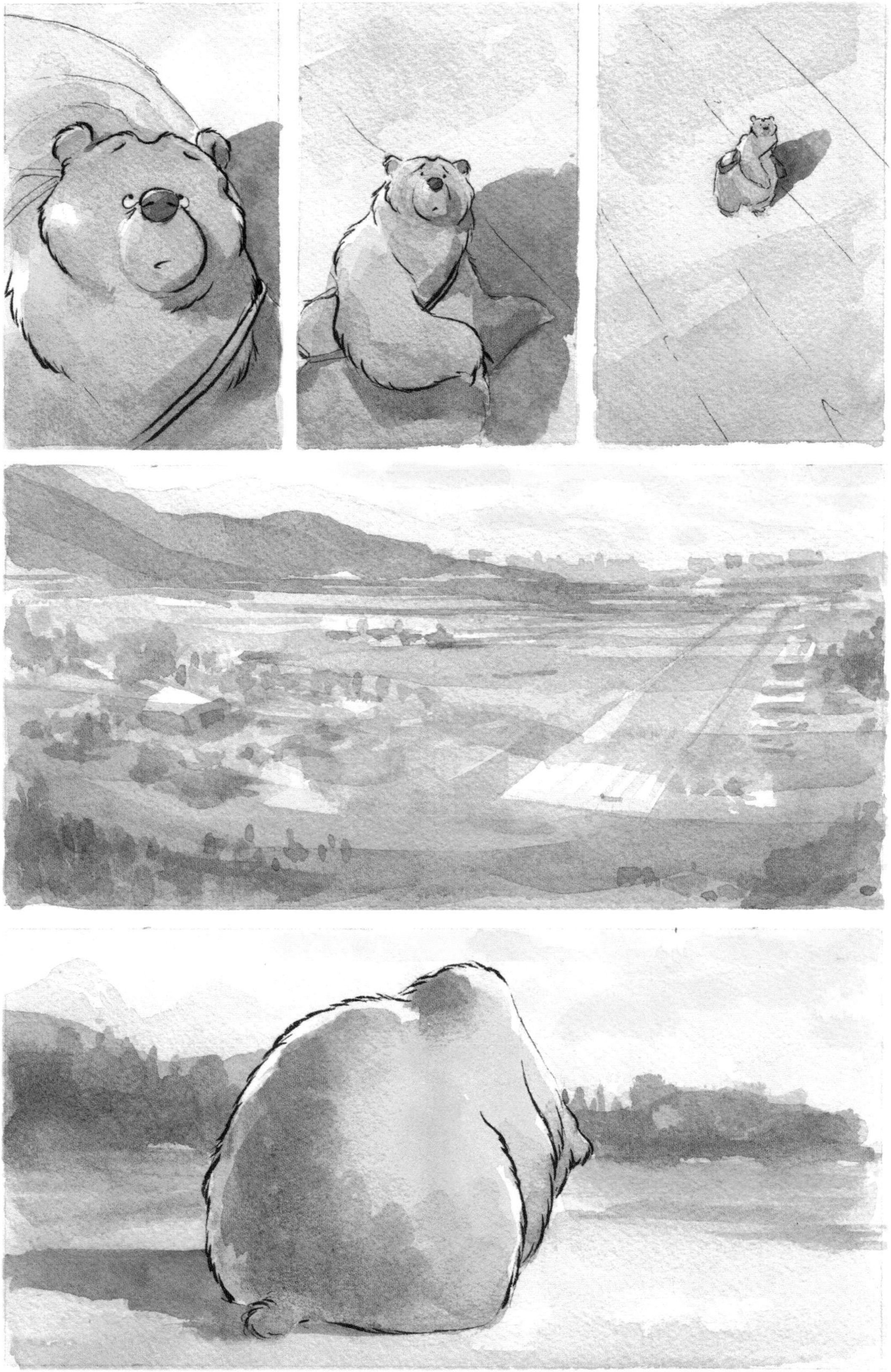

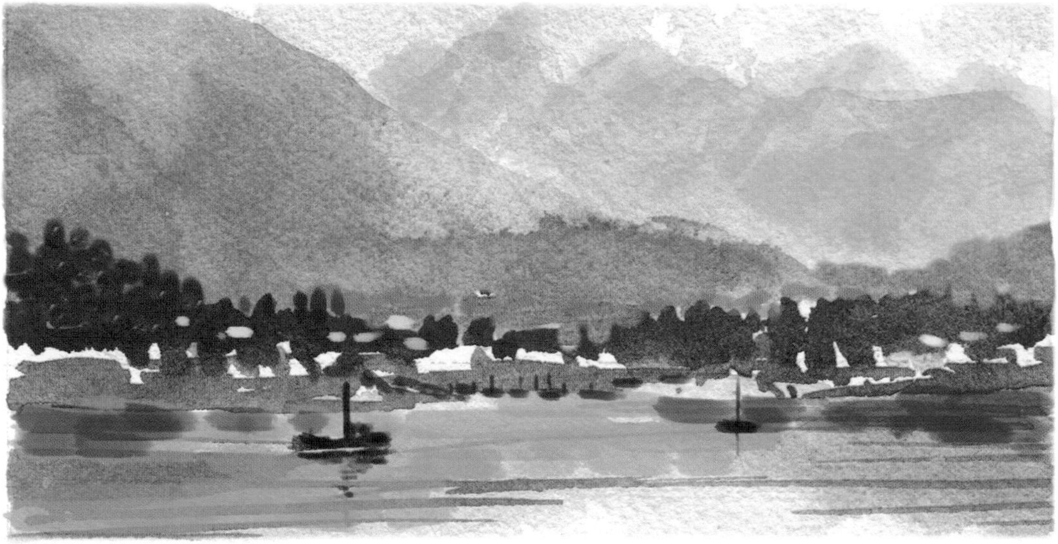

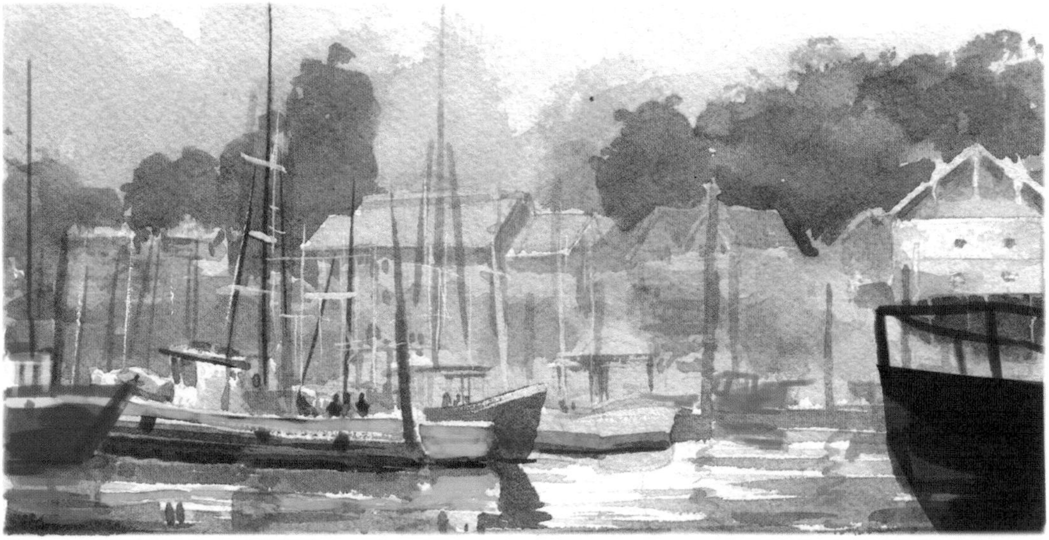

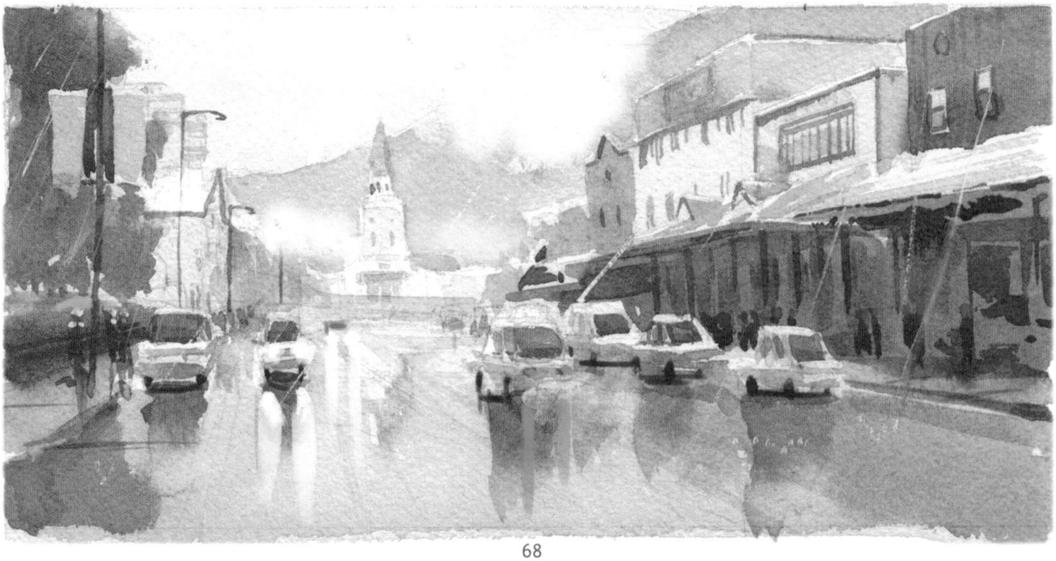

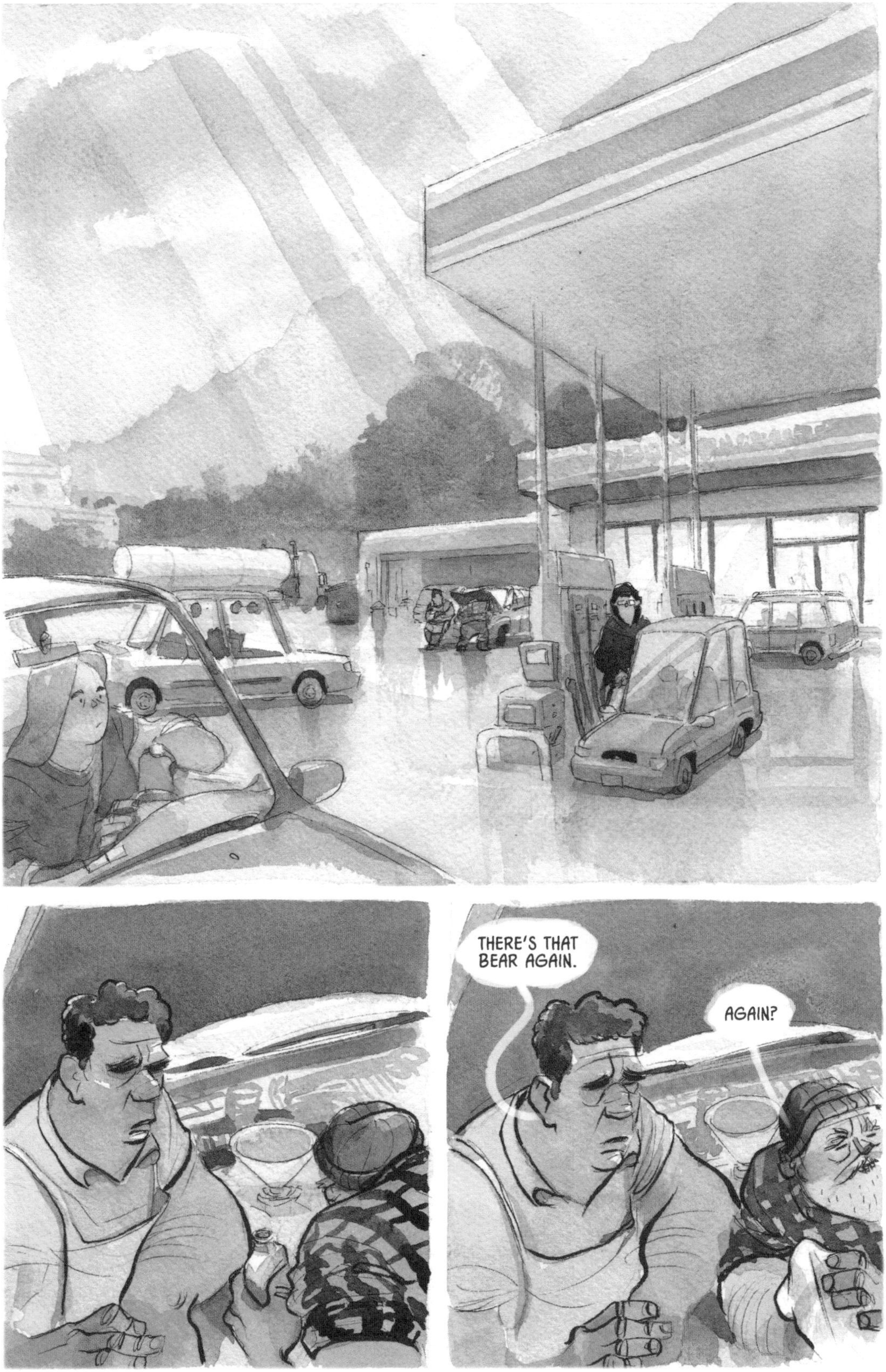
THERE'S THAT BEAR AGAIN.
AGAIN?

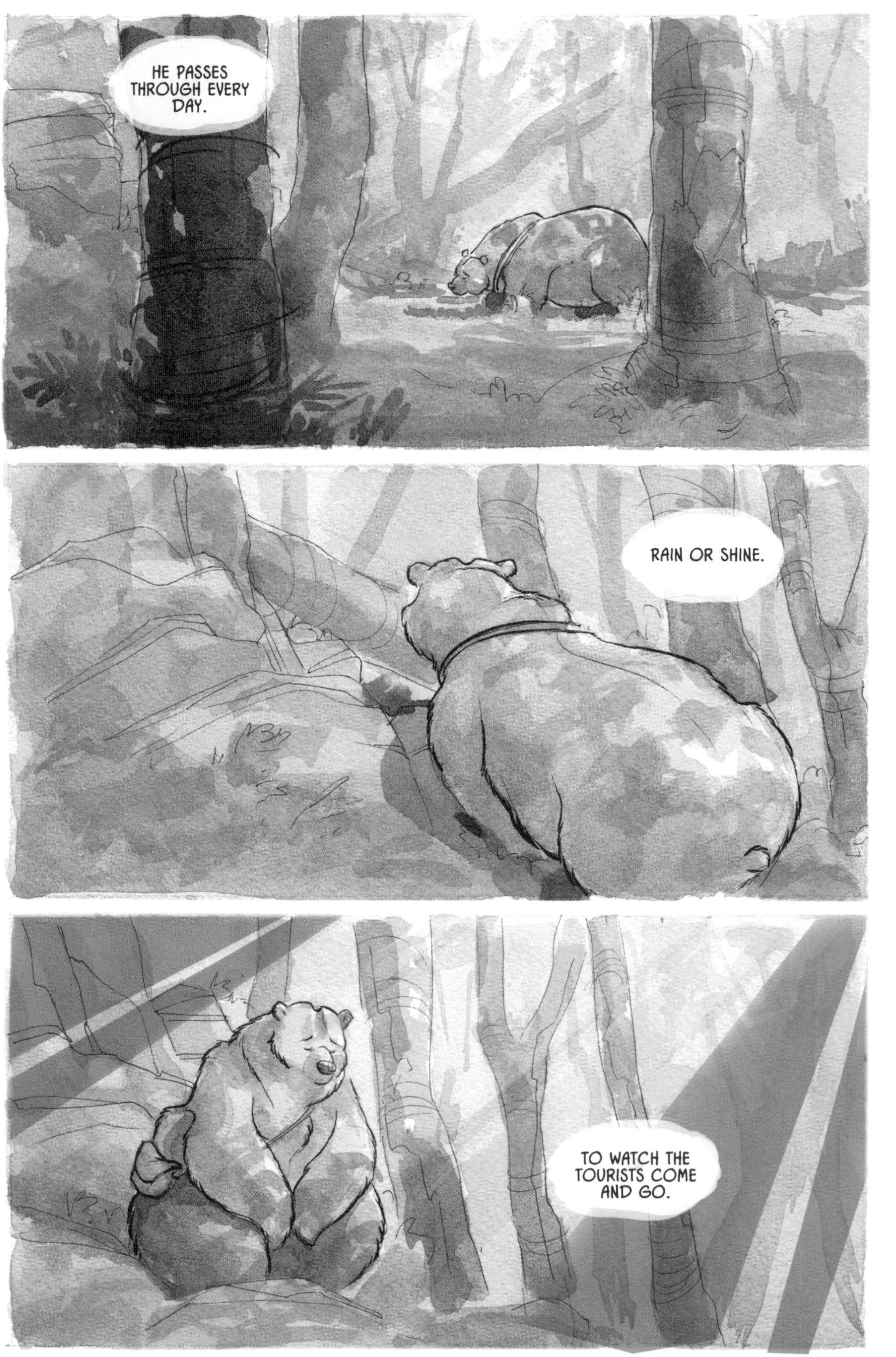
HE PASSES THROUGH EVERY DAY.
RAIN OR SHINE.
TO WATCH THE TOURISTS COME AND GO.

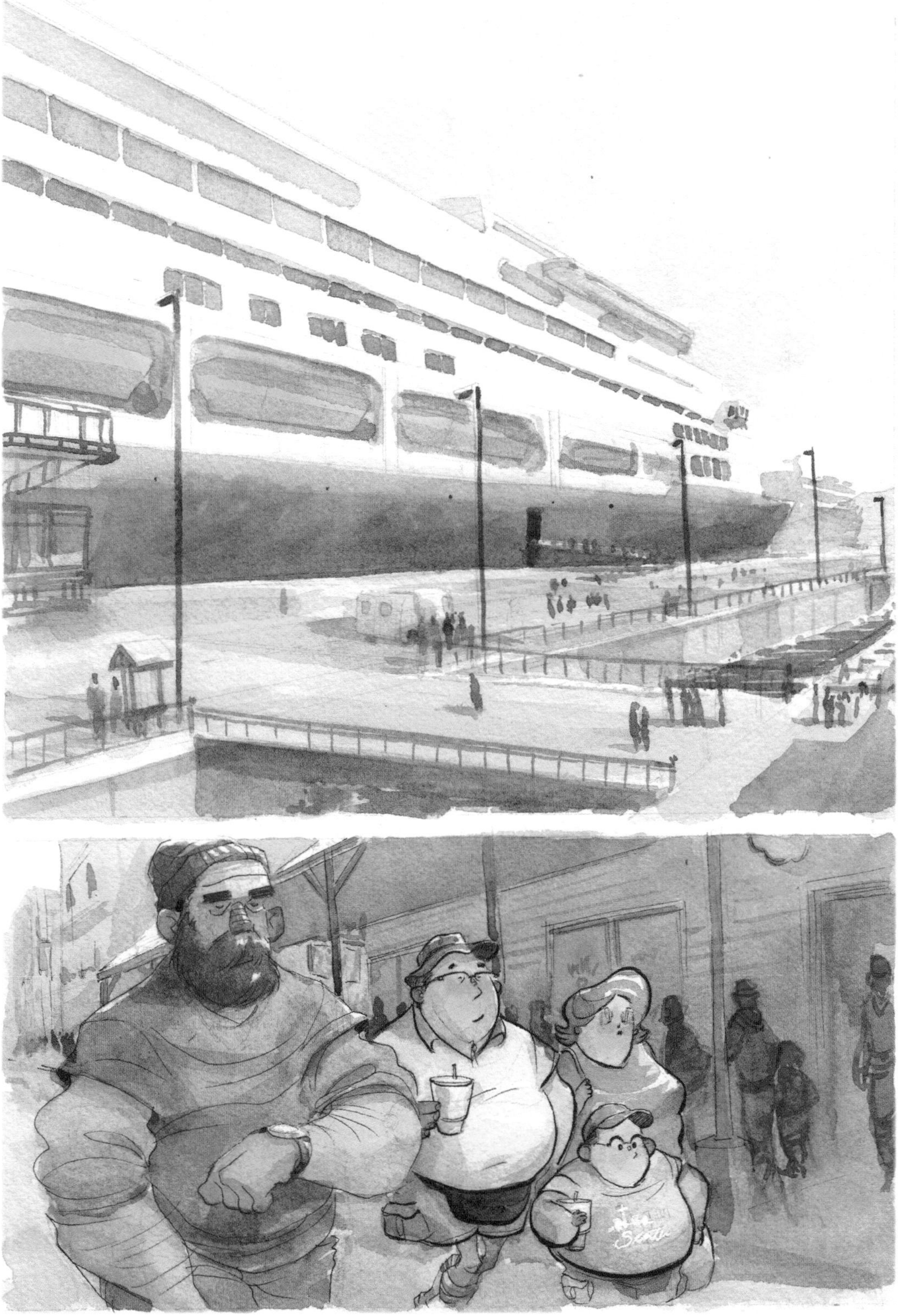

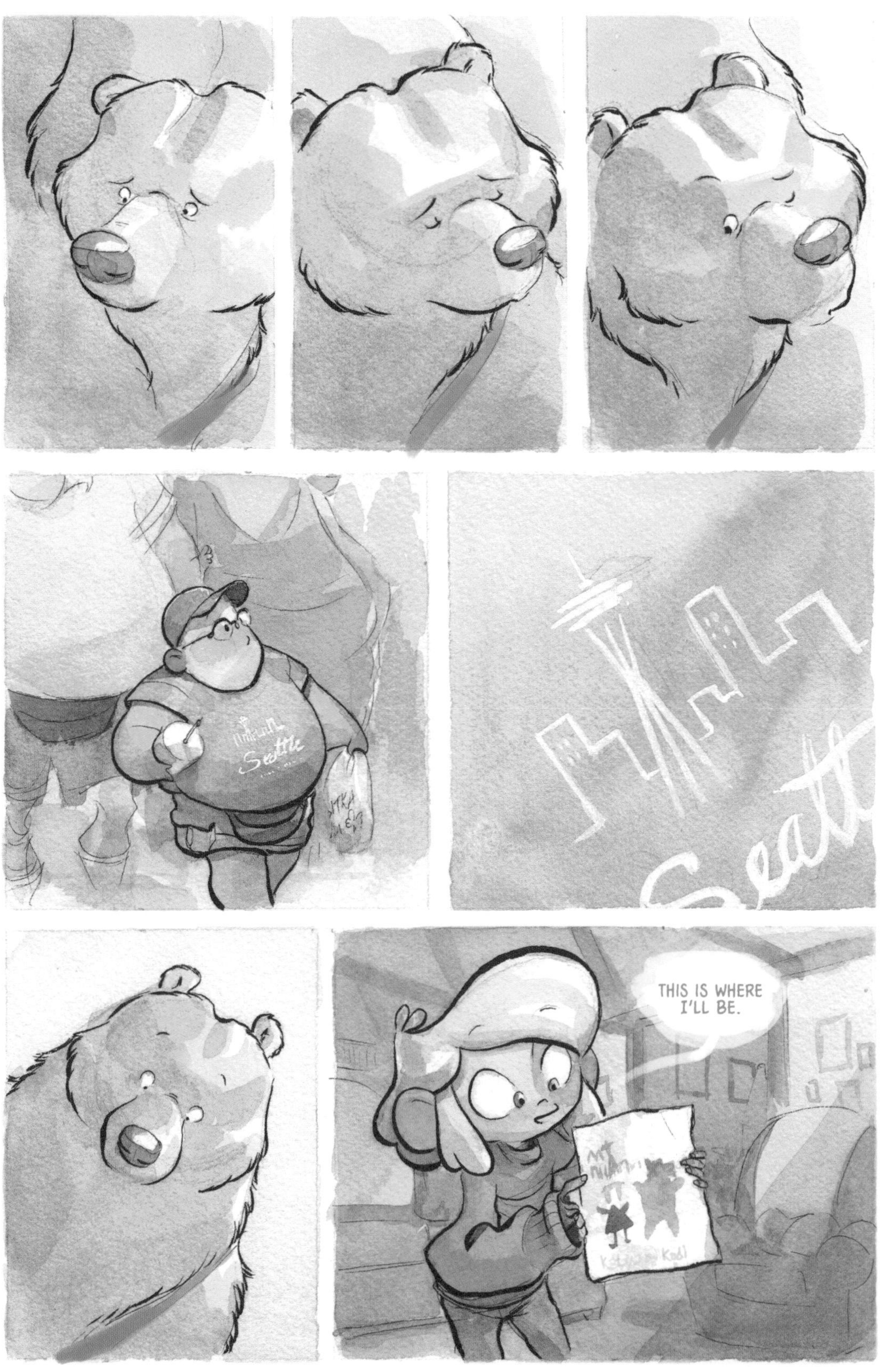
THIS IS WHERE
I'LL BE.

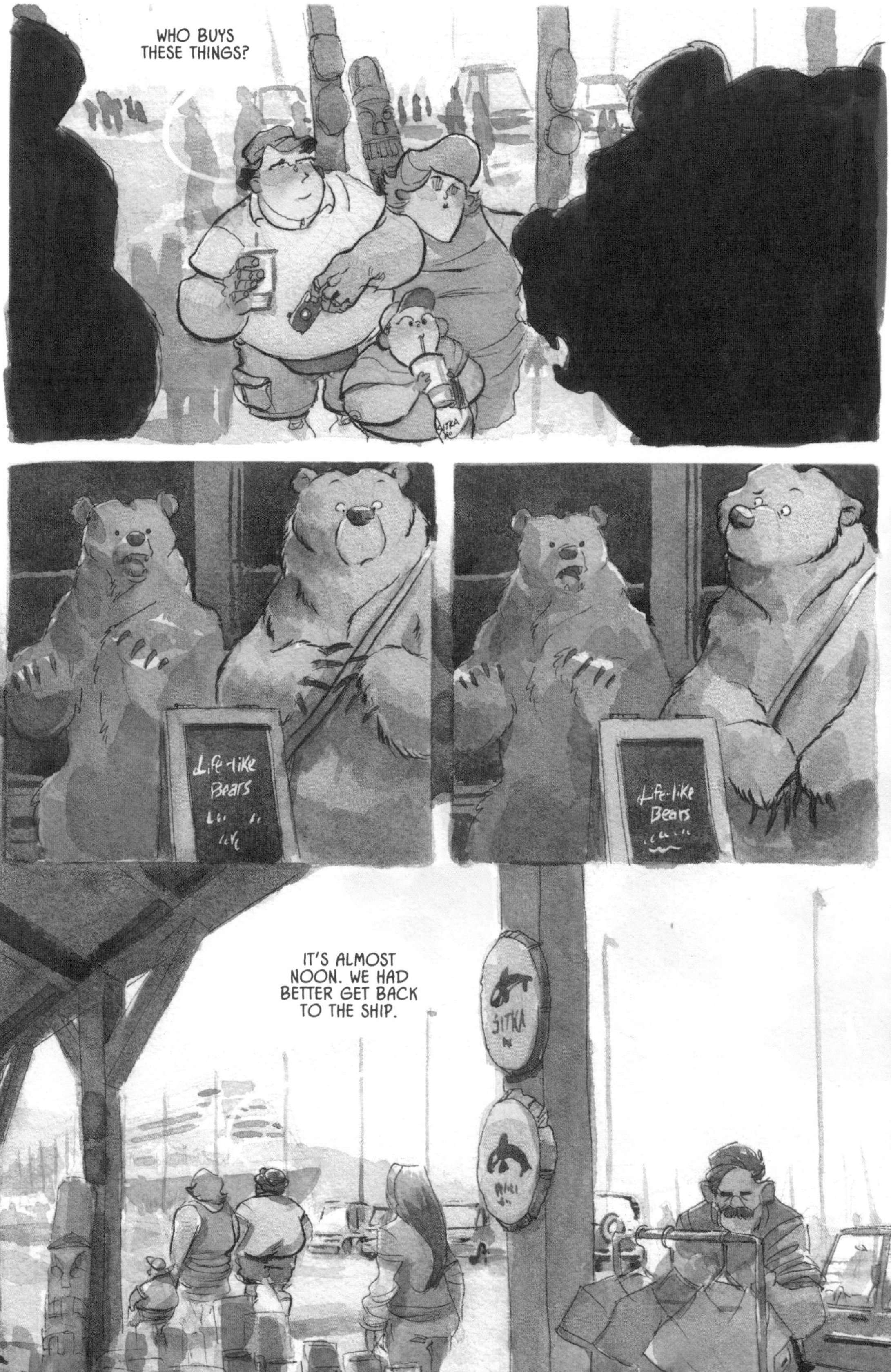
WHO BUYS THESE THINGS?
Life-like Bears
Life-like Bears
IT'S ALMOST NOON. WE HAD BETTER GET BACK TO THE SHIP.
SITKA

THIS IS THE LAST OF THE LOAD. WE'RE ALL SET.

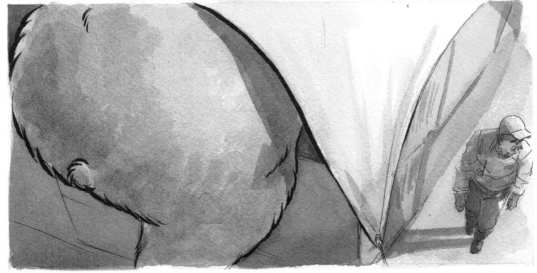

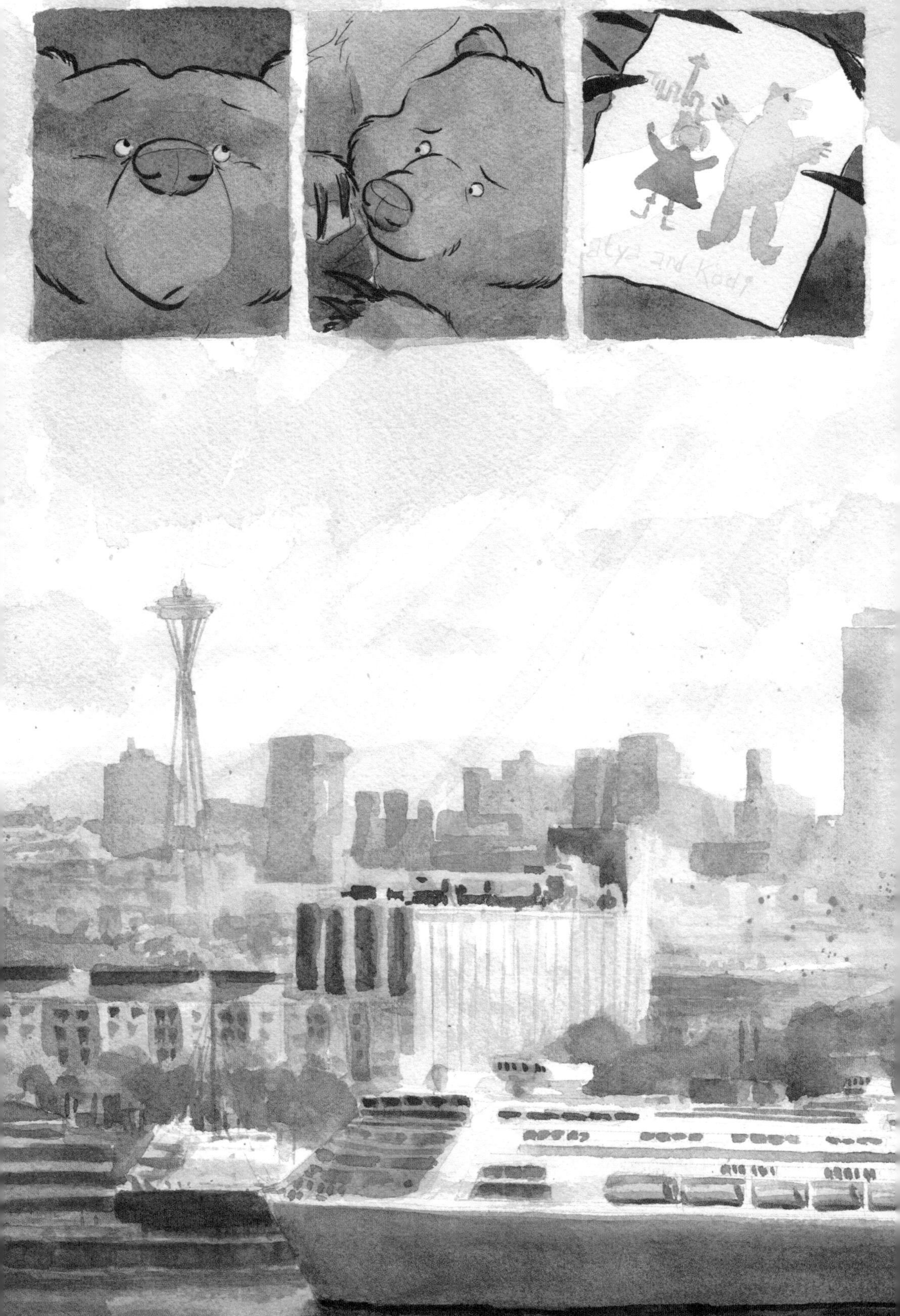
atya and Kodi

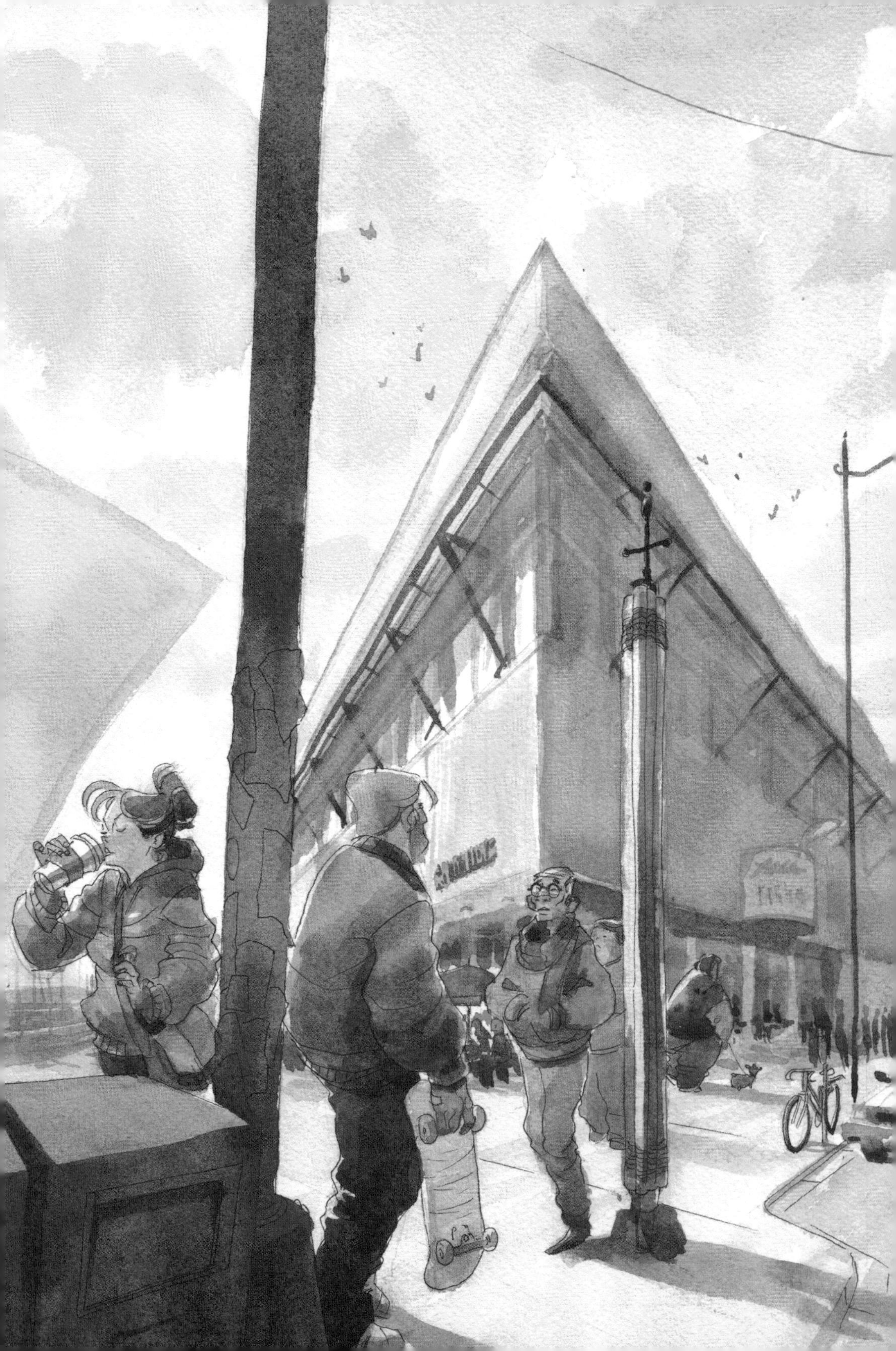

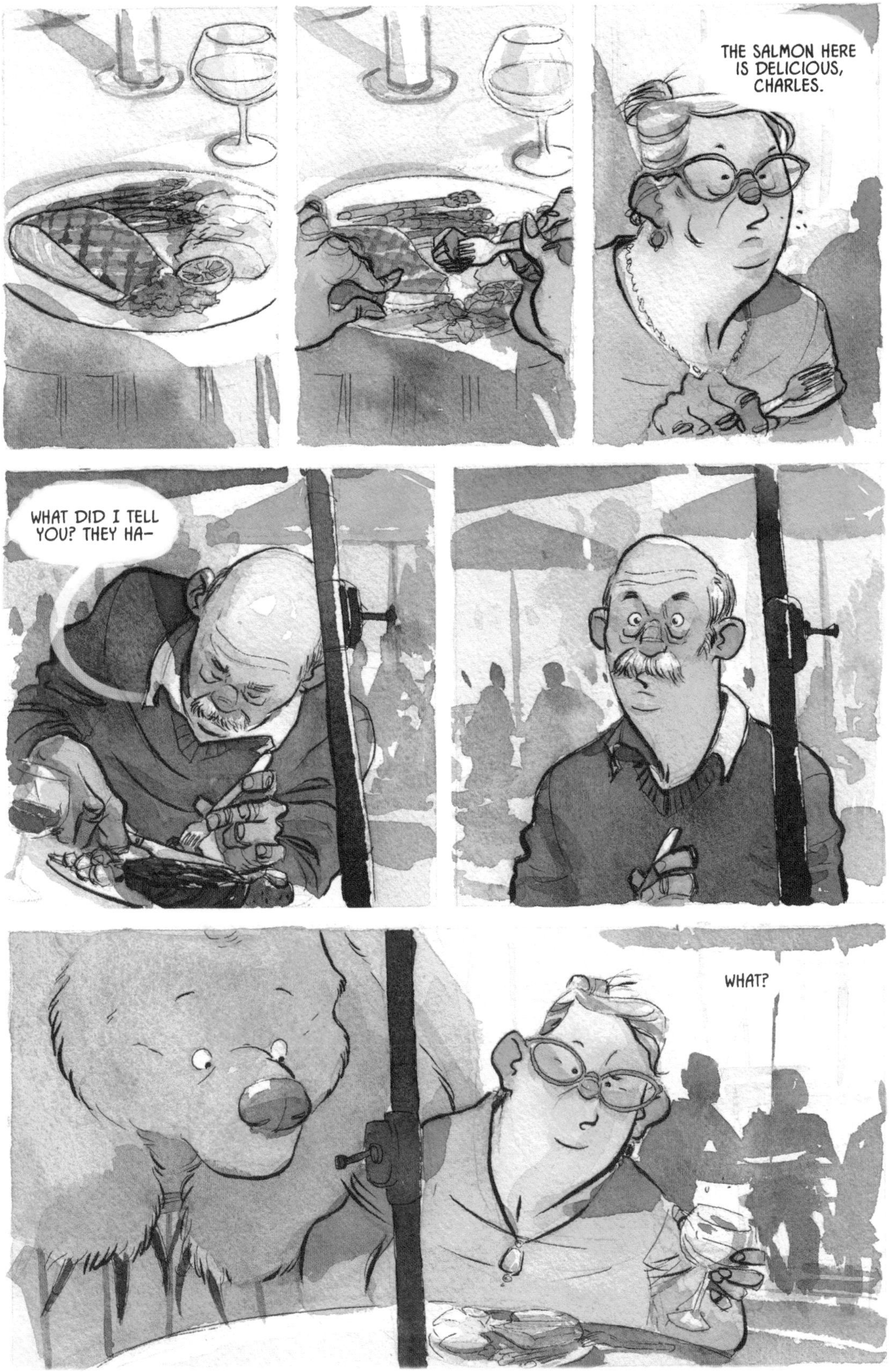
THE SALMON HERE IS DELICIOUS, CHARLES.
WHAT DID I TELL YOU? THEY HA-
WHAT?

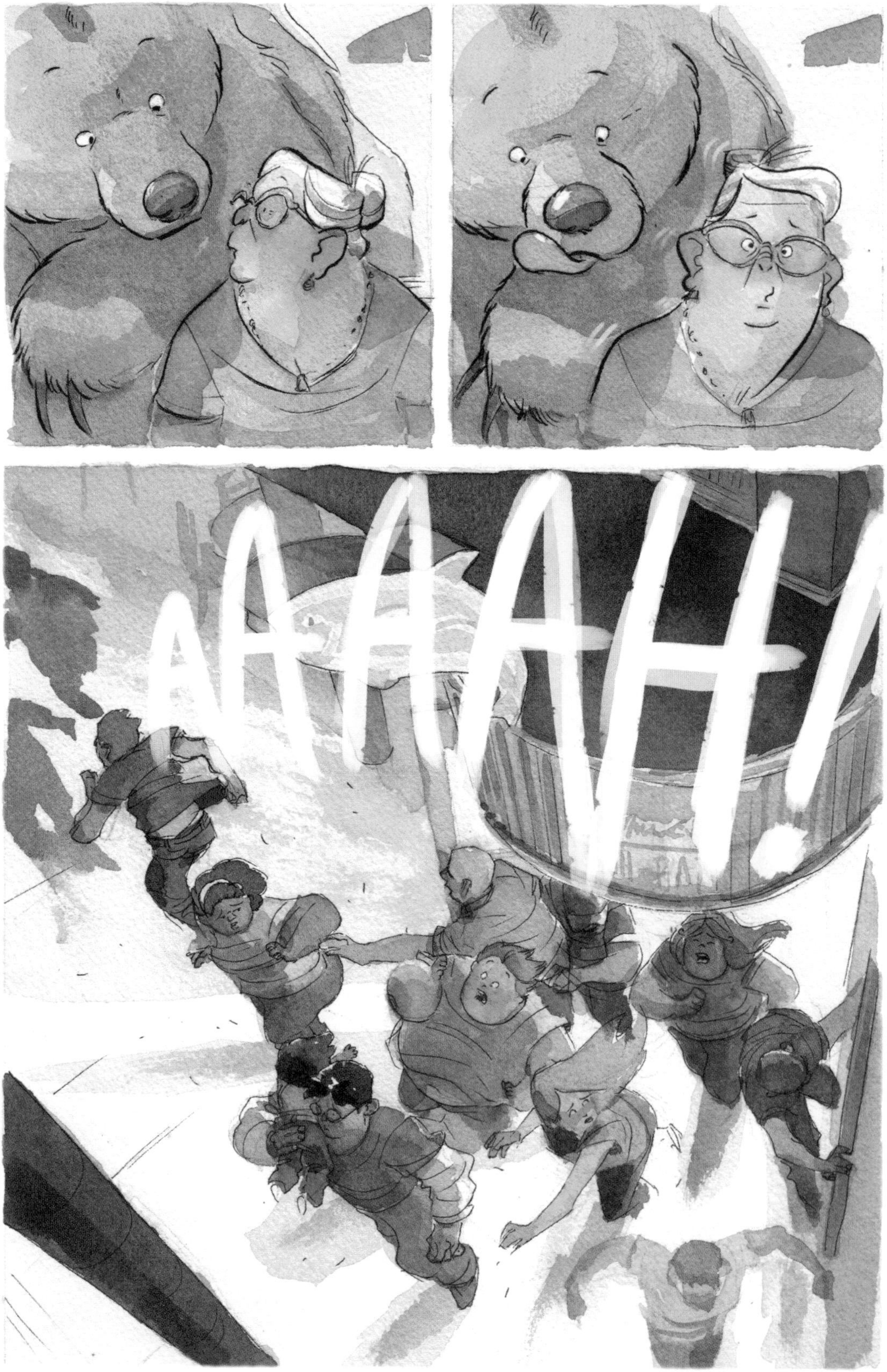
AAAAH!

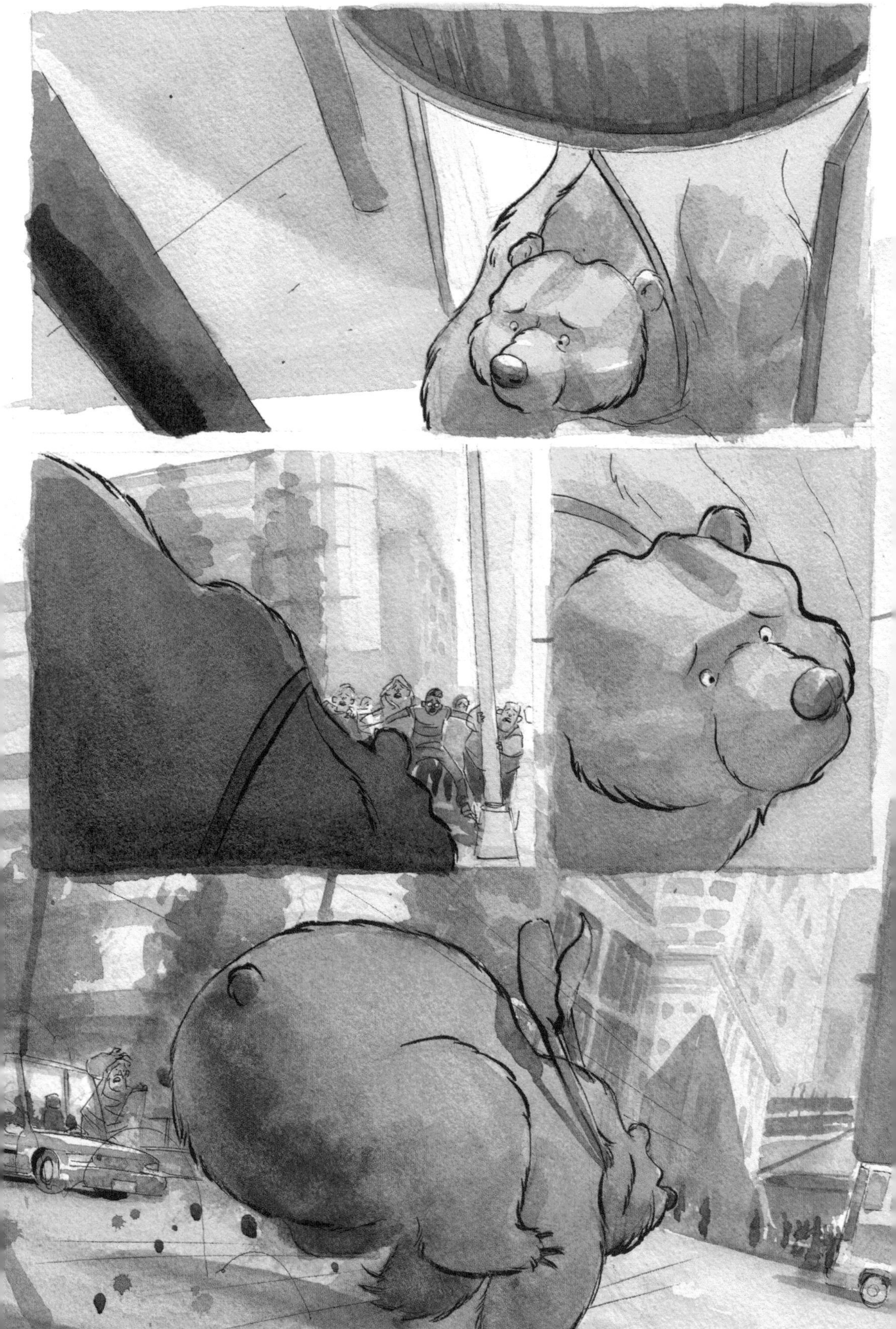

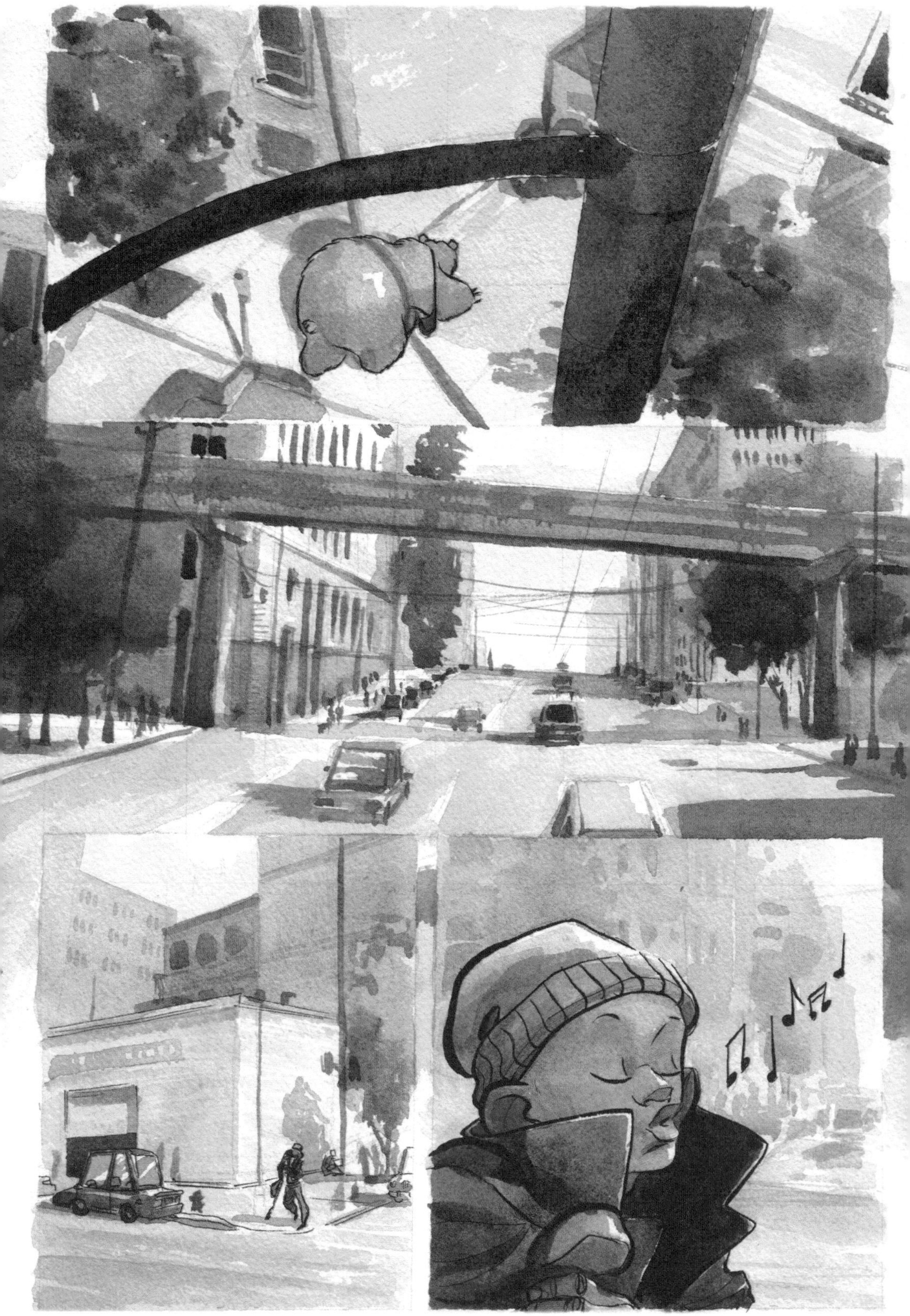

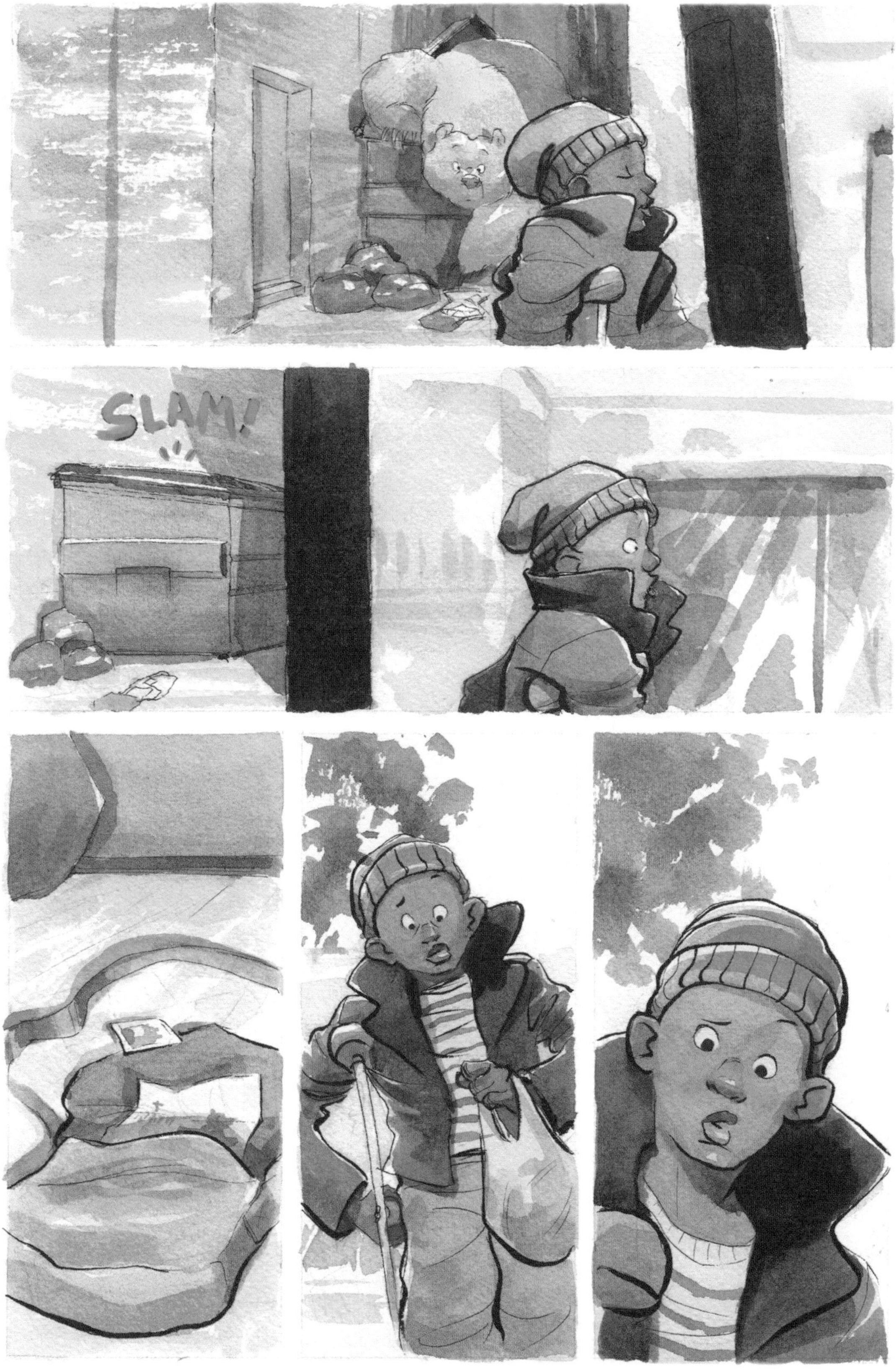
SLAM!

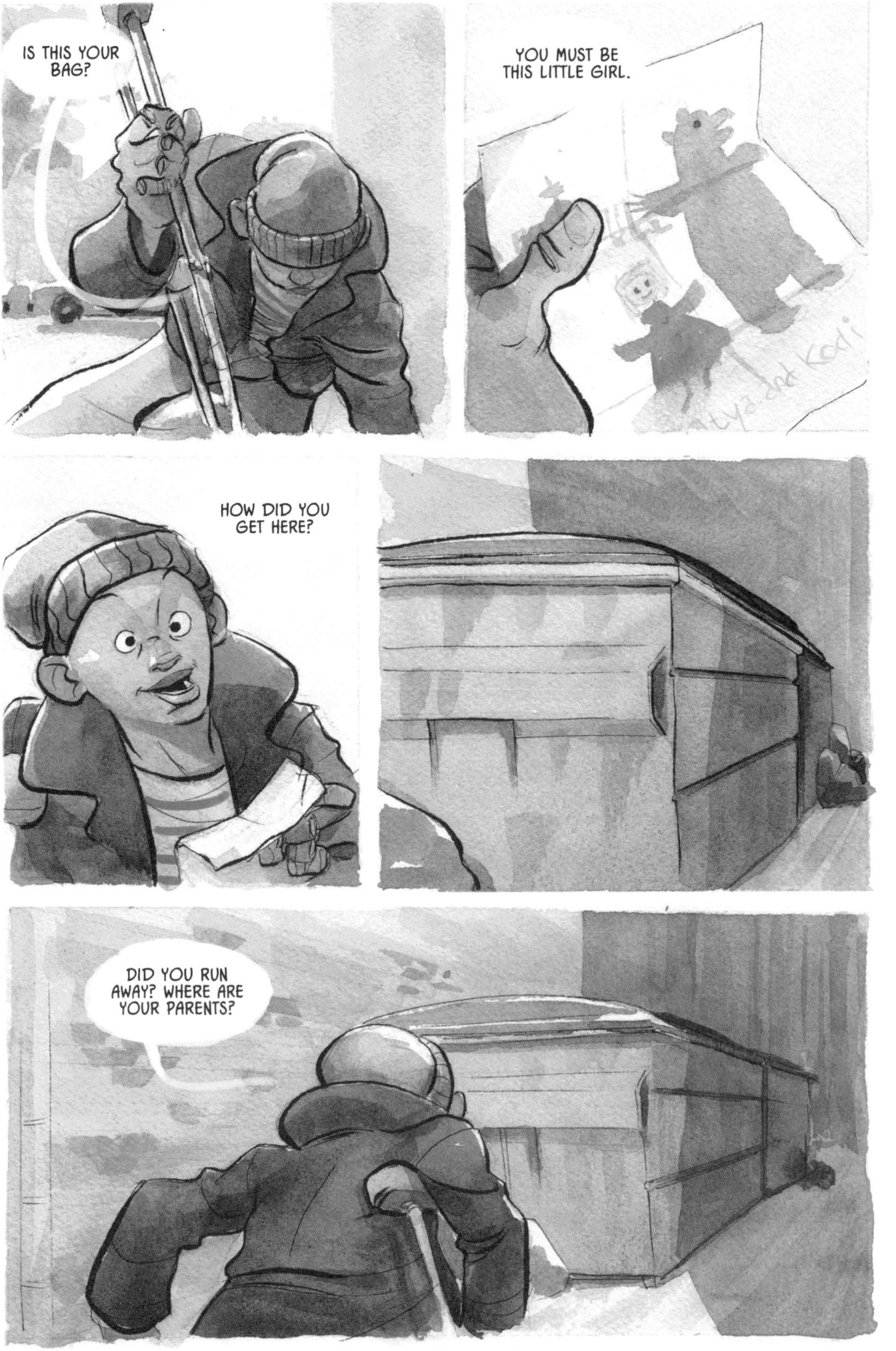
IS THIS YOUR BAG?
YOU MUST BE THIS LITTLE GIRL.
HOW DID YOU GET HERE?
DID YOU RUN AWAY? WHERE ARE YOUR PARENTS?

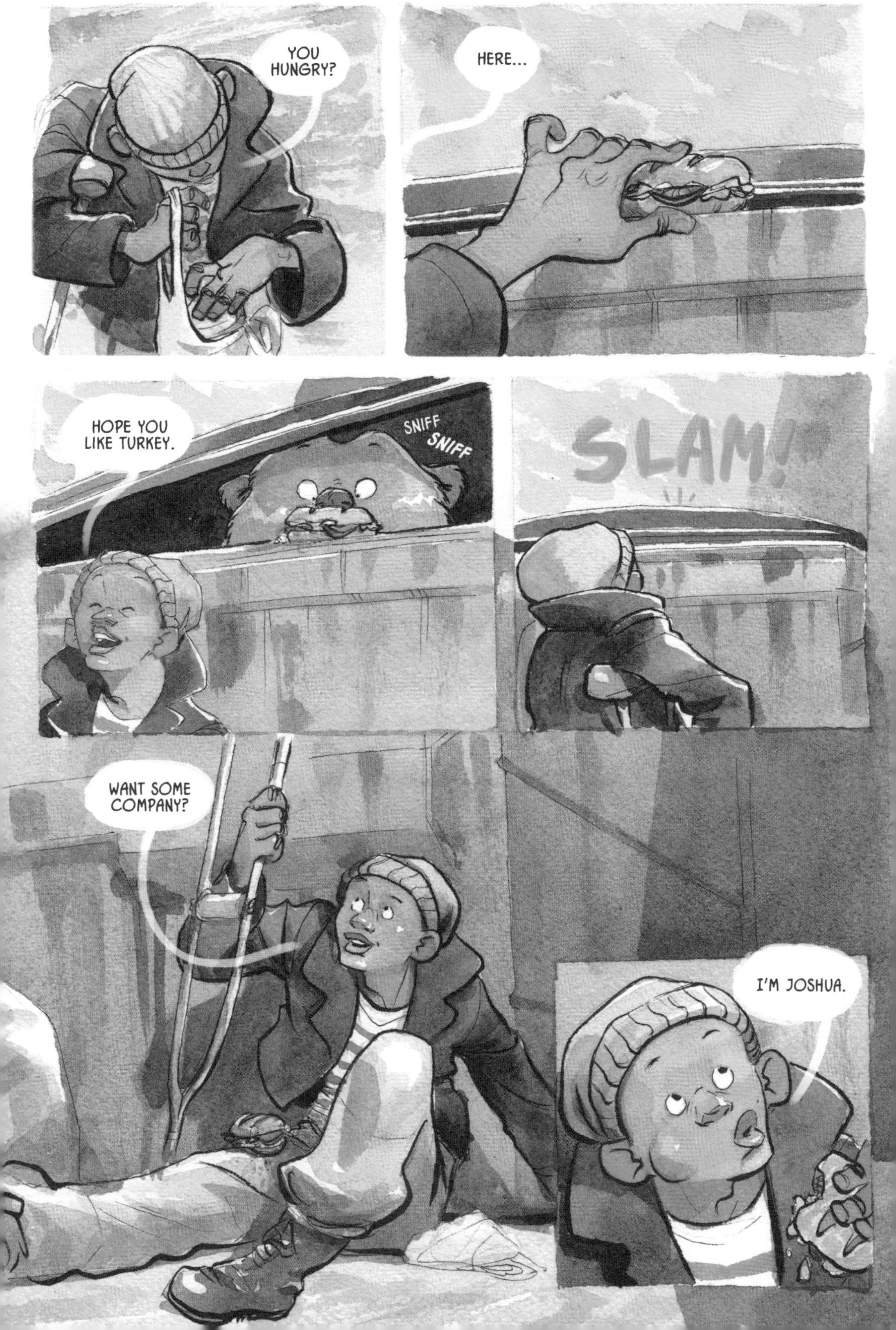
YOU HUNGRY?
HERE...
HOPE YOU LIKE TURKEY.
SNIFF
SNIFF
SLAM!
WANT SOME COMPANY?
I'M JOSHUA.

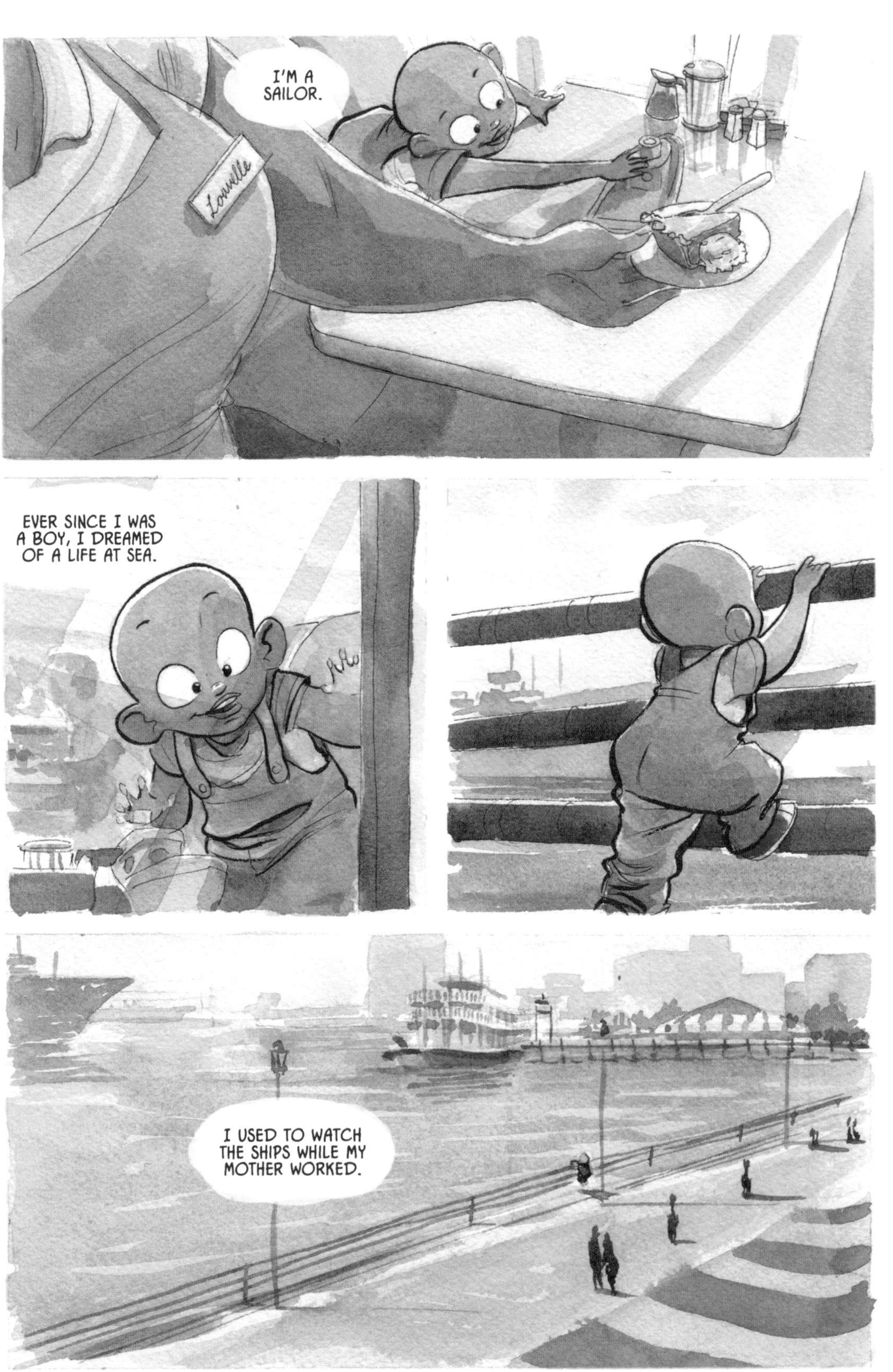
I'M A SAILOR.
EVER SINCE I WAS A BOY, I DREAMED OF A LIFE AT SEA.
I USED TO WATCH THE SHIPS WHILE MY MOTHER WORKED.

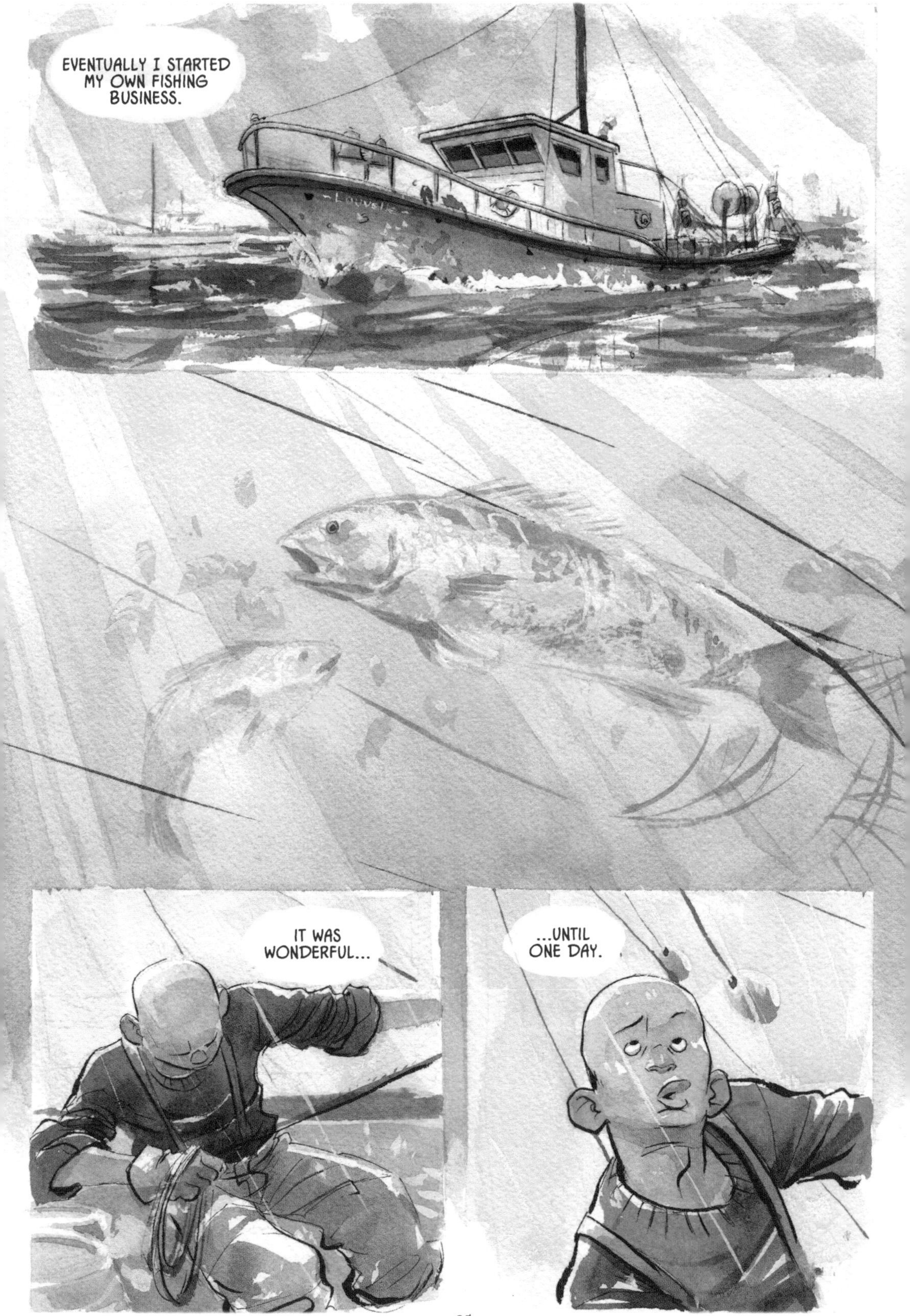
EVENTUALLY I STARTED MY OWN FISHING BUSINESS.
IT WAS WONDERFUL...
...UNTIL ONE DAY.

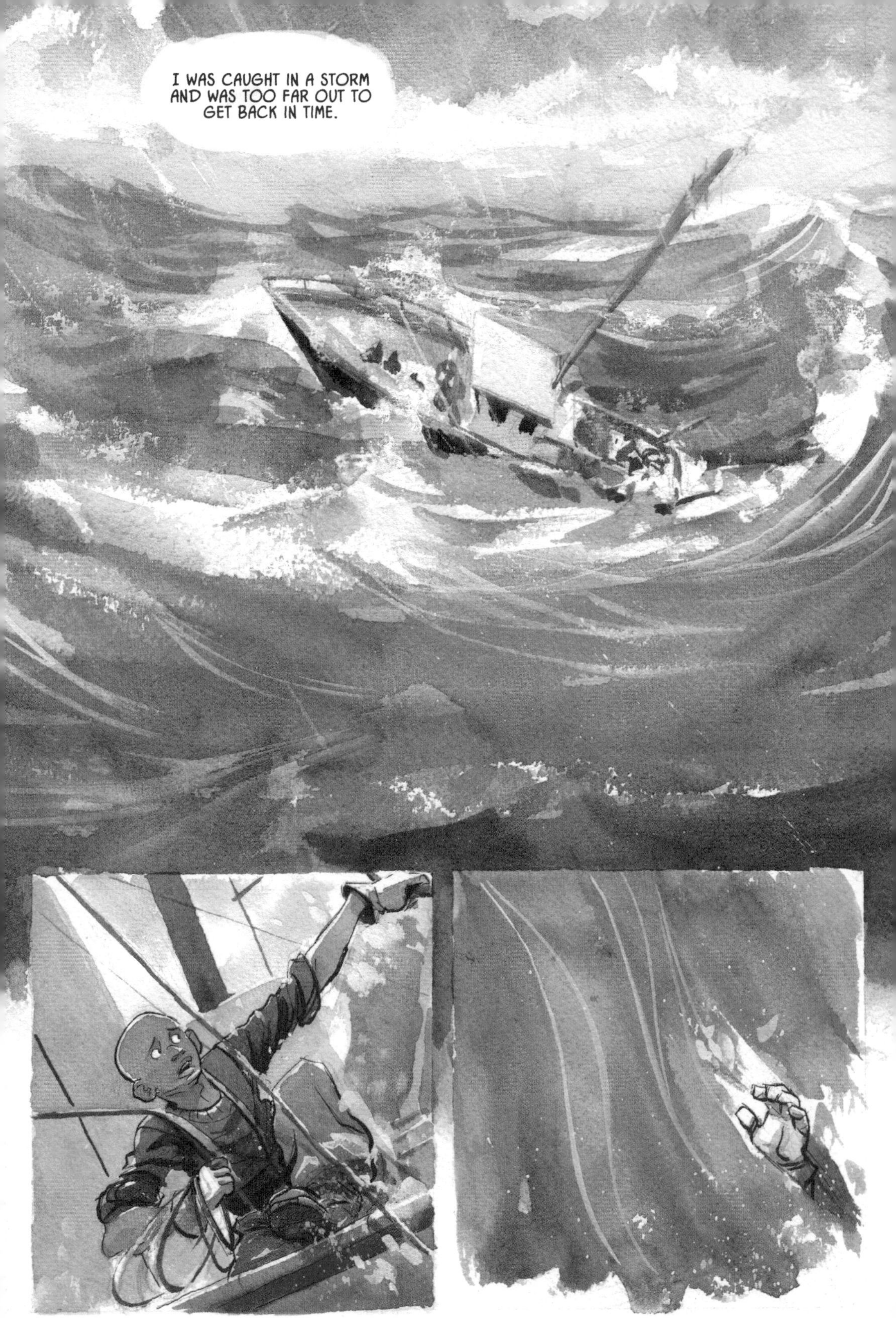
I WAS CAUGHT IN A STORM AND WAS TOO FAR OUT TO GET BACK IN TIME.

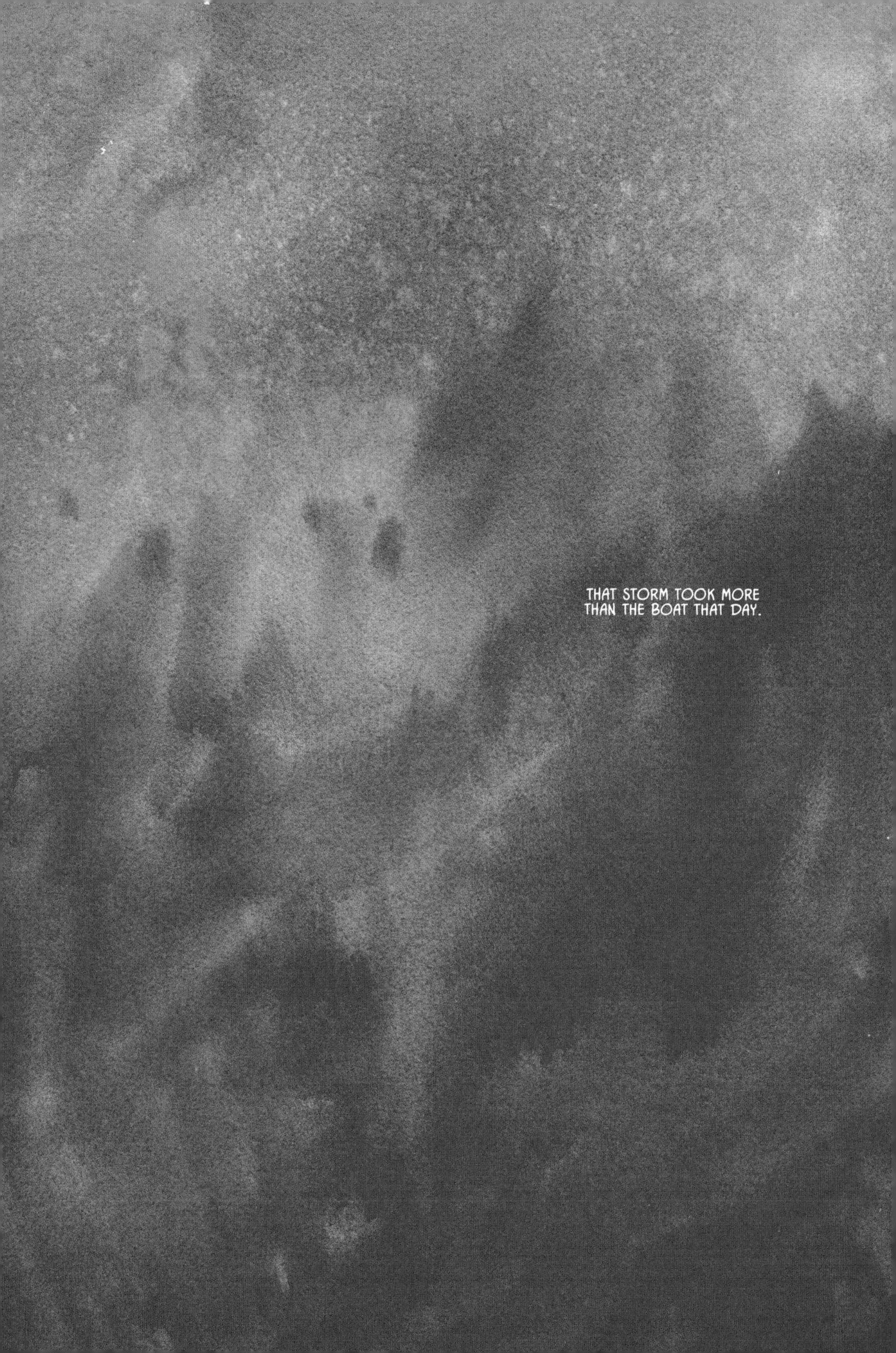
THAT STORM TOOK MORE
THAN THE BOAT THAT DAY.

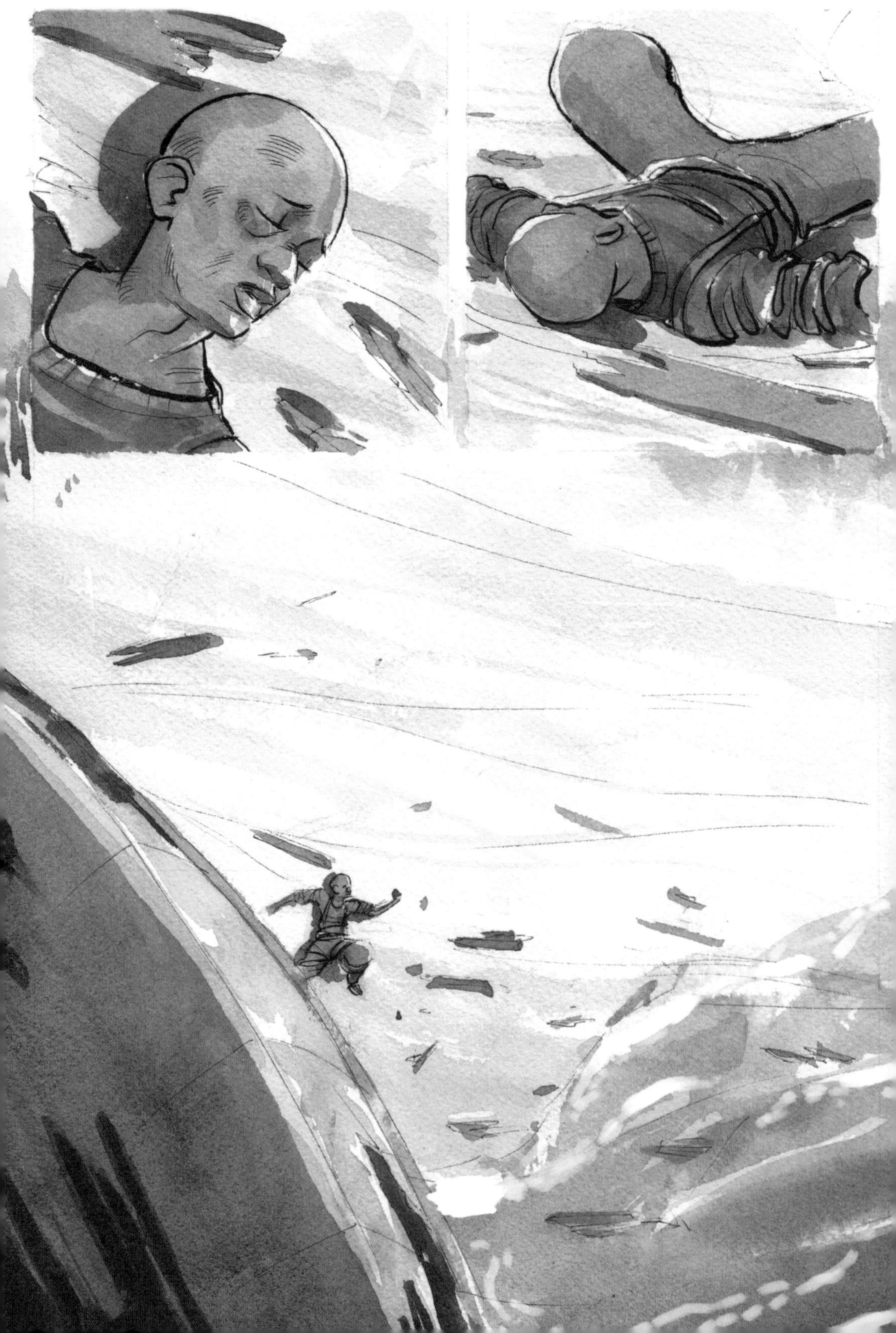

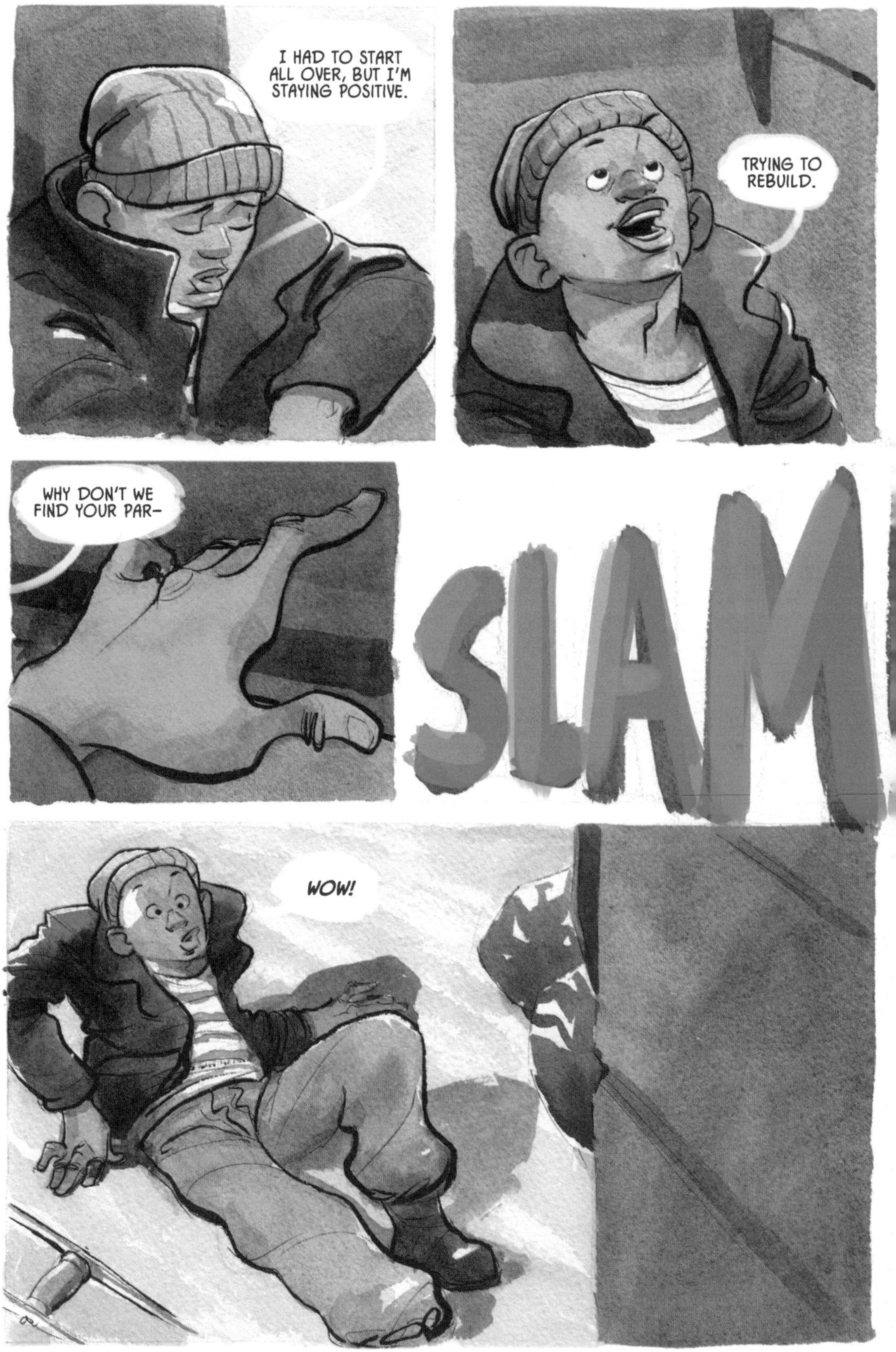
I HAD TO START ALL OVER, BUT I'M STAYING POSITIVE.
TRYING TO REBUILD.
WHY DON'T WE FIND YOUR PAR–
SLAM
WOW!

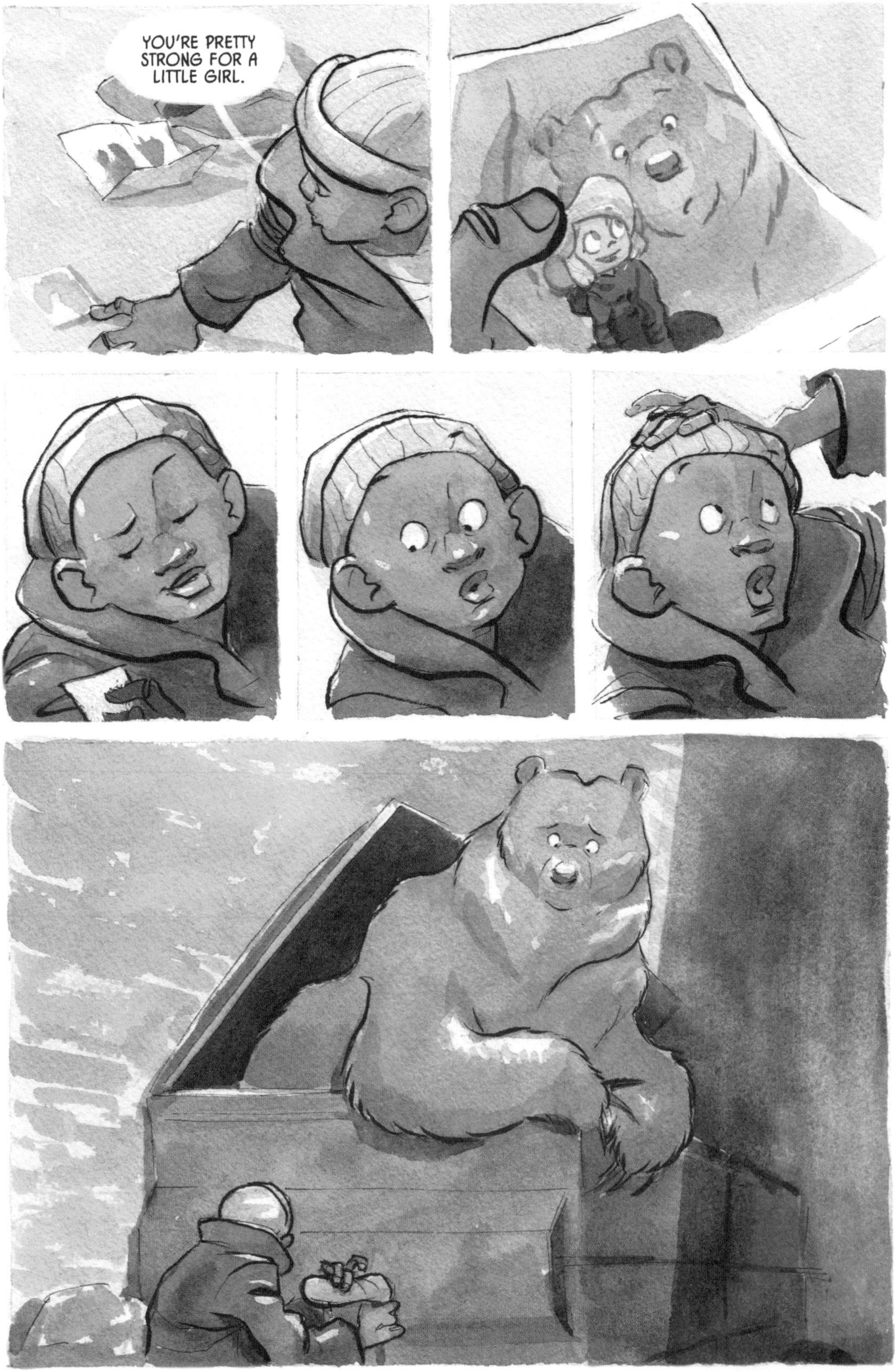
YOU'RE PRETTY STRONG FOR A LITTLE GIRL.

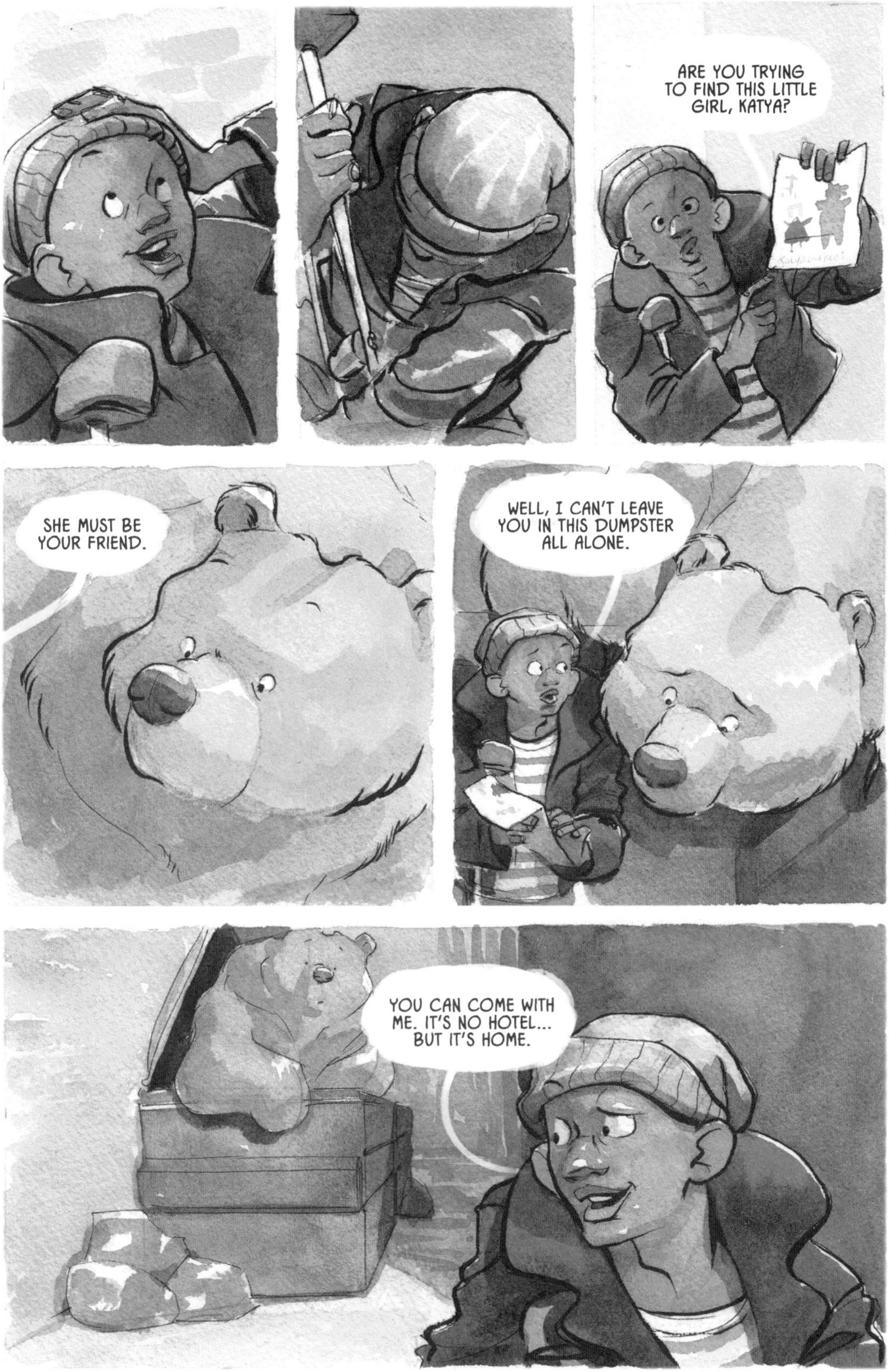
ARE YOU TRYING TO FIND THIS LITTLE GIRL, KATYA?
SHE MUST BE YOUR FRIEND.
WELL, I CAN'T LEAVE YOU IN THIS DUMPSTER ALL ALONE.
YOU CAN COME WITH ME. IT'S NO HOTEL... BUT IT'S HOME.

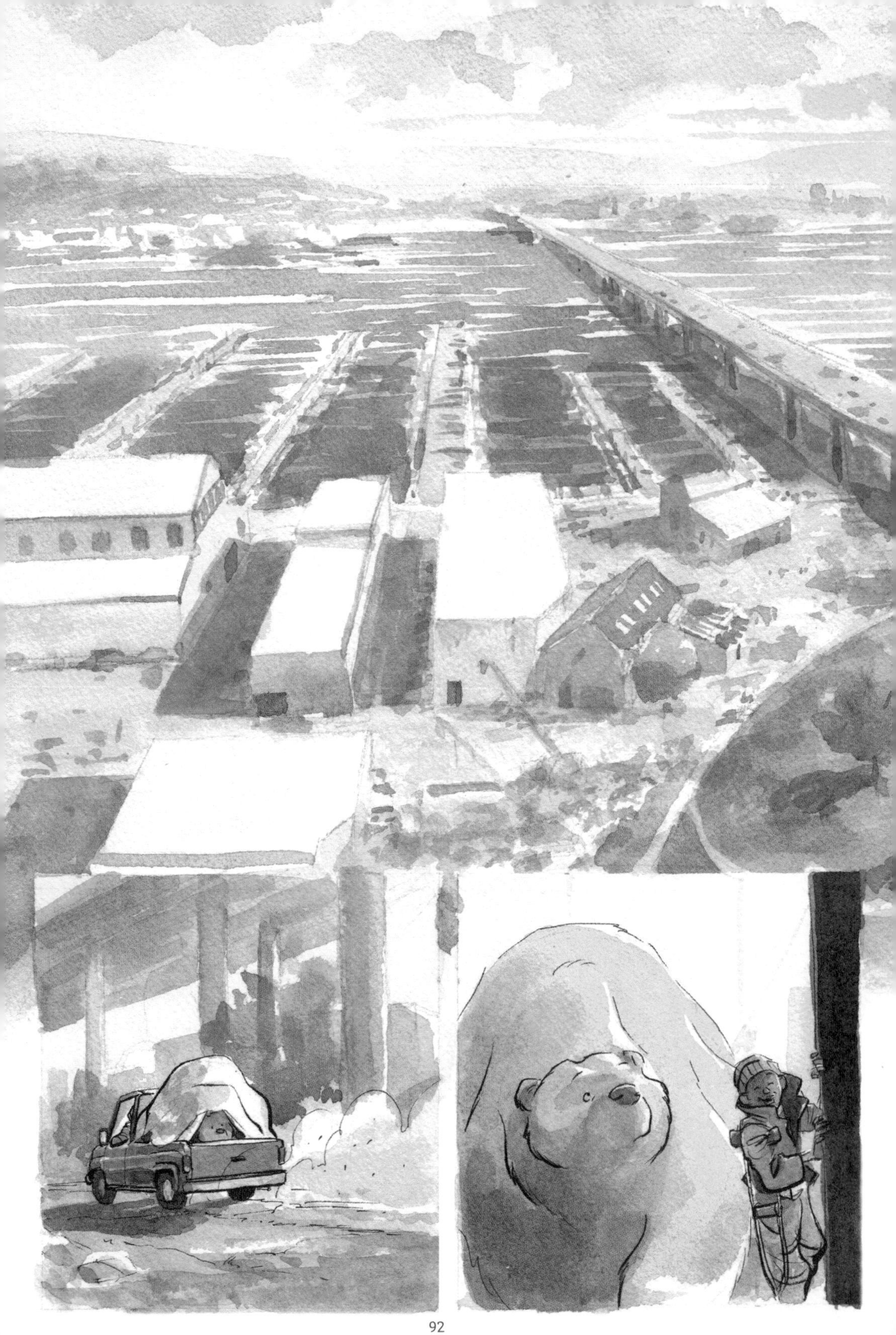

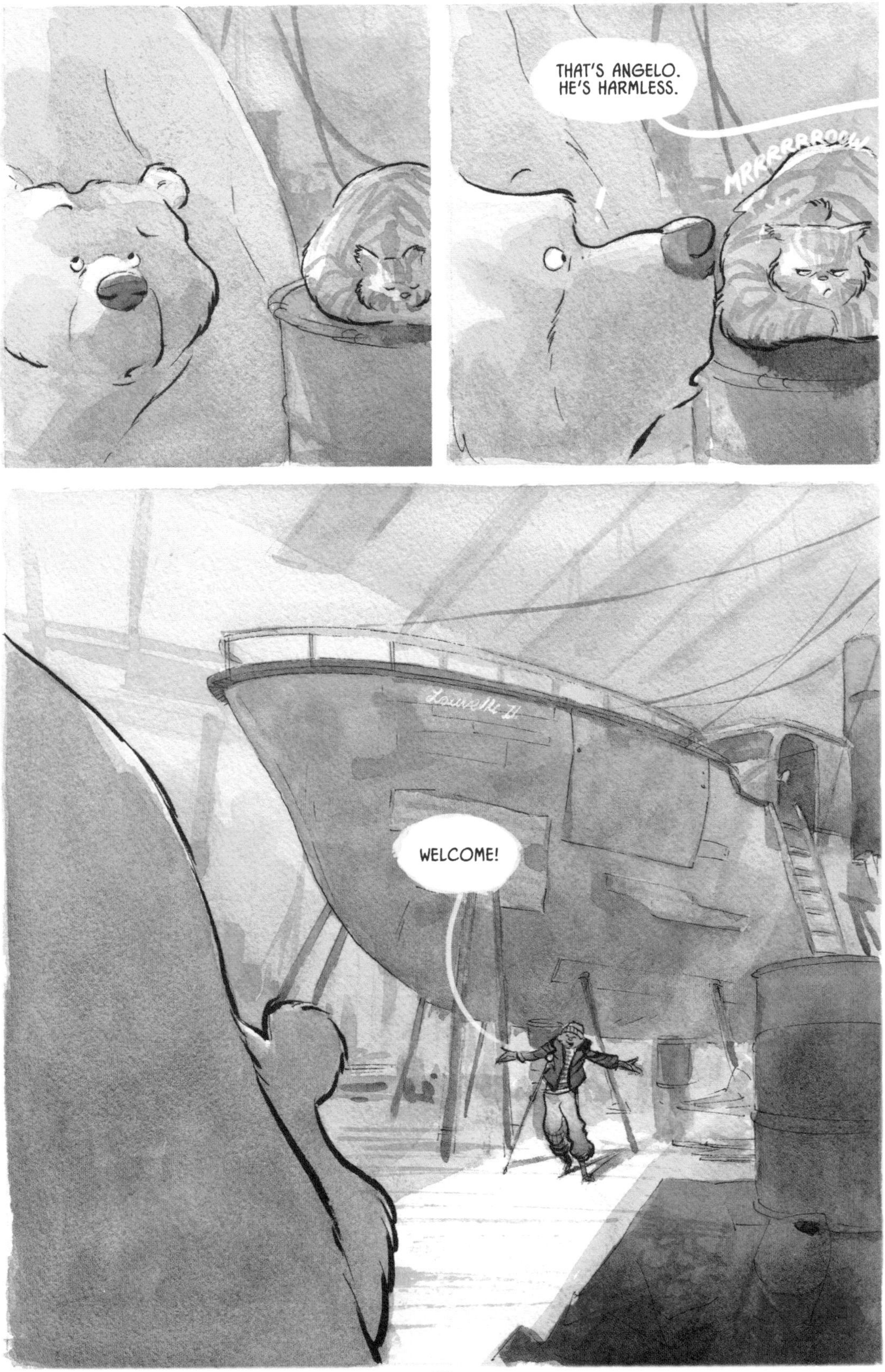
THAT'S ANGELO. HE'S HARMLESS.
!
MRRRRRROOW
WELCOME!

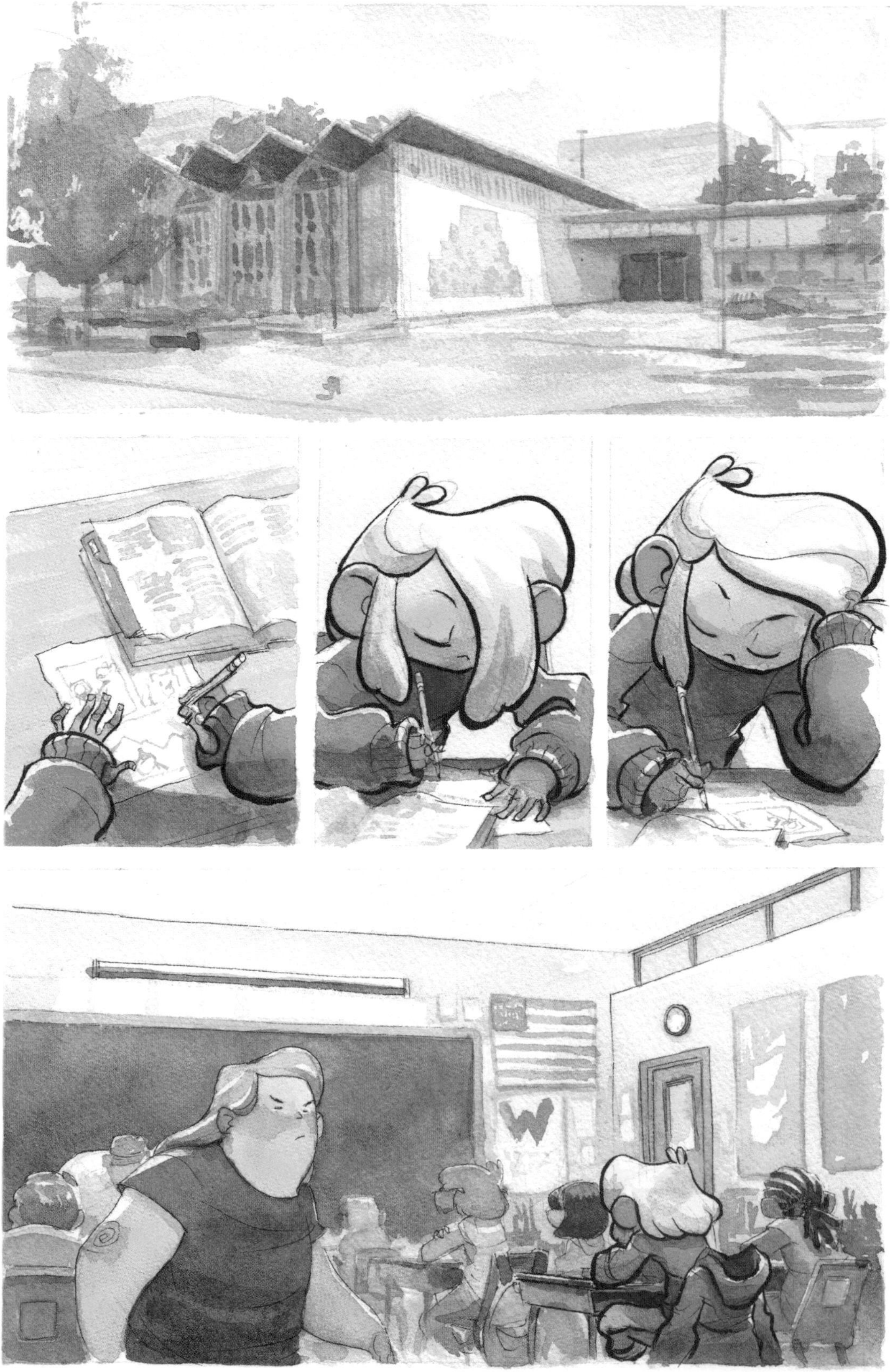
W

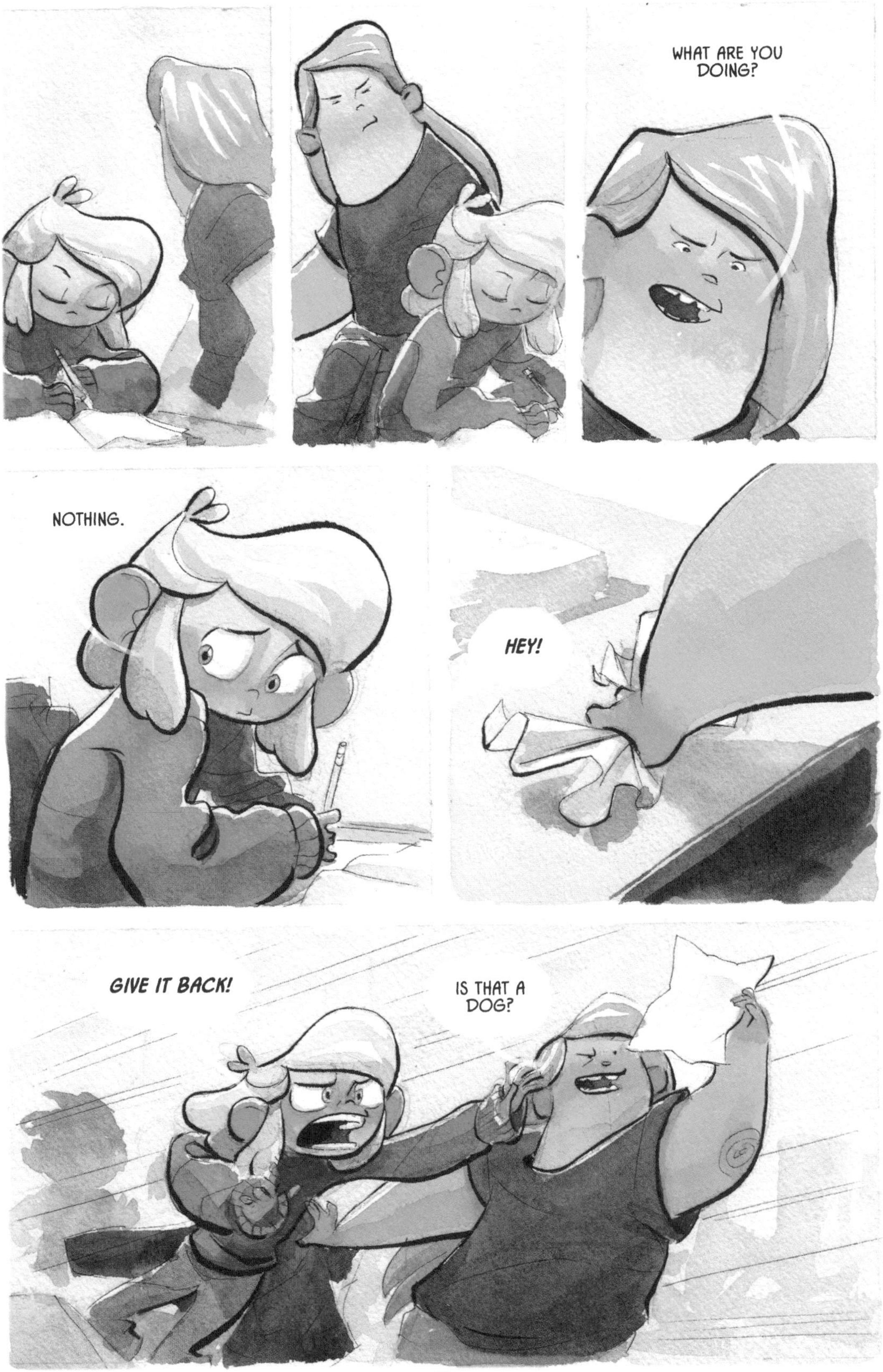
WHAT ARE YOU DOING?
NOTHING.
HEY!
GIVE IT BACK!
IS THAT A DOG?

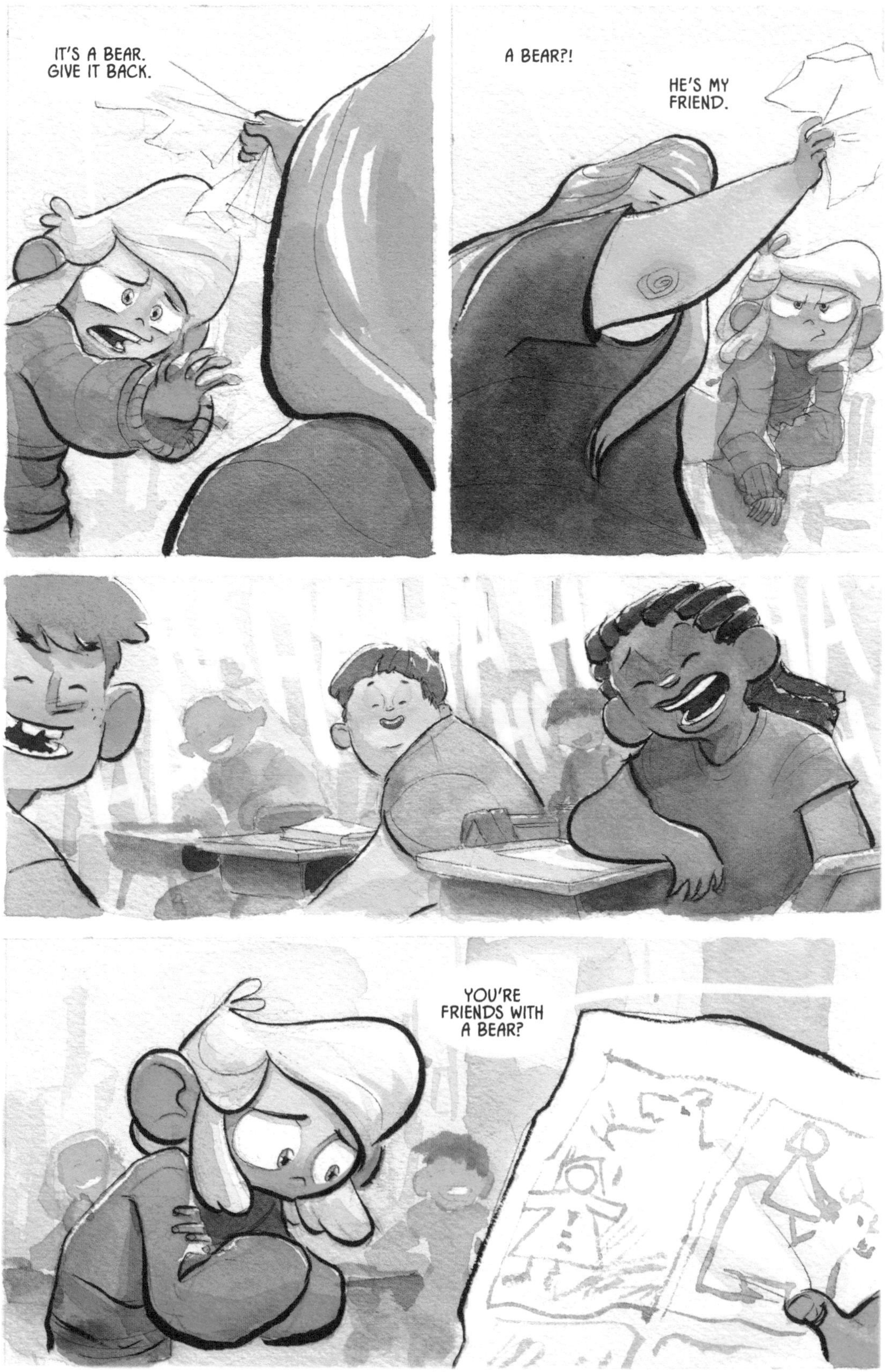
IT'S A BEAR. GIVE IT BACK.
A BEAR?!
HE'S MY FRIEND.
YOU'RE FRIENDS WITH A BEAR?

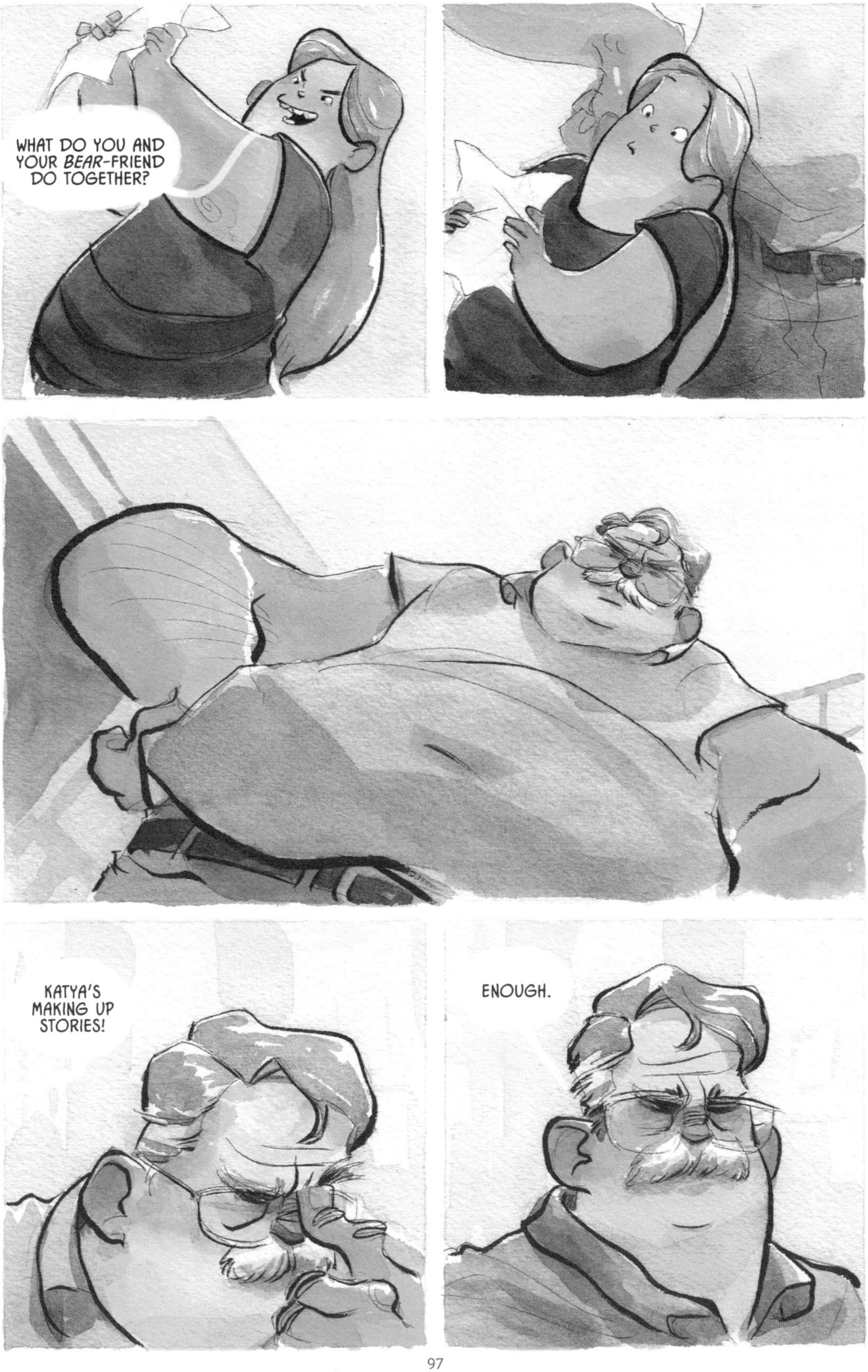
WHAT DO YOU AND YOUR *BEAR*-FRIEND DO TOGETHER?
KATYA'S MAKING UP STORIES!
ENOUGH.

I DIDN'T MAKE IT UP.

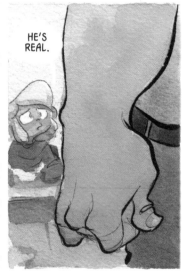

HE'S REAL.

I THINK YOU MAY BE READING TOO MANY COMIC BOOKS.

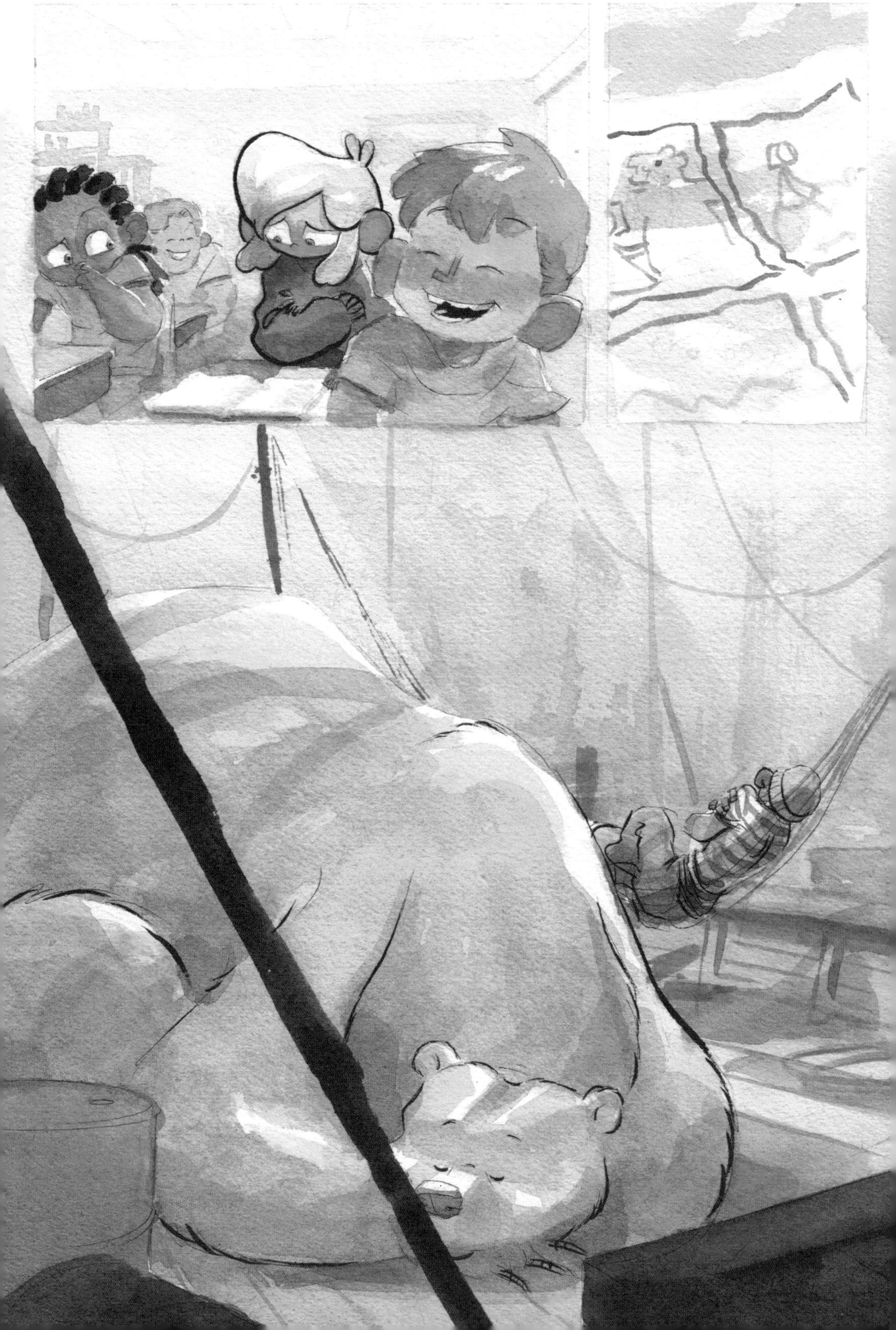

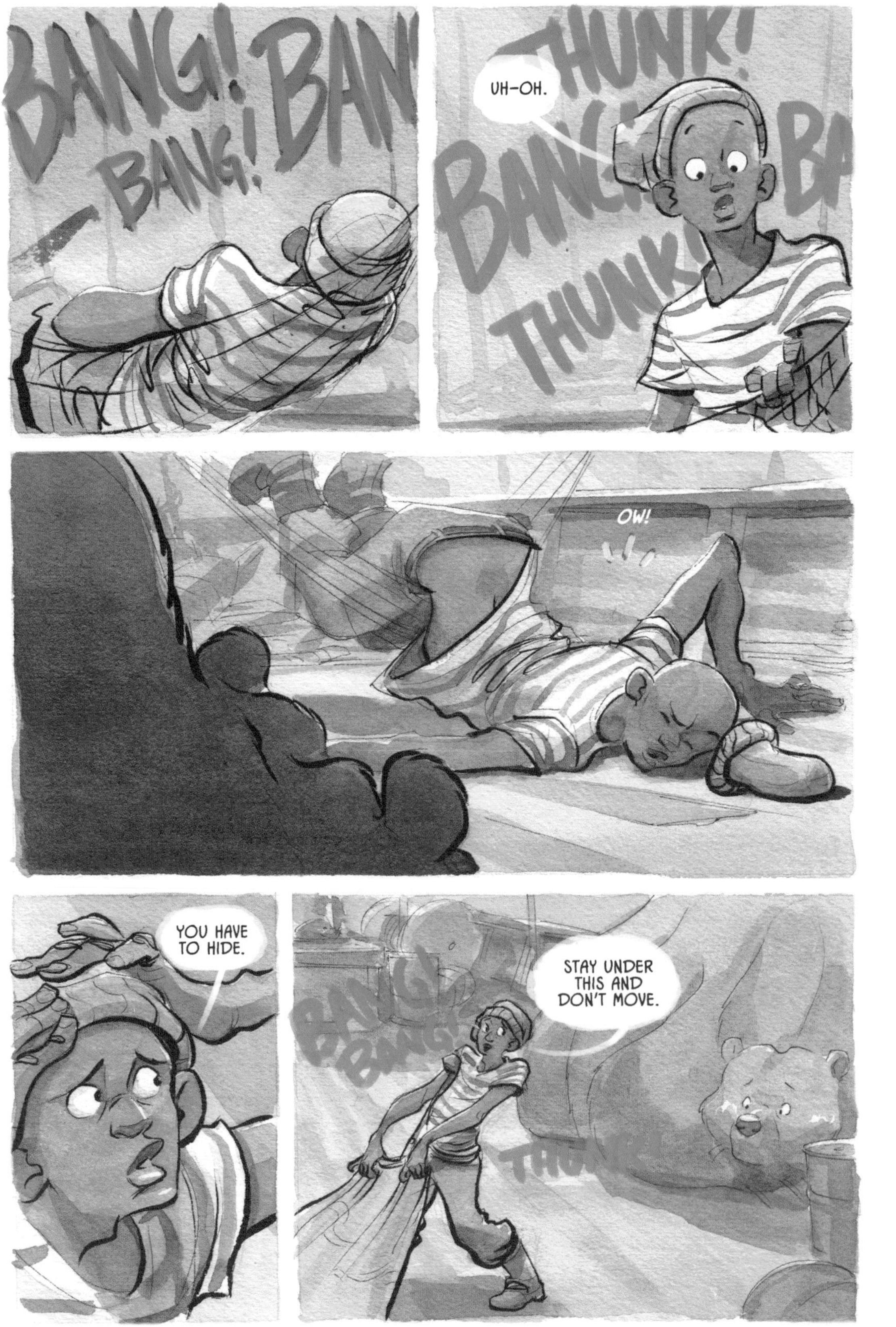
BANG!
BANG!
BAN
UH-OH.
THUNK!
BANG!
THUNK!
OW!
YOU HAVE TO HIDE.
STAY UNDER THIS AND DON'T MOVE.
BANG!
BANG!

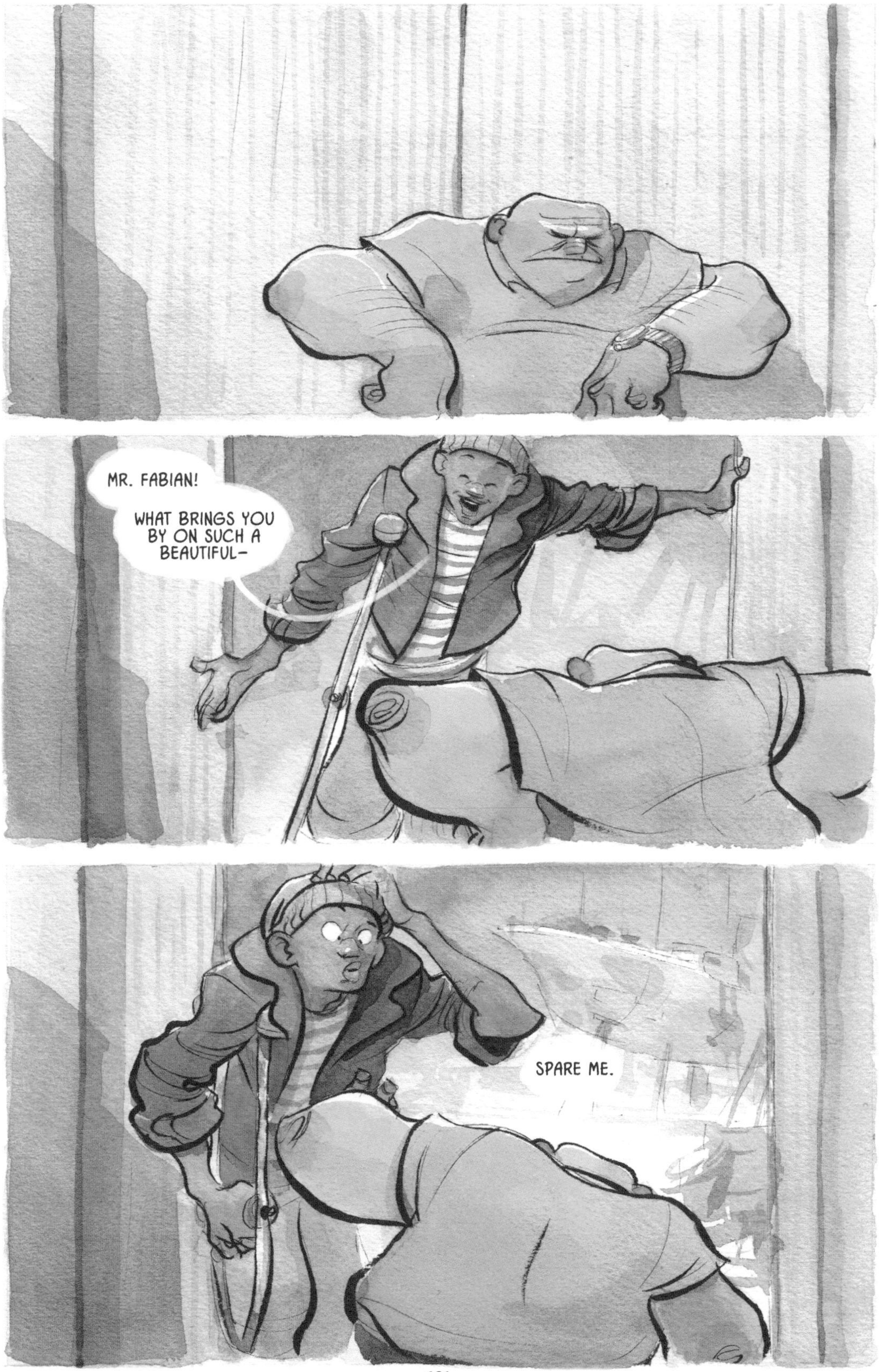
MR. FABIAN!
WHAT BRINGS YOU BY ON SUCH A BEAUTIFUL-
SPARE ME.

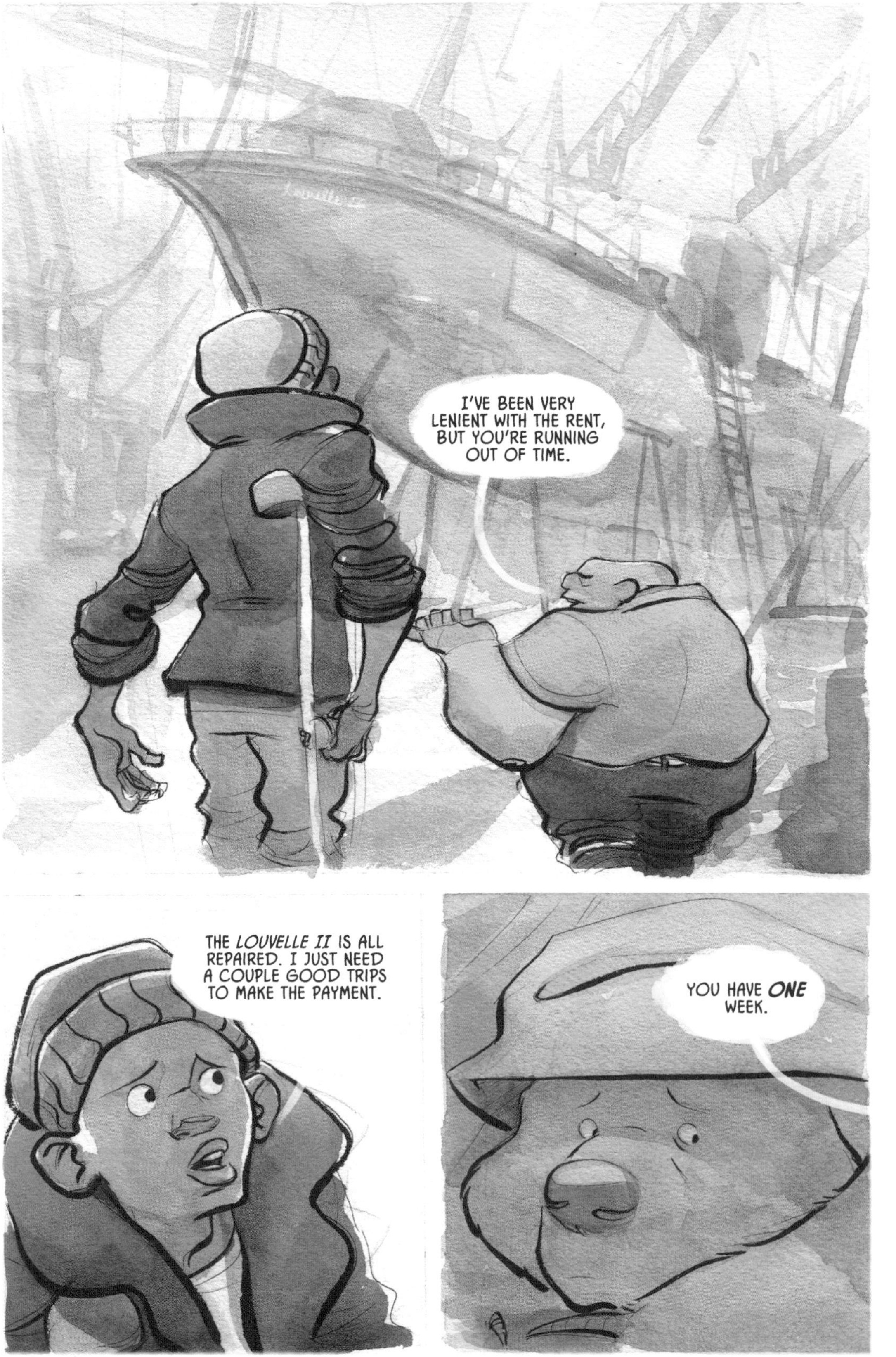
I'VE BEEN VERY LENIENT WITH THE RENT, BUT YOU'RE RUNNING OUT OF TIME.
THE *LOUVELLE II* IS ALL REPAIRED. I JUST NEED A COUPLE GOOD TRIPS TO MAKE THE PAYMENT.
YOU HAVE ***ONE*** WEEK.

IF YOU DON'T—

CLASH!
CLANG!

DID YOU BRING A DOG IN HERE? I SAID NO ANIMALS.

WHAT?

IT WAS PROBABLY JUST A RACCOON.

CRASH!
BANG
CLA

SHATTER SMASH! BANG CLANG! CRASH! SMASH!
CLASH BANG CRAS

A REALLY BIG RACCOON.

I'M GONNA HAVE A LOOK AROUND.

?

WHAT'S UNDER THERE?

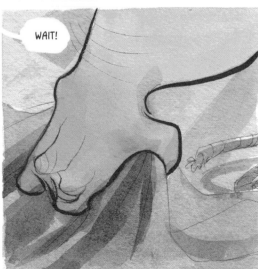

WAIT!

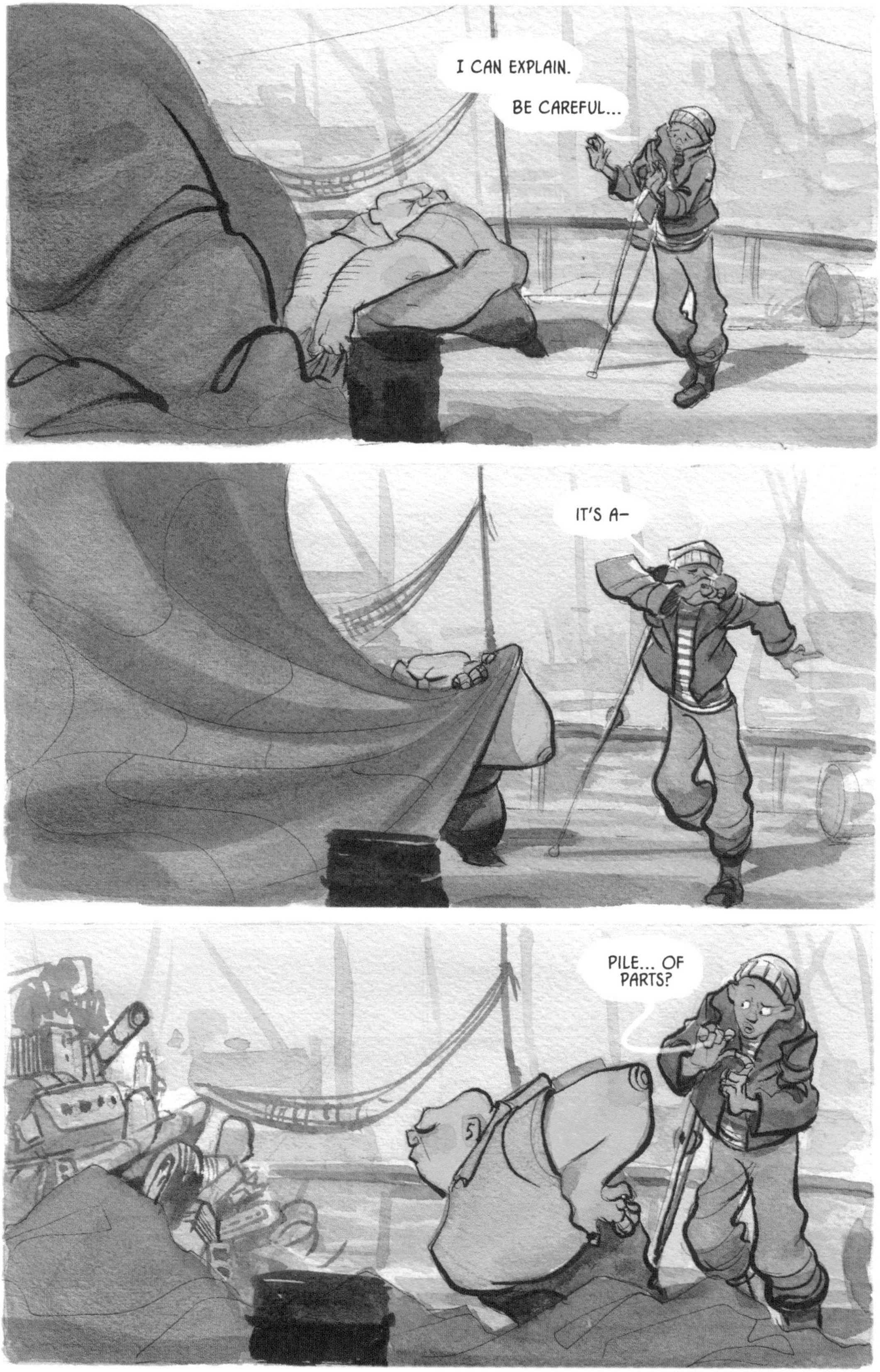
I CAN EXPLAIN.
BE CAREFUL...
IT'S A–
PILE... OF PARTS?

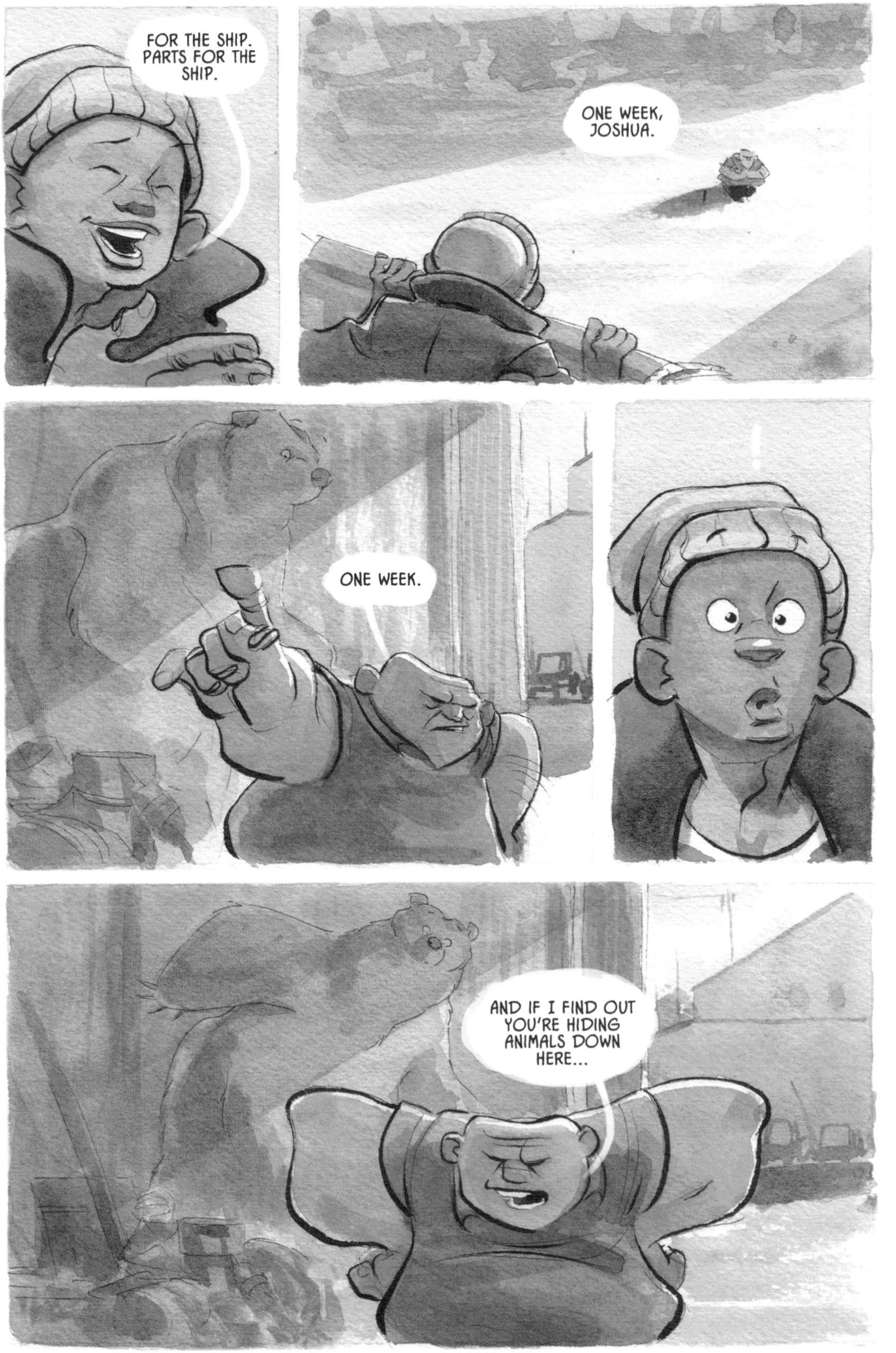
FOR THE SHIP. PARTS FOR THE SHIP.
ONE WEEK, JOSHUA.
ONE WEEK.
!
AND IF I FIND OUT YOU'RE HIDING ANIMALS DOWN HERE...

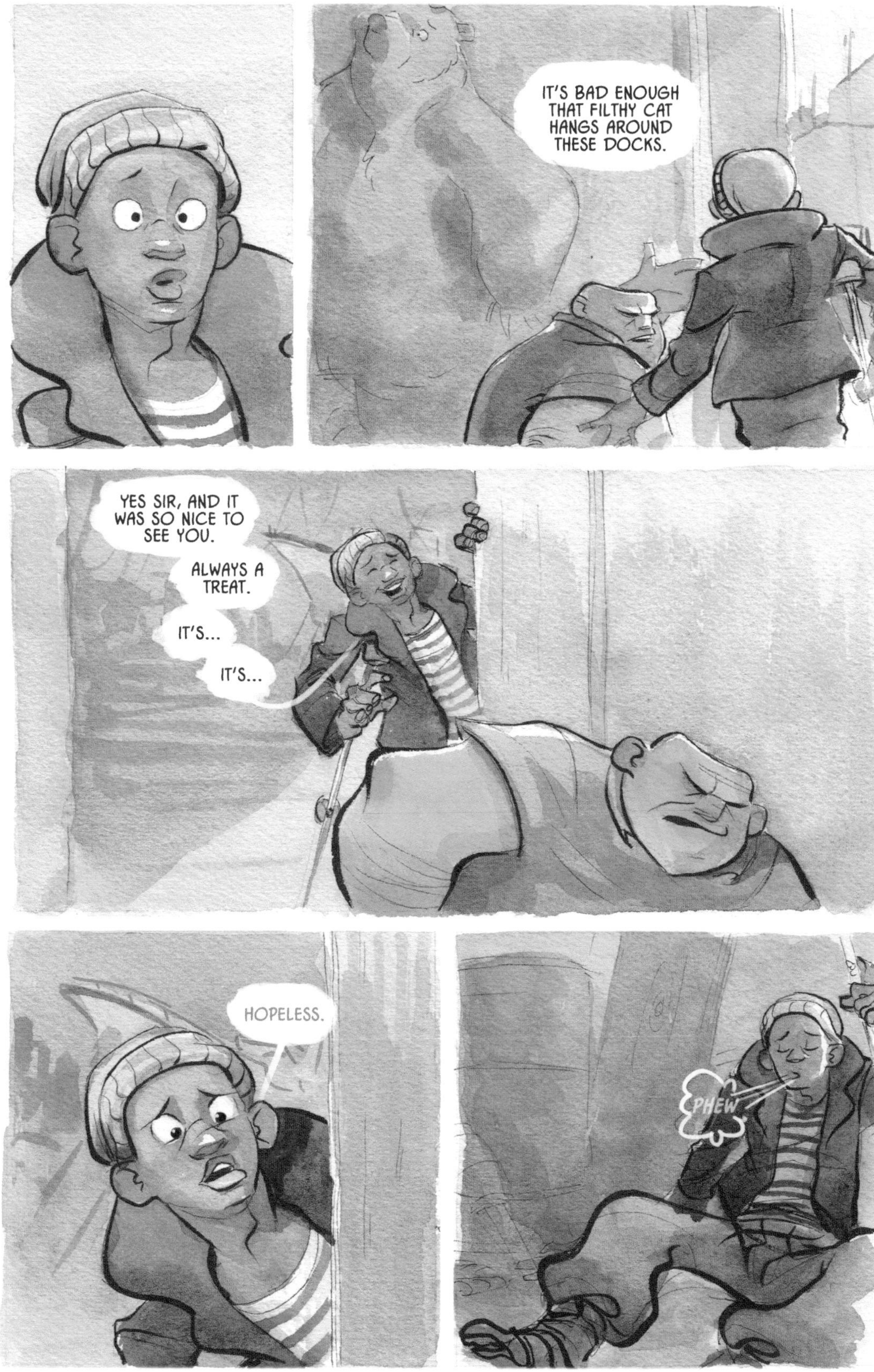
IT'S BAD ENOUGH THAT FILTHY CAT HANGS AROUND THESE DOCKS.
YES SIR, AND IT WAS SO NICE TO SEE YOU.
ALWAYS A TREAT.
IT'S...
IT'S...
HOPELESS.
PHEW

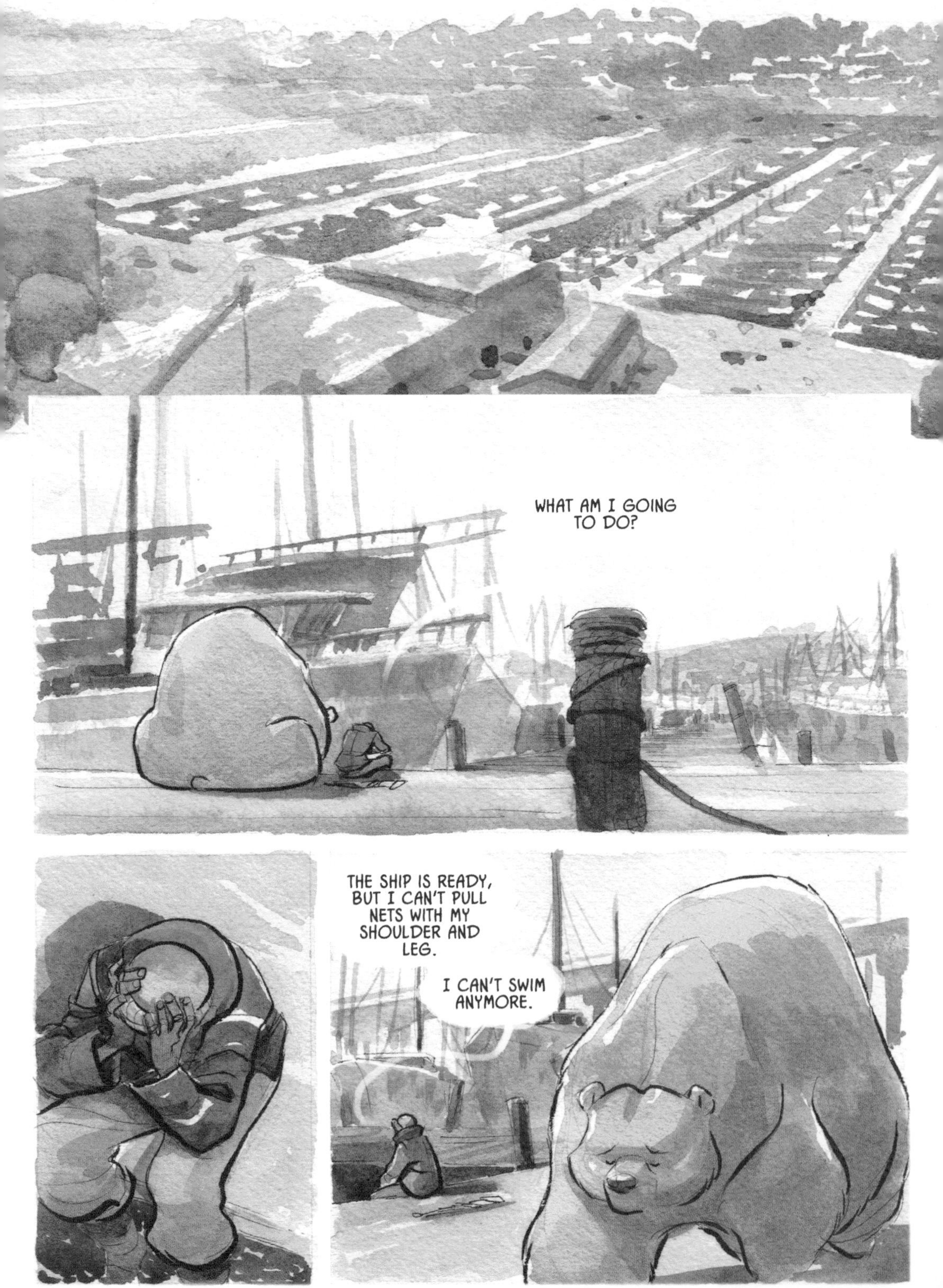
WHAT AM I GOING TO DO?
THE SHIP IS READY, BUT I CAN'T PULL NETS WITH MY SHOULDER AND LEG.
I CAN'T SWIM ANYMORE.

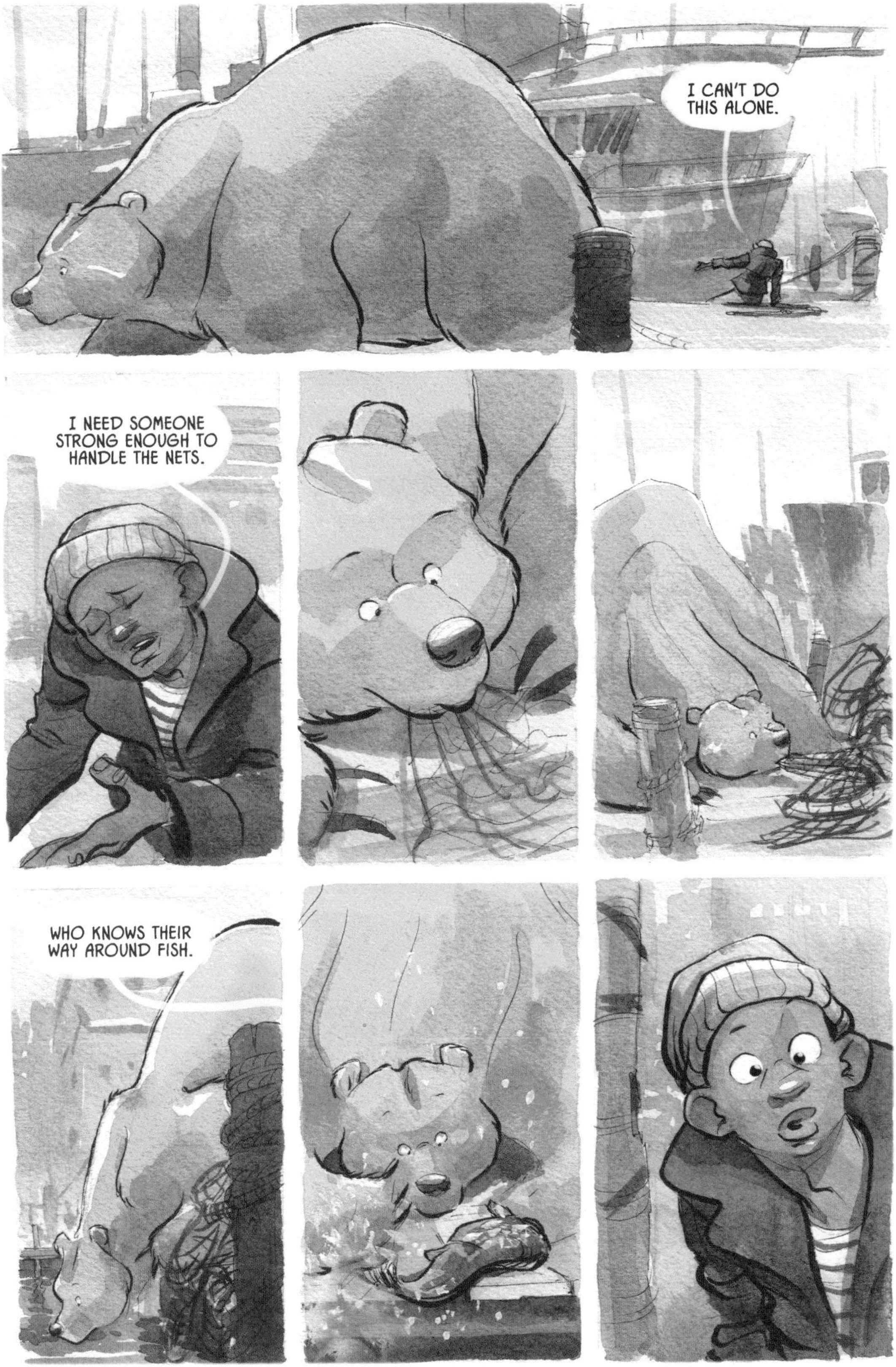
I CAN'T DO THIS ALONE.
I NEED SOMEONE STRONG ENOUGH TO HANDLE THE NETS.
WHO KNOWS THEIR WAY AROUND FISH.

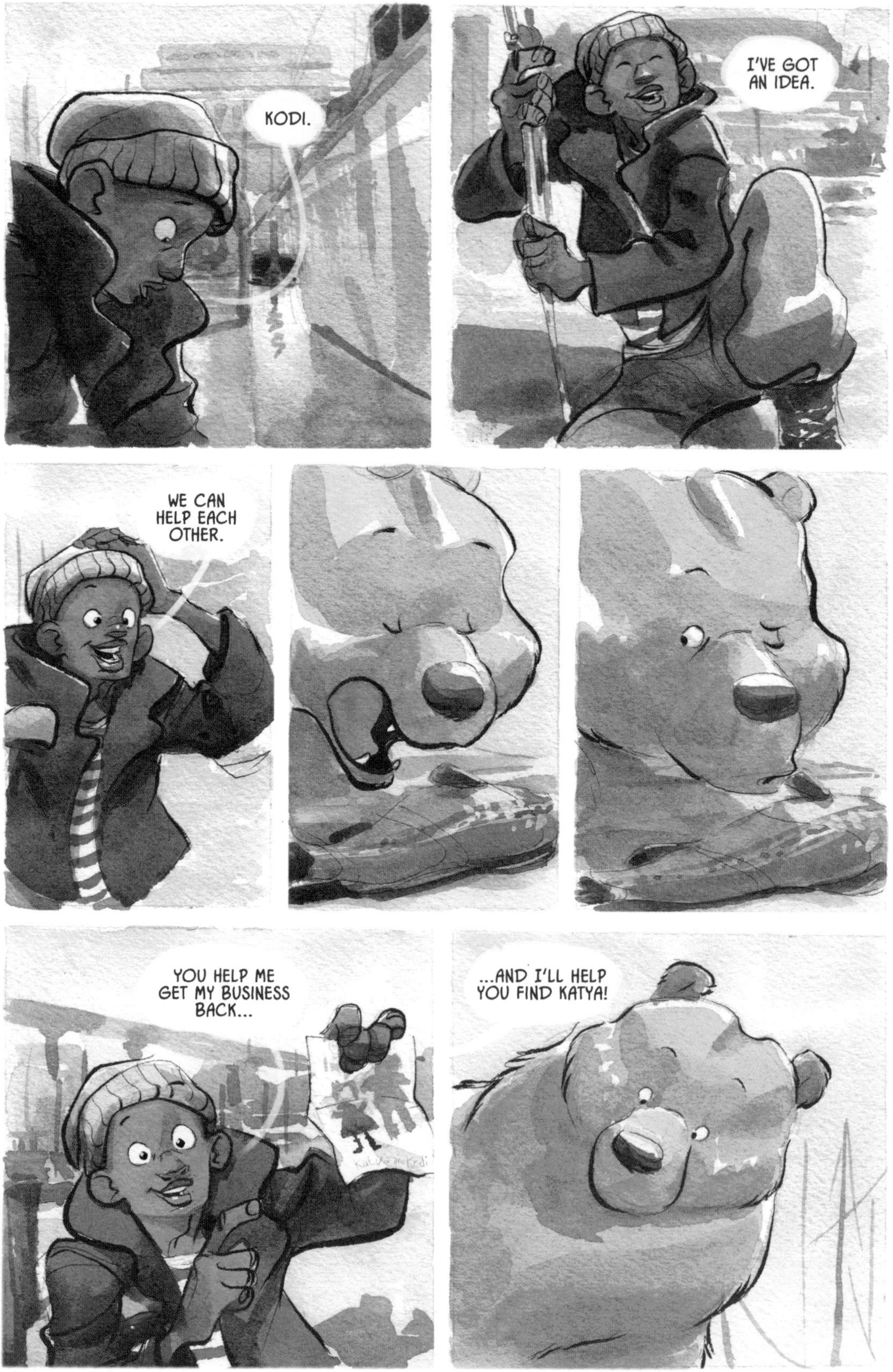
KODI.
I'VE GOT AN IDEA.
WE CAN HELP EACH OTHER.
YOU HELP ME GET MY BUSINESS BACK...
...AND I'LL HELP YOU FIND KATYA!

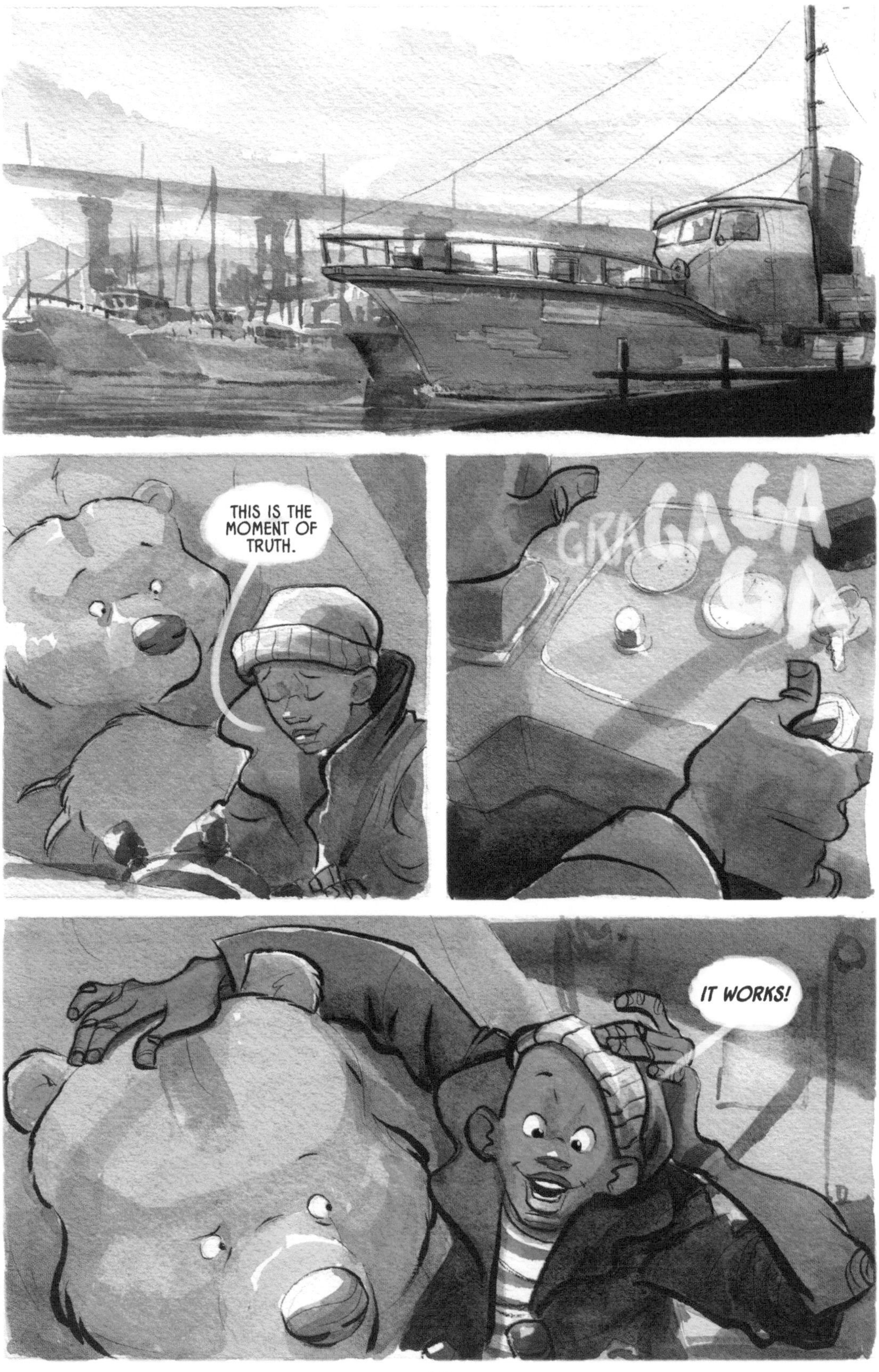
THIS IS THE MOMENT OF TRUTH.
GRAGAGA GA
IT WORKS!

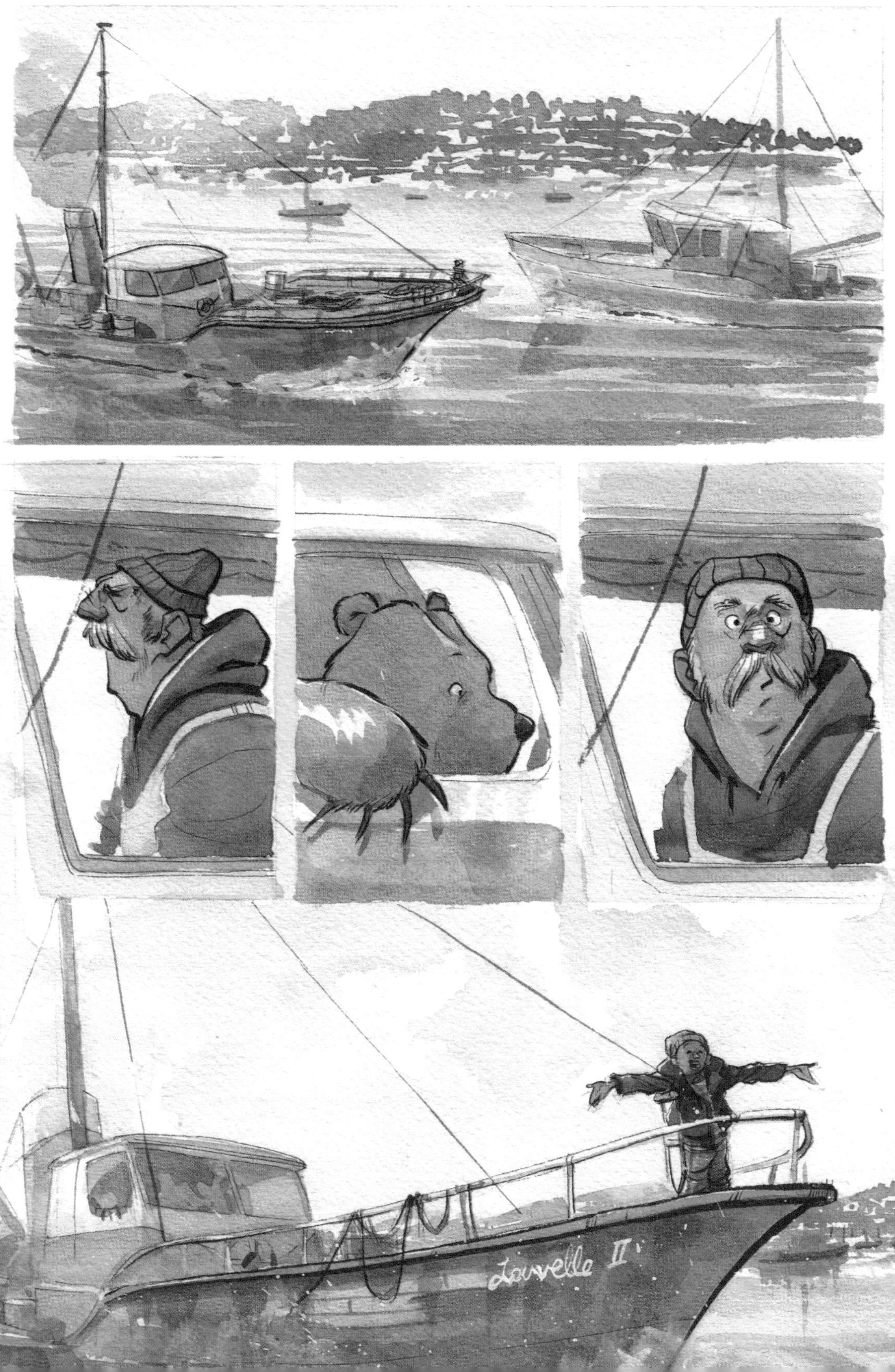
Louvelle II

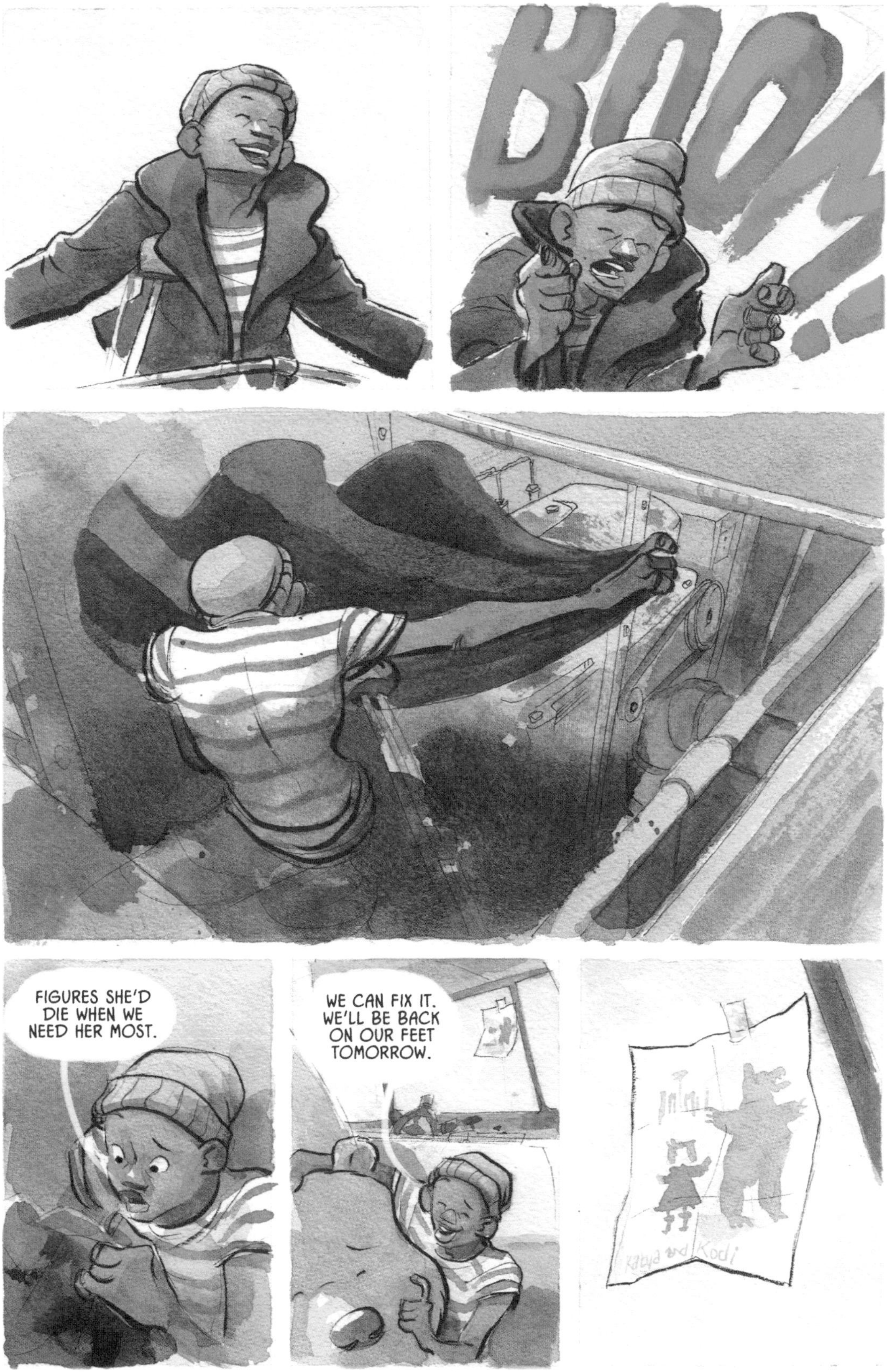
BOOM!!!
FIGURES SHE'D DIE WHEN WE NEED HER MOST.
WE CAN FIX IT. WE'LL BE BACK ON OUR FEET TOMORROW.
Katya and Kodi

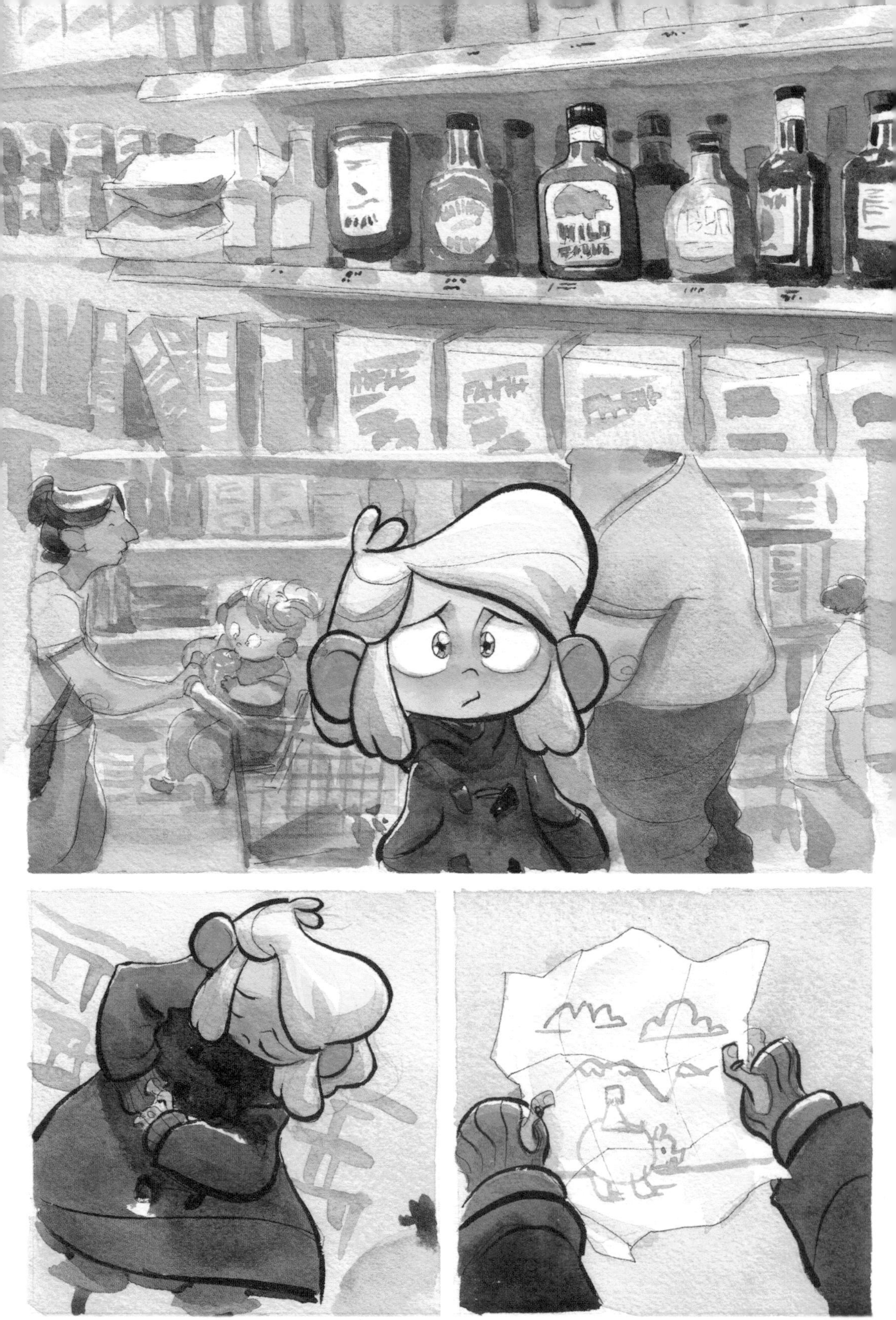
WILD

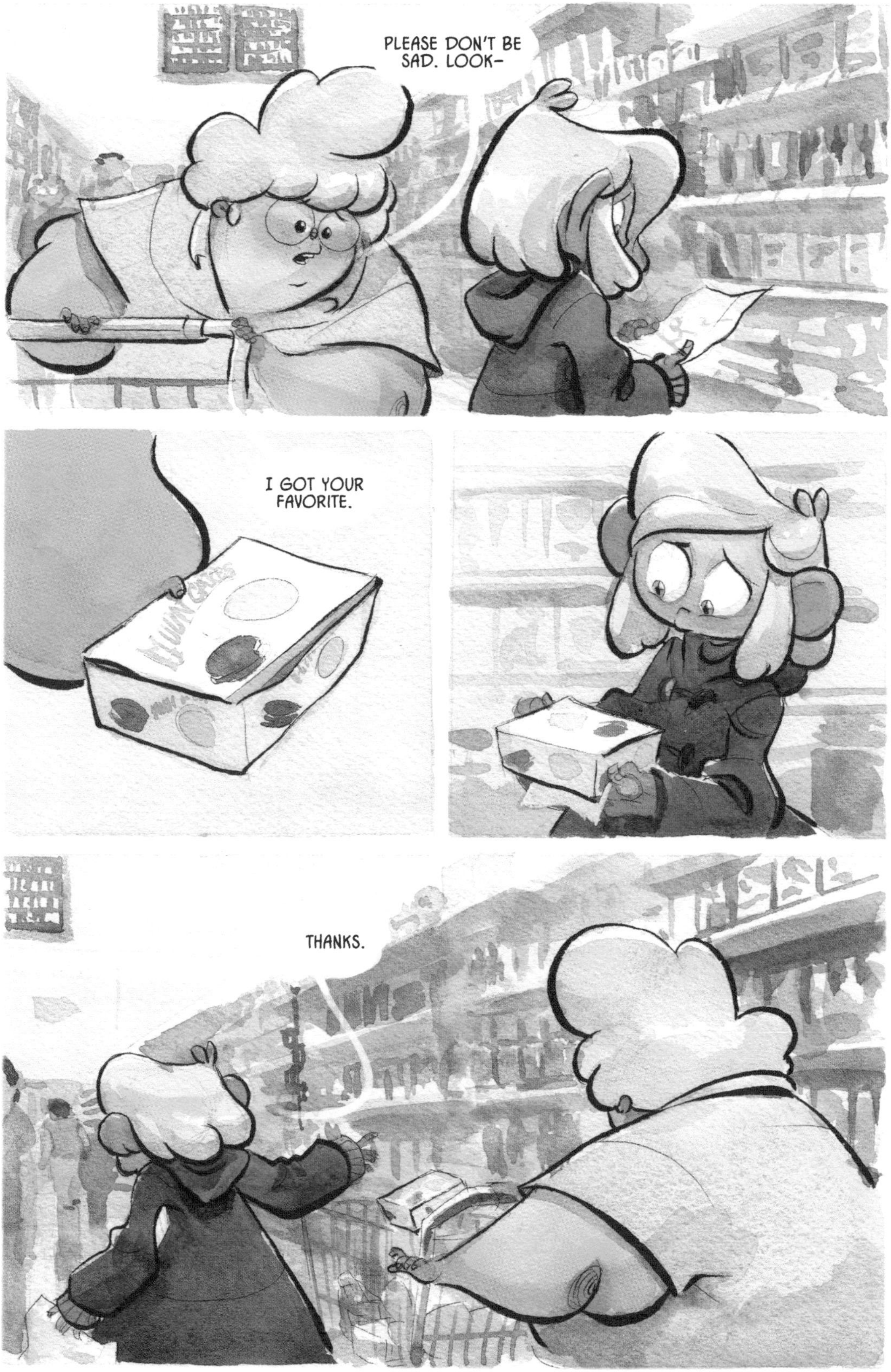
PLEASE DON'T BE SAD. LOOK–
I GOT YOUR FAVORITE.
THANKS.

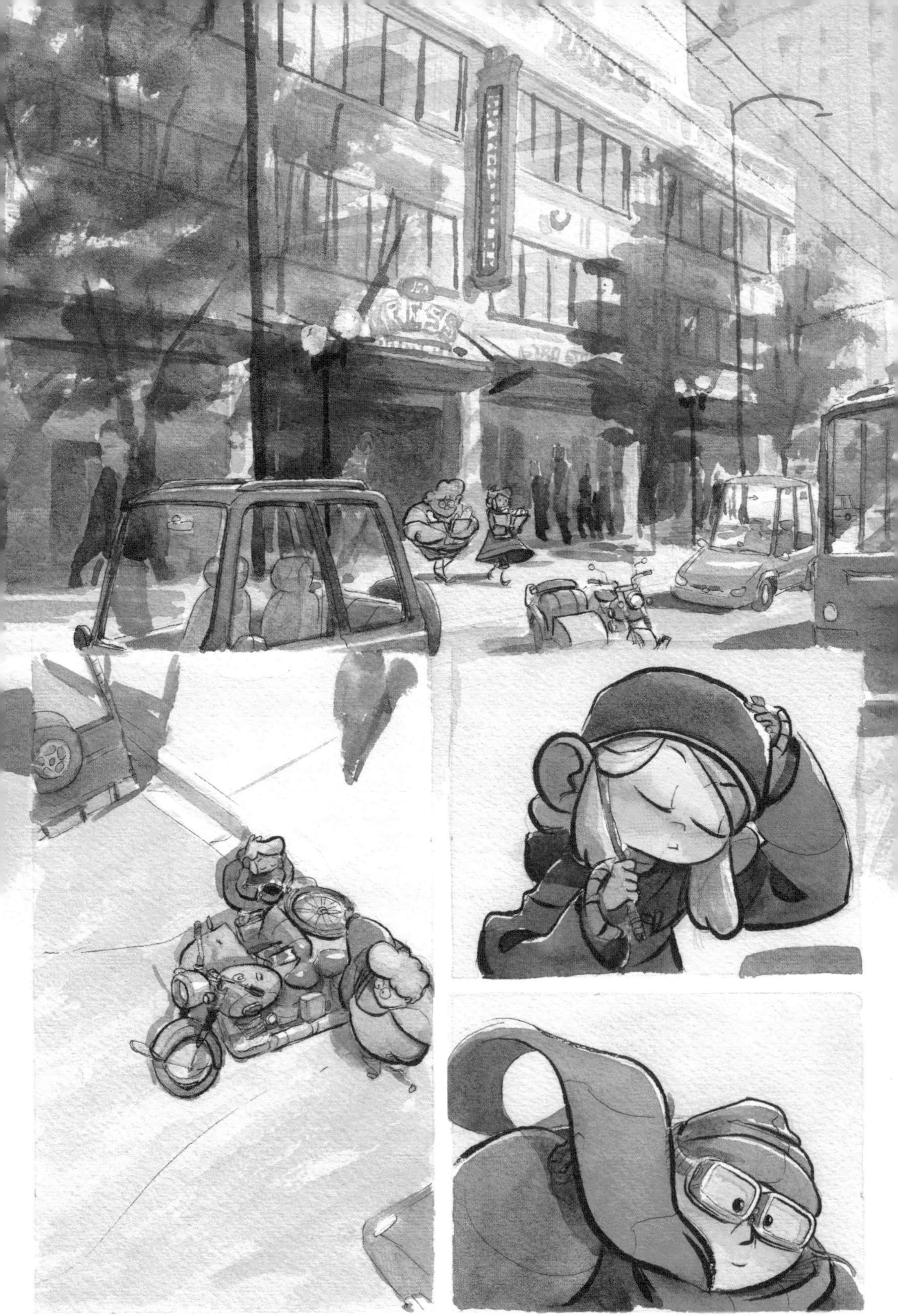

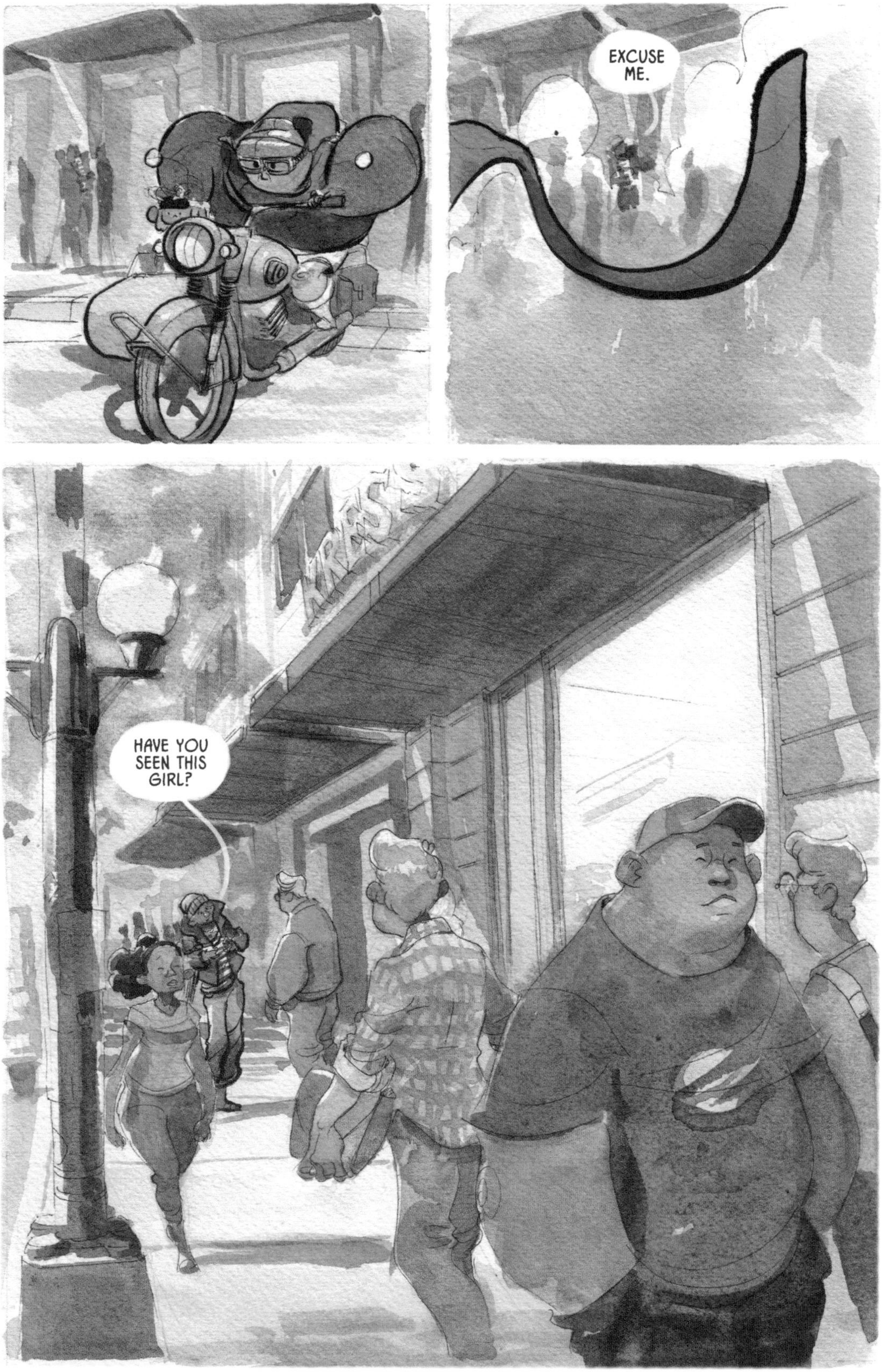
EXCUSE ME.
HAVE YOU SEEN THIS GIRL?

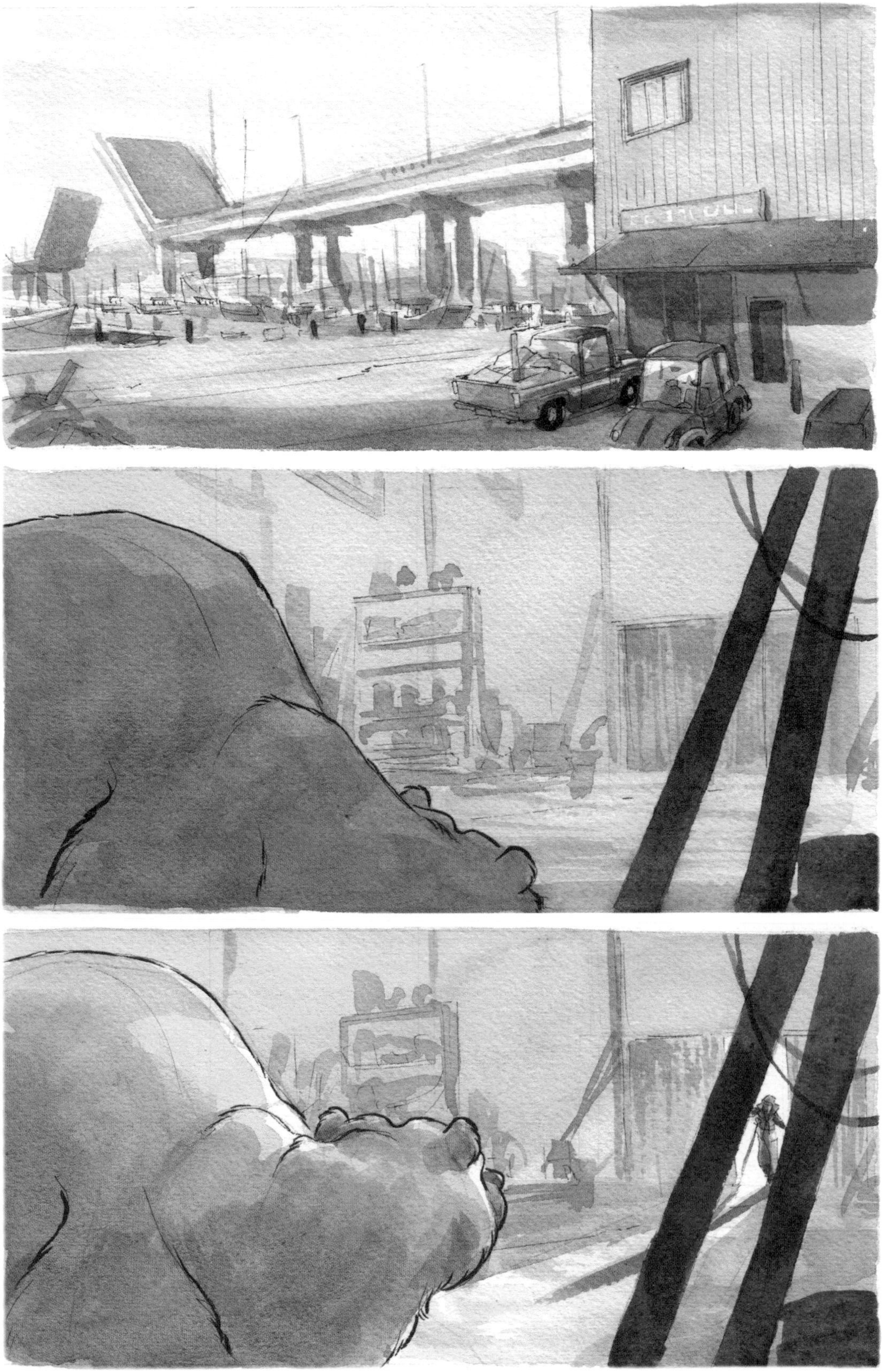

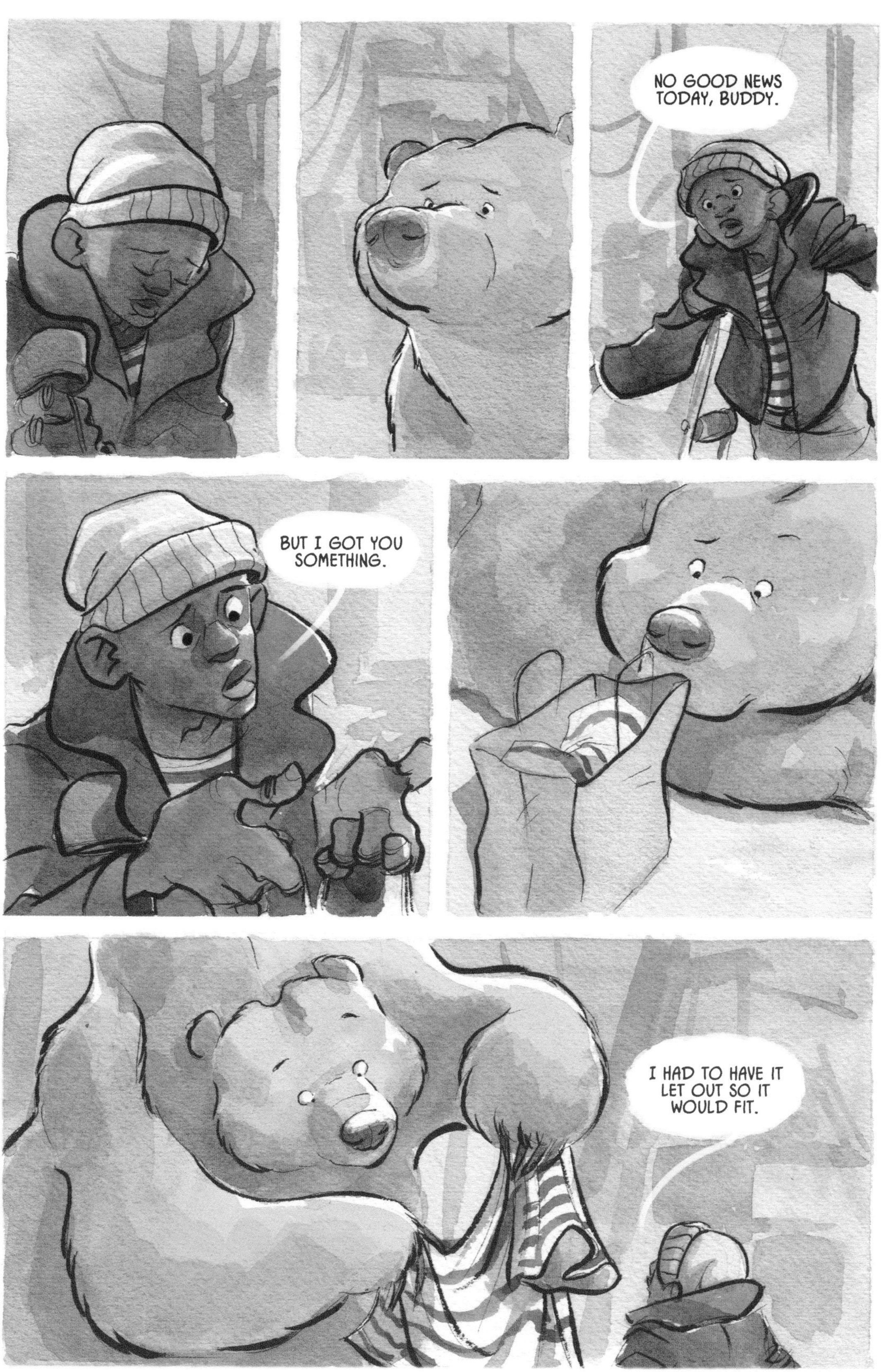
NO GOOD NEWS TODAY, BUDDY.
BUT I GOT YOU SOMETHING.
I HAD TO HAVE IT LET OUT SO IT WOULD FIT.

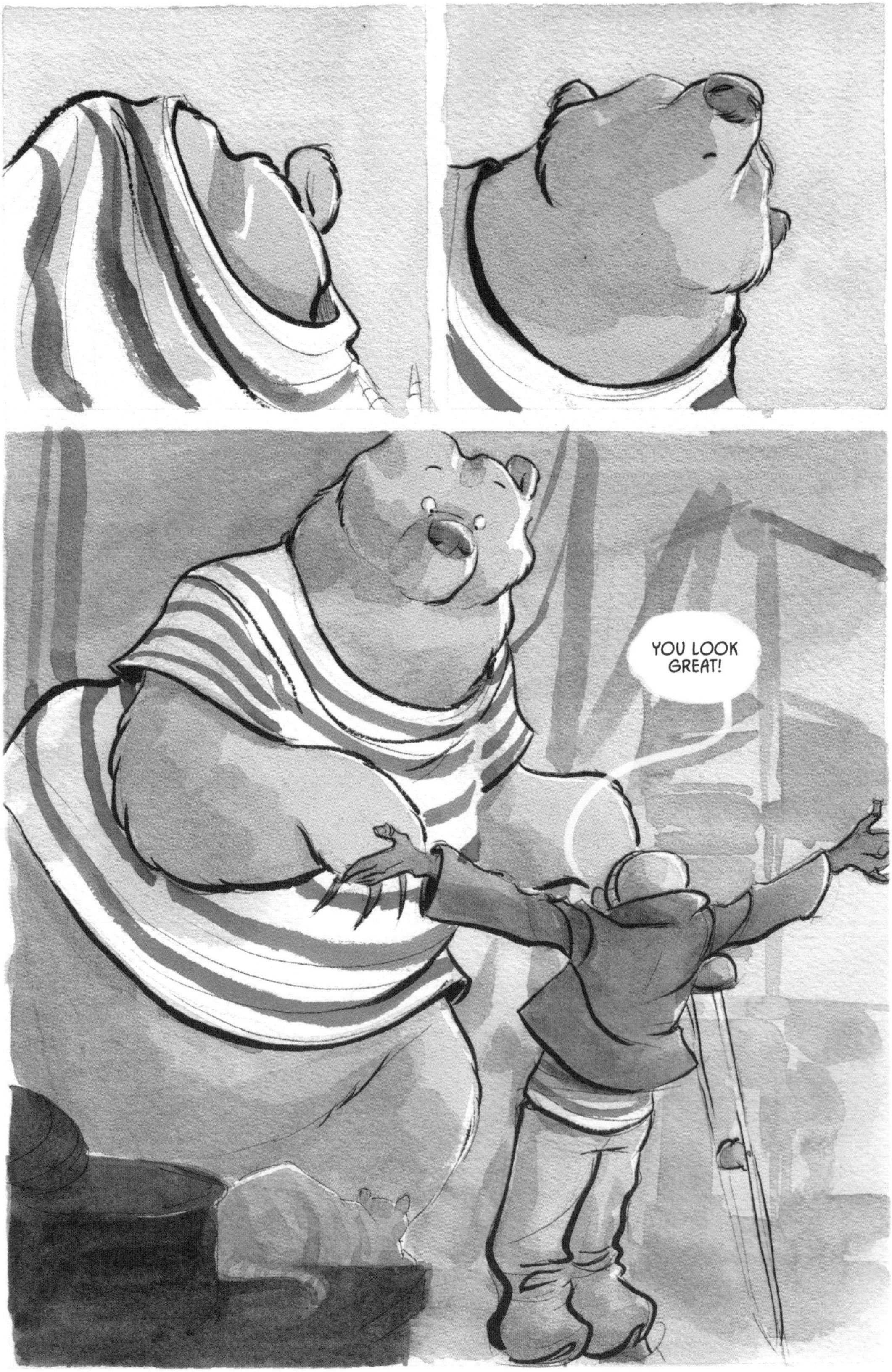
YOU LOOK GREAT!

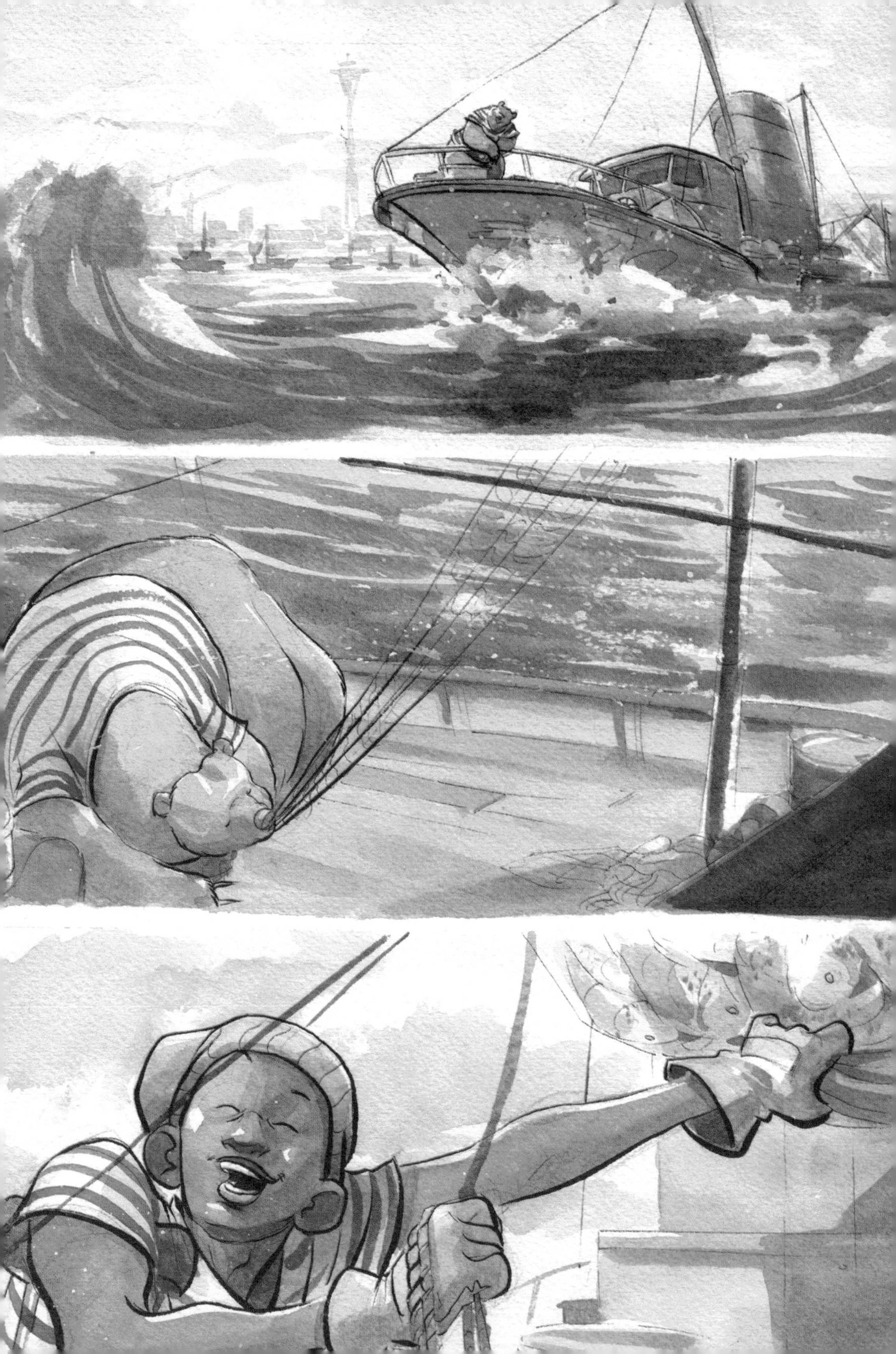

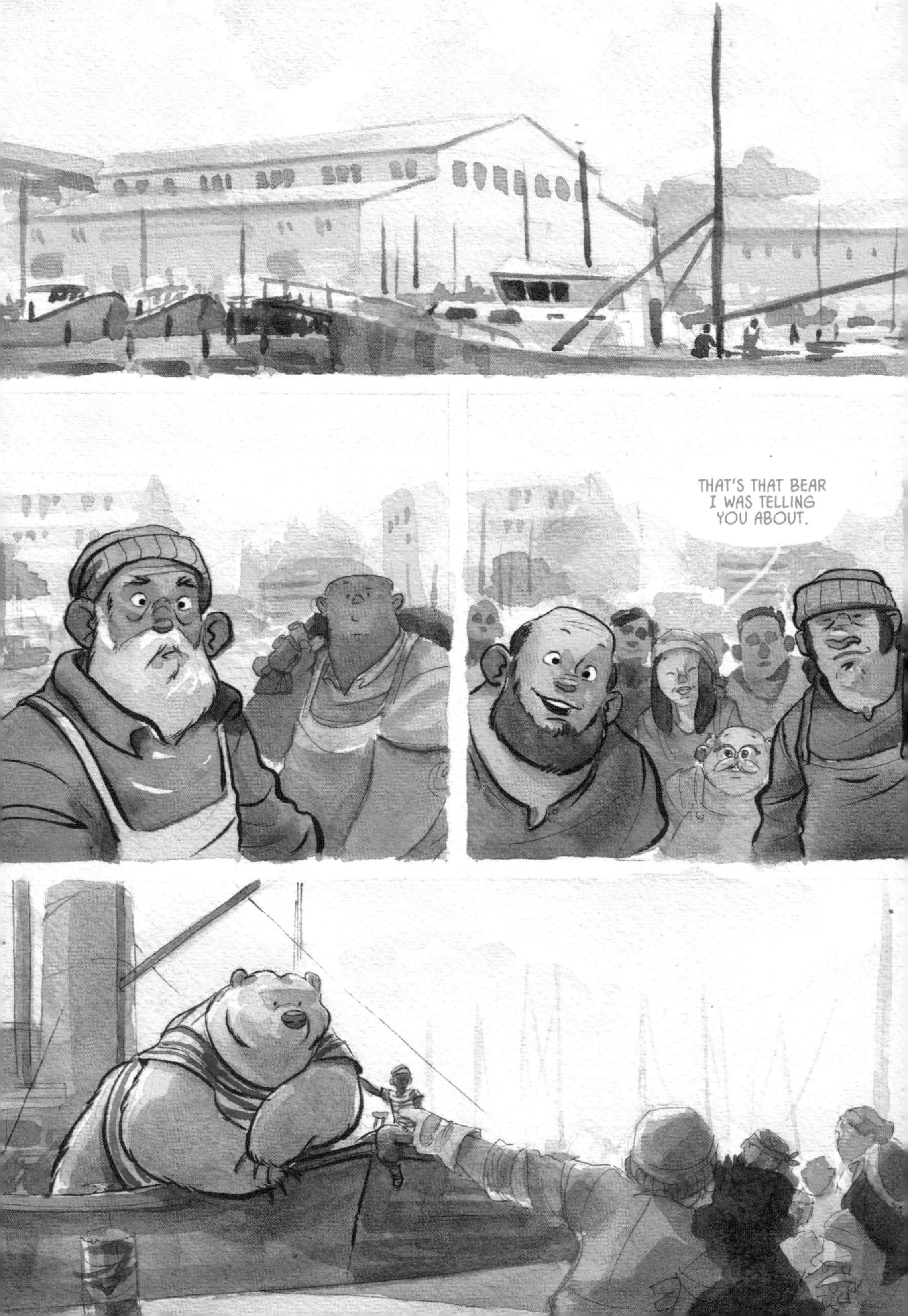
THAT'S THAT BEAR I WAS TELLING YOU ABOUT.

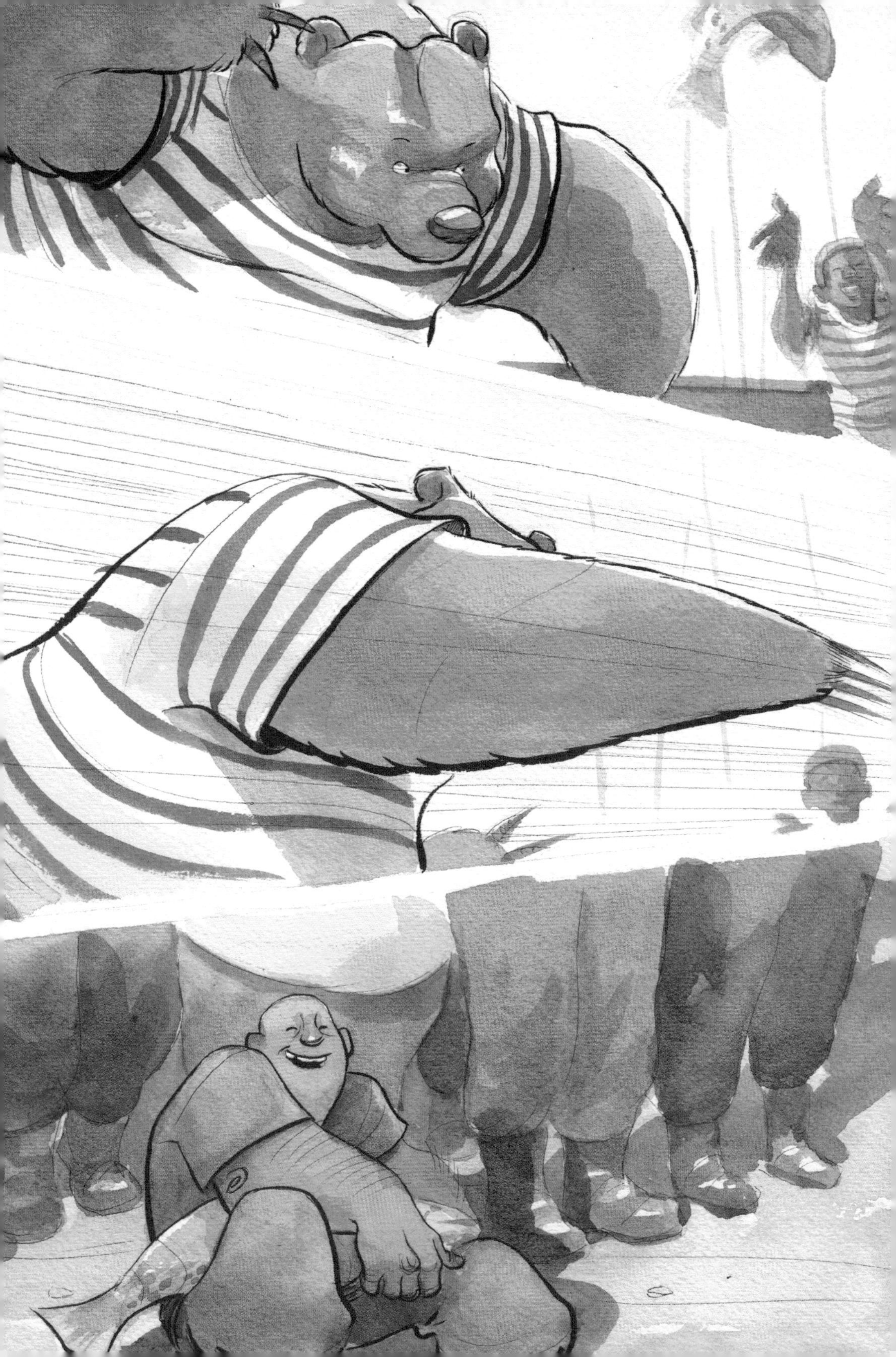

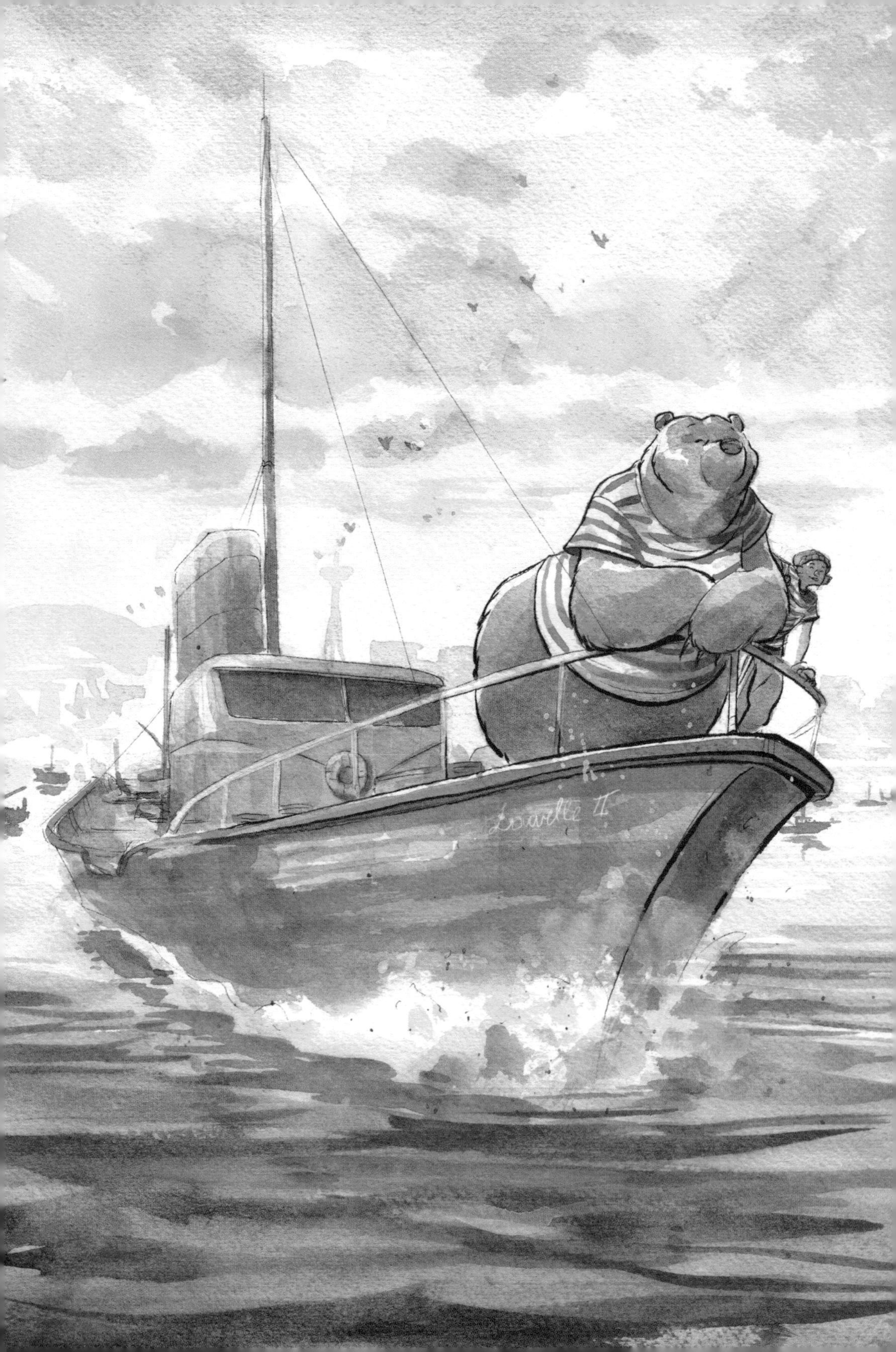

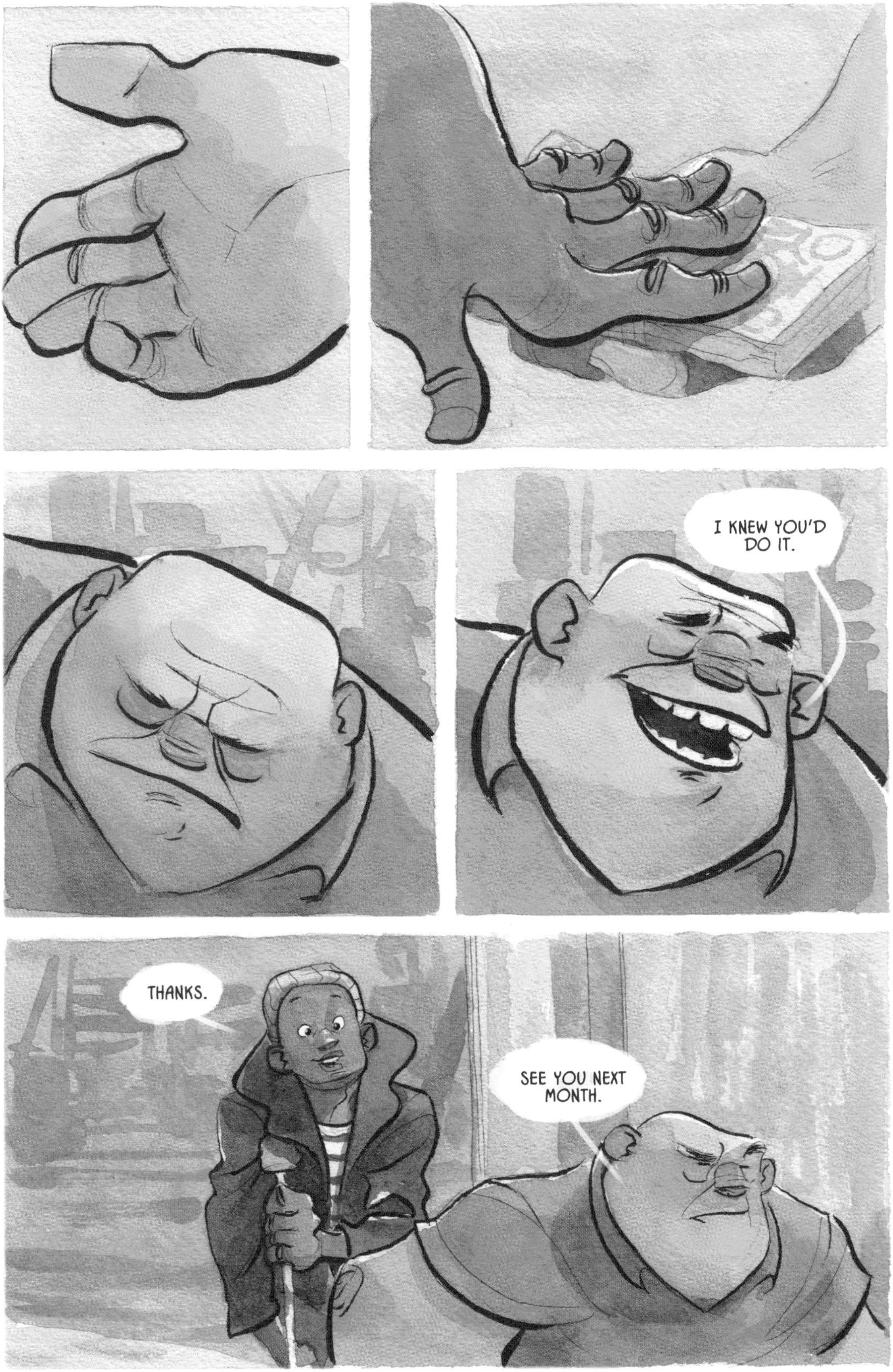
I KNEW YOU'D DO IT.
THANKS.
SEE YOU NEXT MONTH.

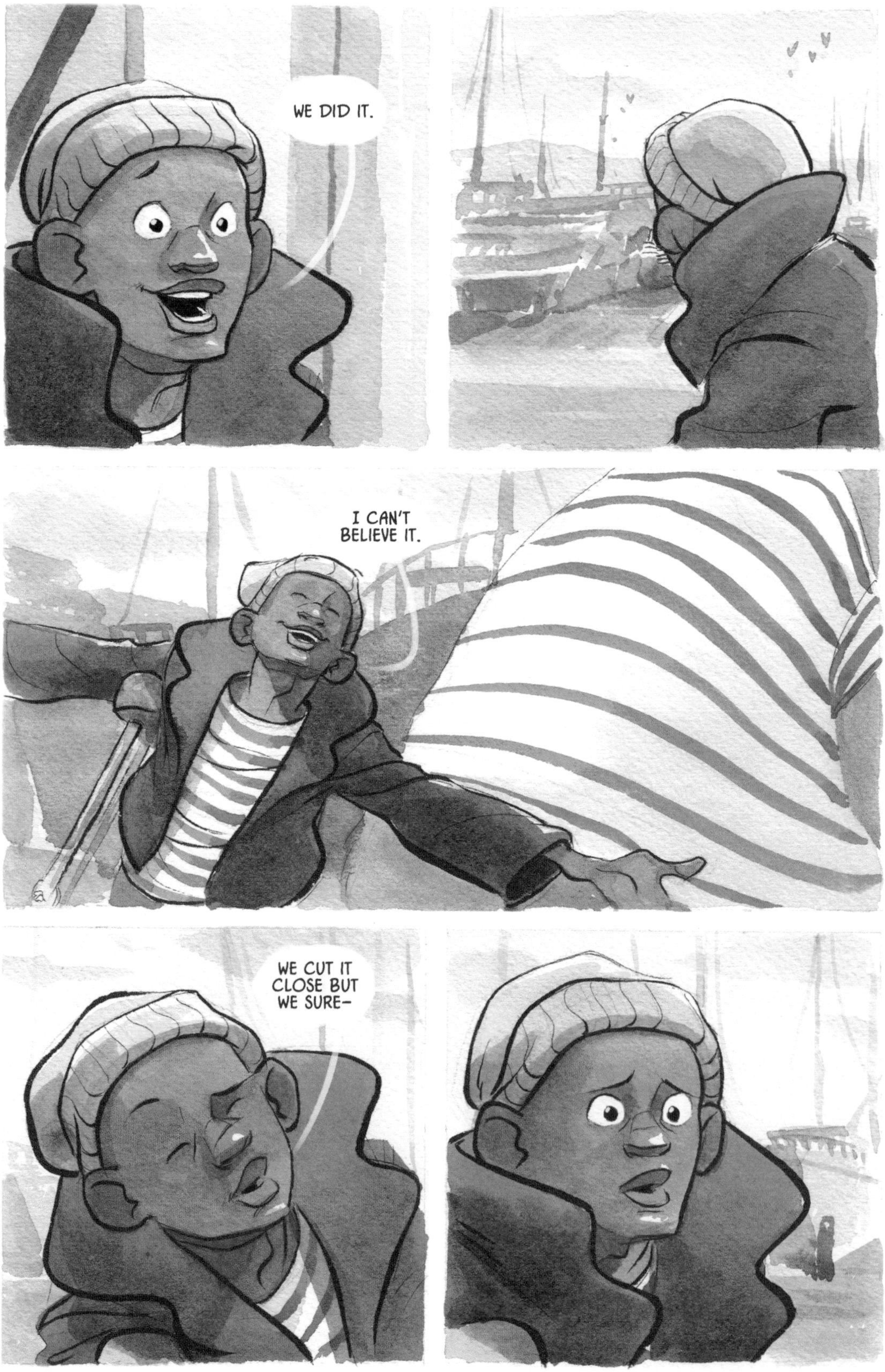
WE DID IT.
I CAN'T BELIEVE IT.
WE CUT IT CLOSE BUT WE SURE–

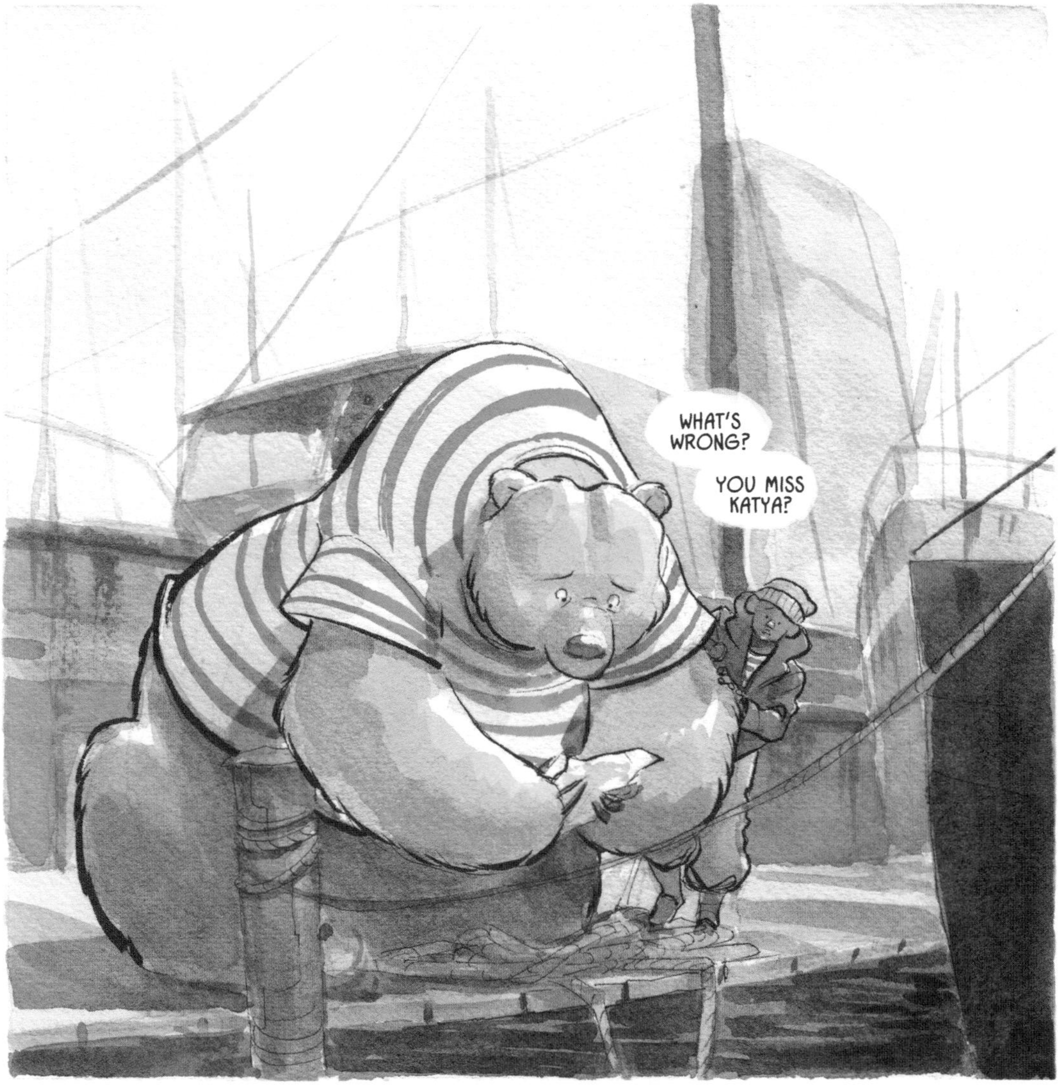
WHAT'S WRONG?
YOU MISS KATYA?

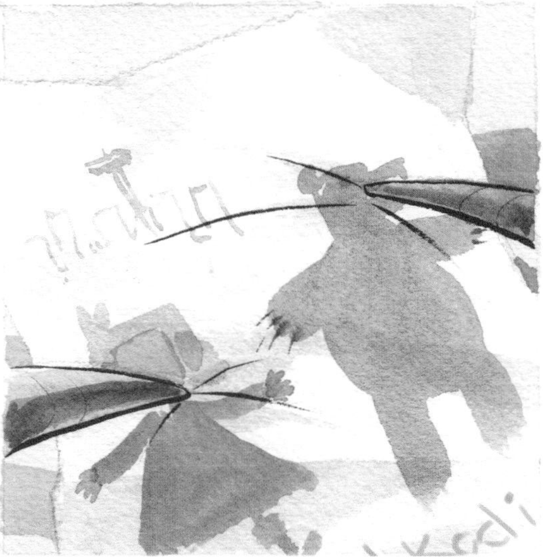

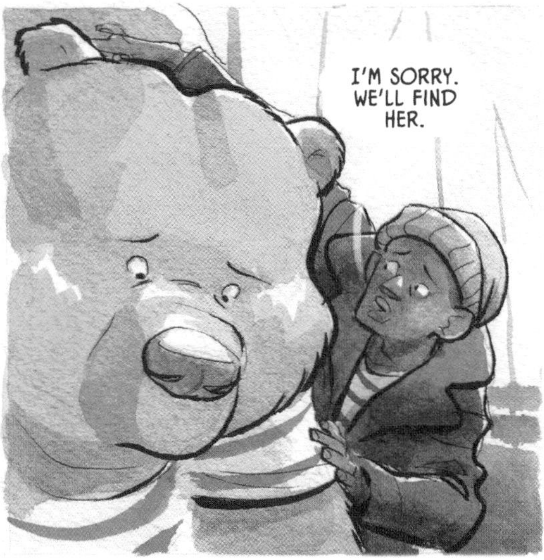
I'M SORRY. WE'LL FIND HER.

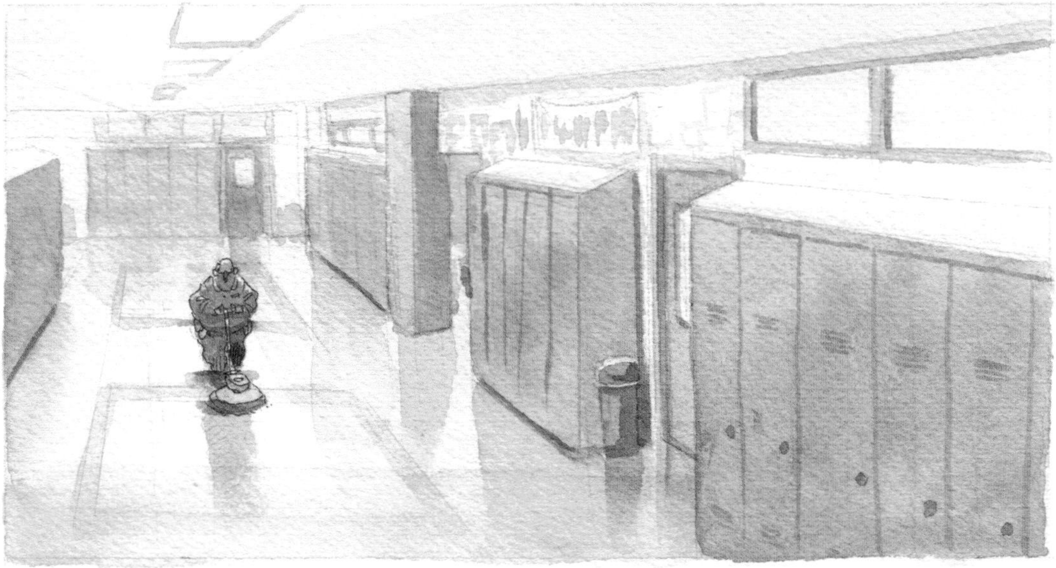

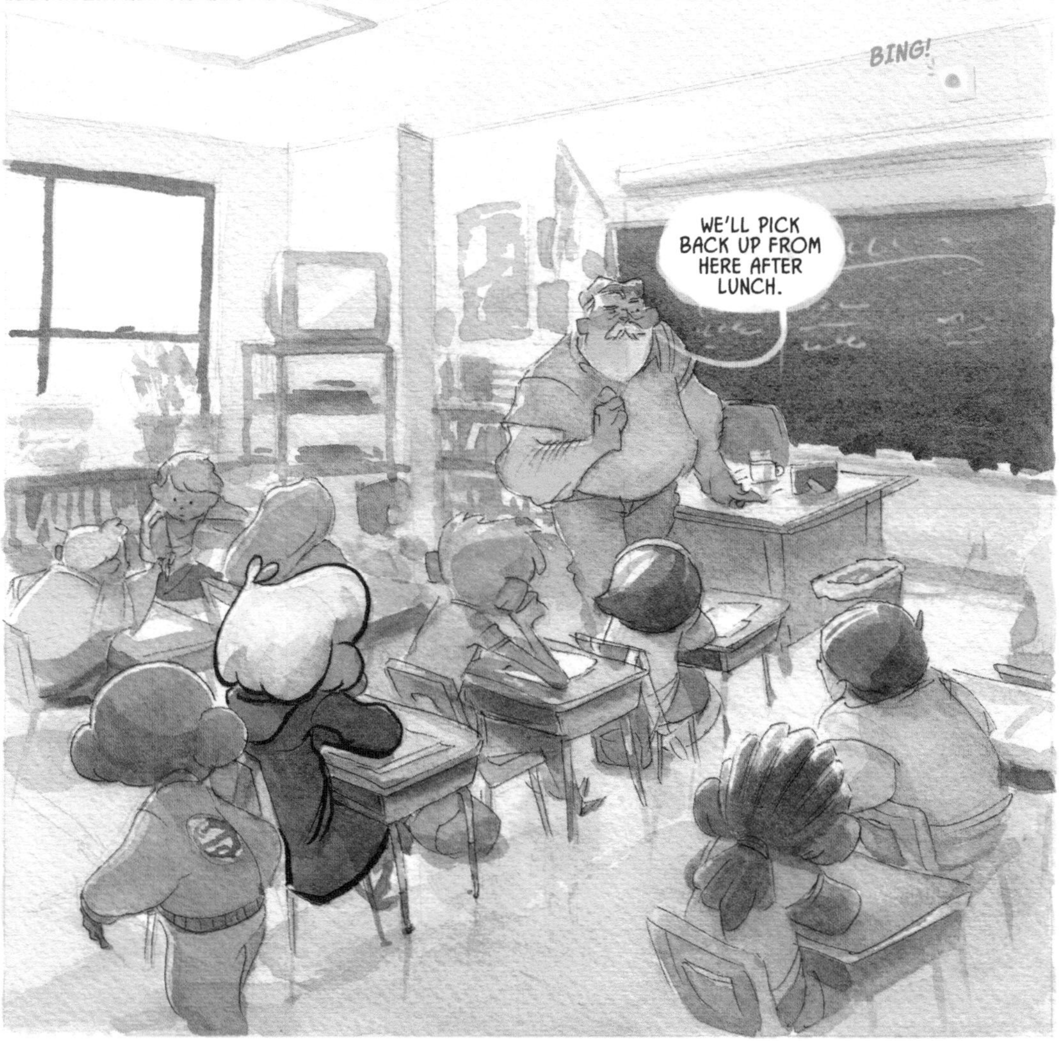
BING!
WE'LL PICK BACK UP FROM HERE AFTER LUNCH.

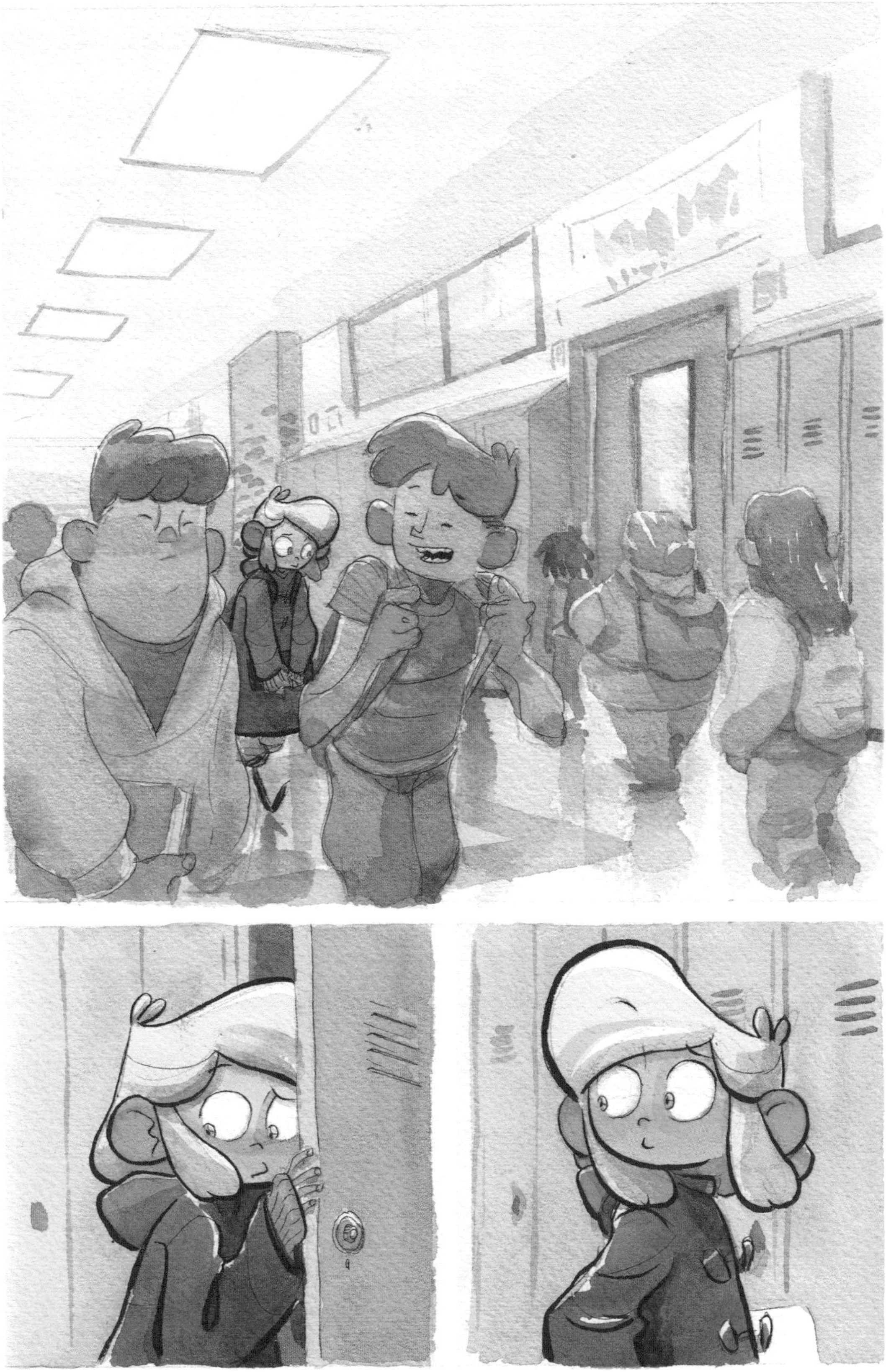

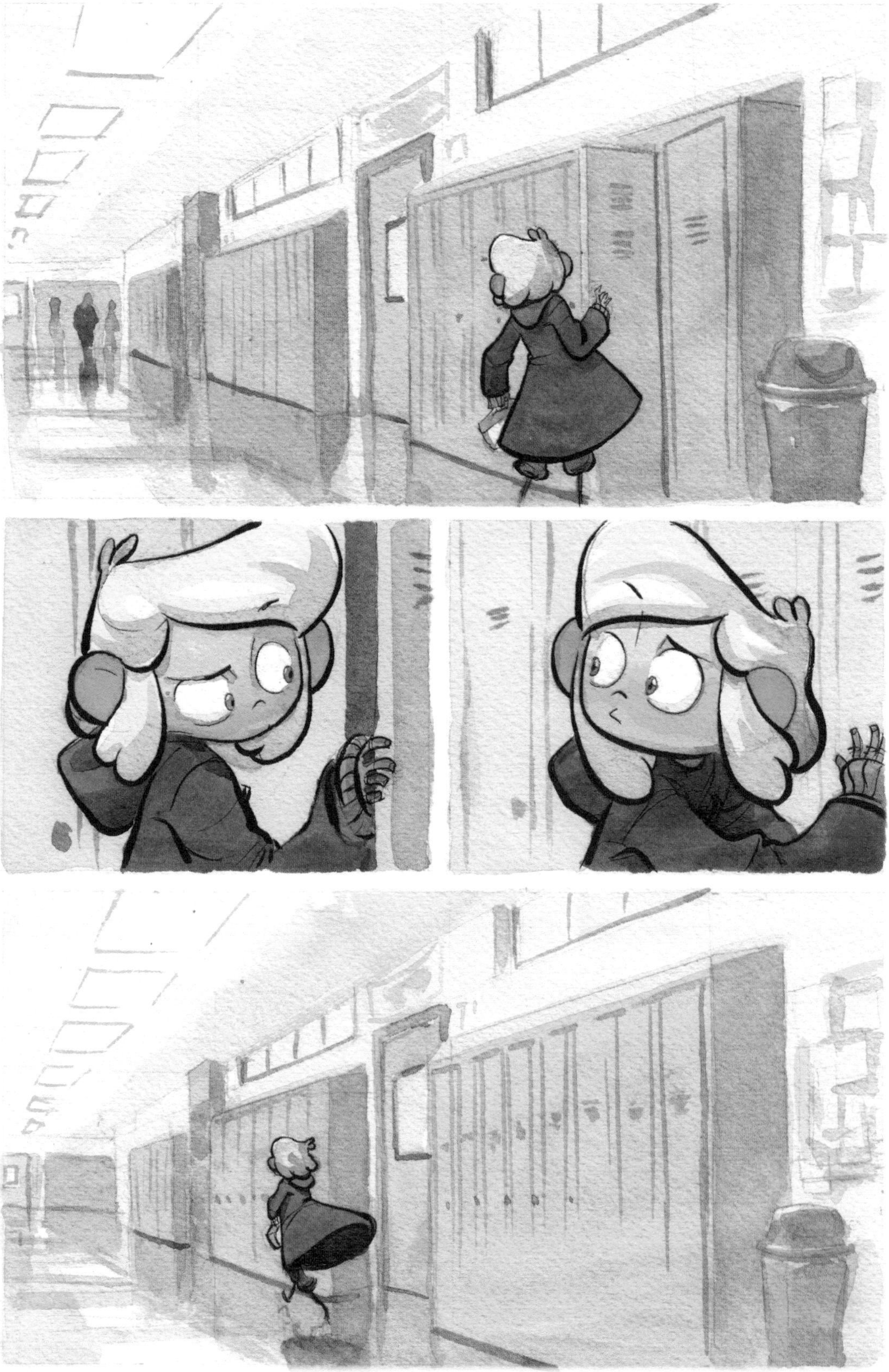

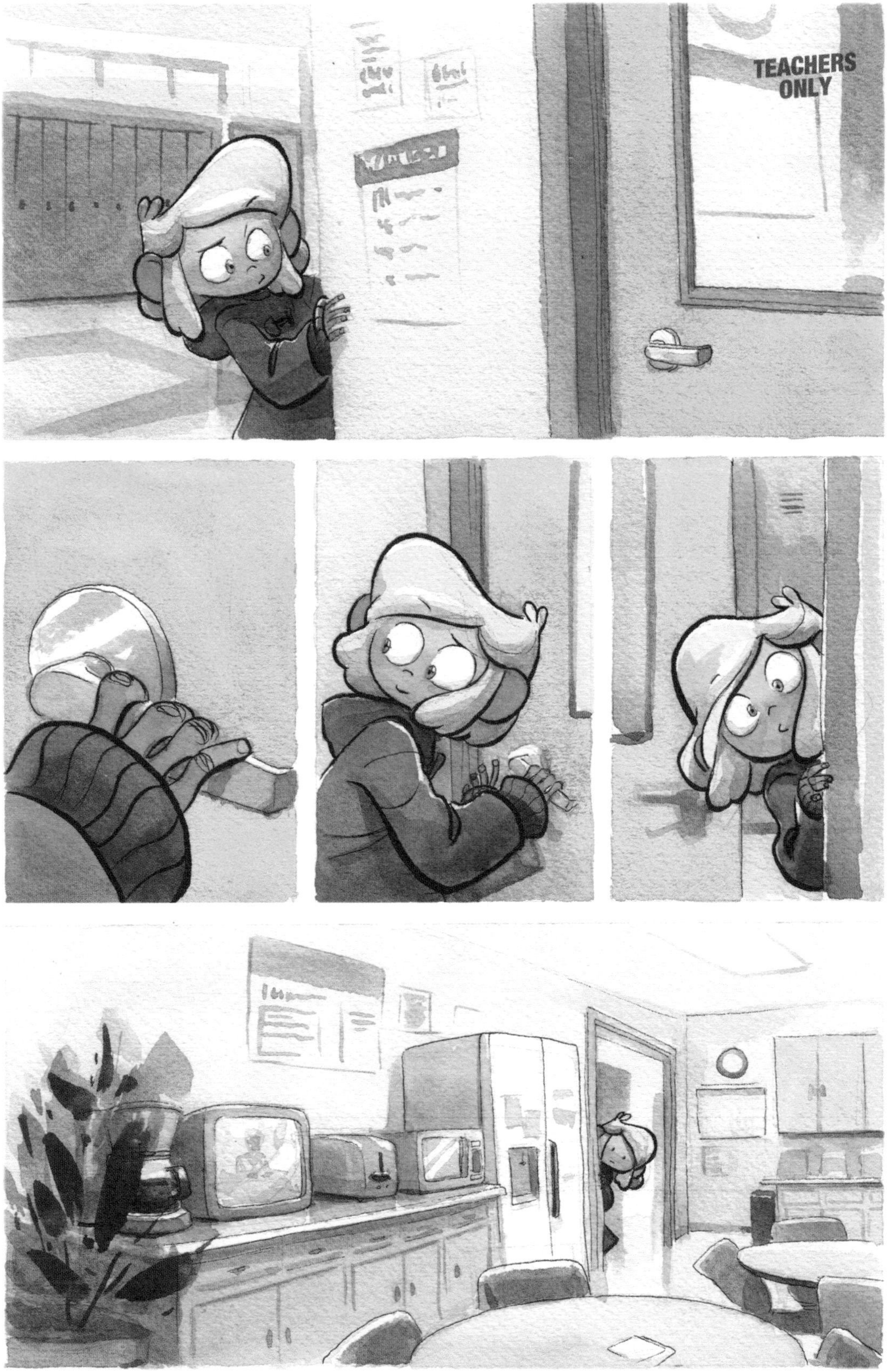
TEACHERS ONLY

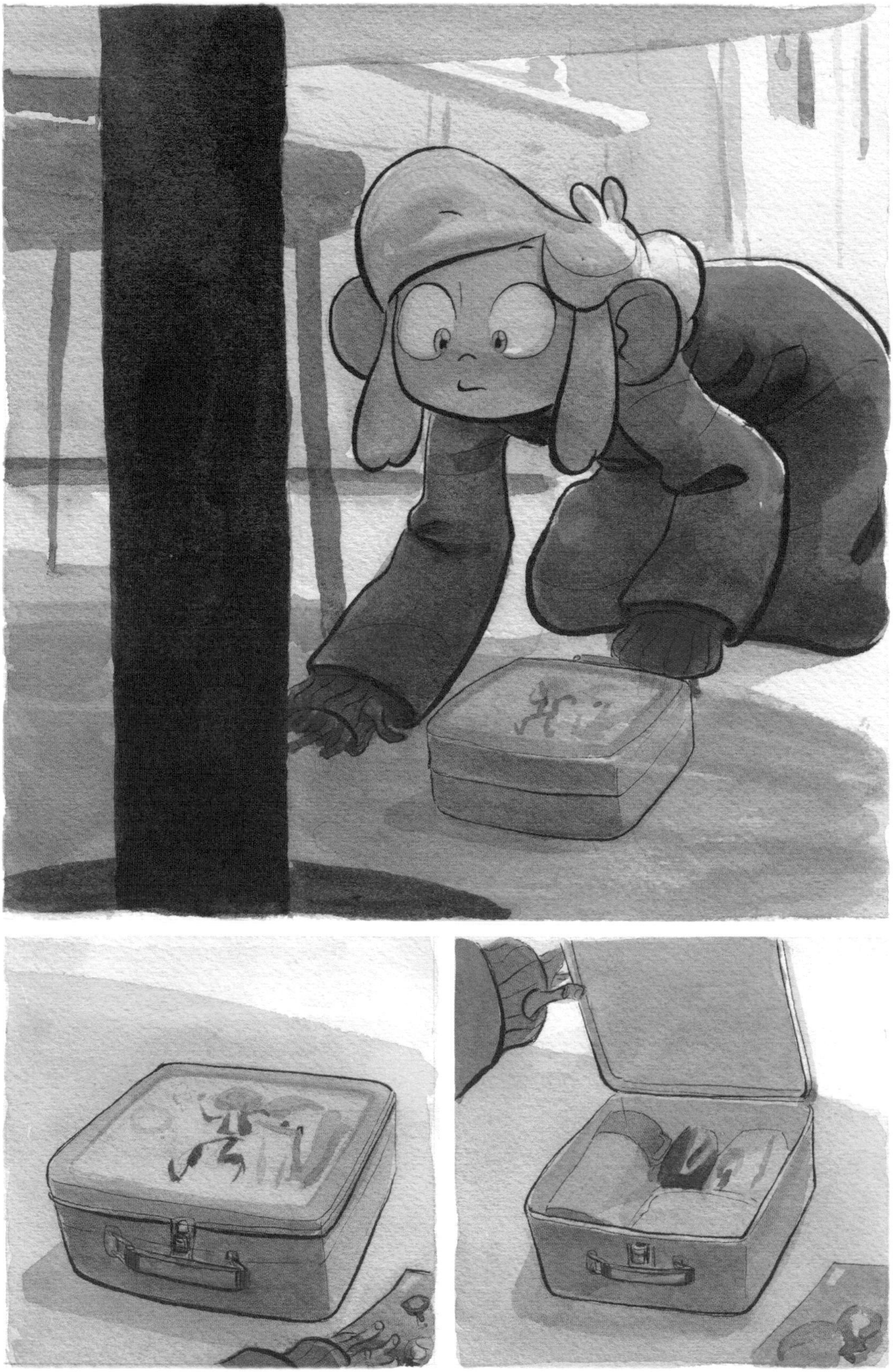

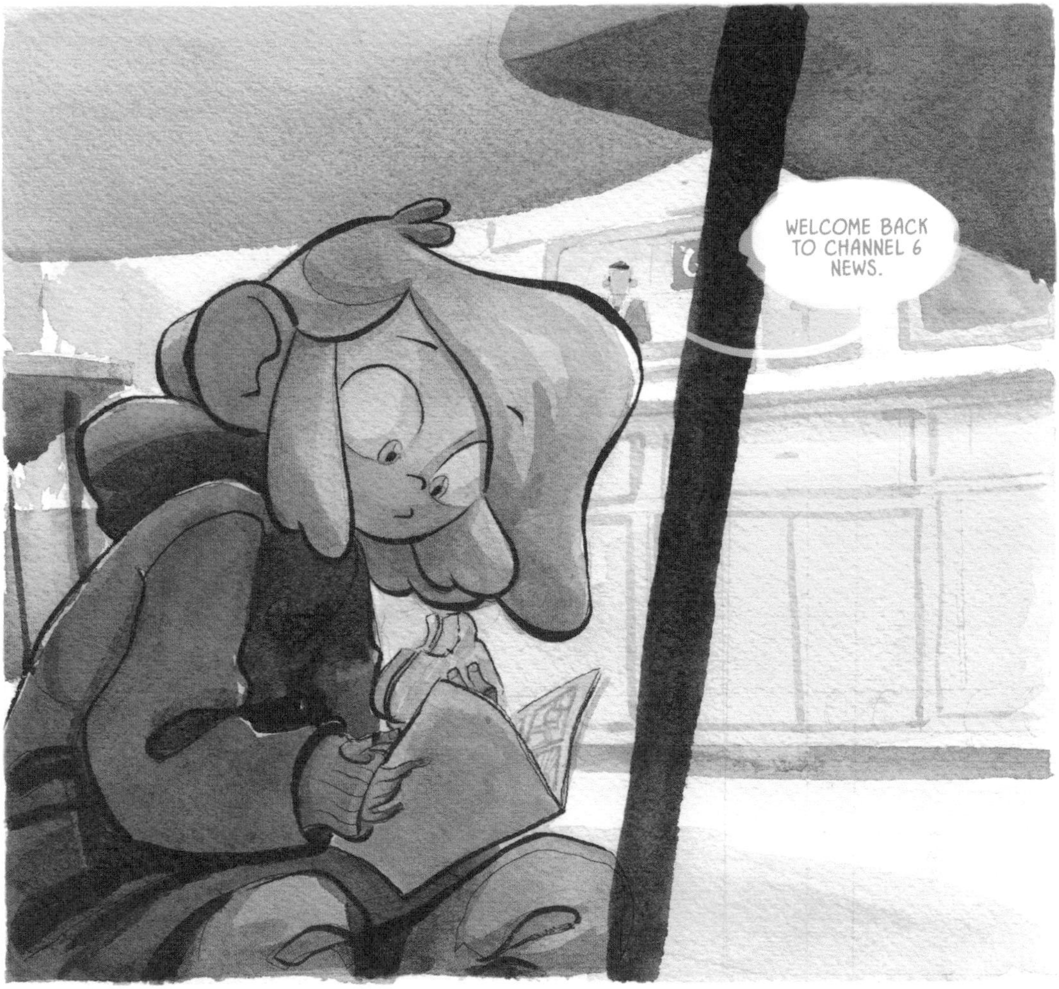
WELCOME BACK TO CHANNEL 6 NEWS.

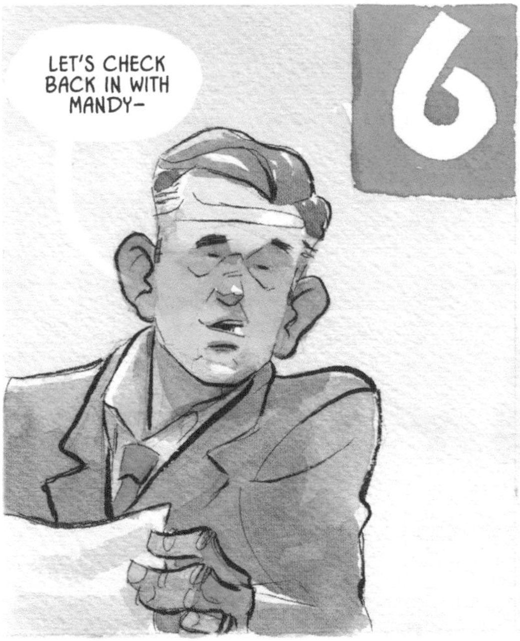
LET'S CHECK BACK IN WITH MANDY–
6

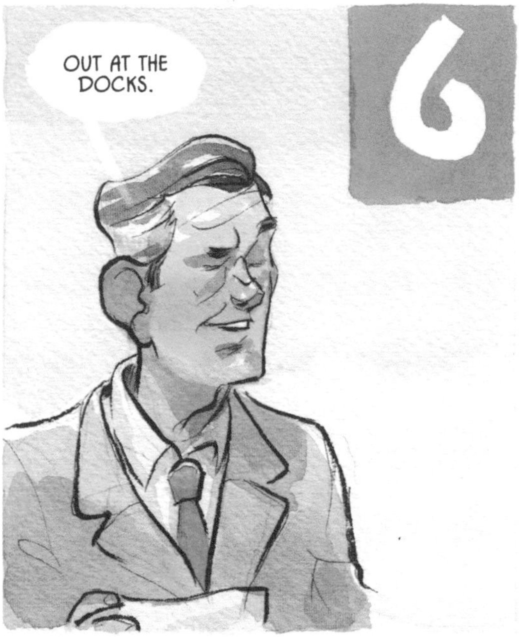
OUT AT THE DOCKS.
6

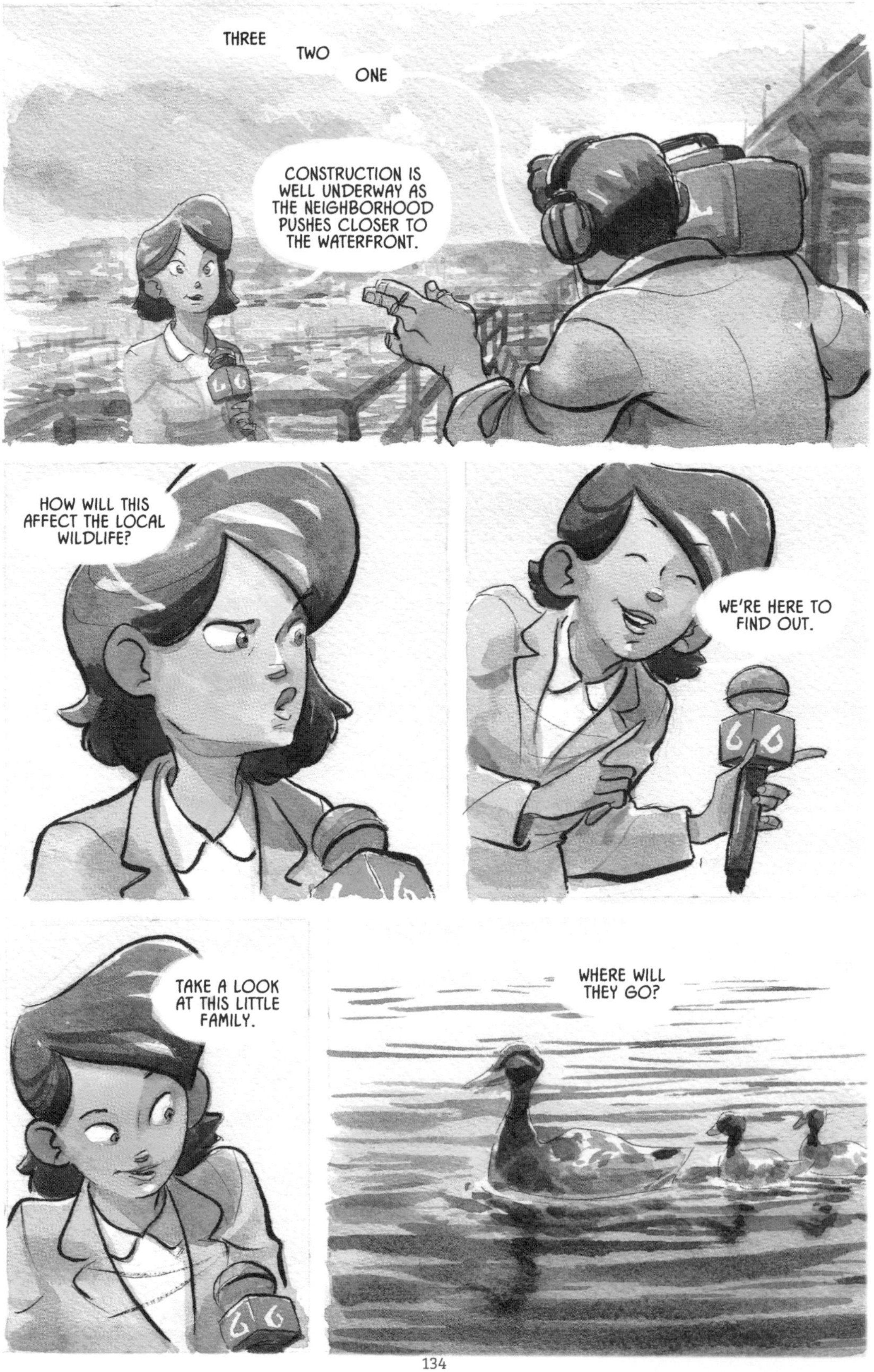
THREE
TWO
ONE
CONSTRUCTION IS WELL UNDERWAY AS THE NEIGHBORHOOD PUSHES CLOSER TO THE WATERFRONT.
HOW WILL THIS AFFECT THE LOCAL WILDLIFE?
WE'RE HERE TO FIND OUT.
TAKE A LOOK AT THIS LITTLE FAMILY.
WHERE WILL THEY GO?

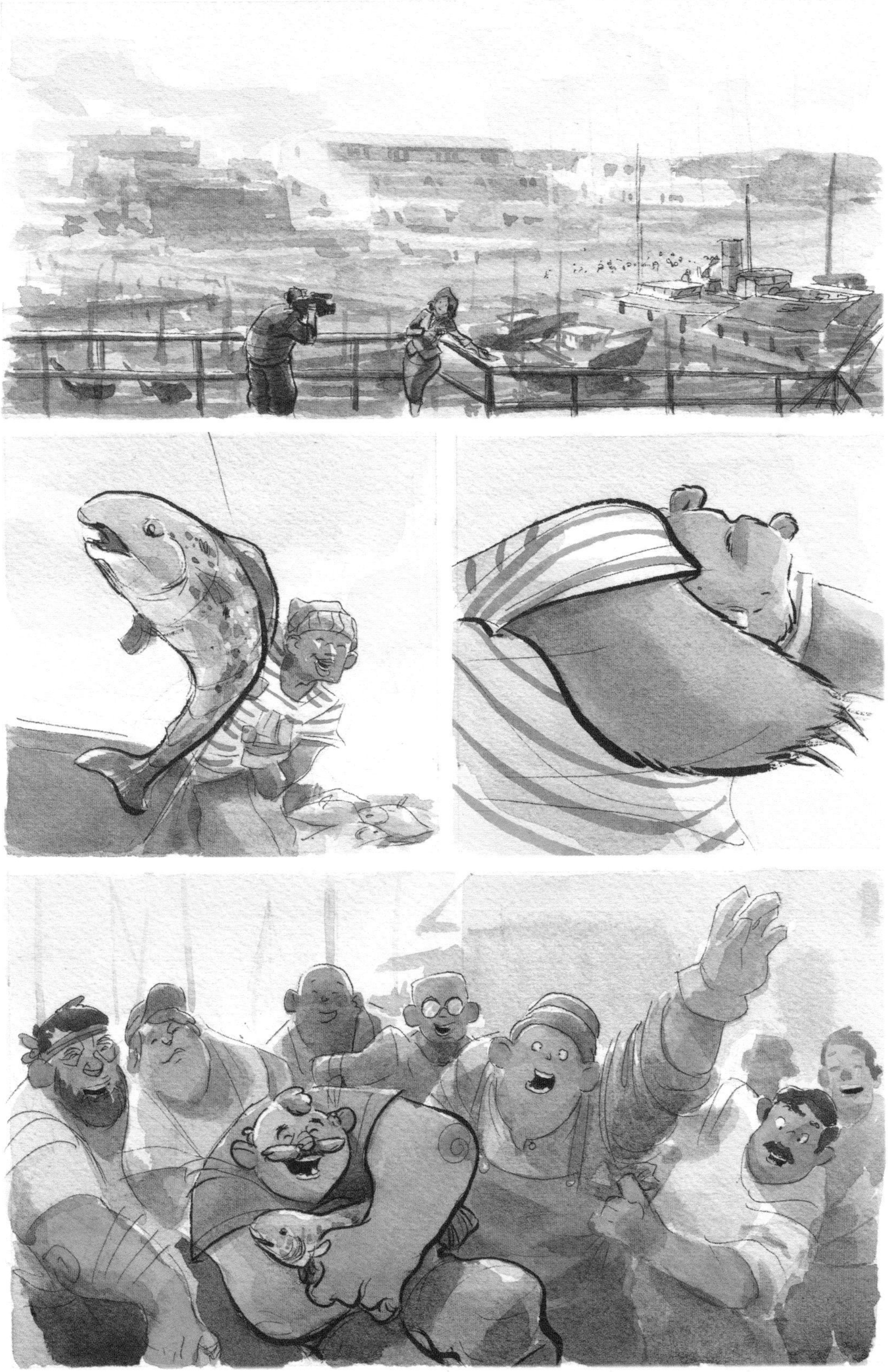

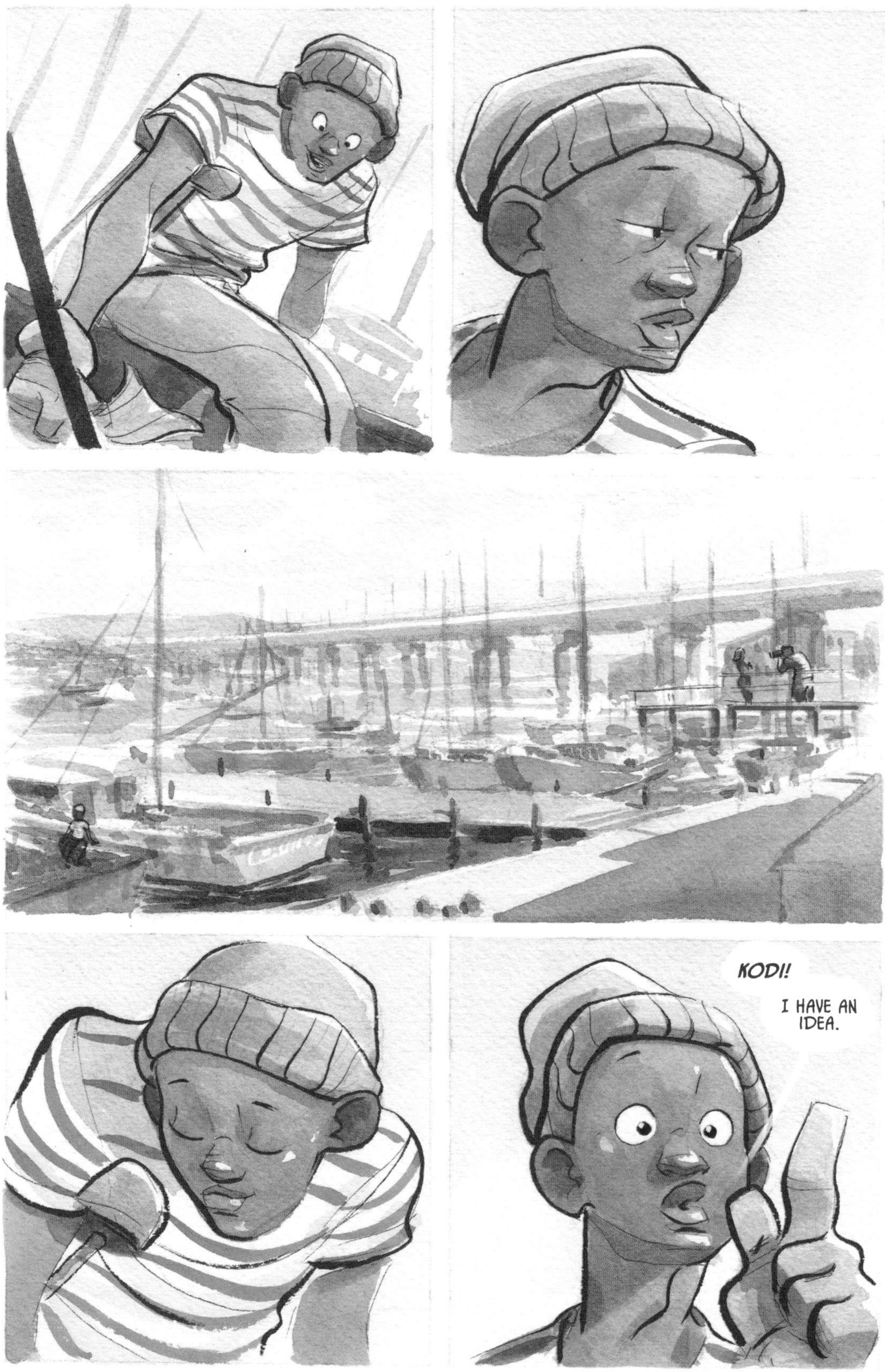
KODI!
I HAVE AN IDEA.

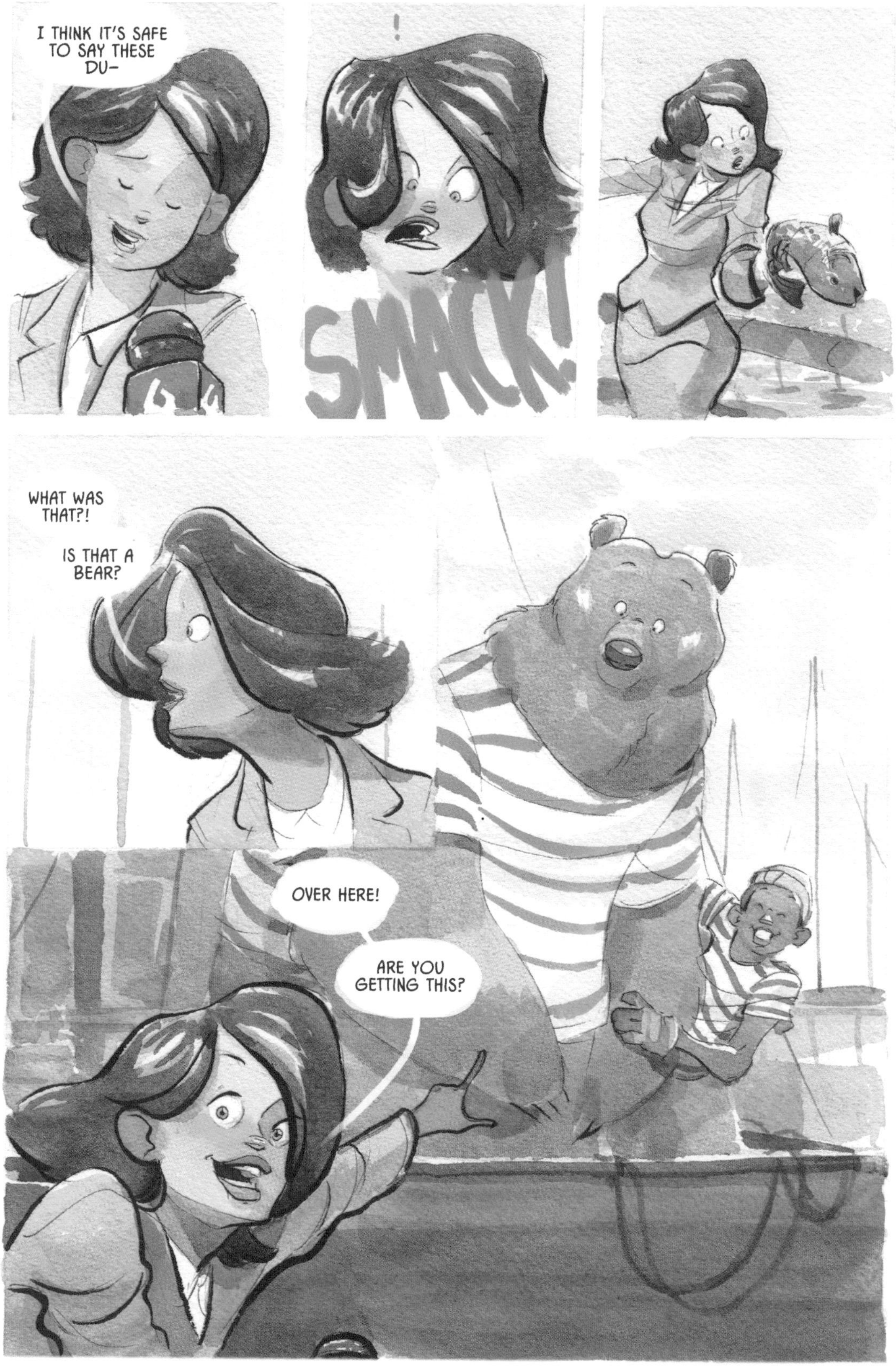
I THINK IT'S SAFE TO SAY THESE DU–
!
SMACK!
WHAT WAS THAT?!
IS THAT A BEAR?
OVER HERE!
ARE YOU GETTING THIS?

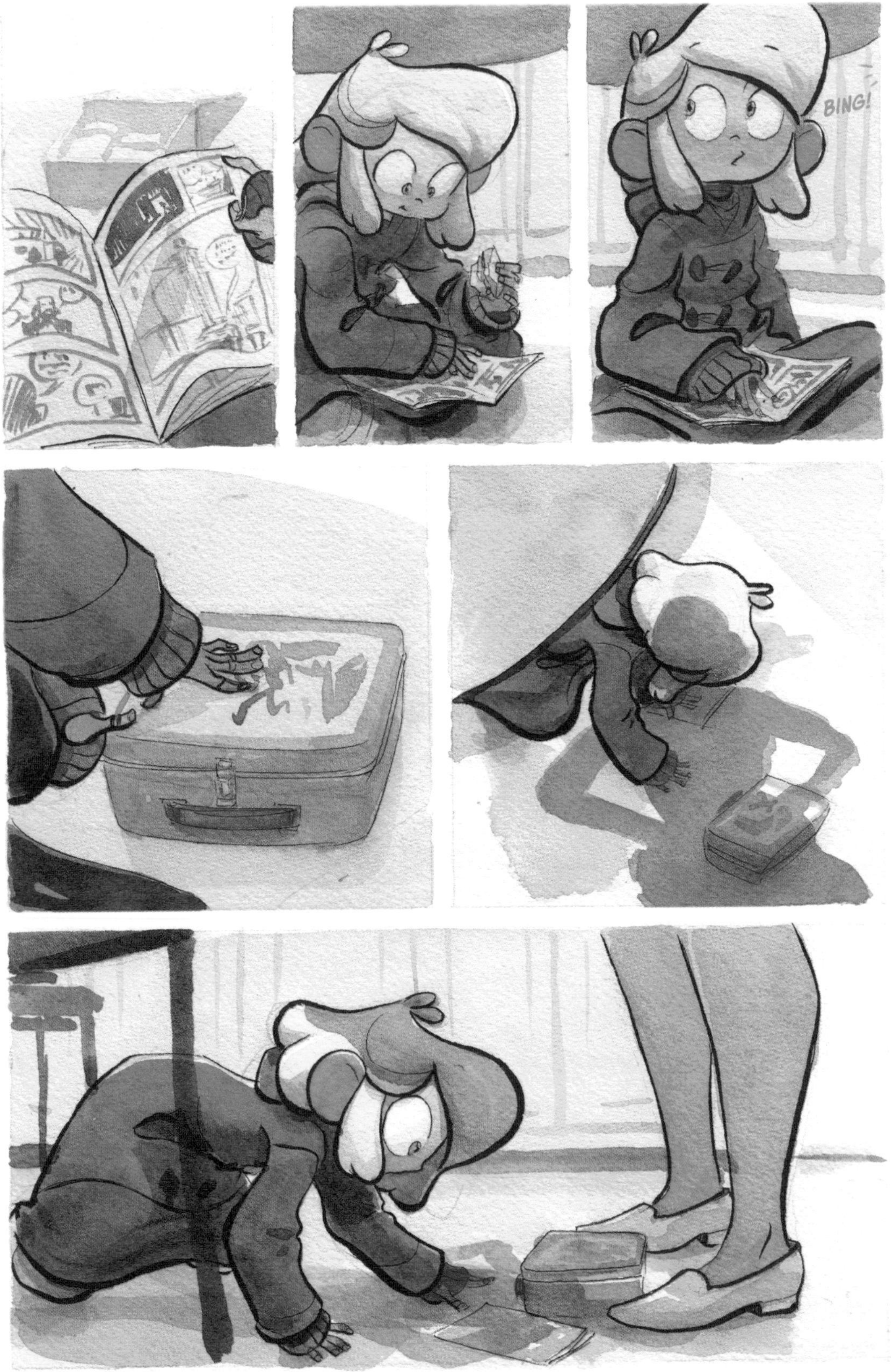
BING!

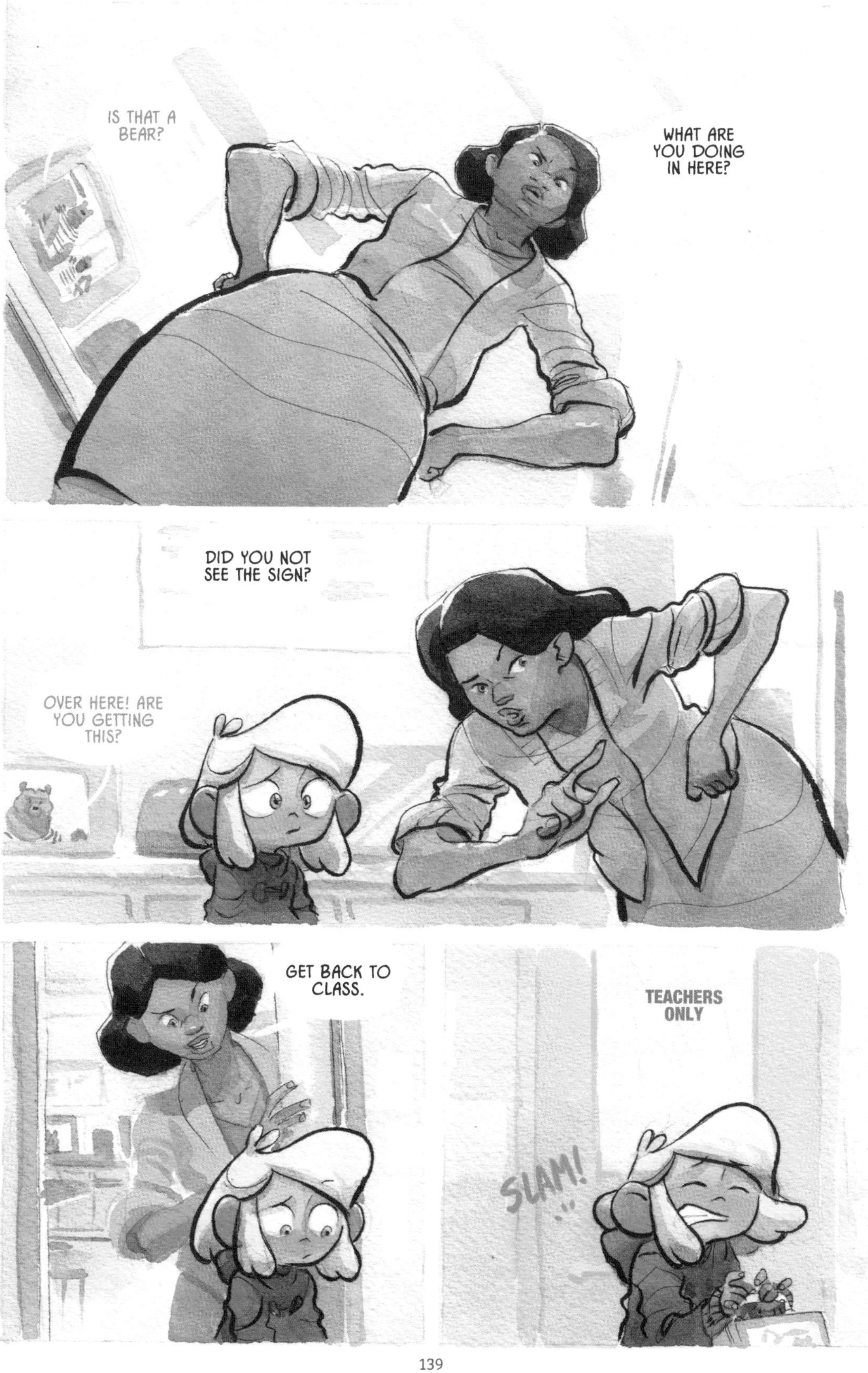
IS THAT A BEAR?
WHAT ARE YOU DOING IN HERE?
DID YOU NOT SEE THE SIGN?
OVER HERE! ARE YOU GETTING THIS?
GET BACK TO CLASS.
TEACHERS ONLY
SLAM!

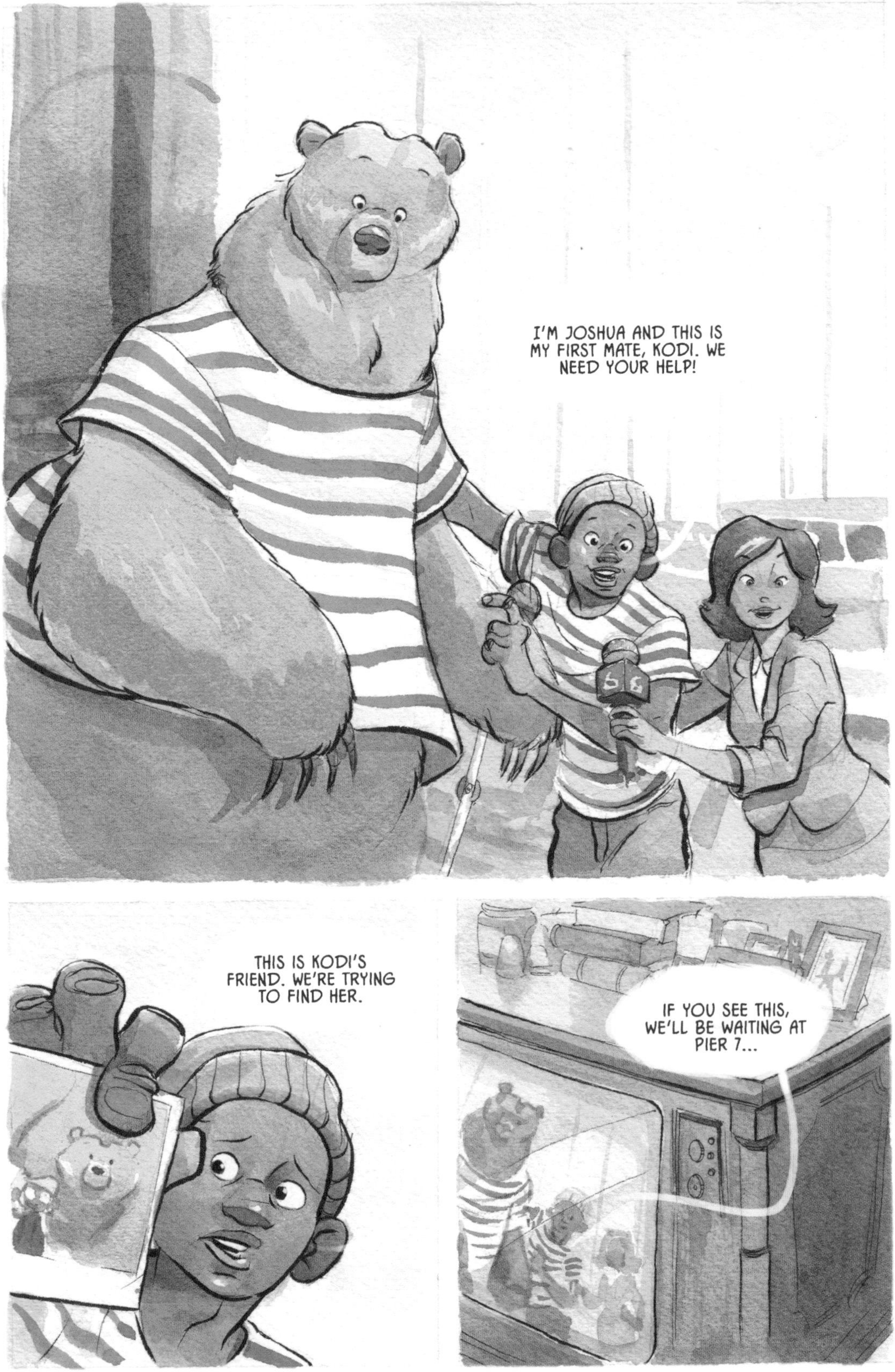
I'M JOSHUA AND THIS IS MY FIRST MATE, KODI. WE NEED YOUR HELP!
THIS IS KODI'S FRIEND. WE'RE TRYING TO FIND HER.
IF YOU SEE THIS, WE'LL BE WAITING AT PIER 7...

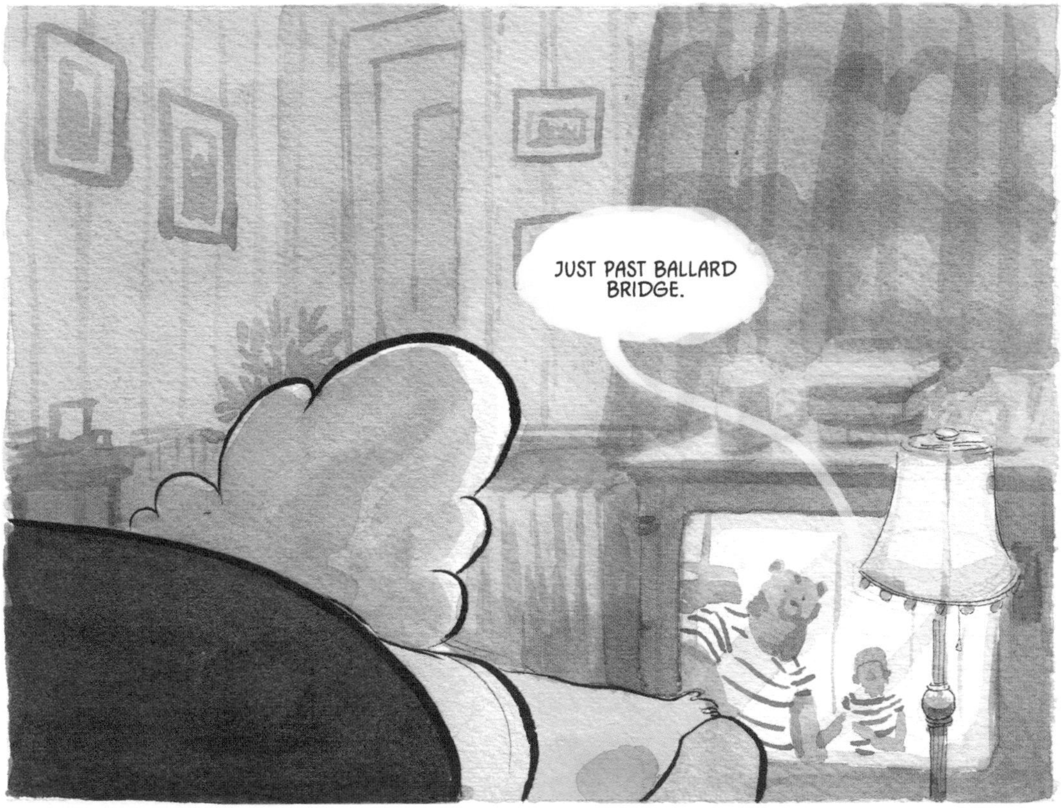
JUST PAST BALLARD BRIDGE.

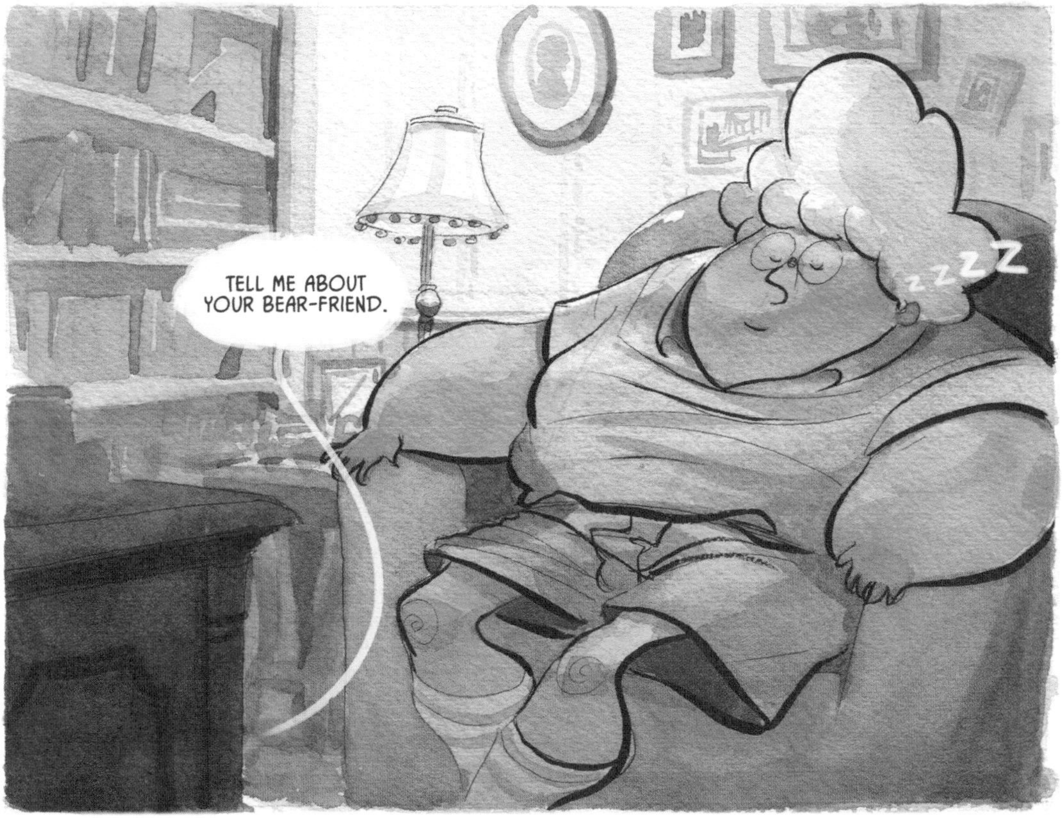
TELL ME ABOUT YOUR BEAR-FRIEND.
z z Z Z

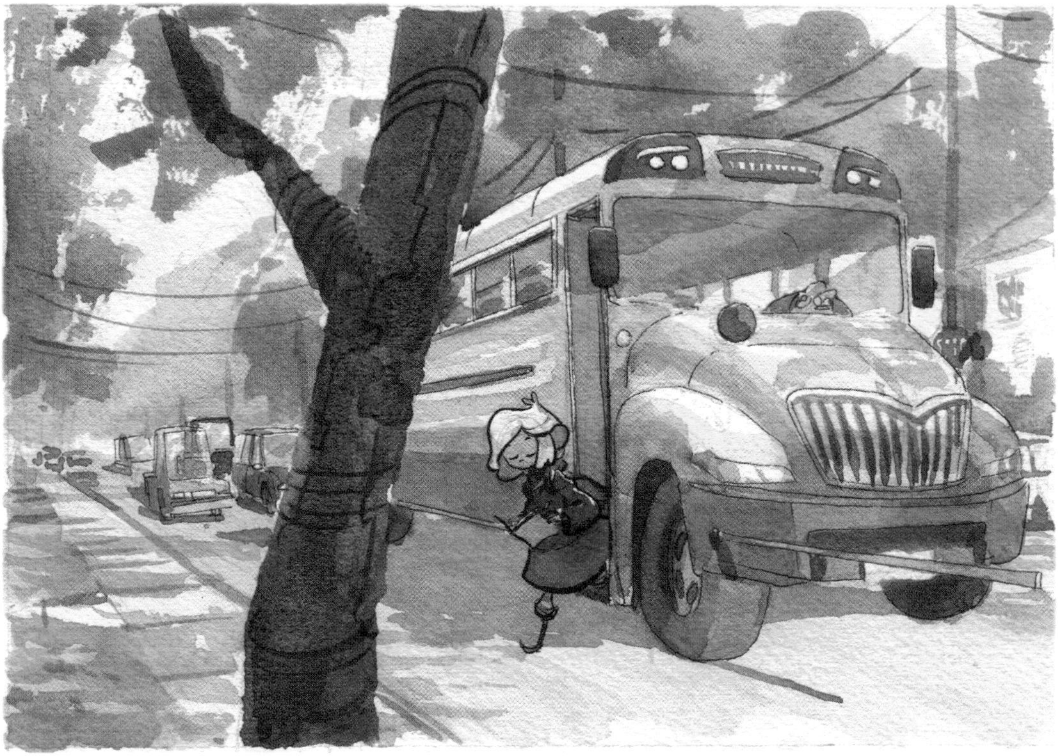
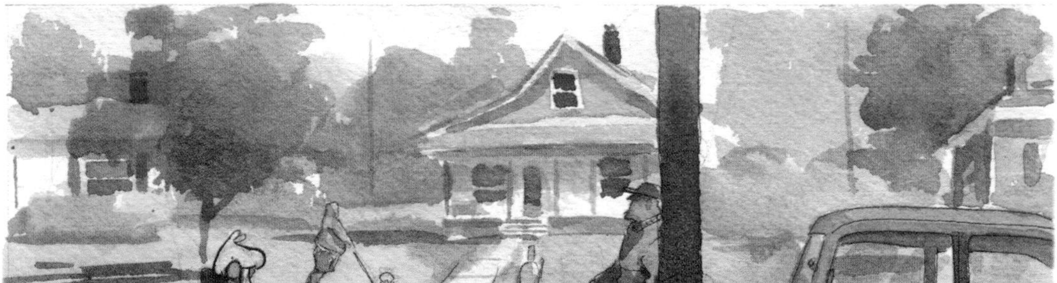
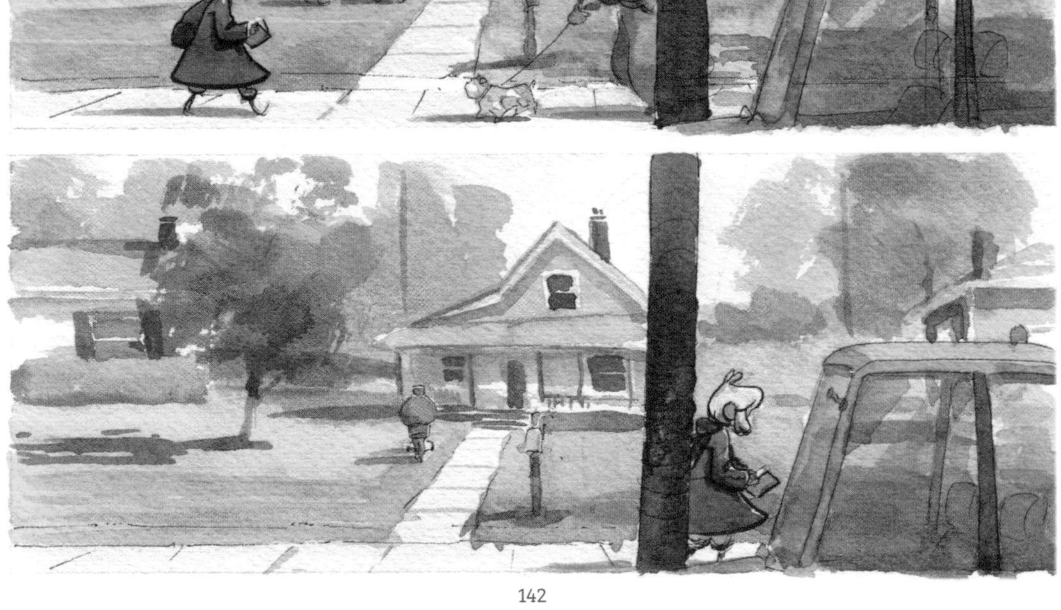

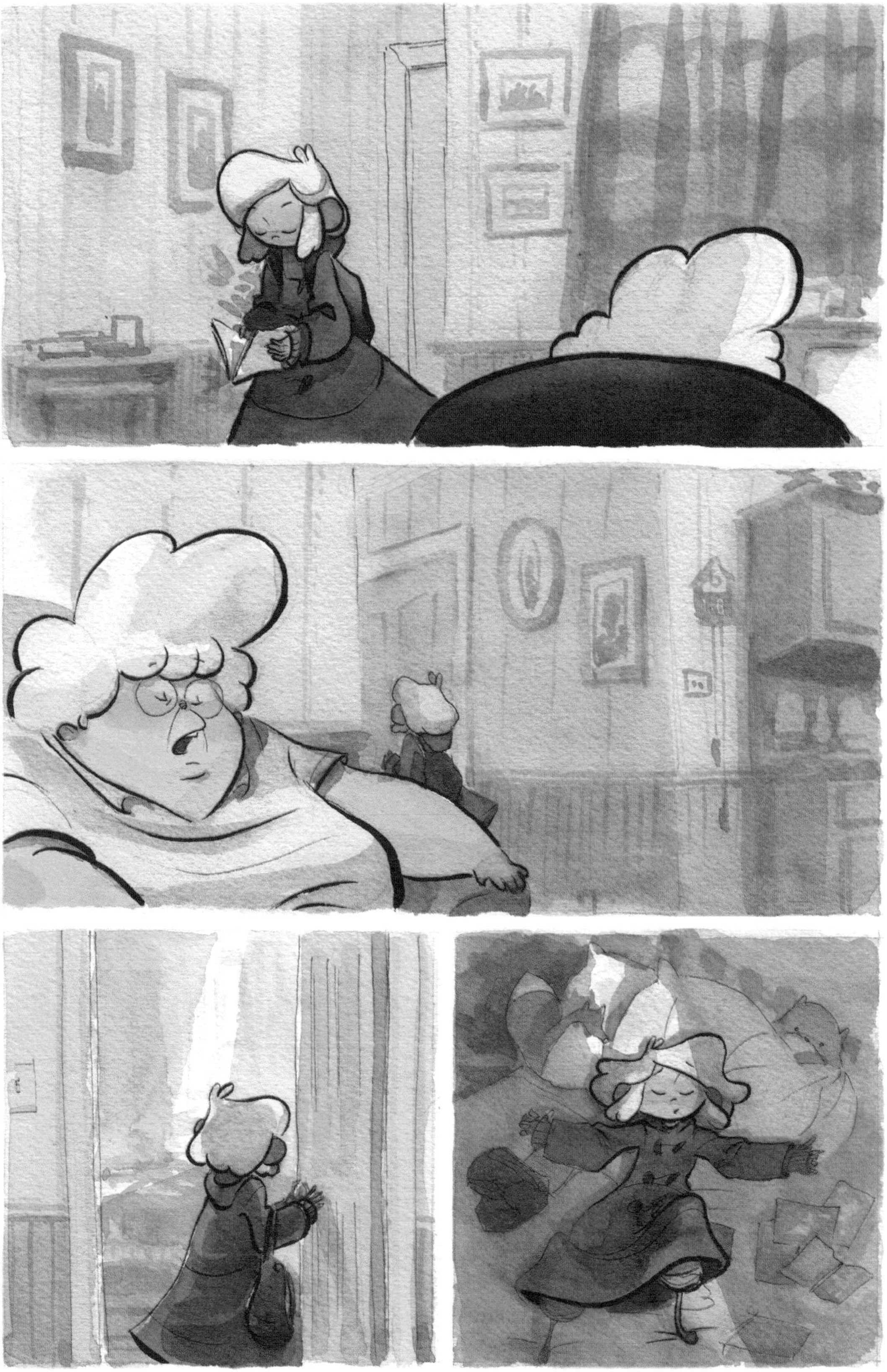

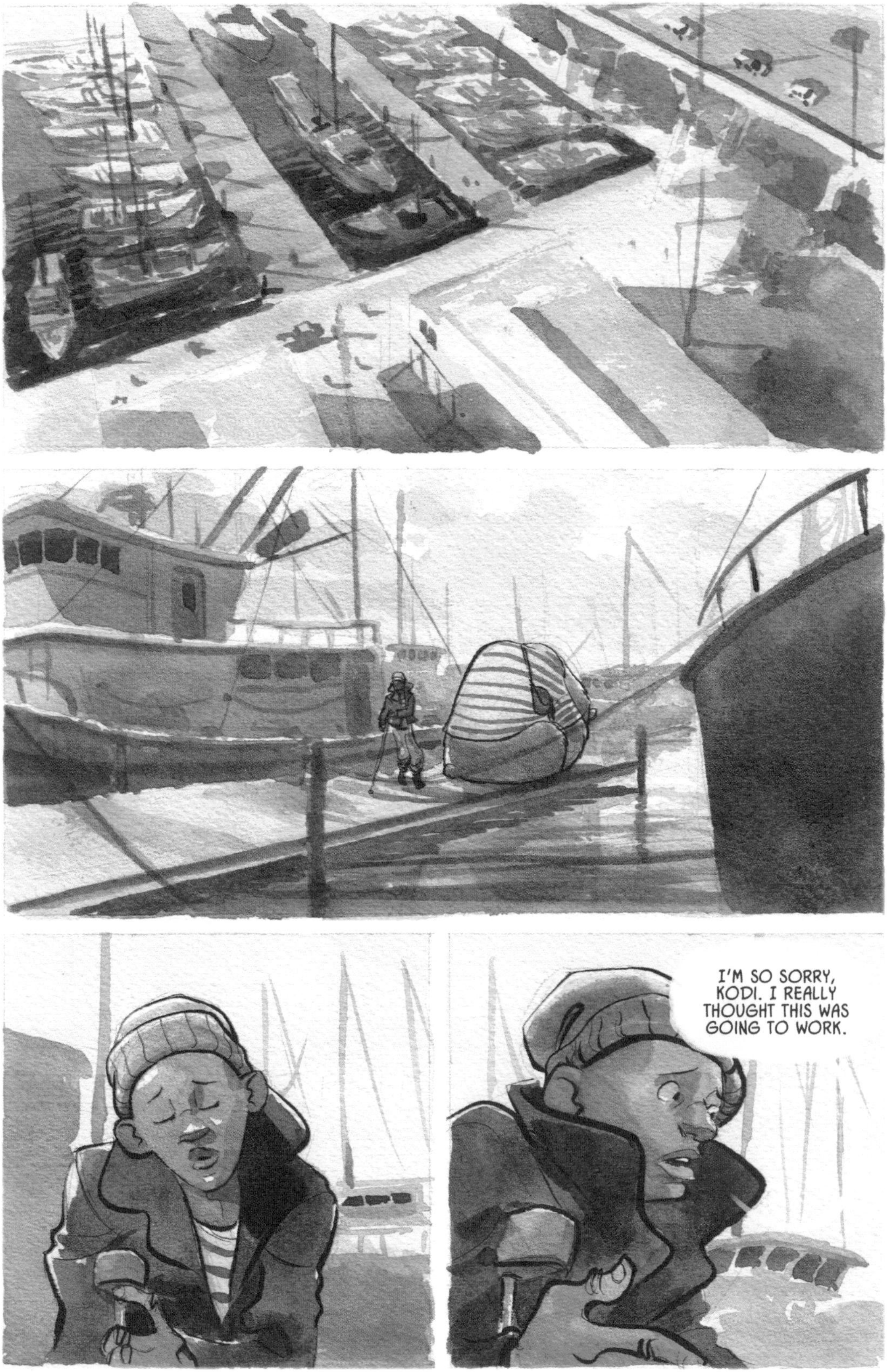
I'M SO SORRY, KODI. I REALLY THOUGHT THIS WAS GOING TO WORK.

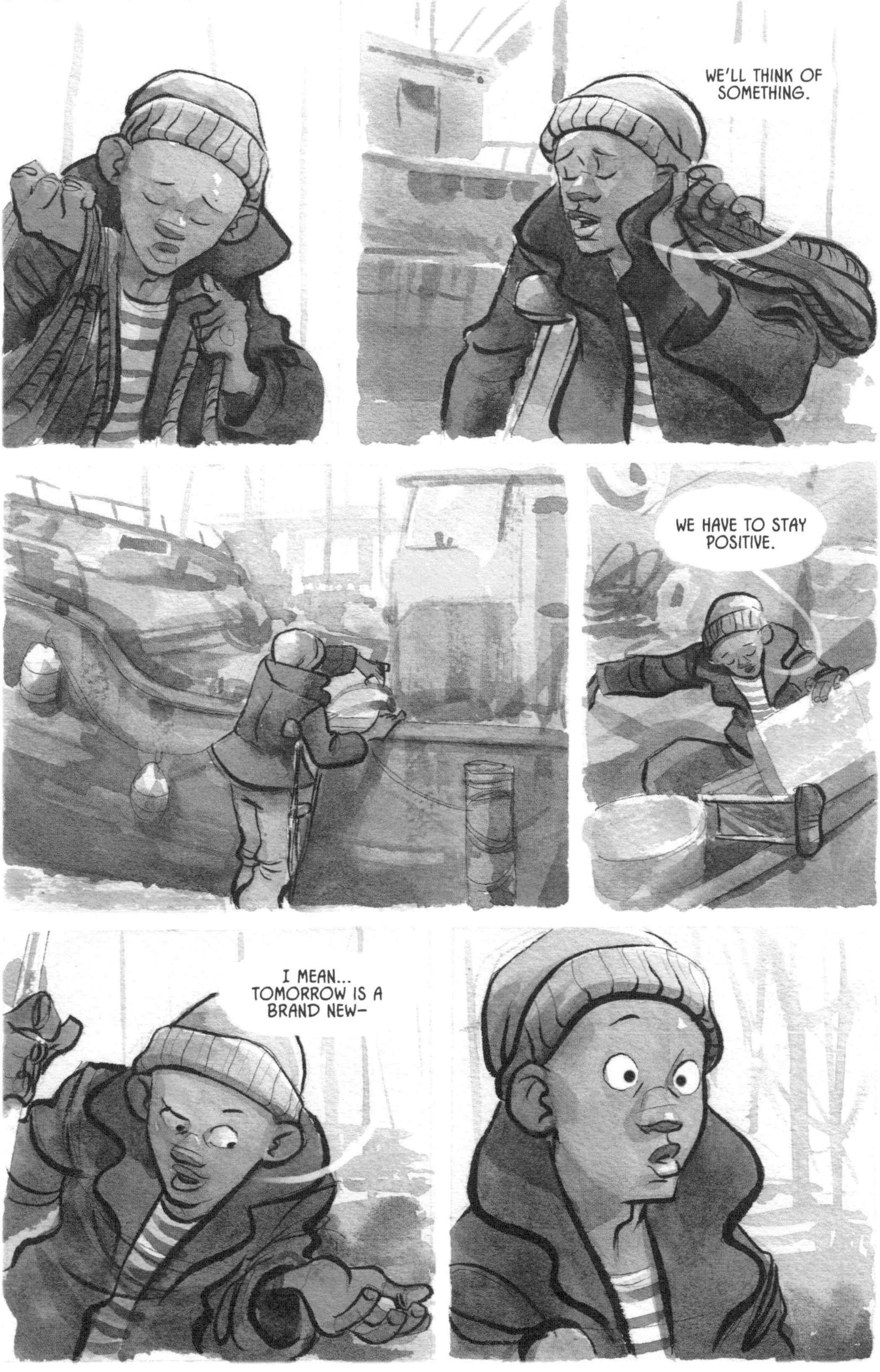
WE'LL THINK OF SOMETHING.
WE HAVE TO STAY POSITIVE.
I MEAN... TOMORROW IS A BRAND NEW–

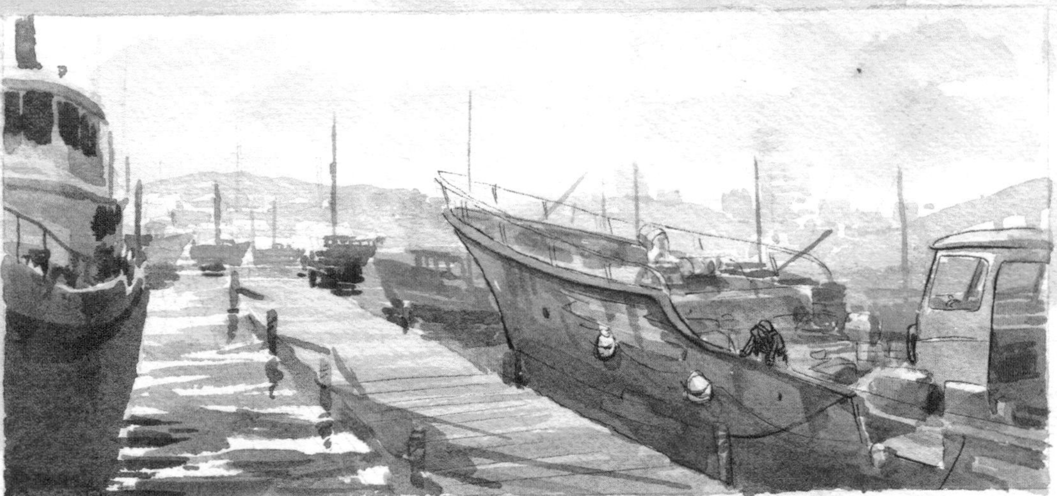

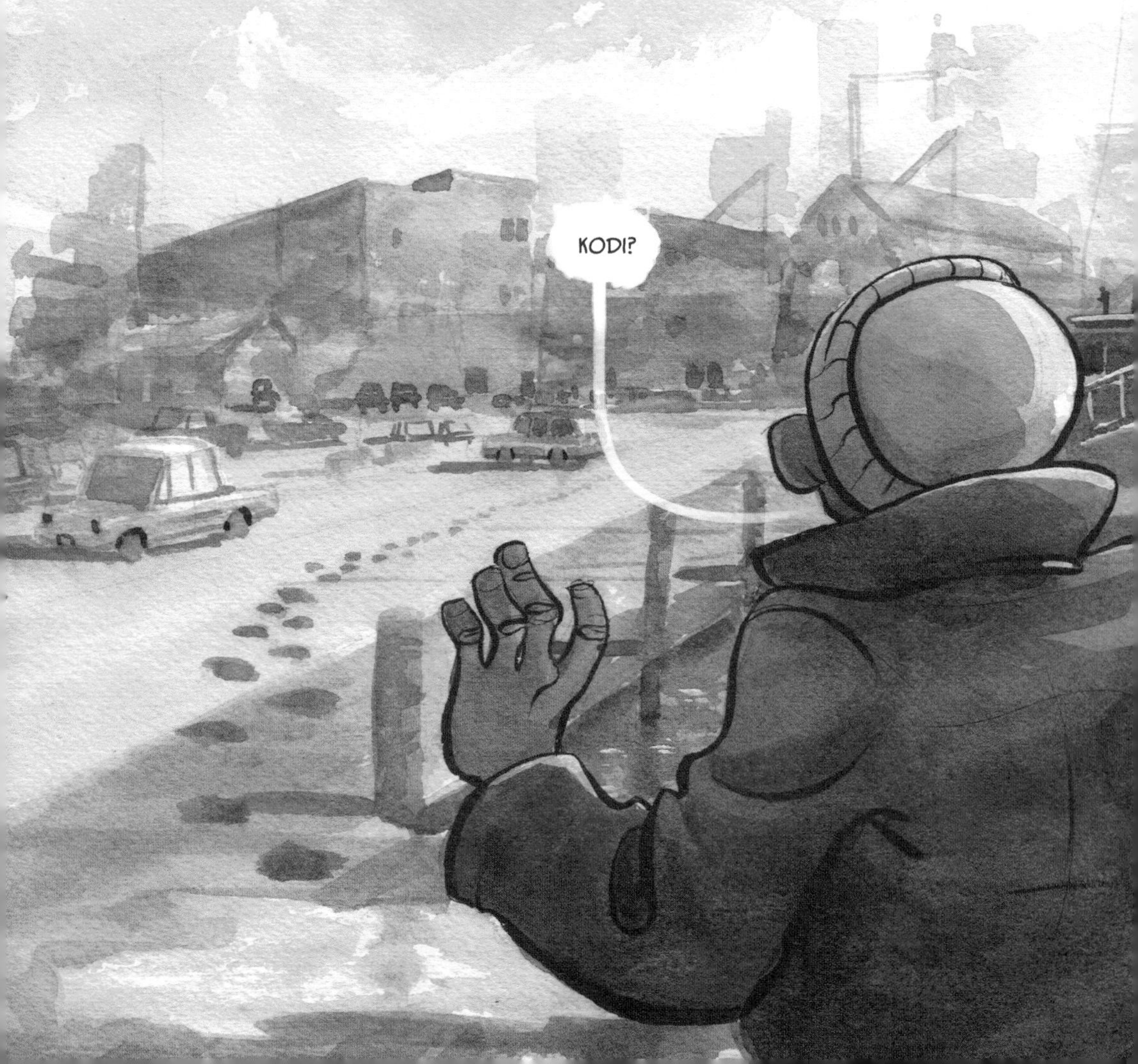
KODI?

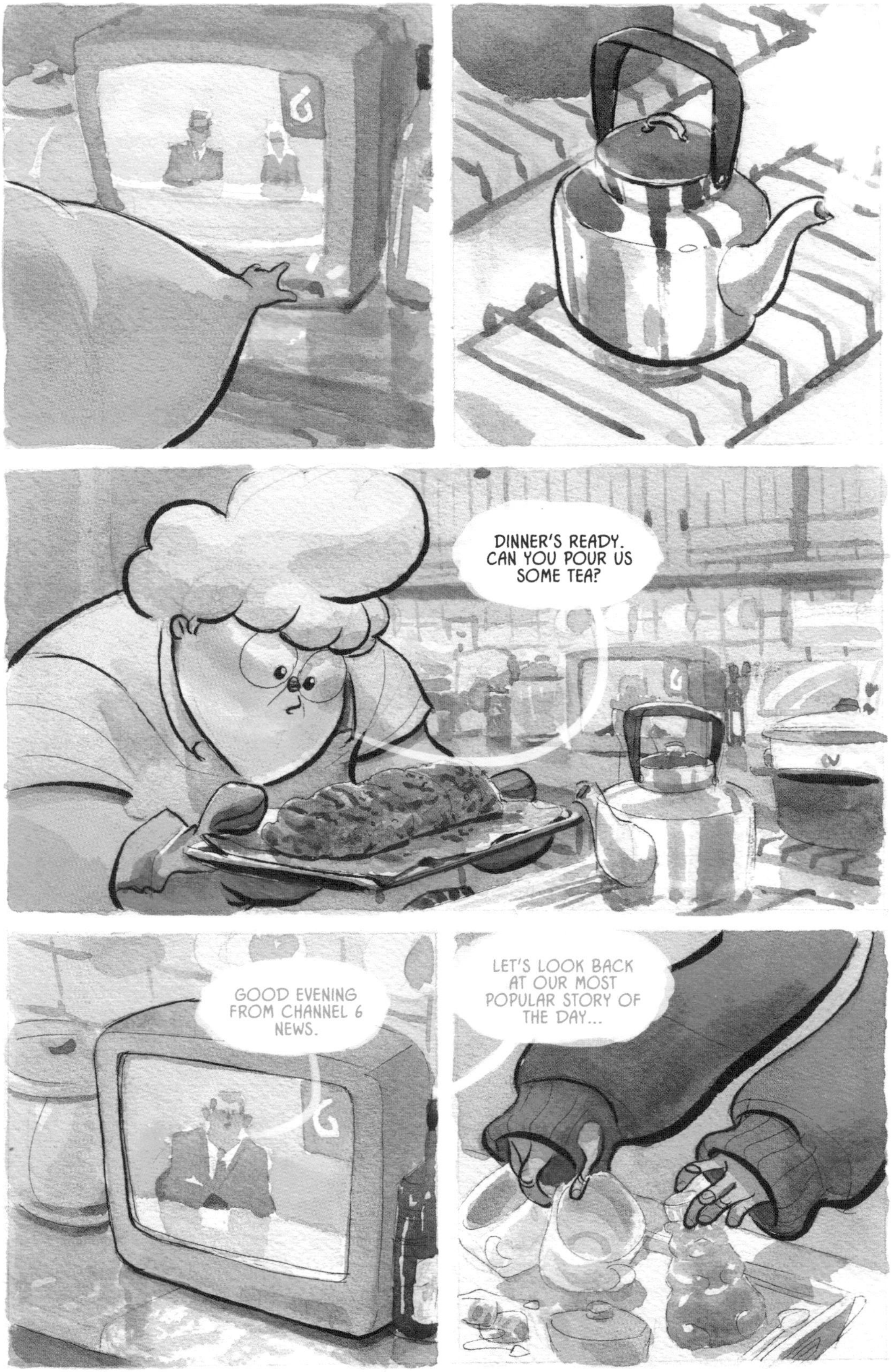
DINNER'S READY. CAN YOU POUR US SOME TEA?
GOOD EVENING FROM CHANNEL 6 NEWS.
LET'S LOOK BACK AT OUR MOST POPULAR STORY OF THE DAY...

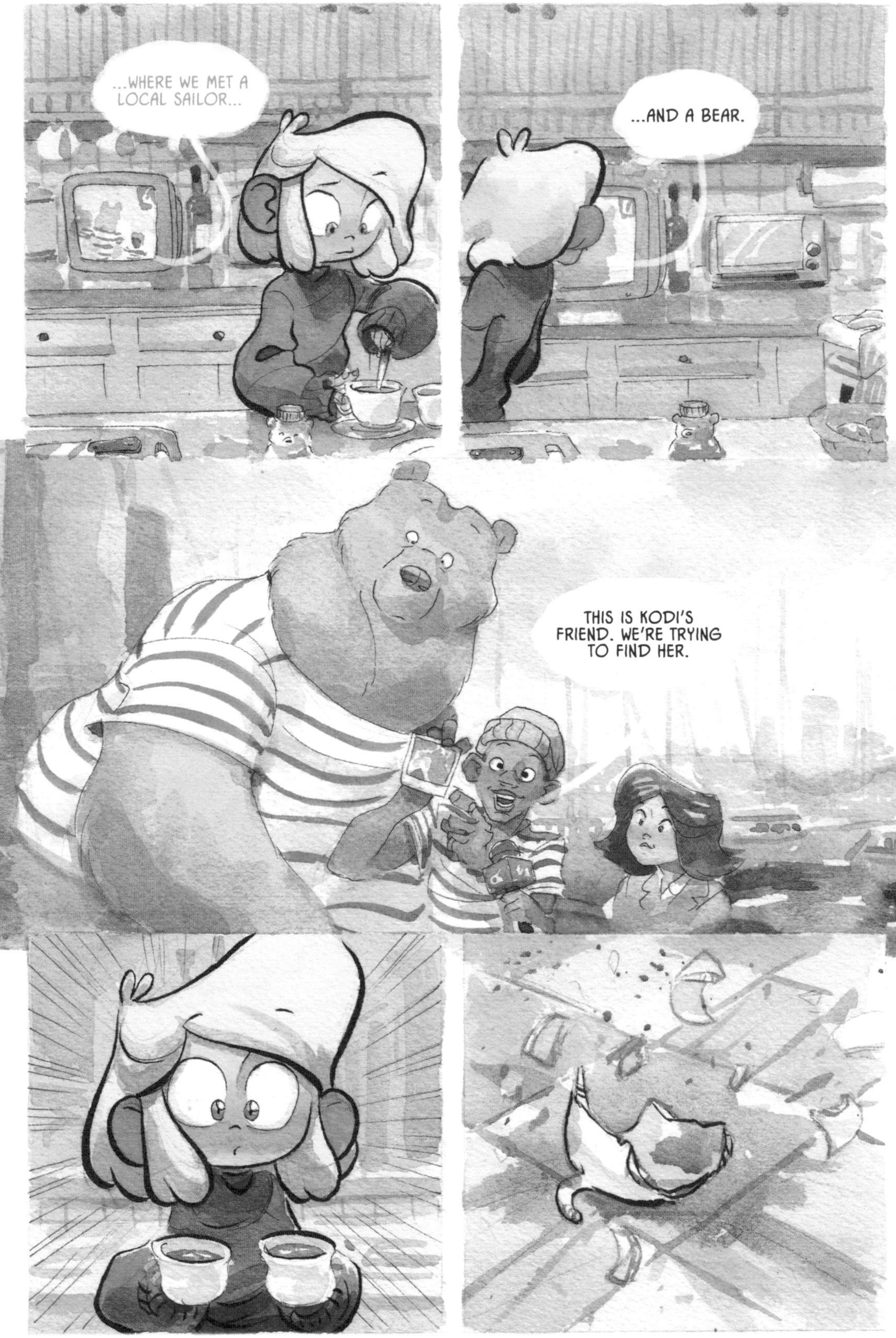
...WHERE WE MET A LOCAL SAILOR...
...AND A BEAR.
THIS IS KODI'S FRIEND. WE'RE TRYING TO FIND HER.

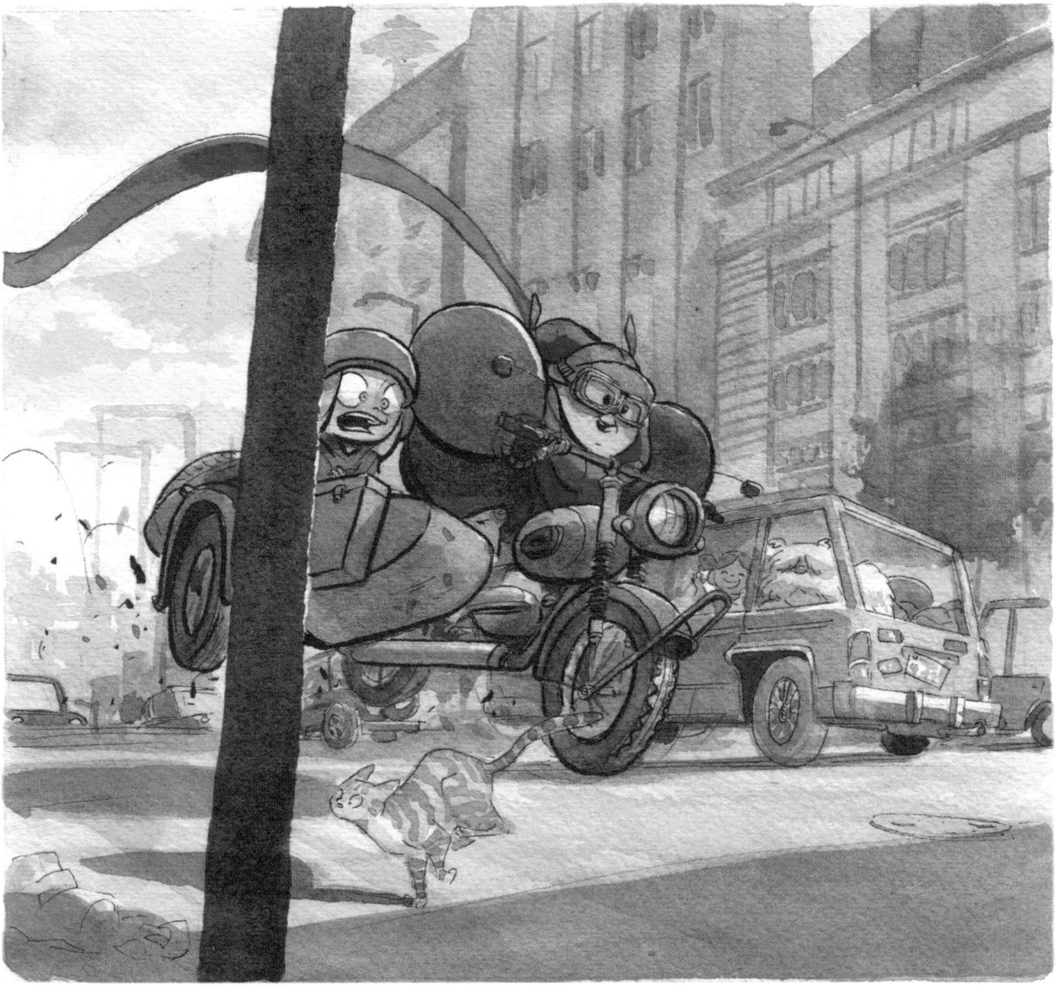

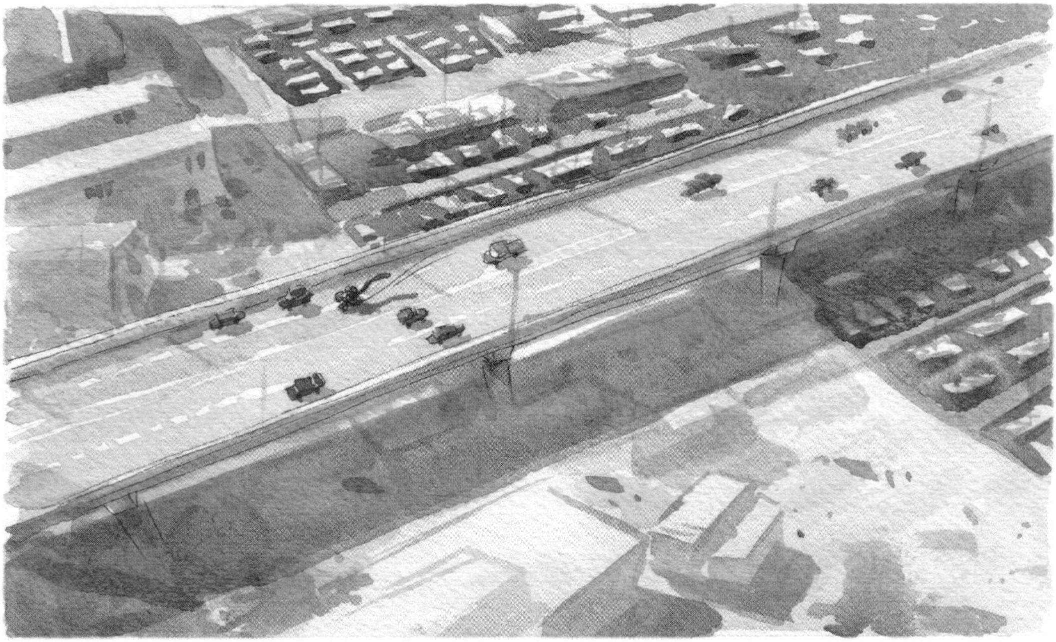

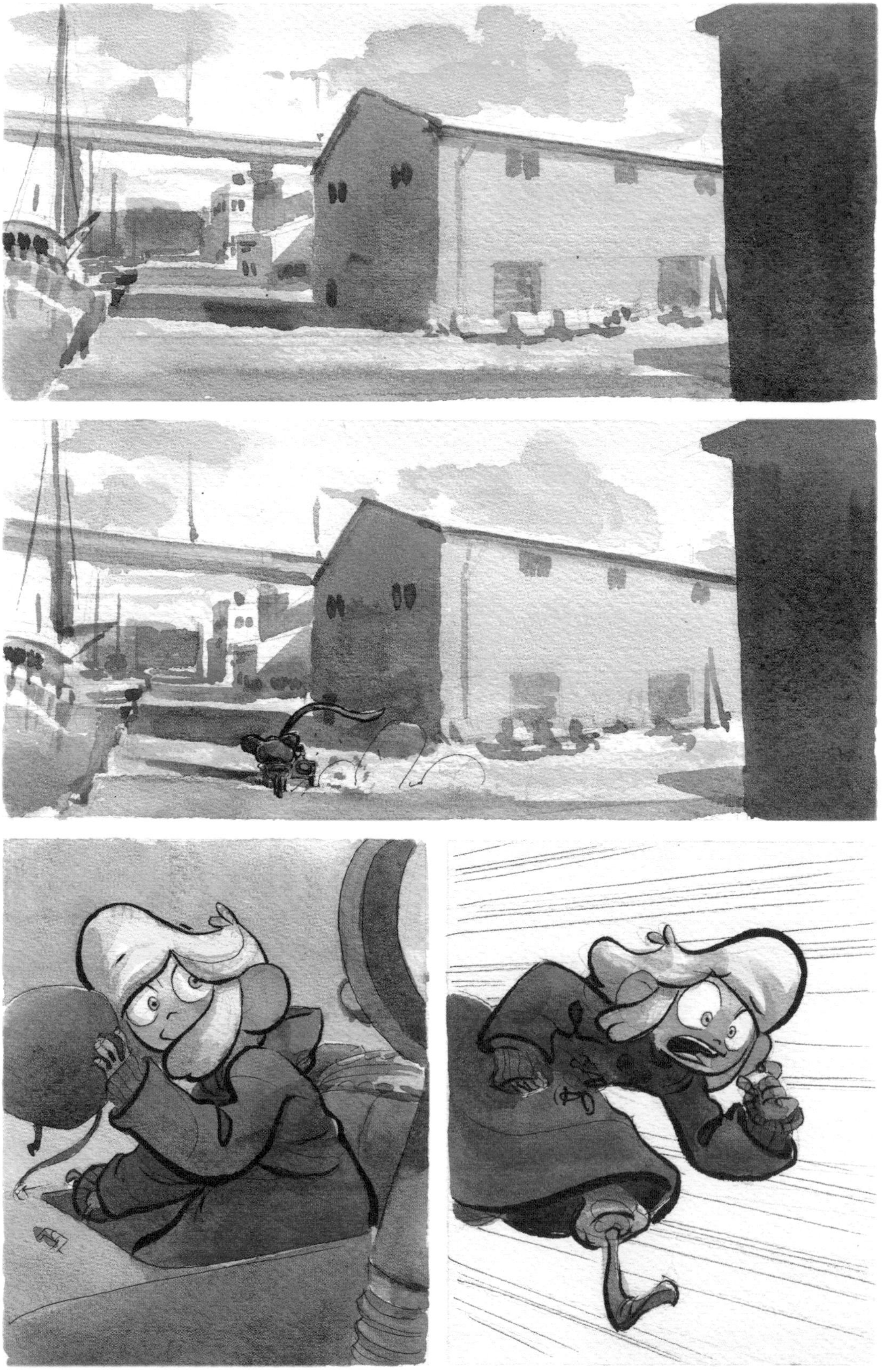

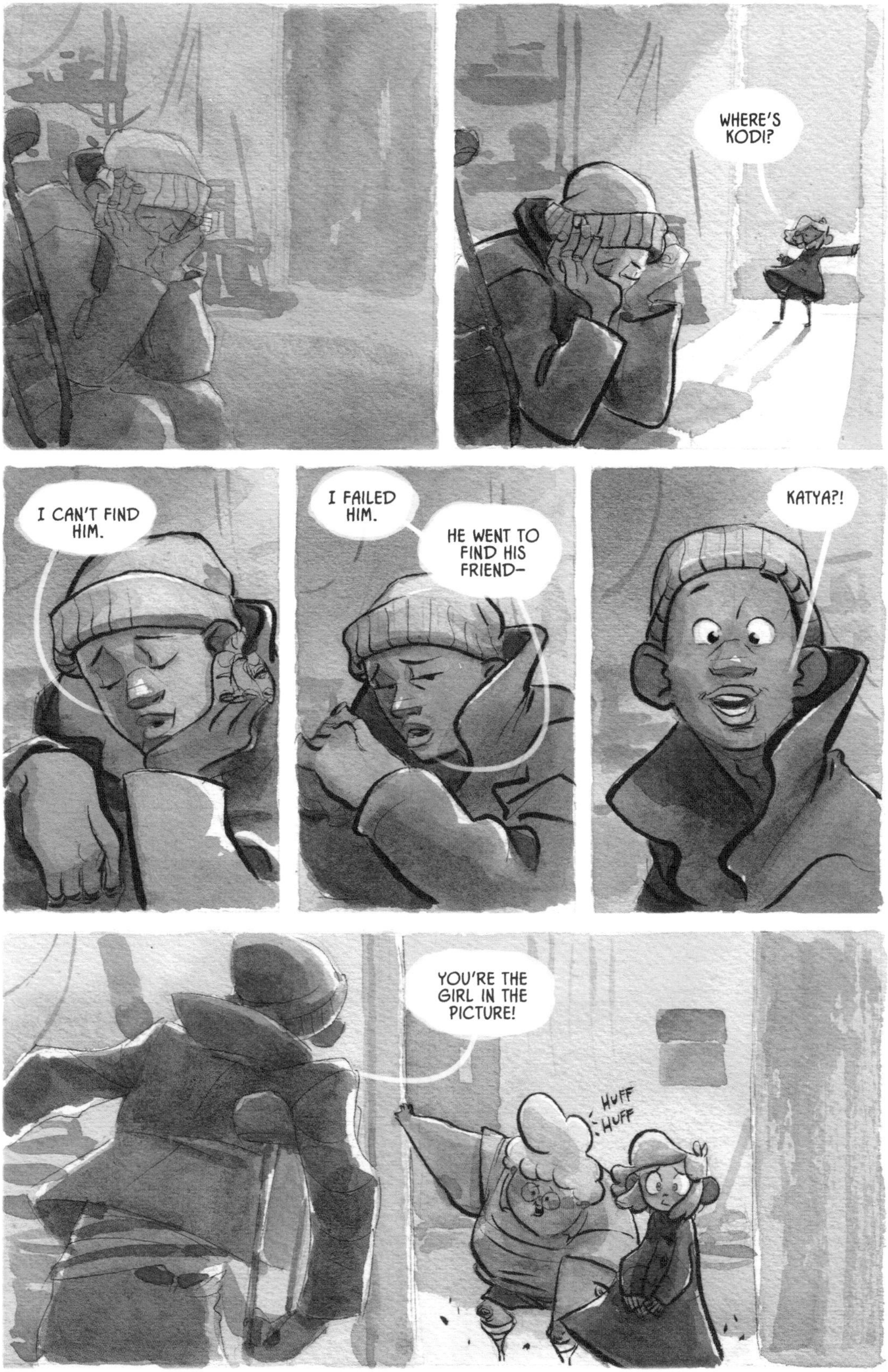
WHERE'S KODI?
I CAN'T FIND HIM.
I FAILED HIM.
HE WENT TO FIND HIS FRIEND–
KATYA?!
YOU'RE THE GIRL IN THE PICTURE!
HUFF HUFF

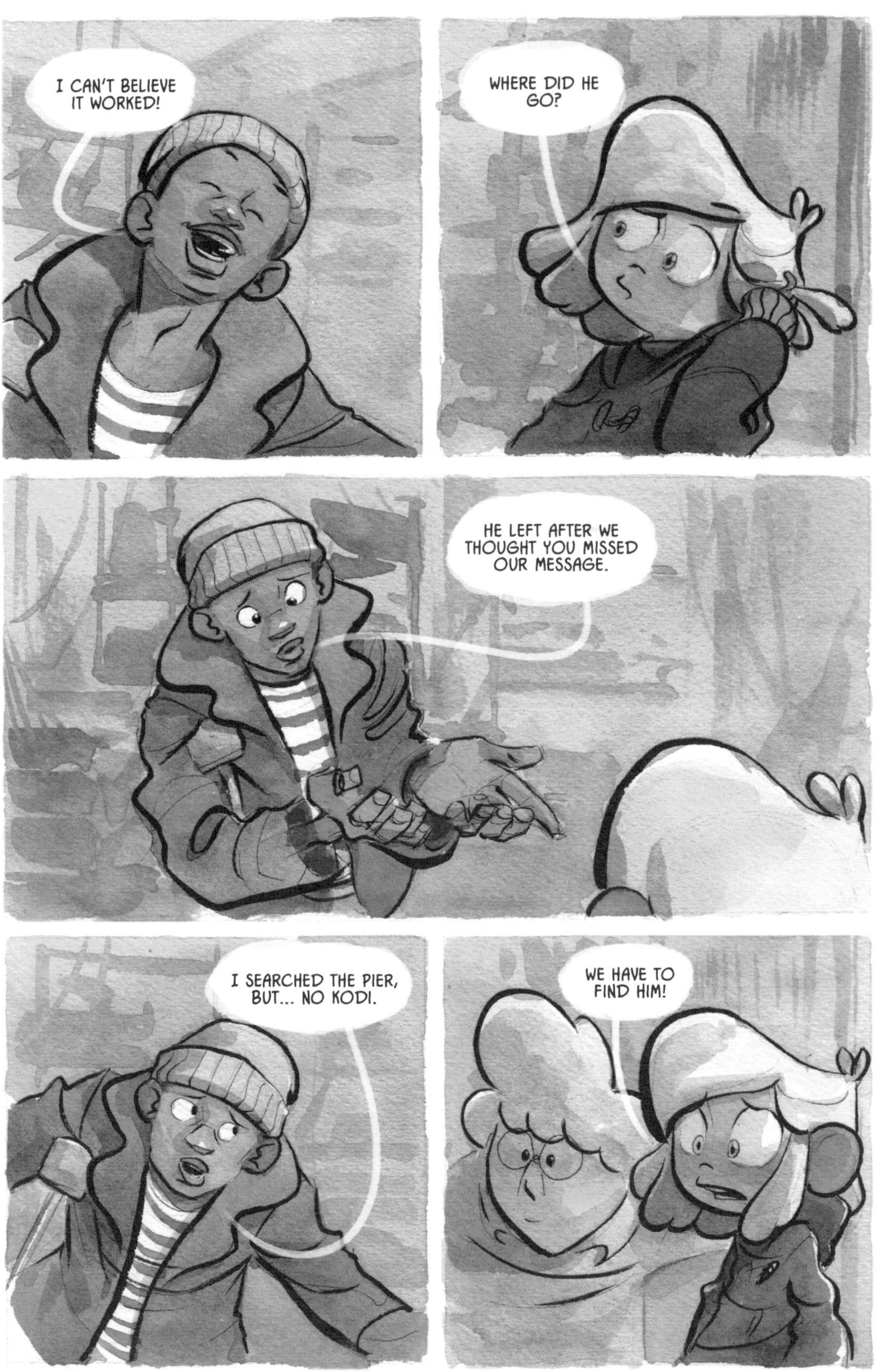
I CAN'T BELIEVE IT WORKED!
WHERE DID HE GO?
HE LEFT AFTER WE THOUGHT YOU MISSED OUR MESSAGE.
I SEARCHED THE PIER, BUT... NO KODI.
WE HAVE TO FIND HIM!

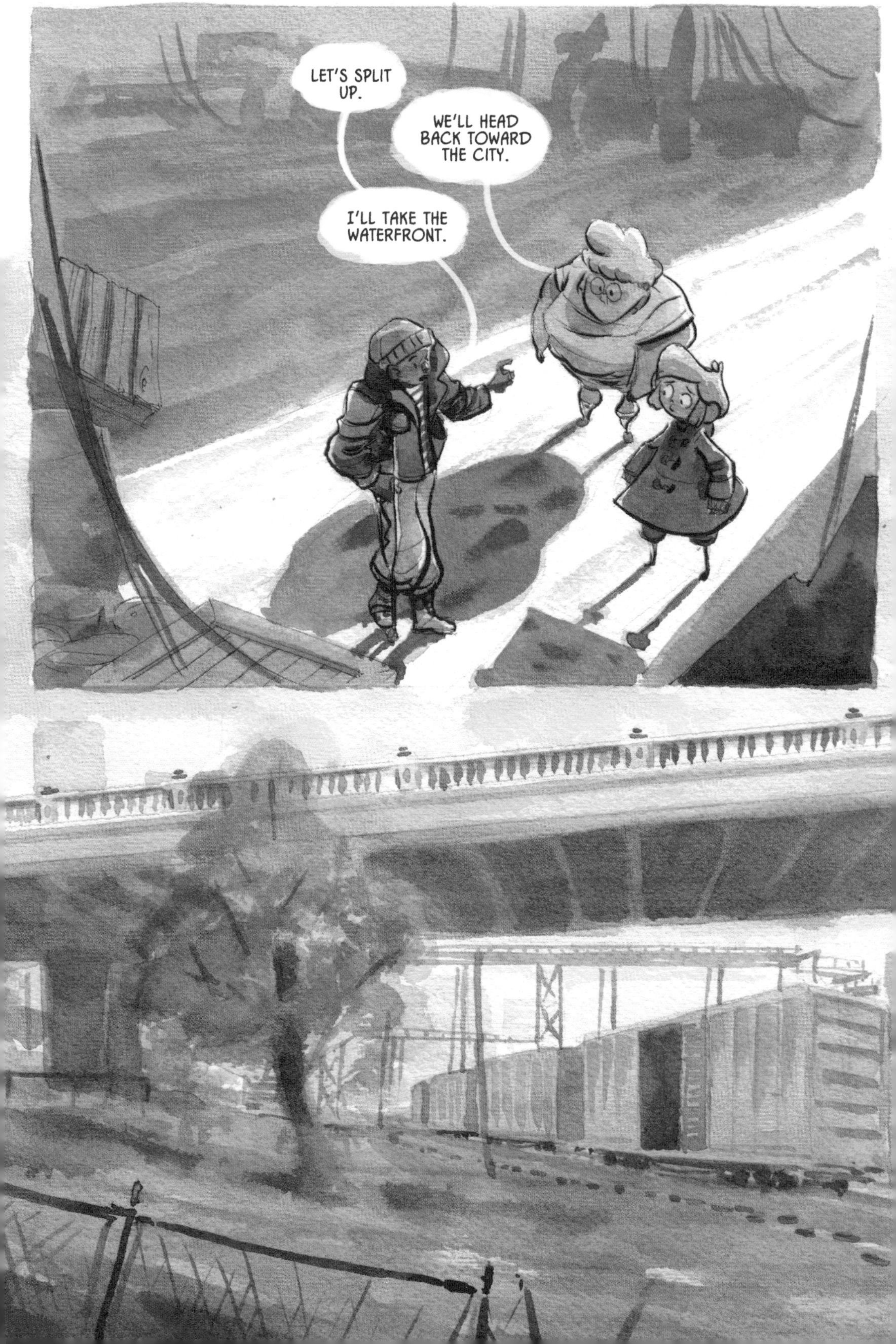
LET'S SPLIT UP.
WE'LL HEAD BACK TOWARD THE CITY.
I'LL TAKE THE WATERFRONT.

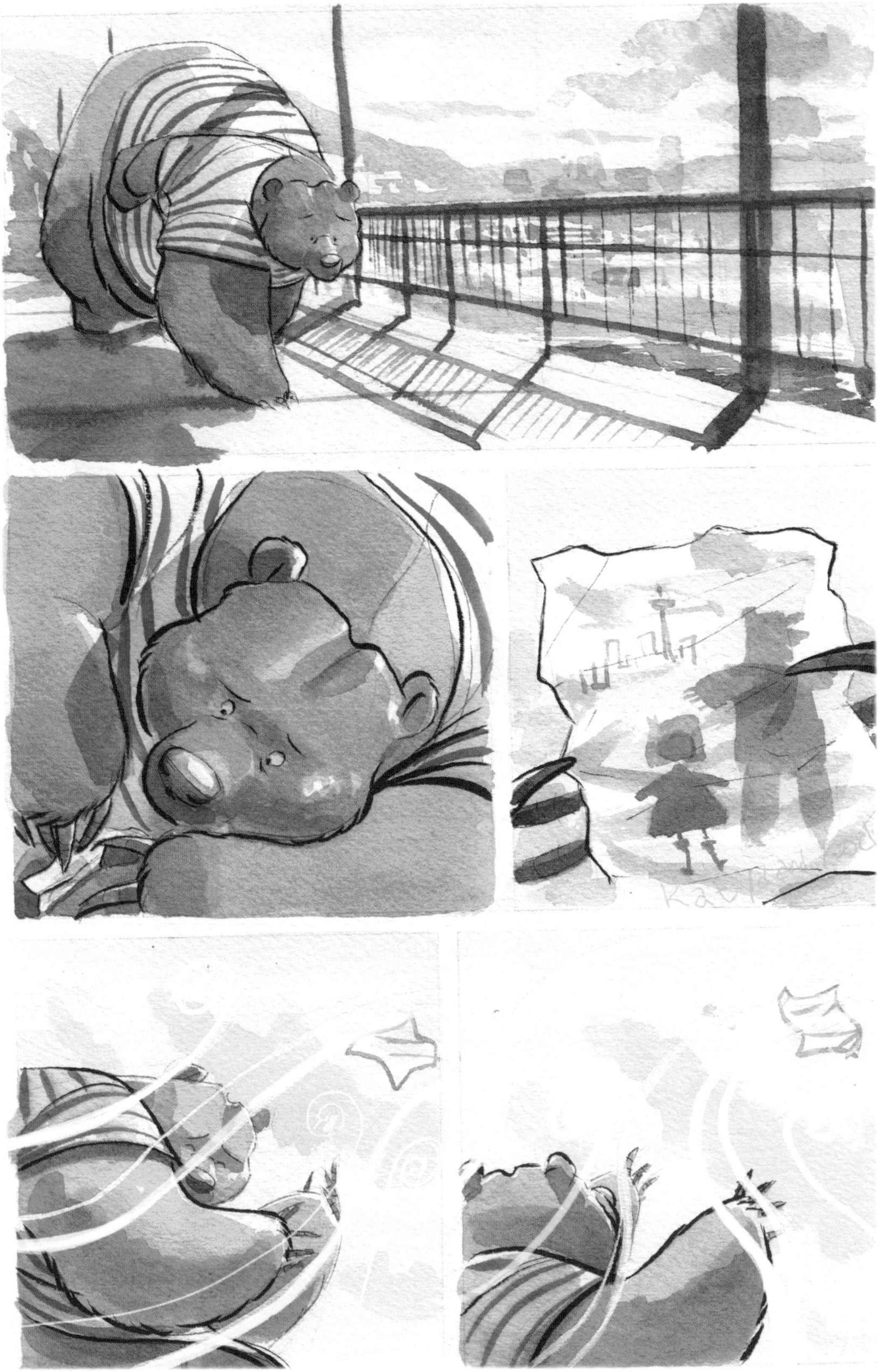

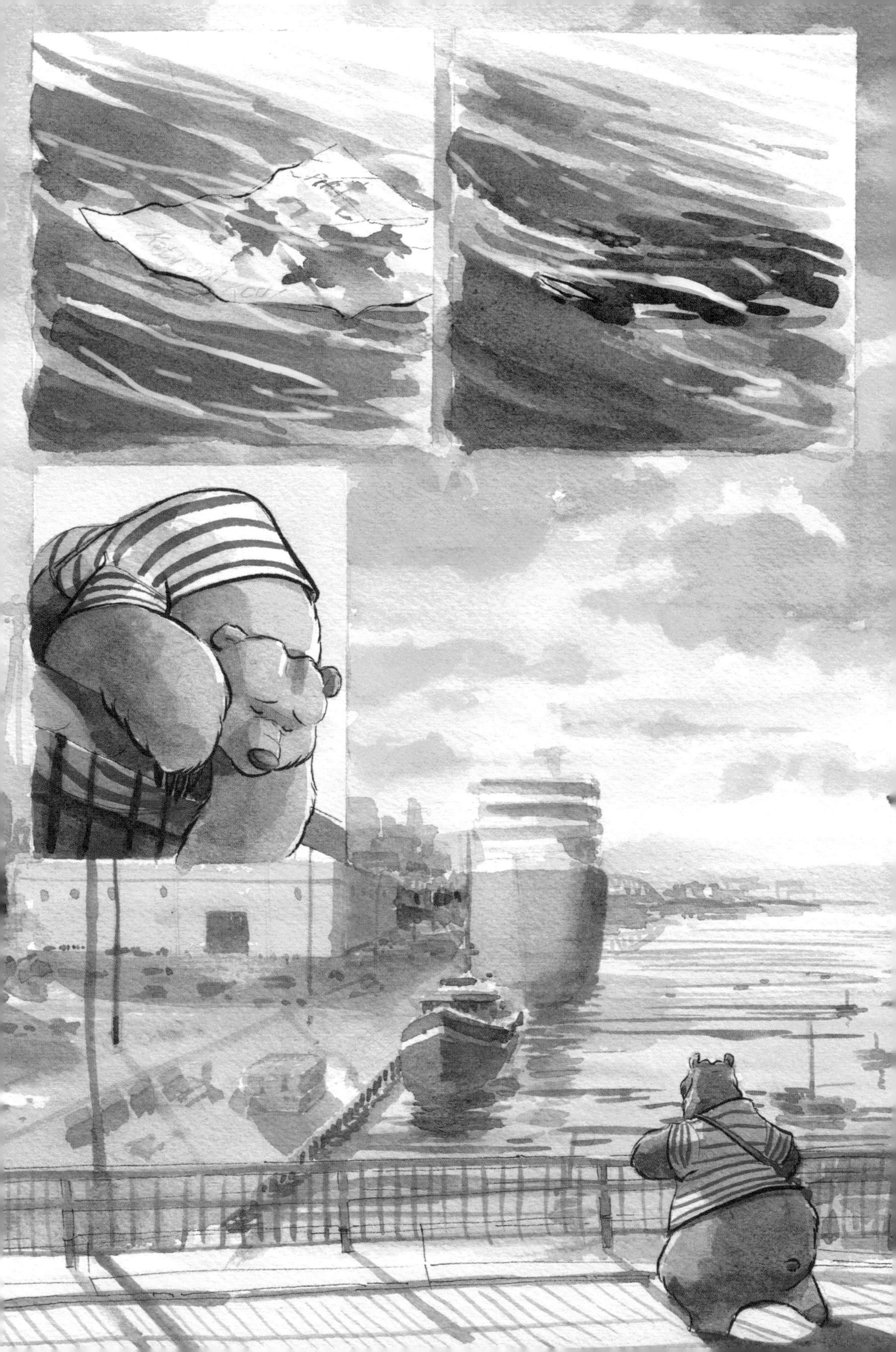

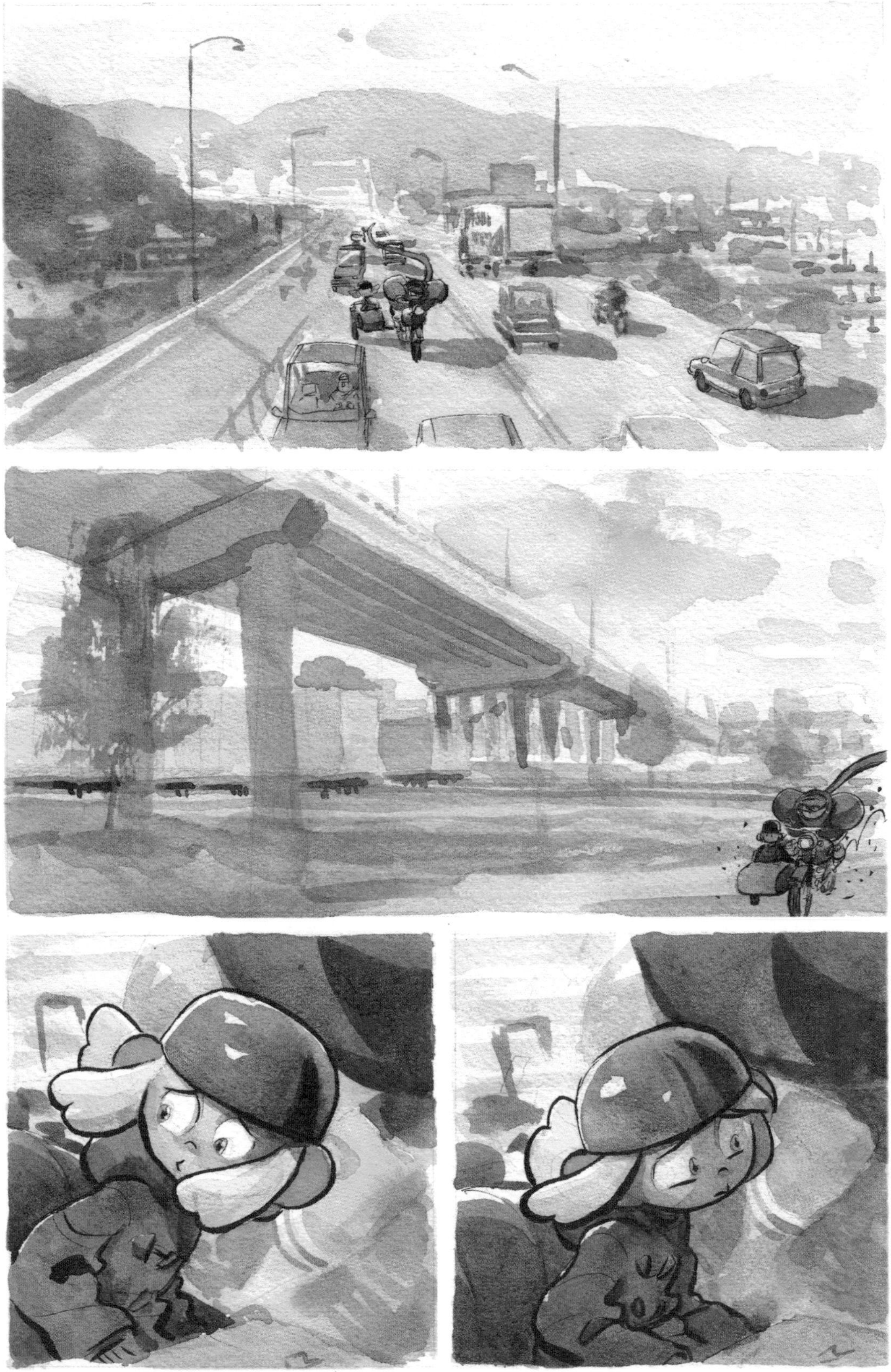

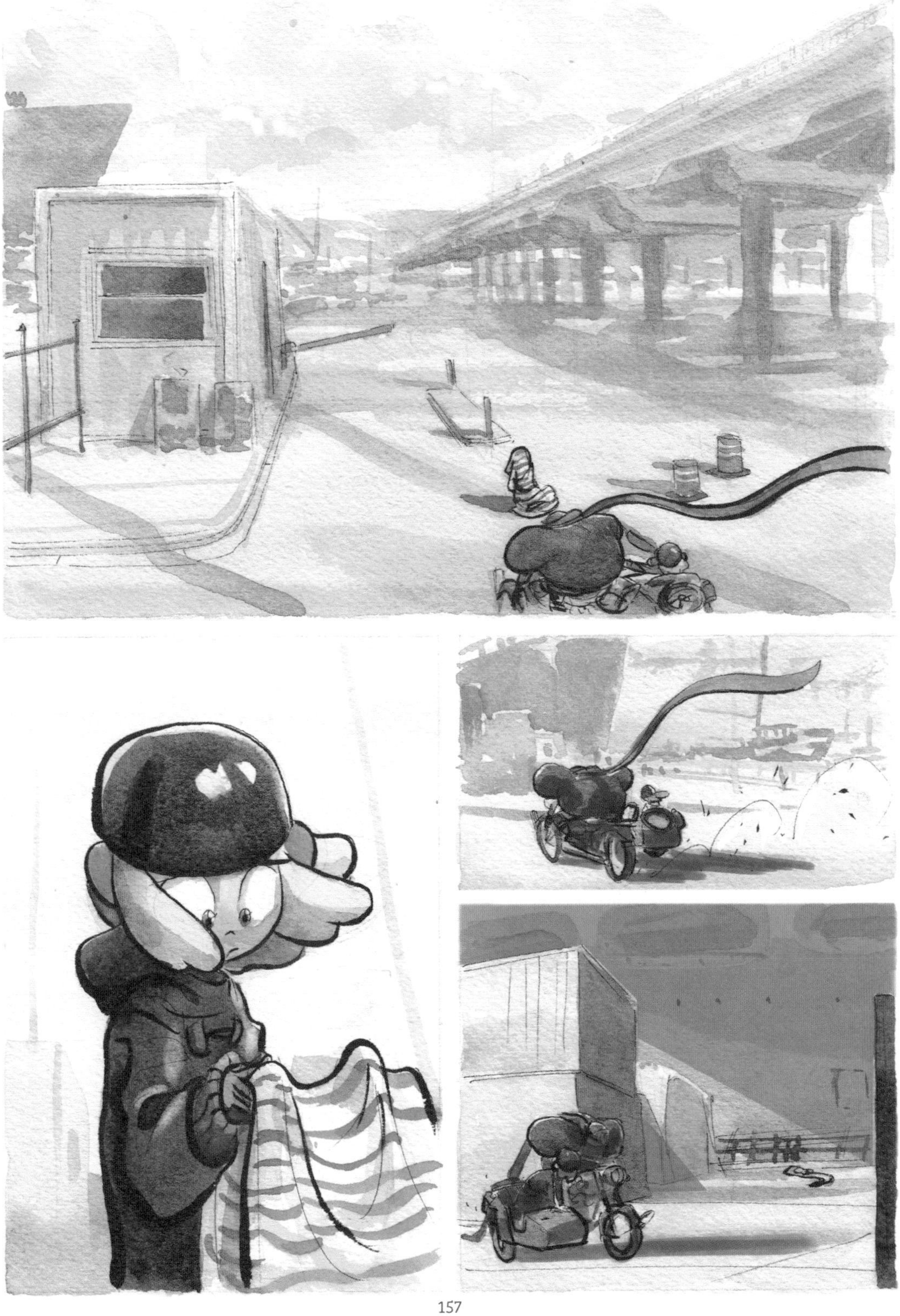

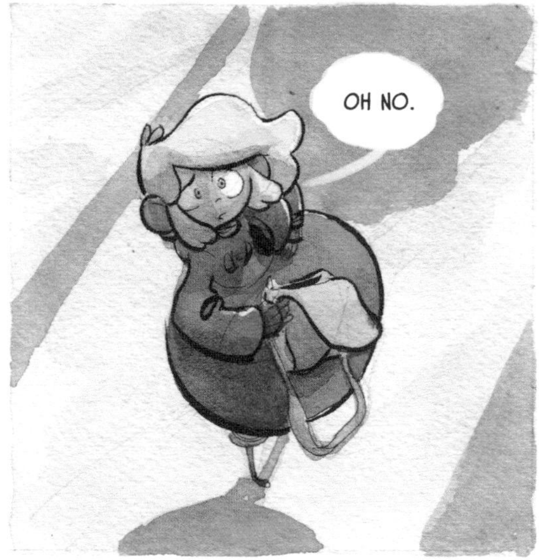
OH NO.

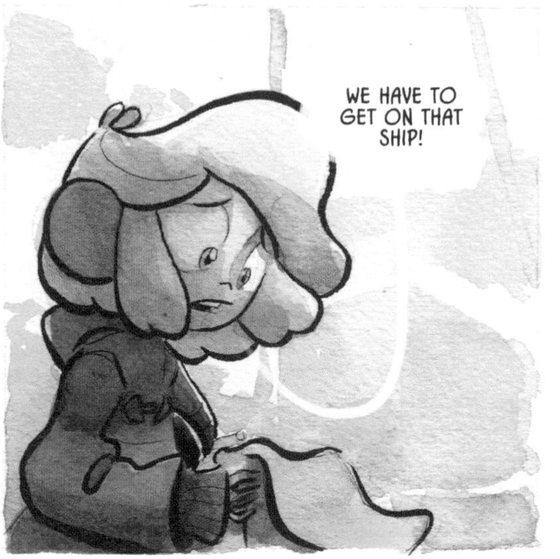
WE HAVE TO GET ON THAT SHIP!

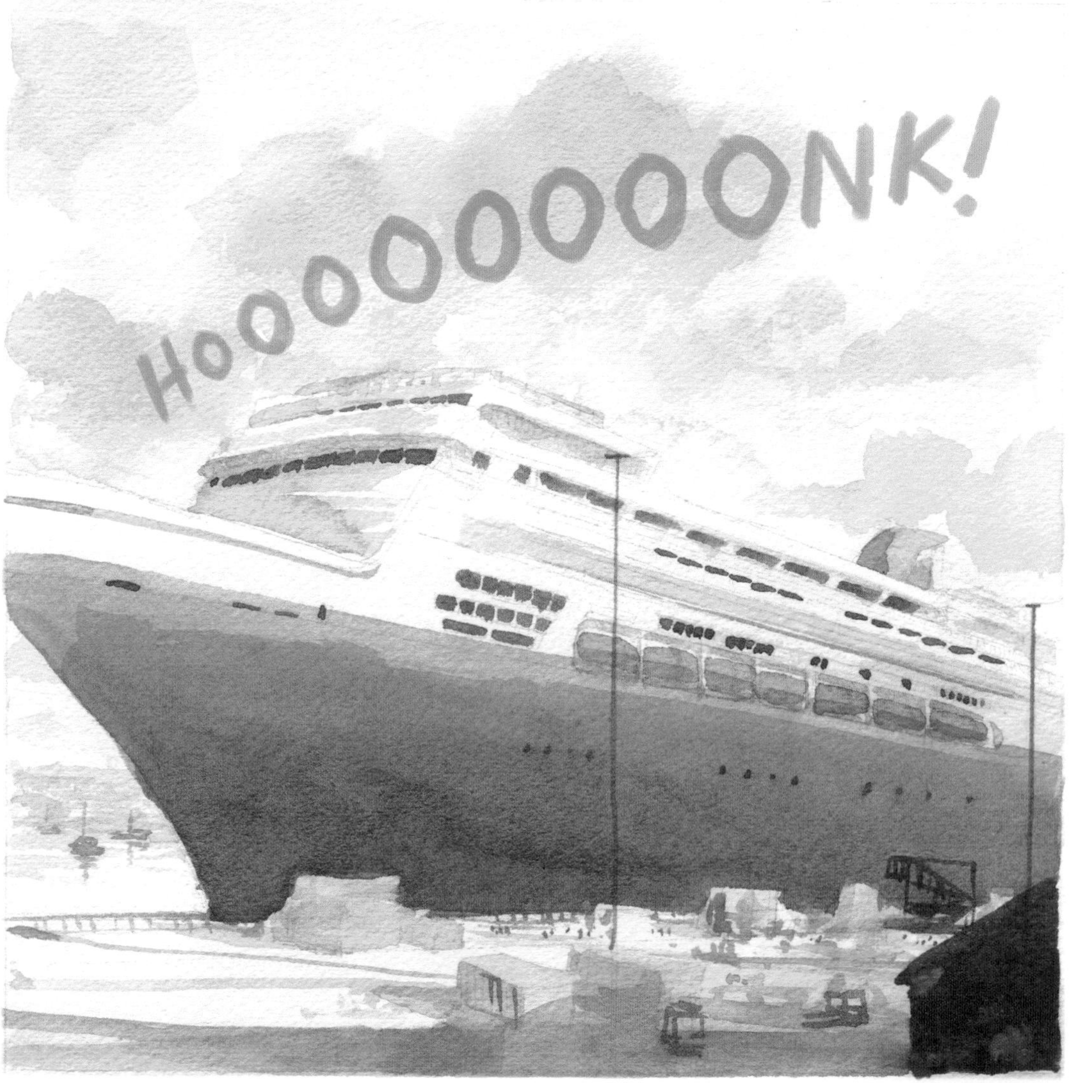
HOOOOOOOONK!

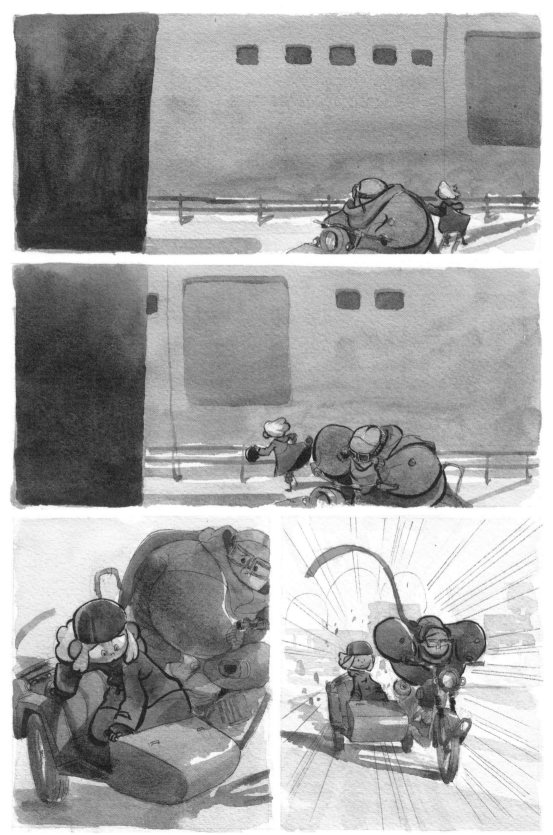

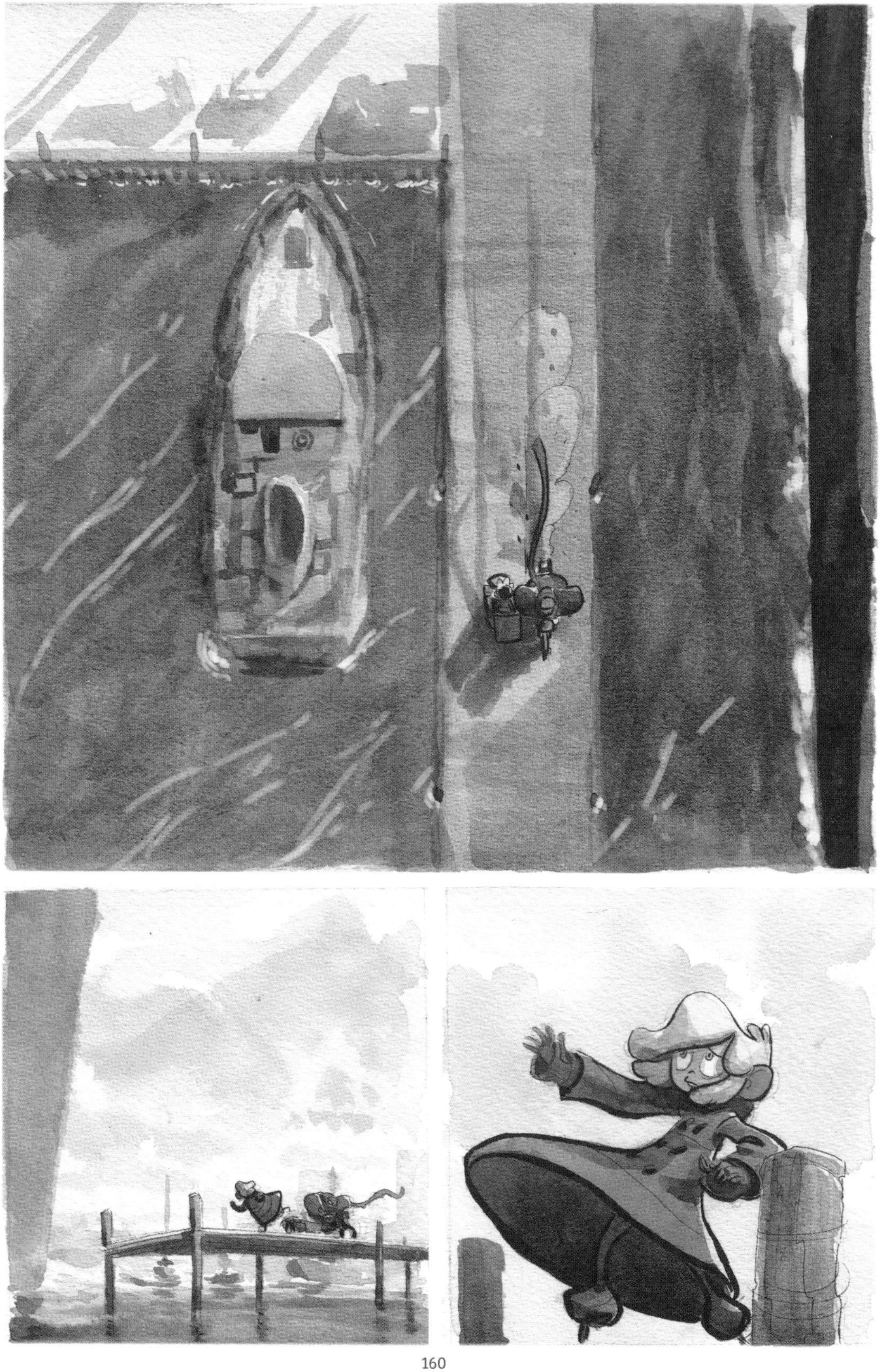

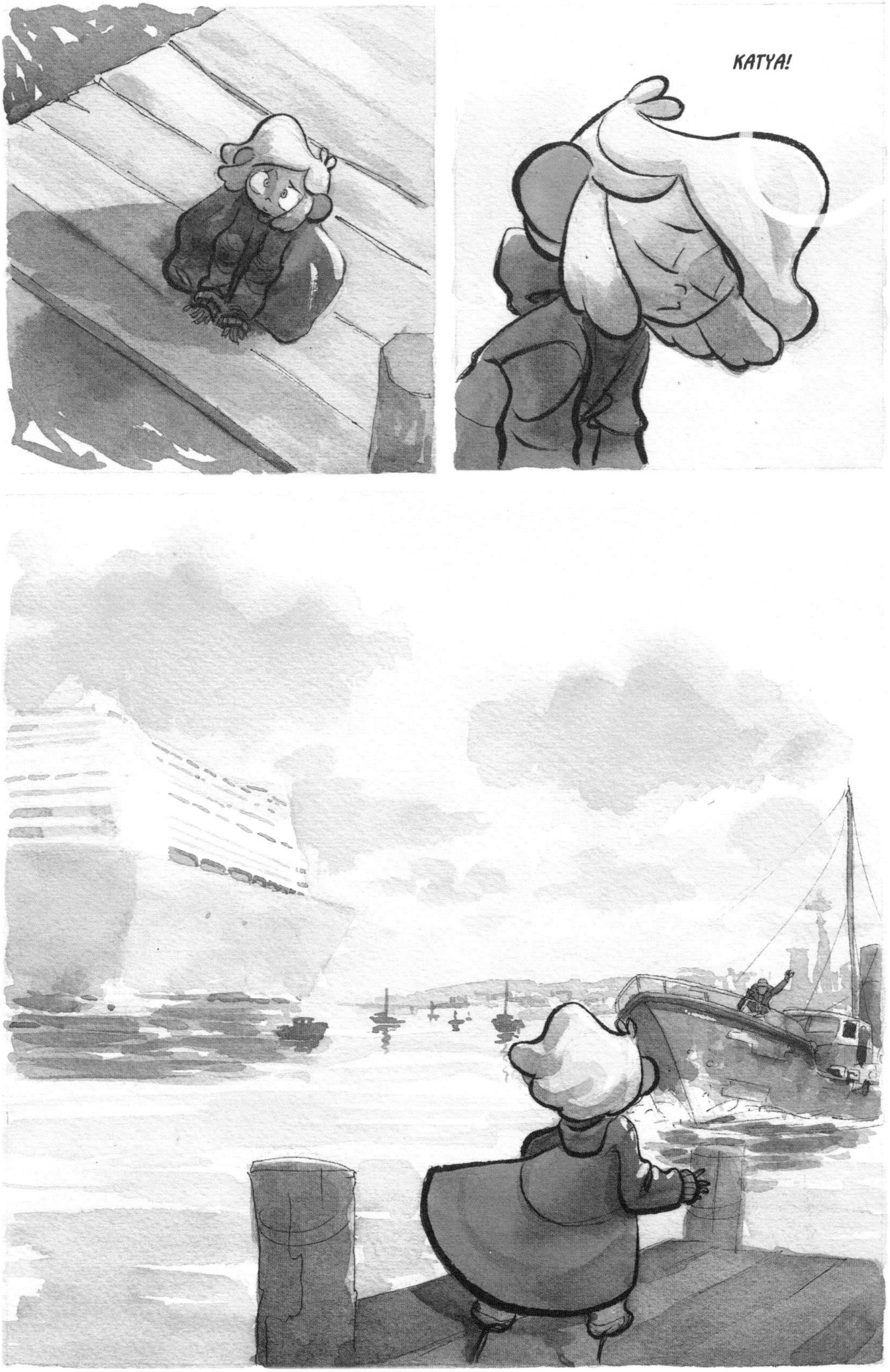
KATYA!

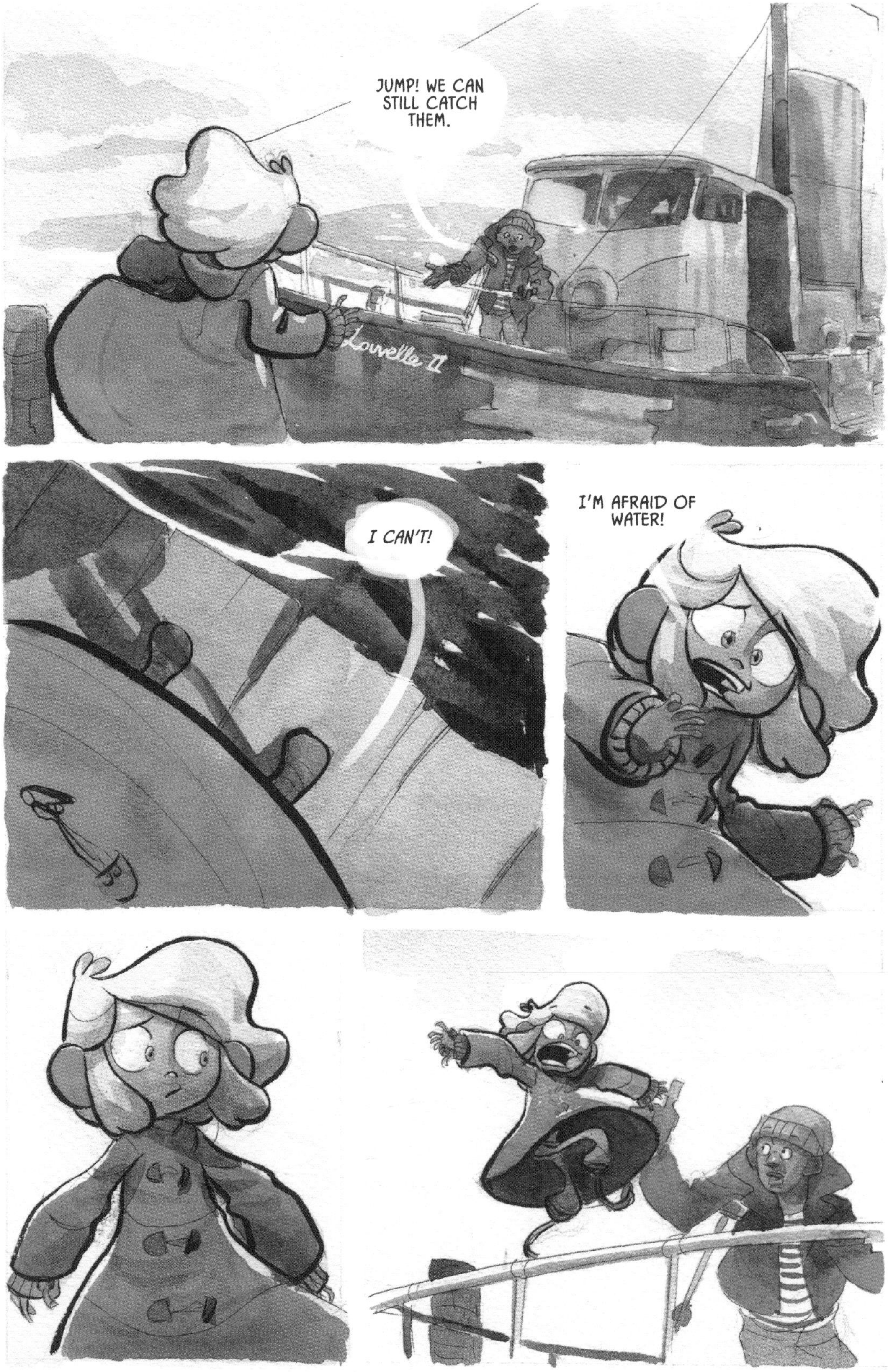
JUMP! WE CAN STILL CATCH THEM.
Louvelle II
I CAN'T!
I'M AFRAID OF WATER!

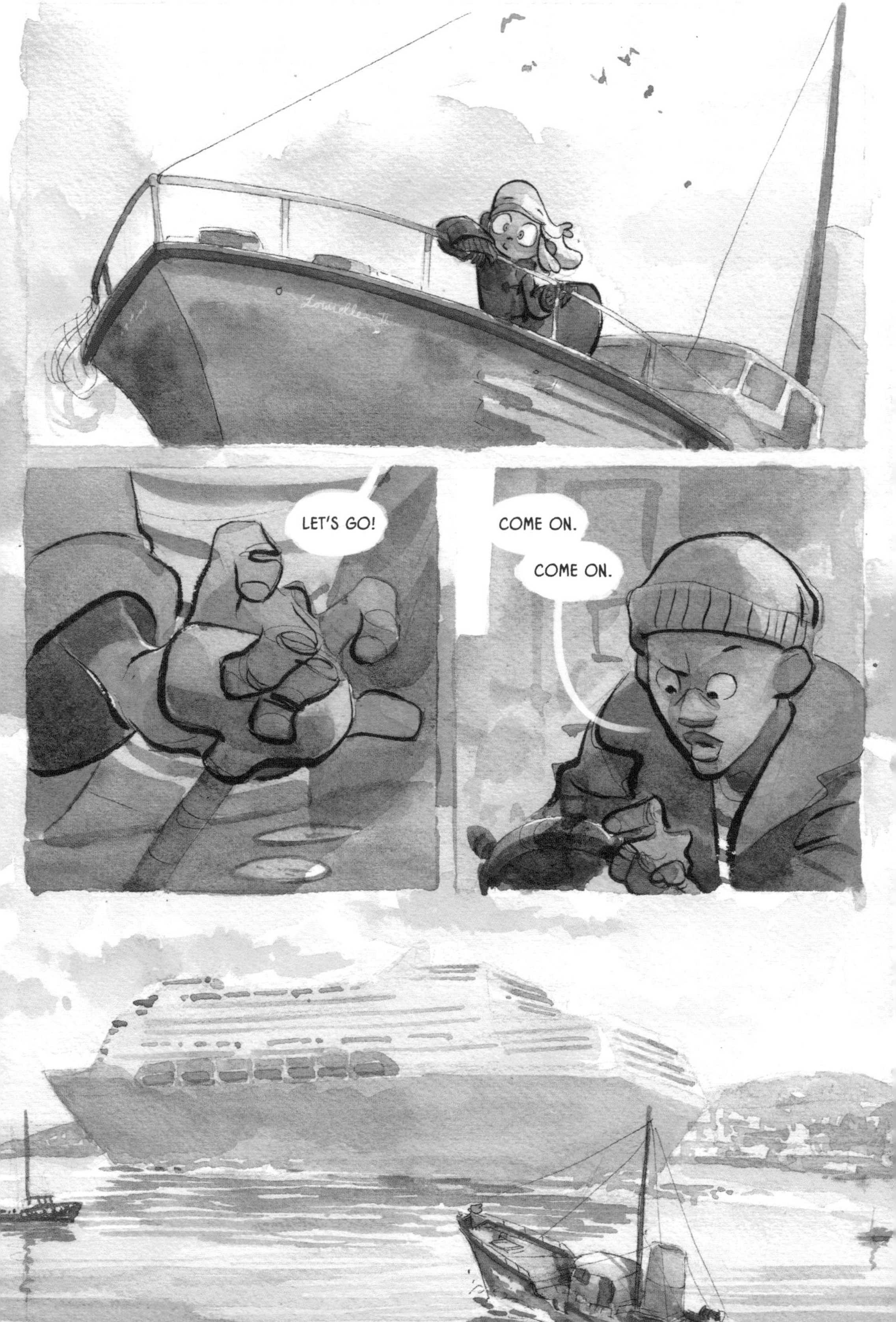
LET'S GO!
COME ON.
COME ON.

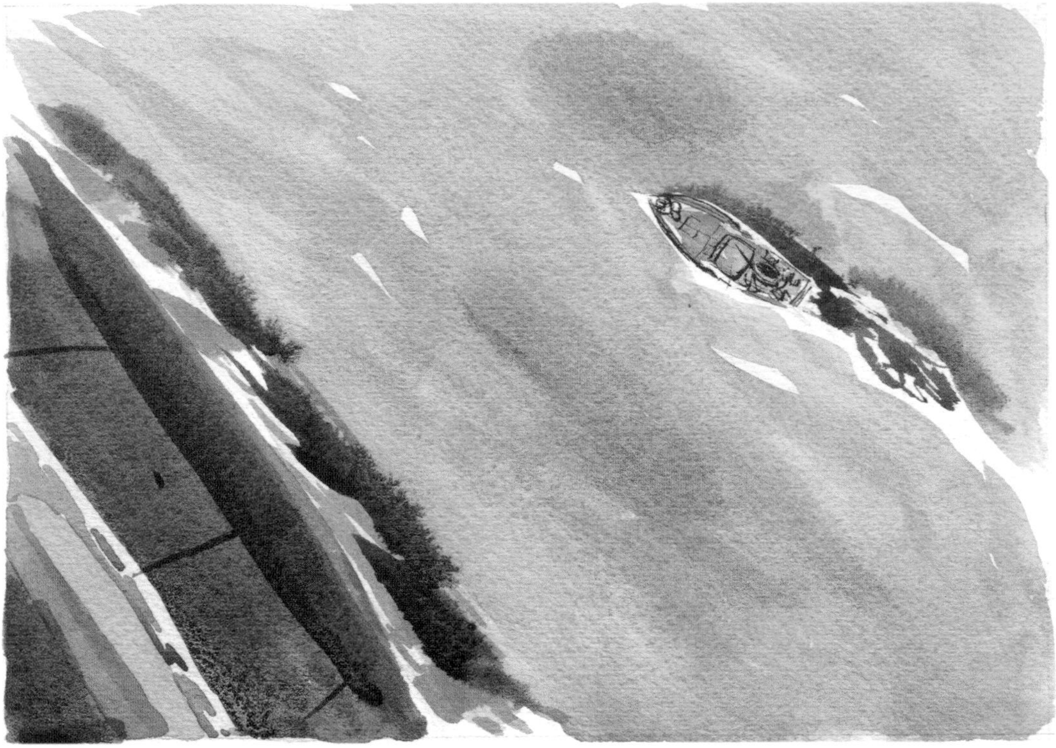

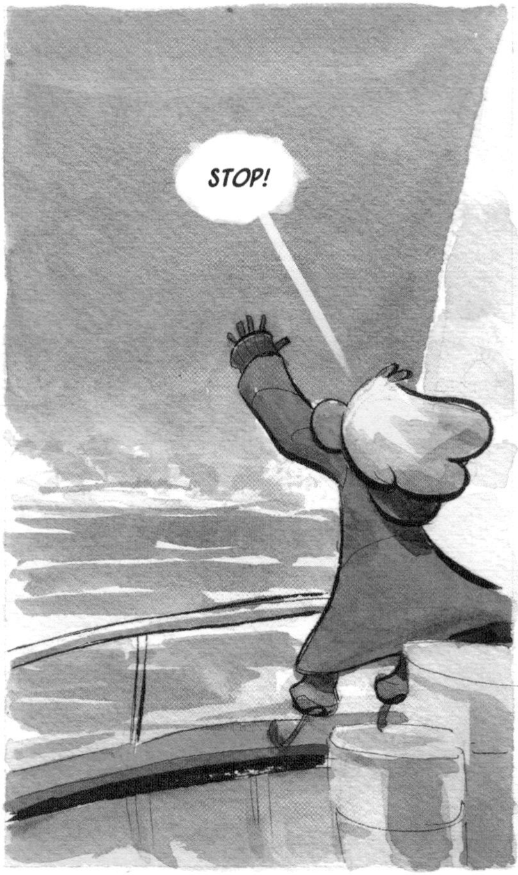
STOP!

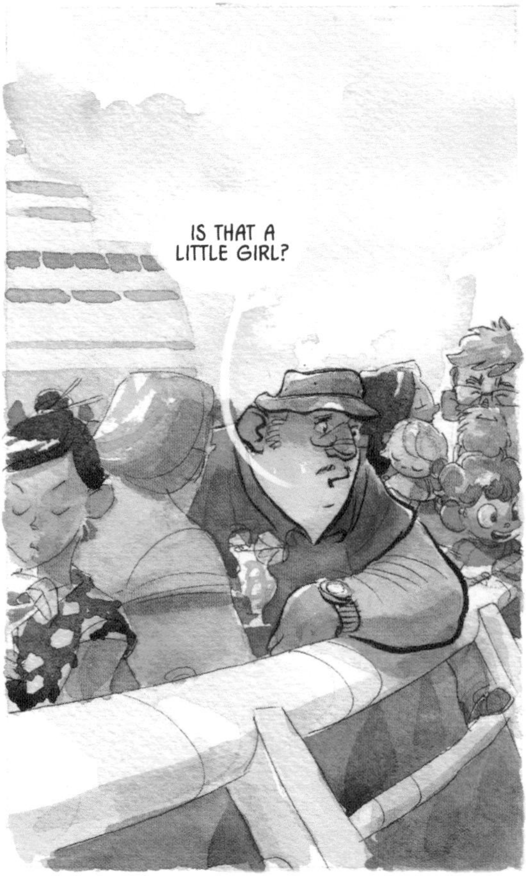
IS THAT A LITTLE GIRL?

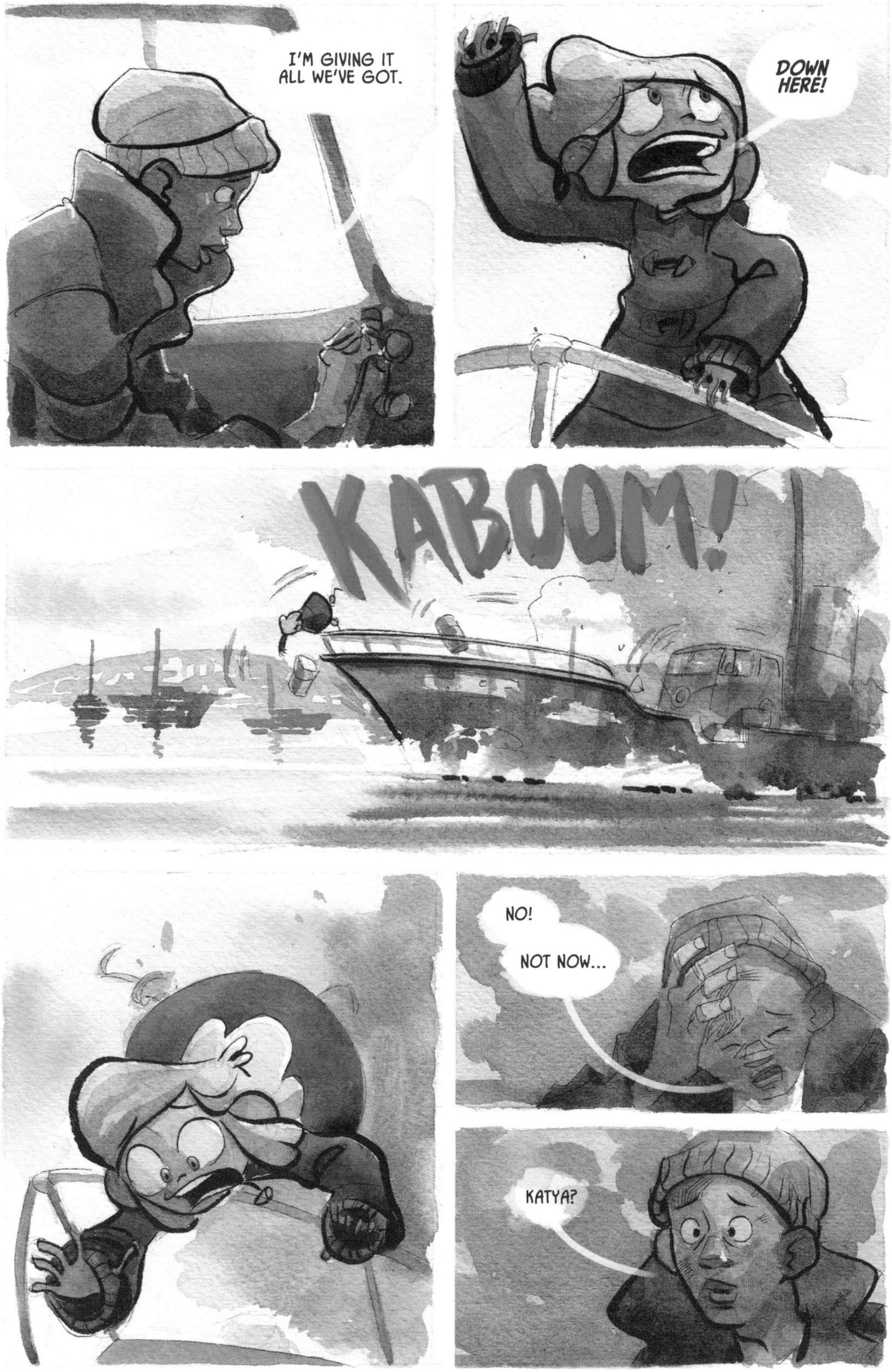
I'M GIVING IT ALL WE'VE GOT.
DOWN HERE!
KABOOM!
NO!
NOT NOW...
KATYA?

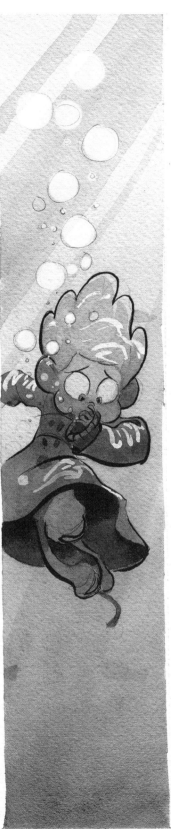

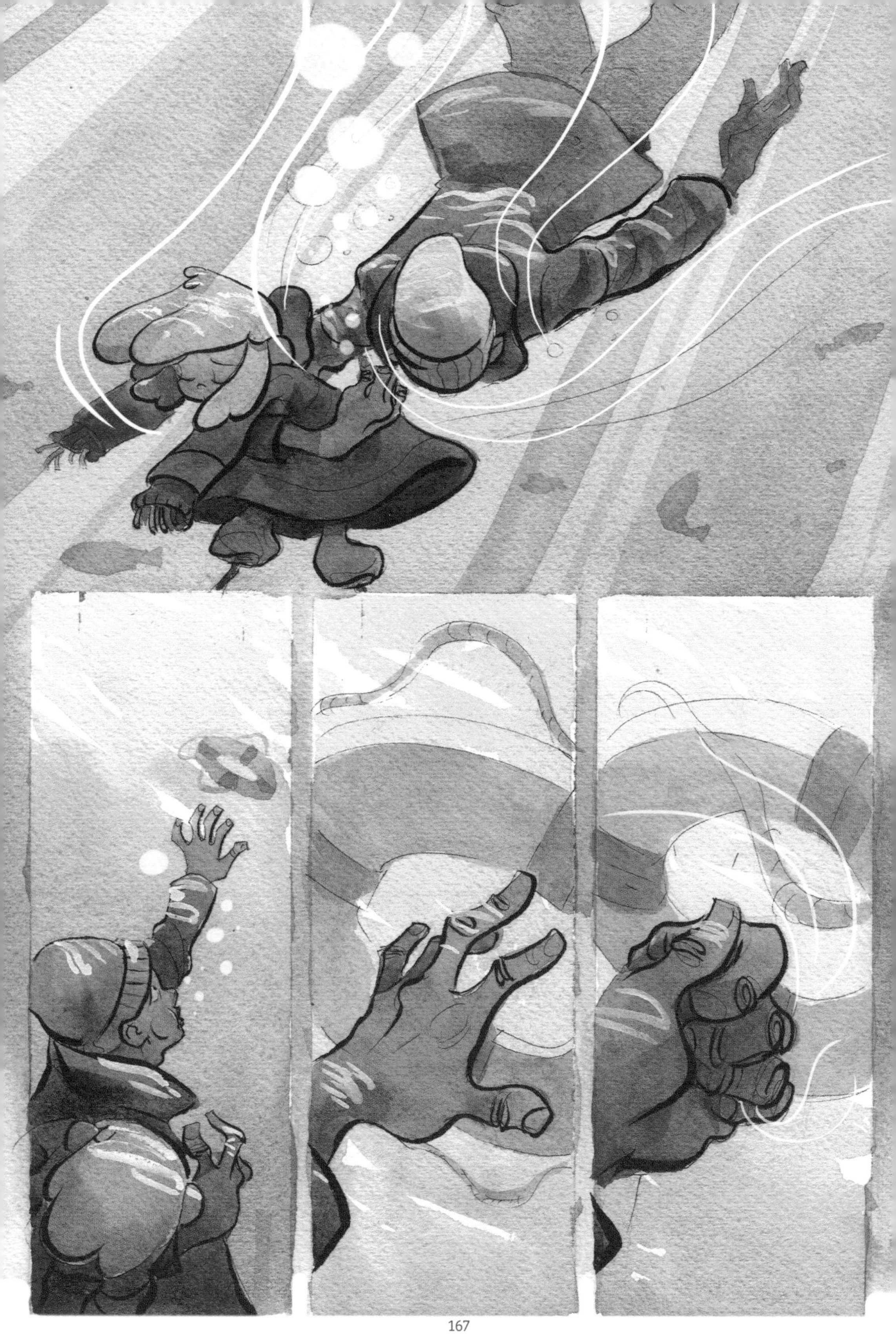

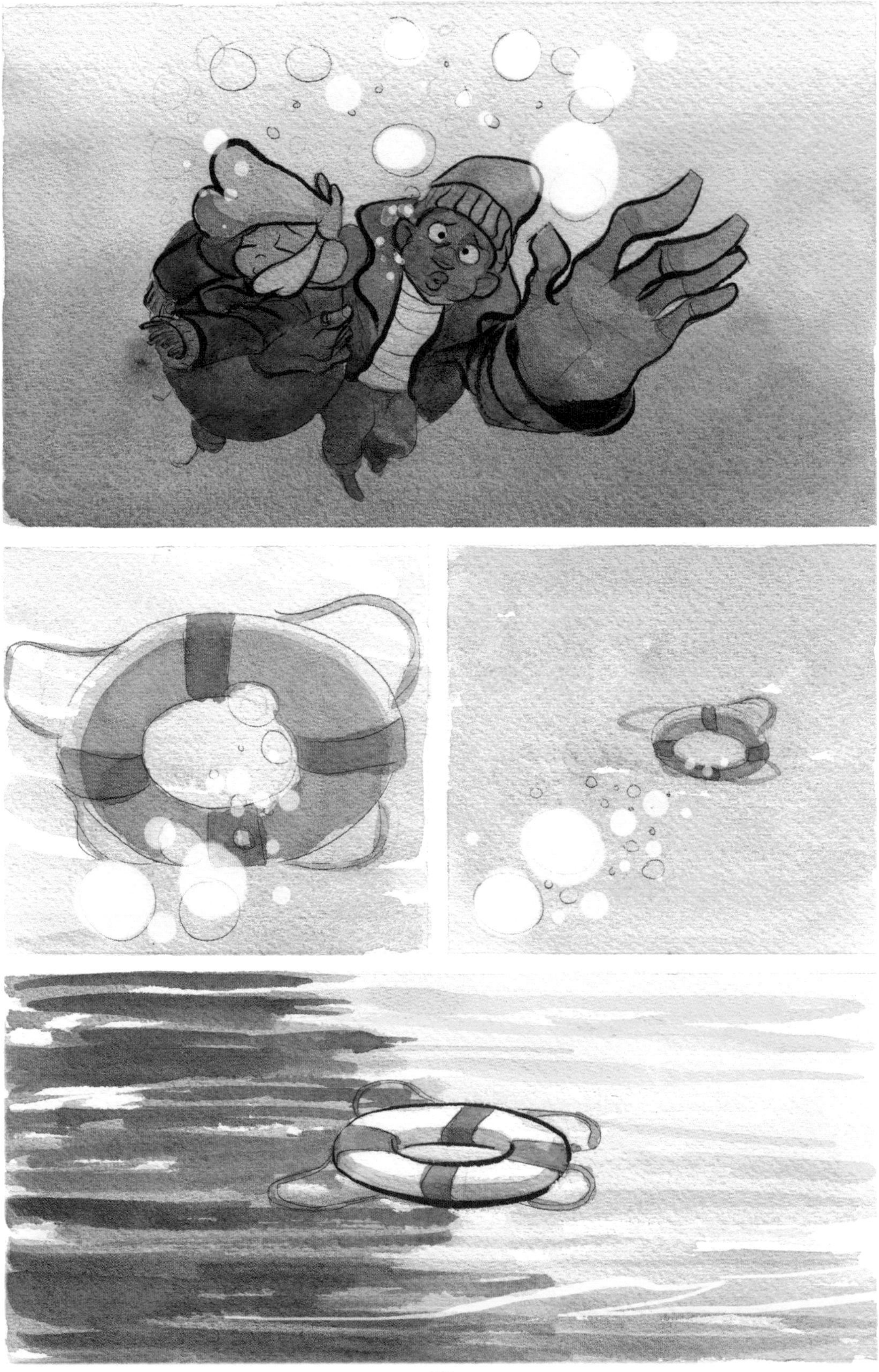

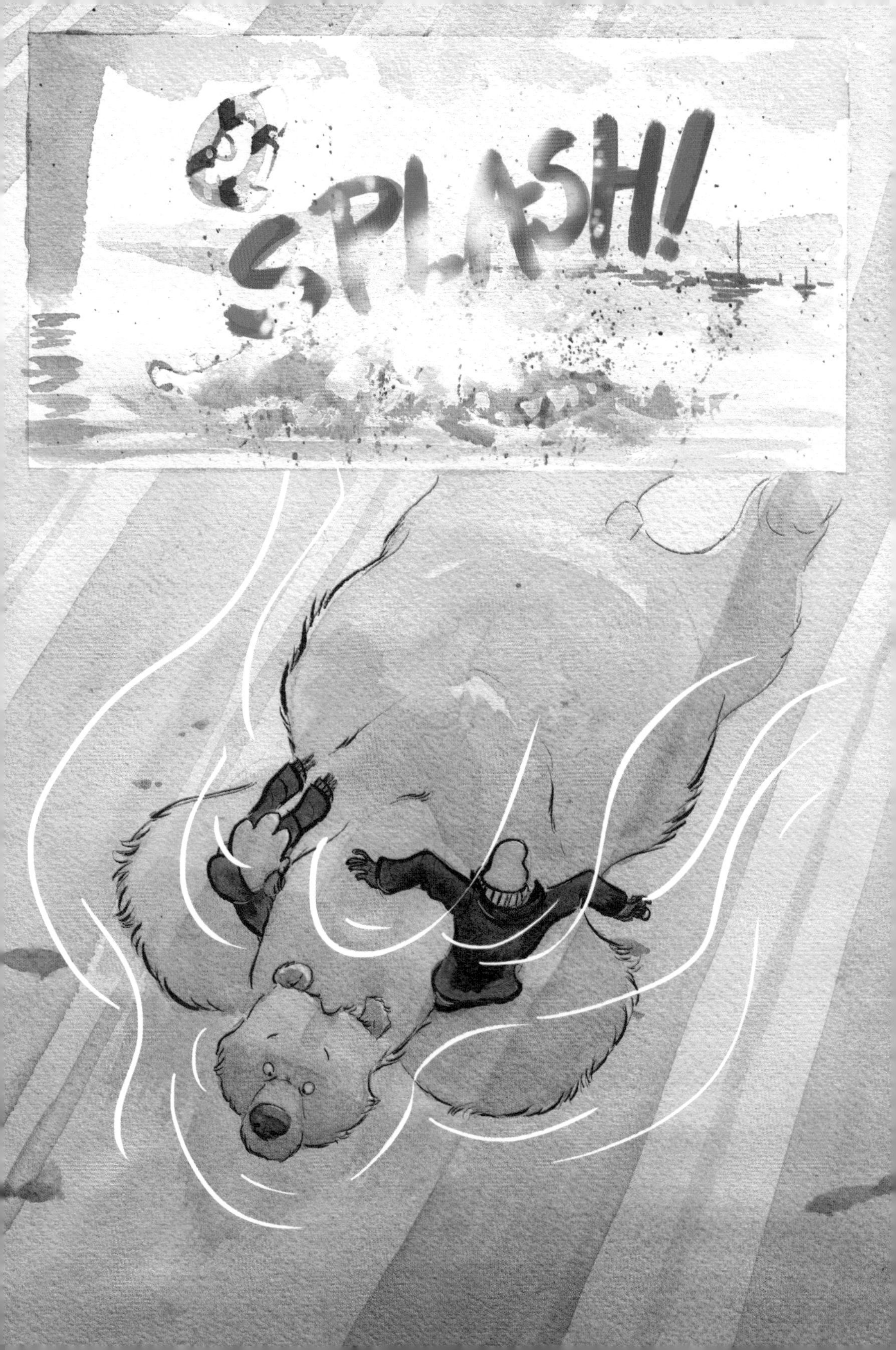
SPLASH!

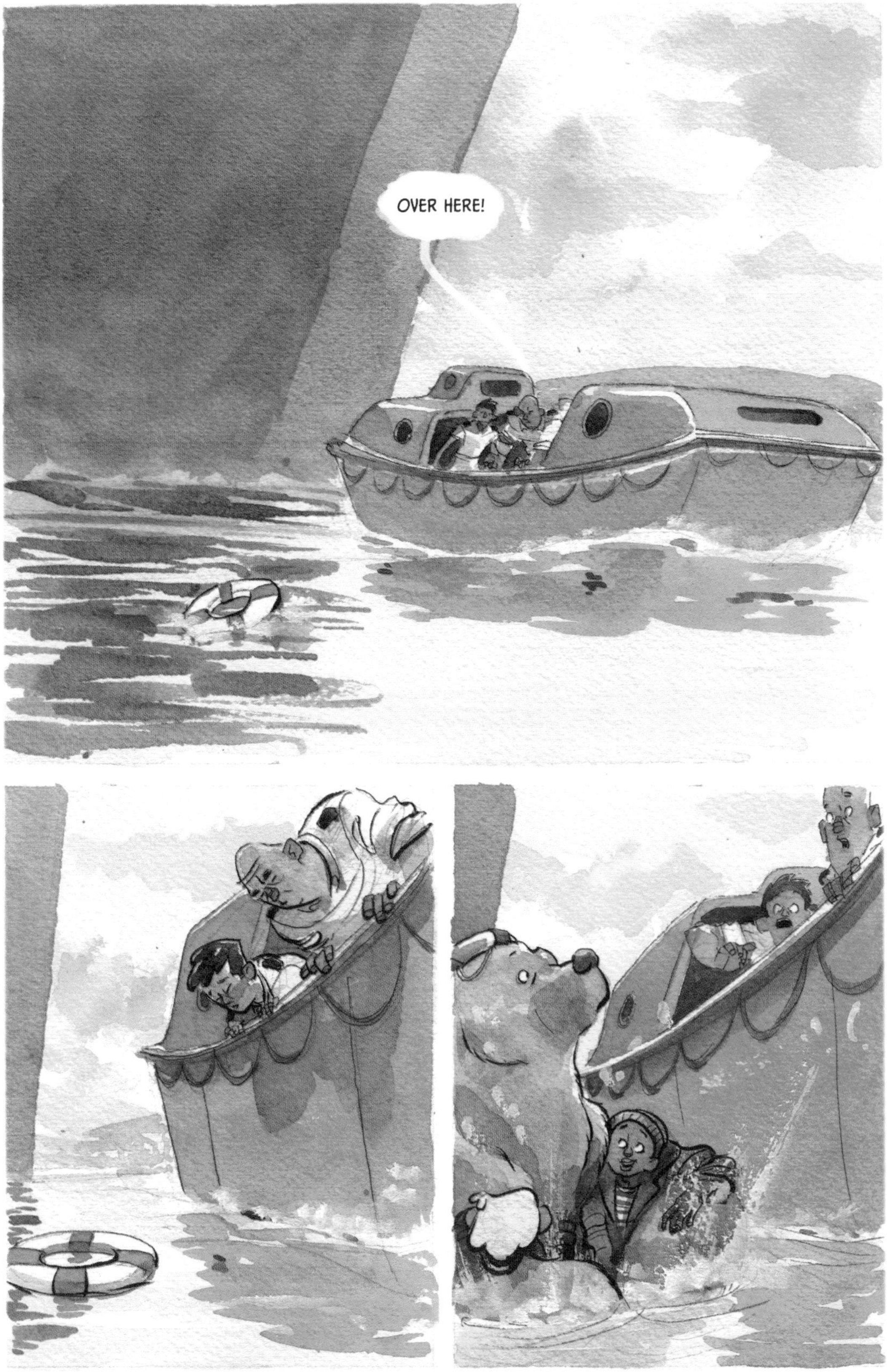
OVER HERE!

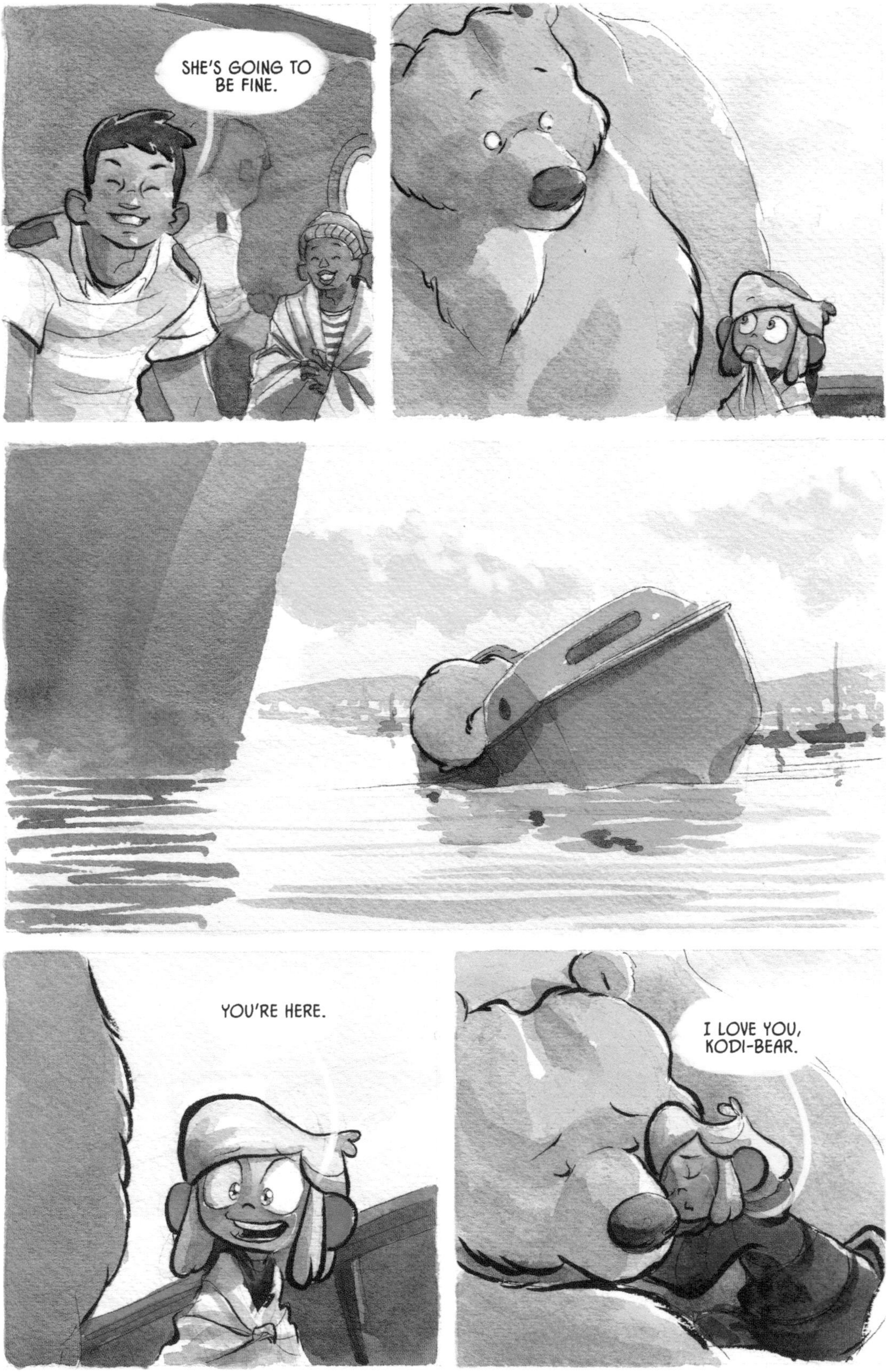
SHE'S GOING TO BE FINE.
YOU'RE HERE.
I LOVE YOU, KODI-BEAR.

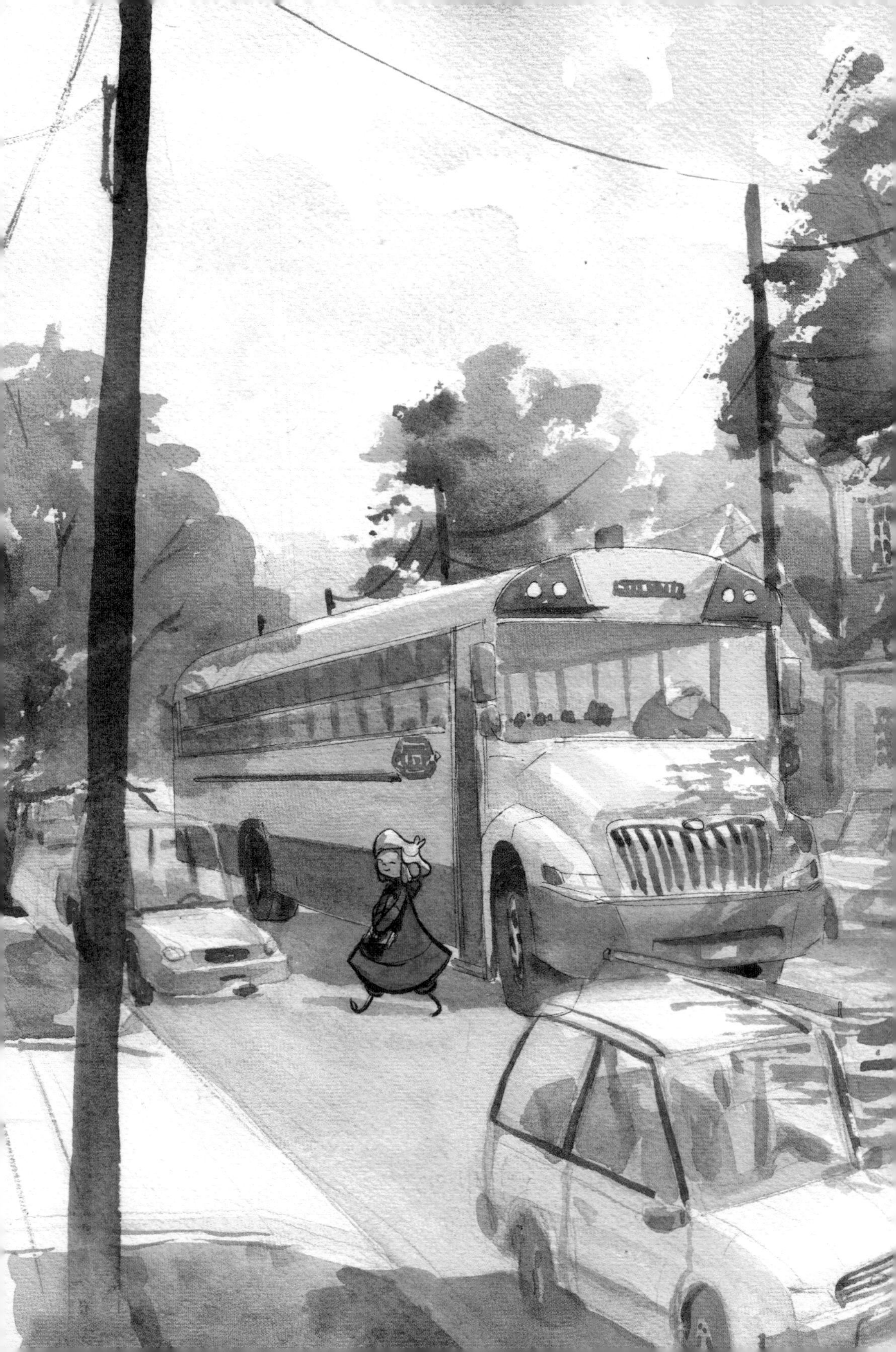

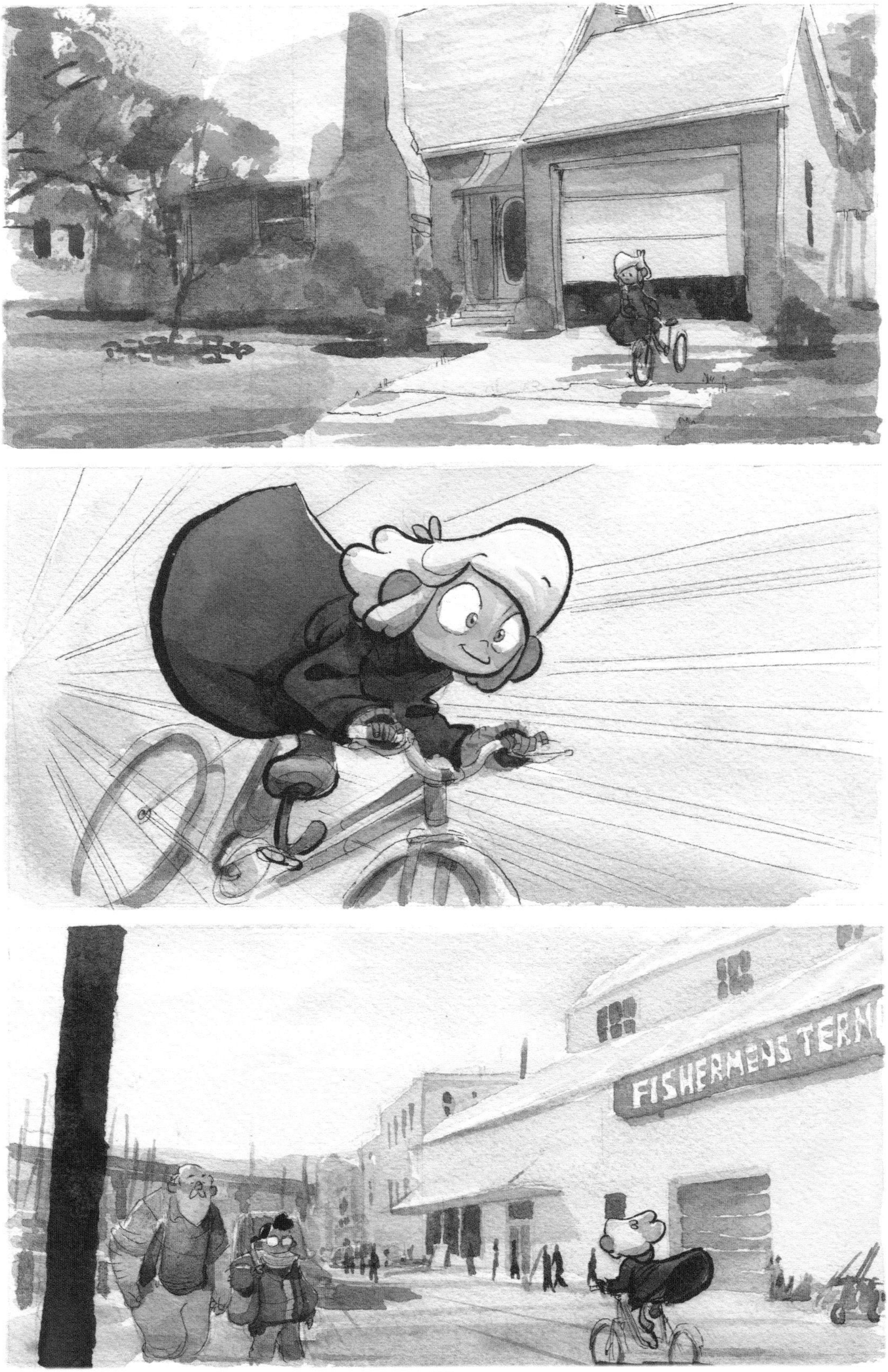
FISHERMENS TER

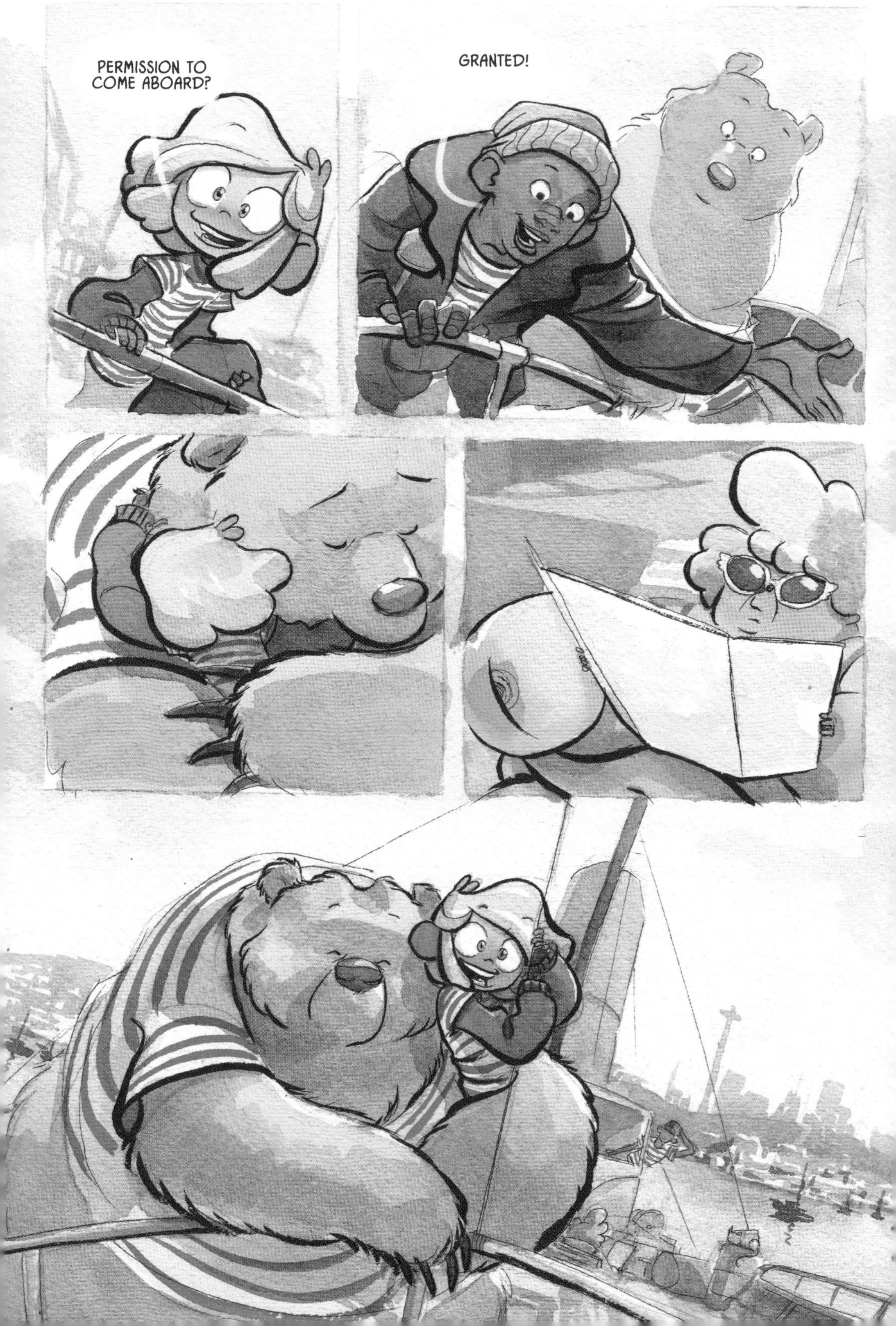
PERMISSION TO COME ABOARD?
GRANTED!

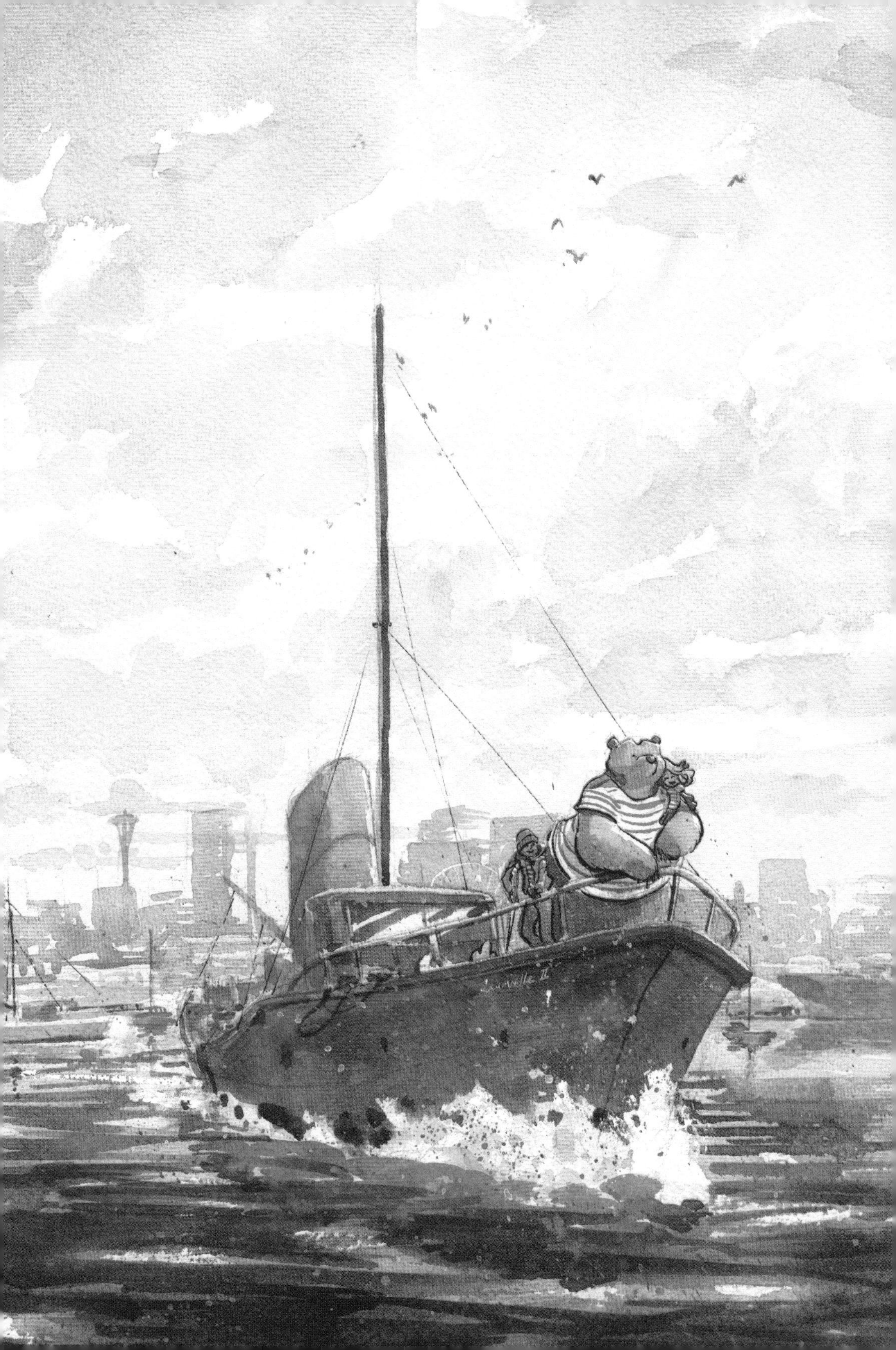

I would not have been able to complete this book without the generous outpouring of time, patience, and positive energy from those around me. For that endless support I want to say a special thank you to Johanna, Oliver, and Vivi Cullum.

Another special thank you to Jennie and Ridge Cullum. Thanks to Justin Cullum, Stefanie, Brian, Nolan, Leah, Henry Ritz, Barbara & Joseph Branch, and Nick & Mary Soroka. Thank you to Kellie Rupard-Schorr and Cathy Magallanez for the gift of art and the ability to follow my bliss.

Thanks to Robert Ullman, Wes Brooks, Duane Ballenger, J. Chris Campbell, Chris Pitzer, Shelton Drum and all of the "Heroes family," Adam and Shawn Daughhetee, Andy Runton, James Gurney, Ben Towle, Brian Ashmore, Zack Rosenberg, and Victor Fuste.

For reference photography help, thank you to Chani Farhaven, Kellie Rupard-Schorr, and Ed Lane.

Special thank you to Chris Staros, Leigh Walton, Gilberto Lazcano and the Top Shelf /IDW crew for their kindness, patience and for taking a chance on me.